SONG FOR CHANCE

SONG FOR CHANCE

A Novel

(♯)

JOHN VAN KIRK

🐔 RED HEN PRESS | *Pasadena, CA*

Book layout and design by Aly Owen
Cover design by Rebecca Buhler

Library of Congress Cataloging-in-Publication Data
Van Kirk, John.
  Song for chance : a novel / John Van Kirk.—First Edition.
    pages cm
  Includes bibliographical references and index.
  ISBN 978-1-59709-267-8 (alk. paper)
  1. Musicians—Fiction. 2. Life change events—Fiction. 3. Psychological fiction.
I. Title.
  PS3611.I753 2013 813'.6—dc23
                    2013003598

The Los Angeles County Arts Commission, the City of Pasadena Cultural Affairs
Division, Sony Pictures Entertainment, the Los Angeles Department of Cultural
Affairs, and the Dwight Stuart Youth Fund partially support Red Hen Press. This
publication was supported in part by an award from the National Endowment
for the Arts.

First Edition
Published by Red Hen Press
www.redhen.org

Acknowledgments

Many friends and colleagues contributed to the writing of this book, some in specific and tangible ways, others simply by being friends. I am grateful especially to my piano teacher, Mila Markun, and my guitar teacher, Scott Stephens. The Rogues were supportive and helpful every step of the way; thank you Laura Treacy Bentley, Shannon Butler, Zoë Ferraris, Charles Lloyd, Marie Manilla, Paul Martin, and Mary Sansom. A number of people served as advance readers, and their comments were invaluable, among them Paul Callicoat, Jane Hill, Ken Shelby, A.E. Stringer, Janet Weinrib, Leo Welch, and Mark Zanter. David Castleberry gave me a free voice lesson, and the Huntington Harmonica Club let me experience firsthand what it's like to front the band. Michele Schiavone copyedited the manuscript in its final stages. My agent, Deborah Schneider, believed in the book and found it a home. Tom Berry has been my teacher in more ways than I can say.

Portions of this book were written at the Virginia Center for the Creative Arts (residency funded by the Mid-Atlantic Arts Foundation), The Writers Colony at Dairy Hollow (residency funded by their Eureka! Fellowship), and the Jentel Artist Residency Program.

Contents

For Karen.

And for Ted: I wish I'd had time to get used to calling you Theo.

I'm not who you want. You think I am, but I'm not. It's true I was in the middle of it all, but I won't be able to give you what you want, tell you what you want to hear. Maybe somebody who was on the outside looking in could tell you, could make it clear, someone who wasn't emotionally involved, but I doubt it. They wouldn't get the power of the emotions without being in there to feel them. And if you're in there feeling them, like I was, you don't have any objectivity. So if you ask me, nobody's going to be able to give you the real explanation, if there even is one. Not me. And not anybody else.

July

Jack Voss heard the pitch change as the engines throttled back before he felt the aircraft decelerate and begin its descent into LaGuardia. He could see the ground now. After almost six hours above an unbroken layer of clouds, the plane was crossing the ragged edge of the undercast, and he took note of the East Coast geography as it came into view, sorting through the maps in his mind, until he caught sight of the Tappan Zee Bridge, and the mental images synced up with the landscape below. Over Manhattan, the afternoon sun glinted off the silvery top of the Chrysler Building, but what struck him, as it had every time he had flown into the city since 9/11, was the empty space in the skyline where the Twin Towers used to be, an ominous reminder that absence could be as powerful as presence, sometimes more so.

Once off the plane, Voss breezed through the airport carrying only his leather jacket and his briefcase. That was one of the advantages of keeping the Manhattan apartment, though he didn't go directly there. Instead he stuck his head into the first cab in line and said, "you know Woodside?"

The driver, tawny dreads spilling from a knit red and purple cap, nodded without turning around. Blasé. Voss climbed in and gave him the address.

"Hey, I know you," the driver said abruptly, having checked him out in the mirror and now turning to face him. "You're Voss. Keyboard man. Ride the Music, baby."

Voss smiled. "That's me," he said.

They pulled out into the flow of traffic.

"You want to listen to some jazz?"

"Sure," Voss said as he tuned in to the pulse of the city, so different from San Francisco, where he had boarded his plane in the gray dawn. He thought of Gershwin for a moment, the car horns in *An American in Paris*, and the Mondrian painting "Broadway Boogie Woogie," which always reminded him a little of a subway map. He watched the driver shuffle through his CDs, a bit apprehensive about what he might be about to hear. People threw the word jazz around these days without much care. The words "smooth jazz" from a radio announcer were enough to make Voss change the station, because he knew what was coming—something soupy and sentimental, Kenny G. or Spyro Gyra. But when the music started, it wasn't soupy at all, rather edgy, crisp, deeply intelligent. He sat back and listened.

"Monk," he said.

"The-lo-ni-us," the driver said, stretching out the syllables.

"Good choice," Voss said. "Very good choice."

(♯)

Artie met him at the door with a familiar smirk and a bear hug, and Voss glimpsed C.C. in T-shirt and underpants scooting down the hall to the bedroom.

"Sorry, Jack," she called over her shoulder. "Still in my undies. Be out in a few minutes. Excuse the mess."

Voss felt immediately at home—his visits with Artie and C.C. always began with her apologizing for the mess, a mess he could never see.

"C'mon in, man," Artie said, stepping back to look him up and down. "God, it's good to see you."

"You, too, dude-san. It's been too long. You've lost weight."

"Yeah," Artie said, looking down at his own sinewy frame. "So I heard you got into Cleveland. The Rock and Roll Hall of Fame. Damn, man." Artie clapped Voss on the shoulder. "Congratulations."

"I was just there to induct Hal," Voss said. "They're not gonna put me in there."

"Shit. Sorry, man. You deserve it, though. And Hal? Nobody would ever have heard of Hal Proteus if it wasn't for you. Vossimilitude put him on the map; everybody knows that."

"Thanks, but I'm not sure that's true. He was a killer bass player, and he could sing. He'd have been somebody whether I was there or not."

"I won't speak ill of the dead," Artie said, "but I never liked him as much as you did. Anyway, come in, sit down." He gestured toward the living room where the television was blaring CNN's coverage of the Democratic convention. "It's just the preliminaries. Shalikashvili's going to start things off. Can I get you a drink?"

"I could use a beer," Voss said. He had been looking forward to this, an ordinary evening, sitting around with old friends, watching TV, no business talk, no need to perform, entertain anybody. During the flight he'd gone over the charts for tomorrow's recording session. He was prepared. Tonight was a night to chill. And it was the last night of the convention—to watch that with Artie would be another treat. The most politically savvy of Voss's friends, Artie was a history buff and political junkie who had read everything from Herodotus to Simon Shama; even back when he and Voss were college roommates he had torn noisily through three newspapers a day, flapping the pages and muttering. He was always ahead of the curve when it came to breaking political news, had predicted Carter's nomination before Voss had heard of Carter, was up on the Contra scandal before it broke, was on to Ross Perot before the mainstream media, and foresaw that Clinton's *bête noire* would be his philandering. "What did I tell you?" he had said when the Lewinski affair came to light.

Artie ushered Voss through the dining room—where the table was piled high with unfolded laundry—into the living room. The low sun shone through the blinds onto the huge television screen, revealing a thick coating of dust. Stacks of books and magazines were heaped up on the end-tables and the floor; on the coffee table, a huge pewter ashtray overflowed with crushed cigarette butts.

"What happened to Frau Cecelia, the cleaning Nazi?" Voss said when Artie came back in with a bottle of Pilsner Urquel. "C.C.'s let you revert to your old habits. Place is starting to look like your room at the Lafayette house back when."

Artie tilted his head and raised his eyebrows as if to say, *yeah, it's my mess.* But there was something else going on beneath the surface that Voss wasn't sure of.

"Is everything okay?" he asked quietly. "Didn't you tell me something about C.C. last winter? Some kind of seizure?"

"Yeah. It's a long story. I'll fill you in later," Artie said. Then he pointed with his chin to the TV. "It's the night of the generals. Brilliant. Did you see Clinton the other night? Unbelievable speech. God, I miss him. If only he could have kept his dick in his pants."

Voss nodded. Somebody on the television said something he didn't catch, and Artie growled, "That's right. Red Meat." He turned back to Voss. "I want to see them go for the jugular," he said, "right for Bush himself. Make it personal, goddamnit."

"Isn't that what they are doing?" Voss said.

"Nah. Very few of them. They're going for the love-fest. John Kerry, war hero slash anti-war hero. Flashback to the hippie days, '68 and '72, and try to make us boomers feel like we've got one last chance to get it right. To change the world like we dreamed when we were kids. Not blow it this time like Humphrey and McGovern did."

C.C. came out about twenty minutes later, pale and older than Voss remembered her. Her hair was pulled back into a tight pony tail, but it looked limp and greasy. She bustled about, serving bowls of chips, plates of cheese and fruit, opening a bottle of pinot grigio. Dinner as such never materialized, but there was enough food that Voss didn't miss it. Artie and C.C. still got high, and joints went around along with the wine. Voss was a little out of practice, and there was no way he could keep up. Artie seemed to interact with the television more than he did with either Voss or C.C. anyway, and after a while Voss just settled back into the couch and let the whole scene wash over him.

"I'm going to go get some cigarettes," C.C. said. "You guys need anything?"

Artie sat up. "Sweetheart, it's late," he said. "Stay here. I'll go."

"No," she said, "you hang with Jack. You guys haven't seen each other in how long?"

"No, it's cool. I'll go. No problem. Back in ten minutes."

"No," C.C. said, "I'll go. It's just around the corner, for Christ's sake. I need the air."

Then Artie seemed to plead with her—Voss had never heard anything like it between them; maybe he was stoned, but he felt desperation, agony in his friend's voice: "Let *me* go, sweetheart, please? C'mon, honey; I'd really rather go myself—or else I'll go *with* you, okay?"

C.C. was having none of it. "That would be rude," she said. Then she turned toward Voss, trying to draw him in as an ally. "He's such a *man*." She turned again, mixing sweetness and recrimination. "Artie, baby, we can't just leave Jack here by himself. What's wrong with you, honey?"

Voss sensed vitriol under their endearments. Finally it emerged. "Okay, fuck it," Artie said. "You go. We'll wait here. Just go to Chino's, okay?"

"Yeah, Chino's," she said, conciliatory, now that she'd gotten her way. "I'll be right back, sweetie. Don't worry."

She closed the door behind her, and Voss heard the deadbolt slide in place. Artie started to roll another joint.

"What was all that about?" Voss asked.

Artie shook his head. "I don't want to talk about it right now, okay? I'm sorry, man."

And the two men sat in front of the blaring television. A half hour passed. The absurd hoopla of the Convention, with the synthetic theme music the network had manufactured for it, went on as before, but Artie made no comment, and Voss felt confused and a little hurt.

When C.C. finally did come back, almost an hour later, she was different—by turns emotional and out of it. She started crying during the short film about Kerry's Vietnam heroism. Artie was clearly disturbed.

Then it was time for Kerry's speech. C.C. teared up again at the salute and the corny "John Kerry, reporting for duty" opening.

"Good theater," Artie said, rousing a little from his funk. "If McGovern had played the war-hero card he might have been able to beat Nixon."

More than a little stoned, and still confused about what was going on between his friends, Voss was briefly distracted by a headline that went by on the crawl. At first all he caught were two words—*Hoboken,* where he was planning to go tomorrow to visit his daughter, Chance, and *suicide.* He waited for it to run by again so he could read the whole thing: *Hoboken: two dead and one held for questioning in botched triple suicide.* Now he fixated on the idea of a triple suicide, not something you heard about very often. Sure there were two-person suicides, doomed lovers usually, and mass events, like Jonestown or Halle-Bopp. It had been almost thirty years since he'd heard about a three-way suicide pact. Not a memory he wanted to pursue.

Then Kerry made his remark about wisdom and strength not having to be mutually exclusive.

"Good," Artie said, slamming his fist down on the table and upsetting the ashtray. "That's what he needs to say."

C.C.—weepy and slurring her words—said, "Thank God. I think he's going to win," then slumped over and passed out.

Artie woke her gently, got her to her feet. She whimpered as he helped her back into the bedroom.

"Is she all right?" Voss asked, when Artie came back.

"She's drunk," Artie said bitterly.

"But she didn't drink that much, did she?"

"Not here."

"What?"

"She didn't go out for cigarettes," Artie said. "She went out for a couple of shots. She might have even brought a bottle back in her purse. I'll have to check."

"But we were drinking here. Why would she go out?"

"It's not enough. You saw how she changed. She could sit and drink wine with us all night. She had to have a couple vodkas. It's what she does now. She's an alcoholic, Jack. A bad one."

"How long has it been like this?"

"Forever," Artie said, bitterly. "I mean . . . you remember even back in the early days, she always drank a lot. You don't do that for twenty or thirty years without . . . consequences." Then his voice changed. "She took a turn after 9/11. Before that, the drinking was pretty much limited to nighttime. Then there was the hysterectomy. . . ."

"Jesus. And the seizure?"

"Seizures," Artie corrected. "She's had three that I know of."

Voss looked at Artie. "Do they know what's causing them?"

"It's the alcohol."

"Oh, God, Artie. I'm so sorry, man. Can you get her help?"

"You think I haven't tried? She won't go."

They sat in silence while the commentators told them what they had already seen and heard, as if it required interpreters.

"What about you?" Voss said. "You talking to anybody about this?"

"Who am I going to talk to?" Artie said.

"Well, me, for one."

"Fuck, man. There's nothing to say."

In the cab from Queens to Manhattan, Voss's head swam. He felt that dizzying perspective shift that happens when something dimly glimpsed in the background suddenly slides into the foreground, massive and looming. How many times had he seen C.C. nod off at the end of the night and thought nothing of it? How many times had Artie failed to show up for a dinner or drink in Manhattan with a vague excuse about C.C. feeling poorly? How could Voss have missed the now-obvious signs? He couldn't name all the fellow musicians he had seen destroyed by drink or drugs over the years, but Artie and C.C. had always seemed apart from that world, immune to those forces that took others down. But no one was immune, he knew that; his own escape from the pharmacopeia of oblivion, as he called it, had been narrow, and he still felt its seductive allure at times.

The doorman at his apartment greeted him warmly despite the lateness of the hour, and when he got out of the elevator and opened his door, he saw the unopened bags of books and clothing he had purchased on his last visit and knew he would open them tomorrow with surprise, like gifts he had left for himself. Perhaps there would be something he could give to his daughter. The answering machine on the telephone was winking eighty-eight.

"Shit," Voss said aloud. "Not here too." He unplugged the machine from the wall and threw it in the garbage.

Before he fell asleep, he thought once again of the headline on the crawl about the suicides in Hoboken and fervently hoped it wasn't going to be a replay of the last time. Though that was almost impossible. The record was out of print, all but forgotten.

♯

The sound was as close to perfect as it was going to get. Gordon had got the buzz out of Javi's bass, Charley B.'s drums were tuned and the mikes adjusted, and Voss was beginning to get the feel of the piano, a well cared-for Baldwin with a light action and a warm tone. Through the window he could see Gordon sit back from the mixing board and just listen.

Voss leaned into the mike and began to sing. Almost immediately his voice went flat; then it cracked. He mashed both hands down on the piano keys and said, "Shit. Whose brilliant idea was it to record this song?"

"I'm pretty sure it was yours, Jack," Charley B. said, leaning his upright bass against its stand.

"Yeah, Jack," said Javier. "You said you liked the shoes thing."

"Right," Voss said. "I liked the shoes. But I guess I didn't really remember the rest of the song. I mean, it's got one great line—the rest, well, Springsteen can pull it off. He does that wailing thing; it's primal. But I'm not that kind of singer, and except for the chorus . . . Jesus, the song is barely articulate. No wonder nobody covers Springsteen."

"Uh, yeah," Javi said, "except for Manfred Mann, and Patti Smith, and Cowboy Junkies . . . who else? Charlie?"

"Stanley Clarke," Charlie said, "and Johnny Cash covered, what was it? 'I'm On Fire.'"

"Okay," Voss said, "but it's not like other people make hits out of them."

"Except for Manfred Mann," they said together.

"C'mon, guys," Gordon cut in from the booth. "Why don't you try it again. If you're worried about the wailing we can dub in a sax later. . . ."

"Yeah, Clarence Clemmons, right?" Voss said. "Give me a break, Gordo. If we need a sax when I'm done, we might as well hang it up."

"Okay, Jack. Bad idea. But you've got to stay with this. Just sing it straight, quiet, whispery, close to the mike. Tom Waits, but melodic. The boys are with you all the way. Javi, even softer with the brushes."

"All right," Voss said. "One more time, but then we move on. If we don't get it this time, we'll come back to it tomorrow." He started the count. Charlie's clear, slow bass line and Javi's laid-back brushwork on the drums seemed to say, *listen close*. Voss came in, his voice low:

When I lost you, honey, sometimes I think I lost my guts, too . . .

Then he filled in the gaps with piano chords, thoughtful, as if he were composing them on the spot.

And I wish God would send me a word,
Send me something I'm afraid to lose . . .

He worked himself into it, still soft on the piano, and let the music carry him into the chorus:

Baby, I swear I'd drive all night again, just to buy you some shoes. . . .

(♯)

Voss had the radio tuned to the Newark jazz station as he maneuvered the rented Porsche around the crowded streets of Hoboken. His leather jacket—a West Coast habit, unnecessary in July on the Atlantic coast—lay on the back seat, and a plastic Strand bag containing a private edition of A. E. Housman's poems had been stowed in the trunk. An old Art Pepper recording came on, making Voss feel a little foolish after his struggles to play much simpler music all afternoon. As he searched for a parking space near Chance's building, he began to wonder if the Porsche was a bad choice. An invitation to vandals and thieves. But his plan was to take her out to the country on Sunday, find a nice twisty road, pull over, step out, and hand her the keys. He knew she would love driving the car. He circled the block twice before he saw someone pull out and leave a space halfway down the street from her apartment.

Walking up the sidewalk, he noticed more expensive cars than on his last visit, a Mini, two BMWs. And the building next to hers had a fresh coat of paint and what looked like new windows. Chance's building was still as run-down as ever on the outside, but the entryway showed signs of improvement—new sheet-rock, spackle, and plaster dust, a fresh coat of paint on the inner security door. He buzzed her and waited. After a minute or so he buzzed again, running through his memory of their last conversation, asking himself if he could have given her the wrong date. It had been a couple of weeks, and she had been unusually hesitant, suggesting that he would be so busy he shouldn't feel obliged to see her. But he had insisted, even telling her to write it down: Friday, between five and six. He hit the buzzer again, but still nothing. This was what cell phones were for, he thought, but his cell was in the car, in his jacket pocket. As he was about to go get it, a young woman in gym shorts, tank top, and running shoes came out through the door. She stared at him for a moment, but she didn't say anything when he grabbed the door before it could latch. He trudged up the three flights to Chance's apartment. On the second floor someone, a child probably, was practicing on an out-of-tune piano, picking his or her way through a G scale in broken time. Voss's eyes caught a flash of yellow as he came to the fourth floor landing and the sight of Chance's door crisscrossed with crime scene tape. The world contracted, as if he had gone momentarily snowblind. Around him all white, before him nothing but this door and a dread that he wouldn't allow to become more specific. He felt his stomach clench. He knocked, his heart in his throat, his hands beginning to shake. Nothing. He turned the doorknob. Pushed. Felt the door flex against the deadbolt at shoulder height. His throat tightened as if he were about to be sick.

Something broke through the periphery. The sound of a deadbolt being drawn back. The door of the next apartment opened a crack, then wide enough to let a thick-bodied woman with gray hair step out onto the landing. "You're Voss, aren't you? She told me you were her father, but I wasn't sure whether to believe her."

Voss swam up out of the empty place he had fallen into, found words: "Yes, I'm Voss. I'm her father. What is this?" He pointed to the yellow tape. "What's going on?"

"Oh, God," the woman said. "You don't know? It was on the news." She looked as if she was going to cry. "You'd better talk to the police. They were here all last night."

"What happened? Is she all right?"

"Oh, God," the woman said again.

"What?" Voss said. "What's going on?"

"Let me get the paper," she said, and she went back inside her apartment, coming out onto the landing a moment later with *The Post*. Voss fell back against the wall and then sank slowly to the floor. Chance's picture was on the front page—her hair wavy, her smile radiant—her yearbook photo. He had a copy of it in a frame in his living room. Next to it, a picture of her boyfriend—another outdated yearbook headshot. The paper would only use shots like these when they couldn't photograph the living person. Below them was a photo of a second young man—Voss thought he recognized him—on each arm a burly police officer. The headline read, "TRIANGLE

OF DEATH." Below the fold was written "BI LOVER CHICKENS OUT," and under the picture of the boy in police custody, "I JUST DID WHAT THEY ASKED." Voss felt himself stop breathing, made himself start again. Slow, deep, regular breaths.

The piano student downstairs continued to practice the G scale, missing the F-sharp on the way down.

(♯)

As Voss pulled into a space in front of the police station, he scraped his back right rim against the curb and bumped the car in front of him. The desk sergeant was putting the phone back in its cradle when Voss bent to the hole in the thick glass. "I'm Jack Voss. Is there somebody here who can tell me about my daughter?"

"Yes, sir," said the officer, a heavyset man with gray hair and a neatly trimmed moustache. "The Lieutenant will see you in just a minute."

Voss glanced down at the phone still under the officer's hand. "You already told him I was here?"

"I recognized you right away, sir. I've been a fan for years—ever since you did that record with the big band—what was it? *Ride the Music*."

"Thanks," Voss said. He was in a daze, nearly in shock, couldn't remember driving to the station. "I need to . . . find out about . . . about my daughter."

"Lieutenant O'Beirne will talk to you," the officer said. "I'll take you back. Step over to the door there, please."

The heavy steel door opened with a loud buzz and an electrometallic *kachunk*. The officer ushered Voss through. "Can I get you some coffee?" he asked.

"Coffee's the last thing I need," Voss said, feeling like he was peaking on bad acid. He took in his surroundings in jagged bits: a green hallway, men and women in blue uniforms, another door, a steel chair with a green vinyl seat, a yellow overhead light, its cover full of dead flies. Someone placed a paper cup of water in front of him. In the distance, he heard the steel door in the lobby open and close, the sound of the electric bolt like a hammer to the skull.

Lt. O'Beirne arrived about five minutes later. He was wearing faded jeans, running shoes, and a dress shirt with the sleeves rolled up.

"Mr. Voss, I'm Patrick O'Beirne," the Lieutenant said, "I'm the detective in charge of the case. I'm very sorry for your loss. We've been trying to reach you."

"My phone . . . I unplugged it last night. Somebody put my numbers up on the internet a couple of days ago, and when I got to my Manhattan apartment the machine was full."

Detective O'Beirne drew a fountain pen from his shirt pocket and opened a small, elegant, leather-bound notebook he'd produced from the back pocket of his jeans. "I'm going to send somebody to your place tomorrow morning to get the tape from that machine," he said. "Maybe there's something on it. And you have another place?"

"I live in California. Carmel."

"Clint Eastwood's town. I'd like you to send me the tape from that phone, too."

"Okay."

"You have a cell?"

"In the car. Nobody's got that number yet. It's brand new."

"Okay. I'll need that number."

"It's on the phone. I don't know what it is."

"All right. We'll get it later." The lieutenant paused for a moment, looked at Voss with practiced compassion. "Do you mind if I ask you some questions about your daughter?"

"I was hoping to ask *you* about her," Voss said.

"Right, but I'm sure you'll understand that I'd like to learn what you know about her recent activities before your memory becomes confused with the events of last night. I promise you I'll tell you all I know, if you just let me ask you some quick questions first."

"Shit, if that's what it's going to take," Voss said, too stunned to argue.

"Good. So . . . when was the last time you spoke with her?"

"A week ago, no, two weeks. I was in California. She called me."

"Can you be more exact? A detail like that might help us," the detective said.

"Jesus, I don't know. Wait, let me think. I did a rock and roll camp north of the city. . . ."

"New York?"

"San Francisco, sorry. I did the camp; that started on Saturday. . . ."

O'Beirne turned back the page on a calendar on his desk and pushed it toward Voss. "The tenth or seventeenth?" he asked.

"I think it was the seventeenth. She called a day or two before that." He put his hands on the sides of his head, closed his eyes for a moment, opened them. "I can't think."

"I understand. Take your time. Did she call you on a weekday, weekend?"

"I'm sorry. I don't remember."

"What time of day was it?"

"Huh? Wait . . . It was in the afternoon. I was home. Getting ready to go to The Cove."

The Lieutenant looked up.

"It's a club where I play sometimes on Friday nights."

"So it was Friday, the sixteenth," the Lieutenant said.

"Yeah, I guess it was."

"Okay. Can you tell me what you spoke about, how the conversation went?"

Voss struggled to remember. He had been out on his deck at the house in Carmel thinking about his set list for the night. Below him, the sea broke on the rocks, a low rumble; behind him, the Monterey pines rustled softly in the mild sea breeze and a hermit thrush sang in a minor key, plaintive, sad. The phone rang, and he let the answering machine pick up, but when he heard Chance's voice, he ran inside to grab the cordless from its cradle.

"Chance, honey, just a sec, let me get the machine. I'm sorry; I was screening—some guy put my number on his website, and I haven't been able to get it changed yet. The phone's been ringing off the hook."

"That's what you get for being famous, Jack," Chance said.

"Yeah, I guess. So, you're home? How was the trip?"

They talked for about fifteen minutes. She told him about her trip. She and her friends had camped in the Rockies, driven across part of Canada, and seen the Northern Lights. They'd had a little trouble coming back into the country, post 9/11 tensions. Chance asked Voss about the Vietnam era— was it like now?

"In a way," Voss said. "But I think we had more hope. As bad as things got, we always believed in a future. It's getting harder and harder to believe in a future anybody would want to live in."

"Yeah, except for the rich," Chance said.

"Well, some would call me rich," Voss said. "But I'm not immune to . . . what would you call it, the *zeitgeist*, this atmosphere of, I don't know what, dark clouds, mistrust, hatred, war. . . ."

"Yeah," Chance said. "I know what you mean."

"Sometimes I don't know how your generation can believe in anything," Voss said.

"Maybe we don't," Chance said.

Both were silent for a moment. Then Voss said, "Hey, I'm gonna be in New York in a couple of weeks."

"Great," she said, but her enthusiasm sounded forced.

"Let's get together. I'll be recording all day, but it's banker's hours. I'll be out of there by around five. I'll take you to dinner. Where would you like to go?"

"Are you sure? You'll be exhausted."

"I insist."

(♯)

The detective nodded as he listened to Voss's account of the phone call. The nib of his pen scratched on the paper of his notebook, a sound you rarely heard anymore.

"Is that all you remember?" O'Beirne asked.

"That's it."

"Why did she call? I mean, was it a regular thing for her to call you on a Friday afternoon—evening, her time—or do you think she called for a particular reason?"

Voss looked at the detective. "She called to tell me she was back from her trip."

"Right," the lieutenant said. "Did she mention Fadil al Muti?"

"Fadil? Oh, Fade. Her boyfriend. I think he was the one who had trouble at the border. They thought he was an Arab or something."

"How about Cornelius Webster—Neil, I think they called him."

"I know Neil. I met him a couple of years ago; he's been Chance's friend since grade school, I think. None of this makes sense. I don't think she said anything about him."

Then O'Beirne told Voss what he knew. It didn't differ much from what Voss had read in the neighbor's paper. Chance and Fade were dead. Both shot with a .22 caliber target pistol. Neil should have been dead, too, or so he said. He was supposed to shoot himself. They were going to do it all together, but they only had the one gun. And Neil claimed that when it was his turn he couldn't do it. Since he'd had the gun in his hand, and all three had their prints on it, there was no way to tell who shot whom. Neil's own statements had been contradictory. There wasn't much else. The three of them had been in Canada a couple of weeks ago, had come back through Buffalo. A customs report said a drug dog had alerted on their vehicle, but it was just a dirty ashtray—they weren't holding—so they sent them on their way. No suicide notes had been found.

"And what about Avery?" Voss asked.

"Mrs. Sheridan?"

"Yes. Chance's mother. My ex-wife."

"We've spoken with her. She was pretty hysterical. Told us it was all your fault."

"Yes," Voss said. "She would."

O'Beirne consulted his notebook. "She said, 'it's that goddamn rock opera all over again.'"

"Shit."

"I don't want a media circus around this any more than you do, Mr. Voss. But you know they're going to dig up everything on you. It's not hard to find. I Googled you, and there's a whole article on the suicides back in '75. My advice is don't talk to anybody. If they can't get a rise out of you, maybe they'll let it drop. But you're going to need a thick skin over the next few weeks."

"Yeah. Thanks."

O'Beirne gave Voss his card. "Call me on your cell as soon as you get out to your car—that way I'll have your number."

"Okay," Voss said listlessly.

"Mr. Voss?" the Lieutenant said after he walked him back out to the front desk, his hand outstretched to shake Voss's hand, a calculated gesture of solidarity. "I'm very sorry about your daughter."

Voss shook his hand automatically.

O'Beirne nodded to the desk sergeant.

The door buzzed and the bolt snapped back like a gunshot.

This had been his turf once, but he hardly recognized it. Everything was so built up that you couldn't see the contours of the landscape anymore. Only for a brief moment, when he ended up on a spur of the turnpike, did he get a glimpse of what was left of the meadows, a place he remembered for the smell it had when he was growing up, a dank, rotten swamp to be avoided. Looking down from the elevated highway he saw the tall reeds, golden in the evening light and rippling in the breeze like soft swells on the sea, and he felt a sudden longing for all the lost landscapes. This one had once stretched for miles in all directions, roadless and frightening, a place that could swallow you up, an infinite dumping ground into which things—including, it was said, bodies left by the mafia—would disappear forever. Tall buildings had sprung up around the edges of the now valuable wetland, six, eight, and ten lane highways arced across it, and to the north the Meadowlands Sports Arena Complex had its own exit ramps.

Voss was searching for signs to Route 3 or Route 46, but the road he was on, in the thick of rush hour traffic, was sweeping him off in the wrong direction, toward the east, where he could see the skyline of the city, noting again the absence of the World Trade Center. As a boy, cutting school to take the train into Manhattan to hang out in the Village, or later, driving in with his friends and band-mates, he had watched the two towers being built. They had become the landmark that the Empire State Building once was. Now the Empire State Building dominated the skyline again, golden in the dying light. He saw an exit for Routes 1 and 9, a familiar road north that would surely intersect with Route 3. The ramp was short, and scanning for signs, he nearly slammed into a delivery van at the bottom. The anti-lock brakes kicked in and he shuddered to a stop, feeling the stomach churn of an adrenaline rush, then the breaking of the vinegary sweat of panic. His hands were shaking.

Half an hour later, after a detour through an unfamiliar neighborhood in Secaucus where he nearly got carried off by the tunnel traffic into the city, he was westbound on 46, far wider than he remembered it, and now lined with an unbroken string of strip malls, car dealerships, diners, filling stations, cineplexes, a Barnes & Noble Superstore, chain restaurants, and remarkably, a tiny roadhouse from years ago, neon beer signs glowing in the windows and two pickup trucks loaded with landscaping gear in the gravel parking lot. Driving cautiously in the right lane, he spied the Park West diner—where he was to meet Avery—just up ahead. Huge and gleaming, it was nothing like he remembered; the sign seemed to be the only part of it that hadn't been completely reconstructed, enlarged, decked out with chrome panels and fluorescent lights.

A hostess in a black sweater with black sequins met him as he passed the cash register. A Muzak version of "MacArthur Park" played in the background.

"I'm meeting someone. She may already be here."

"Would that be her?" the hostess asked, indicating a woman sitting alone in a booth by one of the front windows.

Voss had to look twice. It was Avery and it wasn't. He couldn't believe how old she looked. Not that she was older than him, but he hadn't seen her in so many years and his mental picture of her hadn't changed. As he approached the table, she rose elegantly: heels, perfectly creased slacks, a silk blouse, and hair swept up and away from her carefully made-up face. He didn't know if he should embrace her or shake her hand, but she reached toward him with both hands and he folded her in his arms. Her back was bony and hard, her hair stiff and brittle.

"Hi, Jack," she said, letting him go and stepping back to look at him. "You've stayed young, and I've grown old."

"I fake young," he said. "It's part of my job, and it's getting harder every year."

"I've turned into my mother," Avery said. "A skinny bitch with expensive hair."

"And great posture," he said, smiling.

She smiled back for a moment, but by the time they had seated themselves, she was crying. "What the hell happened?" she asked.

"You told the cops it was my fault," Voss said, shaking his head.

"I'm sorry I said that, Jack. I know you loved her."

"I can't absorb it," he said. "It doesn't compute. I was at Artie and C.C.'s last night, watching the Convention, and it came over the crawl, and I never connected it with her. Then I was at a recording studio all day until I went over there to take her out to dinner, maybe go for a drive."

"She likes that," Avery said. Then, tears flowing, she corrected herself: "Liked it."

He pulled some napkins from the chrome dispenser and handed them to her.

"I don't know what to say," he said. "I know I wasn't around for most of her life. I thought I was honoring your wishes, but maybe I accepted my banishment too easily."

"Not now, Jack," Avery said. "We are where we are. I'm glad you're here."

"Me, too," he said. "I mean, not under these circumstances, but, I don't know. . . ."

"Shut up, Jack," she said gently.

They ordered coffee, a slice of cheesecake for him. He kept looking at her, remembering, recognizing and not recognizing her in the drawn woman before him. She had been heavy the last time he'd seen her, and before that she had been slender and sexy. He'd never known another woman's body as well as he'd come to know hers. He knew where she was ticklish—the crooks of her arms and the backs of her knees; could diagram the constellation of moles on her left shoulder blade—Cassiopeia in the flesh, he used to say; knew that her pinkie toes were so small as to be nearly vestigial. But in many ways this was an entirely different woman before him. Her eyes were the same, almost black with faint gold coronas around the pupils, like eclipsed suns. And seeing her weep was familiar. But she was no longer a girl, and that was how he remembered her.

"You're staring at me," Avery said. "I've gotten old. Get over it."

"No," he said, shaking his head. "I'm sorry. It's just that. . . ." He ran out of words.

"Forget it," she said. "When did you last talk with her?"

"Two weeks ago? I told her I was flying in for a session. I can't believe this. She said she was looking forward to seeing me."

"She always looked forward to seeing you," Avery said. "She was proud of you."

"Incredible."

The waitress delivered their order. First placing the cheesecake in front of Avery, who pushed it across the table to Voss.

"You had certain advantages a parent on the scene doesn't have."

"Yeah, I know. Not being the disciplinarian. Good cop. Like that?"

"That. But also being exotic by not being around much. Your presence was always an event. Special."

"I always tried to support you," he said, realizing it was a lie as soon as he said it.

"You gave her the money to move out, Jack. Paid for her own apartment when she was only nineteen."

"Yes, I did."

"God, I was mad at you for that."

"She was going to move out anyway," Voss said. "I didn't want her in some rat hole."

Avery reached her hand across the table and touched the back of his hand. "I know," she said. "She was like us, when we were that age."

Voss just shook his head.

"Did you know the boys?" she asked.

"I'd met Neil a couple of times, and I met Fade last May. They came out to see me, stayed at the house—you knew that, right? I mean, she told you?"

"What I knew is all a muddle, right now. I should have remembered. She loved going out to see you. Told me all about your place. It scared me. I was afraid she'd move across the country to live with you."

Voss looked down at his plate. "That would have been interesting."

"Huh?"

"I've lived alone so long I have a hard time with visitors, much less a live-in daughter."

"Well, you won't have to worry about it now," Avery said. "Shit. I'm sorry. I've been mad at you for so many years, Jack. But I tried not to let it spill over on to her. I really did."

"I know."

"What were they like when they came out to see you?"

"They were like us when we were traveling in Europe, in Greece. Crazy about each other, always touching, laughing. Two neo-hippies in that little van of his, with sleeping bags and incense, beads hanging from the rear-view mirror."

"Two?"

"Yeah, Chance and Fade."

"Neil wasn't with them?"

"No. They talked about him. He had to work or something. They were going to meet him later, in Portland or Seattle, drive back together."

"Did you get high with them?"

The question was like a well-placed jab, grinding skillfully into an old injury. In the quiet that followed it, Voss could hear a soupy Muzak rendition of the old Isaac Hayes theme from *Shaft*.

"I'm not a druggie," he said. "I haven't been since . . . I haven't been for a long time. But, yes, I did get high with them. Once. It was their stuff, and they offered. It was one of two times I've smoked this year."

"I'm sorry," Avery said, shaking her head. "I don't mean to stab at you, but we've got quite a history."

"Yeah," he said.

"So Neil wasn't with them."

"No. Like I said, they were supposed to meet up later, then cross the country together. They ended up going through Canada, right?"

"Yeah," Avery said. "And something happened."

"What? What do you mean?"

"I don't know exactly. But when they got back they weren't the same."

(♯)

On the way back to the city, Voss noticed a sign for a hobby shop in one of the strip malls he was passing and he pulled in. He wandered the aisles in a daze for a while, settling finally before the plastic model airplanes. The clerk, a man in a flannel shirt and suspenders, watched him closely, rang his purchases up quickly, and began turning lights out as soon as he had run Voss's credit card.

About an hour later Voss was back in his apartment, emptying onto the dining room table a bag which contained tiny paint cans and brushes, a bottle of liquid glue, a tube of Squadron green putty, a razor knife, some sandpaper, and kits of a P-38 Lightning and a P-51 Mustang. He dialed Artie's number on his cell phone and got the machine. He didn't know what to say, so he hung up without leaving a message.

He spread a newspaper out on the table and opened the P-38 box. It was an Italian-made kit, and the instructions were written in four languages.

He had to wear his reading glasses to make out the smaller pieces on their plastic trees. He took the parts into the kitchen, washed them carefully with soapy water, and rinsed them off in the sink, then brought them back into the dining room along with a cutting board. When he was a boy of ten, he would have just started to put the kit together, but now he was adhering to the procedures he and Hal had used later, when, as teenagers, they would get high and build models. Hal had discovered magazines dedicated to model-building, and together they had learned to wash the parts, to use putty when working with ill-fitting pieces, to paint the small parts while they were still on the trees.

He went into the kitchen and grabbed a bottle of Grolsch. In the freezer was a baggy with about a half ounce of pot. A gift from Artie. Voss couldn't remember how long it had been there—a year at least—but he was glad to see it. He couldn't find a pipe or rolling papers. Thinking back again to his teen years, he took a ballpoint pen apart to make a mouthpiece, fashioned a bowl out of aluminum foil, and fired it up. "Here's to you, Hal," he said out loud. "Aw, Chance. What the hell?"

He did not turn on the radio or put a disc in the CD player, but for four silent hours he lost himself in the finicky work of careful construction, trimming parts with the knife, painting cockpit details and the pilot figure, taking care to glue the canopy to the fuselage without grazing the clear plastic. He decided to build the plane with the gear up, and the only place that needed to be filled and sanded was around the landing gear doors. He popped the seal on the putty, and as the green goo oozed out, the smell of solvent triggered a vivid memory of Hal, who liked to catch a big fly and glue it to the seat in place of a pilot, the monstrous head visible under the canopy if you looked closely. He painted the plane silver to match the picture on the box, and set it down to dry overnight. He would put the decals on it tomorrow. Then what? Somewhere in his basement in Carmel was a cardboard box with half a dozen planes he and Hal had built years ago, stowed away in a dusty corner like the memories that went with them.

In the morning, he was expected at the recording studio, but he couldn't imagine playing.

He could hardly think two thoughts in succession.

He had a daughter.

She was a little girl watching *Sesame Street* in German. She waved good-bye without looking at him.

Then she was gone—or he was.

Years later she came back into his life, remotely—a young woman, a different person all together, but still his daughter. As improbable as it seemed, for all the years of separation, she still loved him.

And now she was gone again. For good this time. It didn't make sense.

Time contracted. Hal's death was yesterday instead of back in the '80s. Chance was dead. Avery had been out of his life since Hal died. His parents were dead. Once, asking himself what remained, he would have quickly said his work. But what was he doing now? Singing covers of other people's songs. He hadn't written anything in five years. No, ten. Nothing since *Practice*.

He was tempted to toss the plane into the garbage—it sat there on the table, a reminder of his inability to progress, his entrenchment in the past, his unwillingness to accept the fact of his own aging, reading glasses notwithstanding. The tiny silver plane with its twin tails and the black propellers he had installed so carefully, the canopy so meticulously painted . . . it was a small but insistent recrimination, and even after he'd turned out the light and headed off for bed, it caught the soft glow of the city from the tall windows, and finally, in that last glimpse, the emotion he'd been waiting for came, and the tears, huge, deep sobs, wrenching and childlike. He fairly dove into the bed, curling up still clothed, and rocked himself, and wept.

The Magic Carpet

Two plus one is so much more than three.

A light April rain was falling as the children climbed raucously into three waiting buses. Harold Proczevski, pushing his way through the crowd, was one of the first boys to get on, and he rushed to claim a seat on the right about two-thirds of the way back. Through the rain-streaked window he looked out at the dark red bricks of Saint Mike's, gloomy as always. John Voss got there next, and once the two of them were seated, no one even tried to get the seat between them, which everyone knew would be reserved for Avery Calentine. The three were inseparable, and had been since the third grade—they were now in the fifth. Soon, Sister Aloysius was squeezing her way down the aisle, checking off names on a list.

"Does everyone have a buddy?" she asked in her classroom voice.

"Yes, Sister Aloysius," the boys and girls said in unison.

"You must never separate from your buddy," she said. "We want to make sure everybody who's on the bus this morning is on it this afternoon."

The journey from Union, New Jersey to Rye, New York took about an hour and a half. John, Harold, and Avery—oblivious to everyone else on the bus—played war, snapping their cards down on the table made by Avery's skirt stretched tight across her legs.

"This isn't going to be much fun if it rains all day," John said.

"It's better than being in school," Harold said.

"It's going to clear up," Avery said. "You watch."

But it hadn't cleared up by the time the bus slowed down to pass between the two art deco towers and beneath the arched sign reading "Playland." The amusement park looked dingy in the rain; the roller coaster called The Dragon was closed until the threat of lightning passed, and the lines for most of the indoor attractions were long. John, Harold, and Avery queued up for the Magic Carpet, a fun house built to look like a Moorish castle. They handed over three tickets each—making sure they kept plenty in reserve for The Dragon later, which cost five—and after weaving their way slowly through a crowd-control maze, they climbed aboard a car that took them in. They passed immediately into a dark tunnel with pop-out frights, lots of noise, and the illusion that they were going to crash into walls that would suddenly bang open and allow them through. The skeletons, ghosts, and bats that flew at them were cheap effects, good for a scary moment that they pretended not to have felt; then the short ride delivered them to a landing where they got out of the car and continued on foot. The platform funneled into a narrow, dark hallway. Skulls with glaring eyes appeared at windows; hags and ghouls lit up suddenly and then went dark again as the three friends stepped on and off the triggering mechanisms. Although they were all too big—too old—to admit being frightened by any of this, the occasional rumble of thunder from outside made the experience more unsettling than it would otherwise have been, and they stayed close together. Once, at the loud crack and sizzle of a nearby lightning strike, Avery squealed, grabbed the two boys, and hugged them to her—contact that could never have happened on the playground or anywhere else back home.

Voss would remember this fun house always, two of the rooms in particular. The first was the crooked room. You were delivered to it via a dark, angling hallway and tilting stairs, so that, already disoriented, when you turned the last corner and saw into the room, it appeared to be perfectly ordinary. But when you stepped inside, you felt the floor slope away and you had to lean back to keep from falling. You threaded your way through another maze of handrails, like the mazes outside, turning to find yourself leaning forward and climbing with heavy steps. John tried to get the feel of the floor, to picture in his mind what the angle was exactly, but it wasn't easy or obvious. Certainly if you spilled a drink and watched it flow to one corner or the other, you would see which way the room tilted, but that wouldn't make it appear tilted to your eyes, which were still fooled by the normal looking floor, walls, and ceiling. Two turns into the maze, the angles clicked in, and John made a great point of showing how well he could keep his balance, maneuvering deliberately, hardly touching the rails. Harold and Avery, on the other hand, stumbled and fell over one another carelessly, laughing all the way, so that John felt a bit of a fool, and a little jealous, although he couldn't exactly have said why.

Beyond the crooked room, the hallway led into the great center gallery, filled with flashing lights and the almost musical blare of an arcade. While in memory the crooked room resolved into a kind of mechanical drawing, showing how its tilted floor, walls, and ceiling were installed in the otherwise plumb and level structure, a box propped crookedly in a larger box . . . while in memory the crooked room was analyzed and its mystery explained away, the great hall only grew more wondrous. It was filled with attractions, from fortune-telling machines—which required extra money—and an indoor merry-go-round, to automated games of skill—like Skee-Ball— and tests of balance and strength, and everywhere arrows pointed to the entrance to the magic carpet that gave the entire building its name. John, Harold, and Avery made their way past a photo booth and a sequence of curvy mirrors, laughing at the distorted images of themselves, fat or thin, or fat and thin in different places, and stopped in front of the Barrel-O-Fun, a slowly rotating wooden barrel, a little over five feet in diameter. The challenge was to pass through it without falling. Harold went first, keeping his balance for a brief moment, but falling about halfway through, and then rolling around in the middle as the barrel turned. After he finally crawled out, John, who had been studying the contraption all the while, said, "watch this."

He stepped in, struggling for a moment to time his steps into the side of the barrel that was constantly rolling toward his feet. Then he reached out with his hands, braced himself with arms and legs wide apart, his body forming an X, and soon was upside-down and then rightside-up again. He took a step forward, braced himself again. After four turns, a bit dizzy, he stepped out the other end, wobbly, but proud of his feat.

"My turn," Avery said. She repeated John's maneuver, but as she turned upside-down, her skirt fell up, revealing her white cotton underpants. She squealed, tried to push the skirt back down with one hand, and fell in a heap. After crawling out, she said to the boys, "I'm doing what John did. You guys have to stand guard. And close your eyes when I say."

So, with John Voss at one end and Harold Proczevski at the other, Avery Calentine reentered the rotating drum, braced herself, and began to turn. "Shut your eyes," she said, and then, "Okay, open them." She was coming back around, inching forward as she rotated. "Shut . . . open," she said three more times. Then—yelling "whoo!"—she stepped out wobbling and grabbed John for support, a gesture so unexpected and her trust in him so great, that he staggered and almost fell under her leaning weight. Then he regained his balance, held her up, and felt . . . happy.

From there they went to a jukebox in a soundproof room and played "Runaway," singing along with The Ventures at the top of their lungs. Moments later they crowded into the photo booth, and grinned and clowned for the camera as it flashed four times; then they stood impatiently outside as it slowly cranked out the row of black and white pictures. Voss often thought of that strip of photographic paper with the four gray images in which their childhood faces were frozen forever. He remembered it pinned to the frame of Avery's bedroom mirror in the house she grew up in; remembered her bringing it out of her purse, stiff and curling, to show around years later; and then, at some point, he couldn't say exactly when, it disappeared.

They had been warned to save the actual magic carpet for last, and when they finally went through the doorway with its flashing lights and climbed into a waiting car they found out why. It was a trick. The car took them through a curtain made of cloth strips and then the safety bar lifted and the seat fell out from under them, spilling them onto a huge moving belt, the "Magic Carpet," that bounced down a ramp and deposited them on a cushioned platform back outside. There was no getting back in without paying again.

After lunch—boiled hot dogs and Cokes with crushed ice—the sky cleared, and the roller coaster was opened. John, Harold, and Avery rode it twice in succession, eyes closed the second time, Avery sitting in the middle, six hands held high in the air—her left clasped in Harold's right, her right in John's left—for the entire ride.

They played war again on the way home, a perfect unit of three, immune to the noise of the other children. Were it not for something that happened later, after he and Hal had left Avery at her house and were about to split up to head off to their own homes, Voss would have remembered the entire day as one of perfection.

"Did you look?" Harold asked.

"What?" John said.

"At Avery. Did you look, see her panties?"

"When she fell?"

"No, after, when she went around and around."

"No, I didn't look. I said I wouldn't."

"I did. And it was a good view."

John and Harold could never agree later just whose girlfriend Avery was first—they had both been "Calentine's Valentine" many times. She cheered them on when they performed "Sherry" at a school assembly, John playing his accordion and singing the lead, Hal harmonizing. She went back and forth between the two of them throughout high school. When Harold got his first bass, after seeing Paul McCartney's on the Ed Sullivan Show, and the boys formed a band, Avery was the one who suggested John become Johnny and Harold Hal. When Johnny and The Featherweights started playing gigs at local high school dances, she never missed a show. Sometimes the boys weren't sure whose girl she was on a given night; she would make dates with both of them, as if she liked them equally and never felt jealousy herself or thought either of them would feel it. If they hadn't both been in the band, the question of which one she danced with might have caused problems, but it never came up. She sometimes danced slow songs with boys who asked her, but John and Hal didn't pay attention to it; during the fast songs she was always right in front of the stage, her partner, if she had one, just another member of the free-form dancing crowd, and always gone by the time the show ended and she was helping roll up the cords and pack the mikes.

John was the sweet, sensitive one, Hal the wild risk-taker, and she said she supposed she loved them both. When she started having sex with Hal, telling John she didn't think of him "that way," he was stoical about it, turning his frustration into maudlin poems which were precursors of the songs he would write later. When she turned away from Hal and initiated John into the magic of sex, he was so grateful and delighted that he almost forgot the hurt he'd felt before. Once, after band practice in Hal's basement, the three of them high on pot, she'd jerked them both off in a spontaneous expression of craziness and affection, but afterwards they felt weird about it—at least, Avery and John did—and it never happened again. When they graduated from high school, John still had never had another girlfriend, and he was a little jealous of Hal, who sometimes had two or three at a time. Eventually, Avery was just known as John Voss's girl, although it wasn't anything either of them declared, rather something that just happened, or that's what it was for John. No words of love were ever spoken in those days, although Avery said later that for all the scary attraction of Hal, John had always been the one she really cared for.

In 1970 they had been out of school for two years. Voss worked days in Caruso's Music Store on Route 22, he and Hal shared an apartment in Irvington, and the band was doing well, with two or three gigs a week, moving more and more toward the psychedelic, California sound. They had replaced "Massachusetts" with "Crystal Ship" and began doing a long version of "Magic Carpet Ride" that let Voss cut loose on the organ. Then Mitch Romani, their drummer, received his draft notice.

"What are you going to do when they call you up?" Avery, just home from college for the summer, asked John, as they passed a joint back and forth in his bedroom. The walls and ceiling had been painted midnight blue, batik curtains rose and fell with a light breeze, and Thunderclap Newman was on the radio. John's almost black hair was longer than Avery's, and hung to his shoulders. Both were naked.

"What do you mean what am I going to do? I guess I'll have to go."

"Mitch isn't going."

"Who told you that?"

"I know I'm not supposed to know," she said, handing him the joint. "Don't worry, I'm not going to tell anybody. I know about Hal's heart murmur, too. So he's 4-F. But you're 1-A. They're going to call you up. What are you going to do?"

"I don't know. I haven't really thought about it," John said.

"You have to think about it," Avery said, rising and turning her long back to him to get dressed. He thought he liked watching her put her clothes on as much as he liked watching her take them off.

"What do you want me to do? Go to college? I don't think so. I'm not book-smart like you. I just want to play music."

"What about the Navy or the Air Force?" she said.

"What? Look at me! Do I look like a sailor?" He posed with his hair hanging down over his eyes and the joint held between his teeth.

"You're going to have to do something, John. You want to end up being shot at in a jungle on the other side of the world? I'll tell you what, if you go talk to the Navy or the Air Force recruiter, I'll . . ." She bent down and whispered in his ear even though they were alone in the room.

The Air Force Sergeant didn't seem at all interested in John Voss as a possible recruit, but he let him take the tests. After scoring the results he became much friendlier.

"We might be able to do something for you, son," he said. "You got your high school diploma and you got good scores. They'll probably put you in communications, electronics. It'll be two years active, three years reserve, I can almost guarantee you won't go to Vietnam, and if you do, there's almost no chance you'll get shot at. How soon you want to start training?"

Voss couldn't decide, and let things drag on for several weeks. Mitch headed west, going to Mexico, he said. Two weeks later, while they were auditioning a new drummer for the band, they got the news. Mitch was dead. He had picked up a hitchhiker in Kansas, and the guy had killed him in Arizona.

"He's a casualty of this fucking war just as much as if he went," Hal said, lighting a joint in the cemetery after the burial. "If it wasn't for Vietnam he'd be standing here smoking with us right now. . . ."

Avery, John, and Doug, the guitar player, looked at him.

"Well, not here, obviously," he said, passing the joint to John. "But you know what I mean."

John Voss signed up for the Air Force the next day. A month after that, in basic, with two other Johns in his squad, he became Jack.

After basic and electronics school, they sent Voss to Germany for eighteen months.

"Like Elvis, man," Hal said, when Voss was home on leave before he shipped out.

It was like a year-and-a-half-long summer job. He lived in the barracks, spent most of his off-duty time on base reading books that Avery sent him, barely seeing the country and learning only enough German to order *Weissbier und Bratwurst*. When he came back, he felt as if he had grown up, become someone else, but back in New Jersey it was hard to say how. Little had changed, except that the space he'd occupied before he left seemed to have closed up; there was no room for him now. Hal had taken over Voss's old job at Caruso's and had kept the band going, now The Featherweights. No more Johnny. Hal fronted, and they'd found another guy who played organ. Avery was still away at college, getting ready to graduate and come home to work for her father's accounting firm.

When The Featherweights played a dance at Union High, their old school, Hal invited Voss up on stage. "Remember Johnny?" he said. "When they cut his hair they had to cut his name, too. Here's Jack Voss, people."

The crowd cheered him, but as he was playing the opening riff to "Light My Fire," his signature tune before he joined the Air Force, Voss felt that the song had become passé. Once Hal started singing, though, Voss knew why The Featherweights still played it; his rich baritone was everything Morrison's was, but he had more range and better control. Hal nodded to Voss for the organ ride, and Voss started out with the familiar riffs Ray Manzarek played on the record, but his heart wasn't in it. When he tried to cut the solo short, nobody was watching him for signals. It was Hal's band now. So Voss pressed on, going through the motions, but not feeling it.

Backstage one of his old English teachers grabbed his arm. He thought for a moment he was about to get thrown out of the auditorium, a non-student, no ticket. "I'm with the band," he started to say, but Mr. Farraday spoke first.

"I heard you were back," he shouted into Voss's ear over the sound of the music—they were now playing "Horse with No Name," Hal's bass dominating the guitars. "Come with me. I want to talk to you."

A few minutes later they stood in Mr. Farraday's office. "Welcome back," he said. "So what are your plans?"

"I don't know," Voss said. "I want to get back to playing music. I guess I'll try to get another band together."

"What about college?"

"Naah. You know what I was like in high school. Where'm I gonna go to college?"

"Forrester College in St. Louis."

"What?"

"I spent most of today with a recruiter who's been making the rounds of schools here in New Jersey. It's a progressive school, and they're looking for people just like you."

"What do you mean, people like me?"

"Kids with talent who don't fit the mold. Kids who are more than they look like on paper. Kids whose grades don't reflect the things they might be able to do in the right kind of school. That's you, John."

"How am I going to do college stuff like calculus and French?"

"You won't have to," Mr. Farraday said. "You can major in music. Everything else is up to you. They've done away with general education requirements. You fulfill the music department requirements and the rest is up to you. You can get the rest of your credits in basket-weaving if you want, although if I remember right, you liked to read books and talk about them . . . even if you didn't like to write essays. . . ." He smiled, knowing, friendly. "So you might take an English course or two."

"I'll have to think about it. I mean, I just got out of the Air Force. I wasn't planning on jumping into anything."

"Come back here tomorrow at eleven o'clock. I want you to meet this guy."

"Who? What guy?"

"The guy from the college, from Forrester. He's going to be here again tomorrow, and then he's on his way. I want you to meet him, and I want him to meet you."

"I don't know." Voss could hear Hal's bass in the distance: *bum boma-lahn, bomalahn, bomalahn-a-bee-bahn*—The Allman Brothers' "Whipping Post."

"You doing something else tomorrow at eleven?"

"I guess not."

"Then come. What have you got to lose?"

(♯)

Two and a half months later, Voss was climbing out of a taxi in front of Lockwood Hall, four years older than most of the other freshmen, but looking only slightly less lost. His hair had begun to grow back, and in his Frye boots and tattered skintight jeans he was pretty sure he didn't look like an airman in civvies. He stood in line to get his ID picture taken, stood in line to sign for the keys to his dorm room, stood in line to meet his advisor in the music department, a middle-aged woman who taught piano. She seemed friendly enough, but teacherly, too, and he had doubts about whether he would get along with her.

That evening, people were walking the halls of the dorms, wandering into one another's rooms, meeting and talking. There were lots of guitars, and one guy who looked vaguely familiar and played the harmonica; he thought he was better than he was. And there was a girl who sang beautifully. Voss followed her voice down the hall and into a darkened room that smelled of incense and pot. She was singing her own songs, accompanying herself on a big Guild 12-string. She reminded him of Laura Nyro, and he wanted to get to know her immediately. Not surprisingly, a crowd had already formed around her. Voss sat down on the floor and someone passed him a joint. He took a hit and leaned back. Her mouth went a little crooked when she sang, but everything else about her was perfect, including her voice, like baked apples and cinnamon.

Her name was Jeanette Del Rio, and she turned up in his Music Theory class, which was taught by Dr. Teresa Madison, his advisor. On the first day, the students introduced themselves and talked about their previous training in music. Voss listened to the stories of the young musicians. Most of them played guitar, and there was hardly anyone in the class who had not been in a rock band. Only Jeanette, who had gone to an elite art school in Cincinnati, had studied theory before, and composition. Voss was the only one who had begun with the accordion, the only one who identified himself as a keyboard man, although most of them had taken piano lessons at one time or another. He was also the only one who had been in the service, and some of his classmates looked at him askance when he mentioned it. He didn't mention it again.

On the way back to the dorm after class, he caught up to her. "Jeanette? Is that right?" he said.

"Yeah," she said. "You're Jack Voss, keyboard man."

"Yeah," he said, not sure if she was mocking him. "I heard you the other night. You're good."

"Thanks," she said. "I didn't see you there."

"I hung back," he said.

"You going to play in the jam on Friday?"

"Huh?"

"You didn't hear? They're going to open up the old theater down by the game room. A bunch of people are going to play. You got your gear?"

The game room had three pool tables, a couple of ping-pong tables, and half a dozen pinball machines. The pool tables were dominated by older guys with long hair and full beards who passed joints back and forth and swigged from a gallon jug of Cribari Chablis. The casual games of eight-ball that were played in the afternoon had been replaced by money games of nine-ball. At the far end of the room, a pair of double doors stood open. Voss could hear someone doing a sound check. He hauled his Vox Continental in its gray case stenciled with his name and serial number past the pool tables and toward the sounds. He recognized a couple of people from the other night, including the harmonica player. A heavyset guy with a soul patch had set up a drum kit toward the back of the small stage, and two skinny guys with guitars were tuning up. They all seemed to know each other already, which made Voss feel uncomfortable, but he set down his gear and walked up to them. "It's an open jam, right? Got room for a keyboard?"

"Yeah, great. You a singer? You got a mike?"

"Upstairs. But I don't have a P.A. I could run it through the amp, but it wouldn't be great."

"It's more than we've got," the drummer said. "I'm Mike. And this is, uh, Steve? Is that right?"

"Yeah, Steve. And Kenny over there."

"I'm Jack. I'll be back with my amp and a mike."

They took their time setting up, everybody playing a couple of licks just to let the others know where he was, what he could do. Finally the drummer spoke up: "Why don't we just try a simple blues? Not too fast, room for everybody to play a little."

"How about 'Statesboro Blues,'" Voss said.

"I can't do that Duane Allman lead," Kenny said.

"That's okay. We'll just start with the chords, play with it," Voss said.

"That's the spirit," the drummer said.

He struck the snare and set the tempo. Voss came in softly on the organ, spooky, slow, leaving lots of room for the guitars. Steve started strumming open chords, and they were making music. Kenny was playing too, but he had the volume turned down so low they couldn't hear him.

"Turn it up," Steve shouted at him.

"Give me a minute," he shouted back. They watched him work at his fingering for another few bars—he was all over the fretboard—and then he reached down and cranked the volume. It wasn't Duane Allman's lead, but it filled in the empty spaces in the groove with style, and before long the room began to fill as well.

They had been playing for about half an hour when Voss saw Jeanette come through the door. People were dancing, and she stood in an open place on the floor and moved to the music. Voss was entranced. It was his turn to take a solo, and he took it down low, a pulse in E. Then he let his left hand dance around the middle keys—never taking his eyes off Jeanette. She was moving with her eyes closed, and he imagined he was playing her, that what he did with his fingers was translated into what she did with her body: he could lift her up, make her throw her head back and shake her long hair behind her, or he could lean her forward, make her bend her knees and twist slowly down toward the floor. They were in sync. He picked up the pace, nodding to the drummer to mix it up a bit, and they played together for a few bars, then the guitars came in and Voss backed off, just keeping up that pulse, liquid, a wave for the others to float on. Jeanette's eyes were open again, and she was smiling at him. Voss gave a signal, and they closed the song on the beat. Whap. And people were hooting and clapping.

"You were in a band before, weren't you?" Steve asked.

"He wasn't in a band," Kenny said, "he led the band. Didn't you."

Voss smiled, feeling good. "It was back in Jersey, a couple of years ago now. We called ourselves Johnny and The Featherweights," he said. "I was Johnny."

"Johnny, huh?" It was Jeanette. "I thought it was Jack."

He smiled again. "It is now."

"Well, I'll say this," she said. "You are a keyboard man."

Voss smiled back at her and was about to say something, when he saw Steve's hand slip casually, possessively, around her, gripping her left arm and pulling her toward him for a kiss. She kissed him back and then wriggled away.

"You going to sing?" she asked.

It wasn't clear who she was talking to, and nobody answered.

"Jack," she said. "You sing, right? You going to sing?"

"I don't know," Voss said. "I'm getting kind of tired."

"C'mon, man," Steve said. "It's early. Let's smoke a joint and play some more."

"And you can sing something," Kenny said.

They got the harmonica player to watch their equipment and went up to Steve's room to smoke. Jeanette moved around the room as if it were hers, taking her shoes off and slipping them under the bed and then lighting candles. Steve sat cross-legged on the bed with an inlaid wooden box on his lap. He rolled a joint expertly, lit it, took a hit, and passed it to Voss.

"Michuacan," he croaked.

Voss took a hit and passed it to Mike. The joint made its way around the room. When it got to Jeanette, she took a deep hit, then turned the joint around, put it in her mouth lit end first, and shotgunned Steve, who leaned in close and inhaled the thick smoke through his nose.

"Do Jack," Steve said, through clenched teeth.

Jeanette smiled, moved off the bed and bent over Voss. She drew deep on the joint, turned it around and put it in her mouth, and shotgunned Voss just as she had Steve. It was like kissing without touching, her body hovering over his, pouring her breath into his lungs, and Voss felt like he was falling through space, the twin intoxicants of the pot and the woman dissolving the solid ground beneath him. He closed his eyes, and as she stepped away he felt her hair brush across his face.

Back downstairs, the harmonica player who had kept an eye on their gear came up to Voss. "You don't remember me, do you?"

Voss looked at him—long hair and a wispy beard, tan cowboy boots, and a western shirt. "I'm sorry?"

"Hank Bowman. I'm Mike Romani's friend. Mitch's brother. I heard you guys play lots of times."

"Right," Voss said, though he still didn't remember him. "You want to get up and play?"

"I can do 'Traintime.'"

"Why not?" Voss said.

Hank Bowman could make the harmonica wail, but his sense of time needed work both in terms of tempo and how long to play. Finally, he ceded the mike to Jeanette, who performed a couple of her own songs, one solo and one with the guys backing her. She sang about a place she'd dreamt of once but could never find in the world. Her apples and cinnamon voice turned to a sound of hunger and longing.

When Jeanette stepped off the stage, the boys looked to Voss to call the next song.

"How about 'Season of the Witch?'" he said.

He had played the original Donovan version many times with The Featherweights; now—given new life by Al Kooper and Stephen Stills—it was one of the few from those days that didn't sound dated or passé. He had to make an effort to avoid slipping into the Donovan voice and accent he used to mimic, but he thought he pulled it off. Steve and Kenny called for "Saint Stephen." Voss didn't know it. He had never played a Grateful Dead song in his life, although once he got the chords he could fill in easily. Looking out into the small crowd, he saw that many of them were singing along.

On Monday, Jeanette sat next to Voss in Theory. "You were great the other night," she said.

"So were you."

"Do you write?"

"I've written a couple of poems I tried to put to music, but I never managed to sell them to the guys in the band. "

"Can I see them sometime?"

"I don't know. I've heard your stuff. You know what you're doing."

"Maybe I could help you set them to music," she said.

Dr. Madison arrived busily, and before he had a chance to reply they were knee deep in Buckthorne's *Musical Theory and Practice*. After class, Jeanette put her hand on Voss's shoulder. "I gotta run. See you Wednesday. Bring your poems." And then she was off. He watched her as she went down the hall, jogging a few steps, then walking, then jogging again. Her floating hair was echoed by the soft, calf-length skirt that swirled around her knees.

He sat in his dorm room paging through the old notebooks that contained his poems. He would never let Jeanette see the notebooks themselves, embarrassing adolescent documents, filled with doodles and awkward sketches along with pathetic attempts at lyrics. He could see now why the guys in the band didn't want to play any of them—they were terrible. Even the best, a tender portrait of his grandmother, had no real chorus or refrain, sounded more like a bad country song than anything he would want to play. The rest were sad attempts to write about alienation, about how hard it was to be young in a world run by old men. The one about the war in Vietnam was just a mass of clichés, phrases lifted from Abbie Hoffman, Jerry Rubin, and Dick Gregory. So he took out a new notebook and tried to write something that didn't sound like high school angst. *I was a stranger till I met her,* he began. *A stranger wherever I went. . . .*

He was still writing about alienation, but now he had concrete experiences to relate—his loneliness and disconnection in Germany, his sense of not belonging when he came back. And the chorus came from that moment when Jeanette had shotgunned him up in Steve's room: *She breathed into me, and the floor fell away. Now I'm floating free, and I don't know what to say.*

"I guess 'heaven-sent' is kind of a cliché," Voss said to Jeanette when she looked up from reading it.

"That's okay," she said. "Songs use clichés all the time. Do you have music for it?"

"Not yet," Voss said. "I've tried a couple of ways of singing it. I don't know if I like any of them."

She looked at him, her head cocked a little. "When did you write it?"

"Last night," Voss said.

"Is it about somebody in particular?"

"Yeah," he said, "somebody I just met a couple of days ago."

(♯)

It was to be his third piano lesson, but when Voss got to the studio, his teacher wasn't there. A note taped to the door told him to go to Dr. Madison's office.

Although she was his advisor and Theory teacher, Voss wondered if she knew his name—the advising session had been a rushed few moments at a folding table in the hallway outside the registrar's office on his first day, and in her class he had sat in the back, trying to lie low, but occasionally rolling his eyes and whispering sarcastic comments to Jeanette.

"Hello, Mr. Voss," she said. A thin woman in her thirties with an interesting face, not pretty but intelligent looking, she gestured for him to come into the room, which was dominated by a grand piano. Bookcases covered the walls, and a small desk was wedged into the corner nearest the door.

"Where's Roger?" Voss asked.

"Mr. Innsbruck has had to leave us. I'll be taking over your lessons. What book are you using?"

"We've just been working up some songs," Voss said. "No book. I've been playing for a long time."

"That's about what I expected," Dr. Madison said. "Piano class is not about learning *songs*. It's not your fault, but we'll have to get back on track." She pointed to the piano bench. "Please sit down."

On the music stand, a three-ring binder lay open to a Chopin etude.

"Play this, then."

Voss looked at the music. "I don't know it."

"That's all right. Let's see how your sight-reading is."

"But . . ."

"Just play it," she said. "Take your time."

He could not remember the last time he had been asked to sight-read. Probably when he took accordion lessons as a little kid. He placed his fingers lightly on the keys, looked again at the staves before him, then turned to her. "I can't do it," he said. "If you give me some time, sure, but not cold."

"All right," she said. "Then show me what you can play. Something that will tell me where you are. Not your most difficult piece, necessarily. Something you are proud of, something you feel confident with, but not something so simple that anybody could play it."

He addressed the piano, an aged Steinway with grainy ivory keys. Dr. Madison stood a little to his right. Again, he was taken back to his accordion lessons: the music before him, Mr. Jensen standing there, watching. Goddamn. Mr. Jensen would do that to him at least once a lesson. And invariably the result was the same. Voss would stumble through, almost every other note a mistake. "You don't learn to read," Mr. Jensen would say. "You play from memory and by ear. You will never get anywhere that way." The first half was true, but he could play, he reminded himself. Everybody said he could play.

"Okay. Here's a piece I know pretty well. I usually play it on the organ."

He began to play "Whiter Shade of Pale," screwing it up almost immediately.

"Whoa," he said. "I'm really not used to this kind of action. Give me a minute."

He played a couple of scales, just getting the feel of the instrument; it felt stiff, unresponsive to his fingers, so used to the keys of an electric organ, which he now realized were more like the buttons of an accordion than the keys of a real piano. If he didn't hit these keys hard enough they didn't sound at all. Even the feel of the old ivory, not smooth like the plastic keys he was used to, but rough and grainy as a welltrodden wood floor, was unfamiliar and uncomfortable. He began to play on the yellowed keys. It was work. He soldiered through the song and then sat back with a sigh.

"You were fighting the piano," she said.

"Yeah," he said, "and it was fighting back."

She smiled for the first time. It was a nice smile, but he had a sense that it warned of something bad to come.

"Do you want to hear what I think?" she asked, continuing without waiting for his answer, "you're not going to like it, I'm afraid."

He took a breath.

"You have talent, but you lack technique. You've got a bit of flash and a good sense of rhythm, which is a real asset, but you have some bad habits that we will have to fix if you really want to progress. I can help you with that, but it's going to be painful. Some of it is going to be tedious, and some of it will be physically demanding."

Voss was visibly shaken. He had pivoted on the piano bench and was leaning back with his arms crossed in front of his chest. He hadn't felt so humbled since basic training. Dr. Madison watched him. He leaned forward as if to speak, and she interrupted him before he could begin.

"Don't say anything yet. Think about it over the weekend. I've read your application file. And, of course, I've seen you in my class. I know you have done well by your music, and I know you are a little older and more experienced than most of the other students here. You find much of this tiresome. You could skip this whole college business, and you would probably be able to work as a practicing musician, playing dances, clubs, living from hand to mouth. And you know what? If you do everything I ask you to do, learn to read music . . ."

Again Voss started to speak, but she stopped him. ". . . I mean really read music, sight-read . . . and perfect your hand posture, strengthen your left hand, extend your repertoire, clarify your timing, and go deeper into your real self in your playing. . . . If you do all those things, you will still be able to work in the same sorts of places. I can't guarantee you anything more. But you will be a better musician."

His roommate was rolling a joint when he got back to the dorm.

"She wants me to start again from the beginning," he said. "Fuck, man. It's bullshit. Who the hell does she think she is?"

"Who she is, is a Cliburn prize finalist who can play the ass off the piano," Artie said, lighting the joint and handing it to Voss. "If she had bigger hands, she'd probably be in some philharmonic somewhere, or else touring the world."

"What? How do you know this shit?"

"It was in the program for a recital she gave in the summer," Artie said. "The prize, I mean. Everybody knows about the hands—I read that Liszt could stretch an octave and a half."

"I don't give a shit if she's the reincarnation of Beethoven himself. It's bullshit what she wants me to do."

"Give her a chance. You can always quit later if you really think she has nothing to teach you."

Voss should have known not to trust someone who left her boyfriend so easily, but when she came to him, Jeanette was like nothing he'd ever experienced before. The promise he'd felt her breathe into him that night of the jam was fulfilled in ways he could not have imagined. He felt things he'd never felt with Avery or the occasional *Frauleins* he'd been with when he was stationed in Germany. It wasn't what she would do to him—though she did things he hadn't even thought of—it was how she responded to his touch. For the first time Voss felt like a great lover. Avery had always complimented him when he'd asked her how it had been for her, but with Jeanette, he didn't have to ask. It was obvious. She writhed and bucked and shuddered, and he was hooked. Sometimes at night they would have sex when Artie was in the room, slipping into bed in the dark after he had gone to sleep, trying their best to be quiet, and never quite succeeding. And sometimes in the middle of the day, when Artie or Jeanette's roommate was in class and they had a room to themselves, Jeanette would strip off her clothes and dance for him until he couldn't stand it anymore. He had it bad. Just remembering some of their sessions would give him a hard-on, and he had to be careful not to think about her in class.

Then Christmas came and she was gone. Back to Steve. Voss was caught completely by surprise, and it felt like he'd been hit by a car that came out of nowhere. He remembered years ago when Avery and Hal had begun having sex and he'd felt left out. This was worse. He and Artie got quietly drunk together.

"You're the music man, Jack," Artie said as they played pinball in the game room. "Look around. You could take your pick."

"I don't want my pick," Voss said. "I want Jeanette."

And by Valentine's Day she was with him again, though he later kicked himself for taking her back. When spring break came, she convinced Voss that if he wanted to have her he would have to let her be with Steve from time to time, but understand that that didn't affect her love for him. And then she went with Steve to Florida.

"You're going to hate yourself for letting her do this to you," Artie said to him.

"Yeah, probably," Voss said. "But you don't know what she does to me."

"I've got a pretty good idea," Artie said. "I'm not that heavy a sleeper."

And when she came back from Florida she seemed to have even more sexual energy than before. She wore him out.

Then in May she started going out with a third guy and dumped Voss and Steve both.

"I'm sorry," she said, in the corner booth of The Bear's Den, the college snackbar. "But I warned you. I'm not the kind of woman who stays."

"You told me you loved me," he whispered angrily.

"I did," she said.

"Yeah," he said. "Maybe someday I'll be able to use the past tense when I say that, too. Fuck this. Have a nice life."

He marched out feeling everyone's eyes on him.

The following August he and Artie, Hank Bowman, the harmonica player, and a couple of other friends moved into the Lafayette house, a massive old place a few miles off campus. A few days before classes started, Jeanette called him there.

"I'm at the airport," she said. "I've got Jimi Hendrix's greatest hits with me, and I'd really like to see you, if you don't mind picking me up."

"Jimi Hendrix's greatest hits" was code for hits of purple haze.

She practically leapt into his arms when he got out of the car to help her with her bags.

"I missed you all summer," she said as he was navigating the ramps back to the highway. "I didn't know how much I loved you. I don't think I know how to stop loving you."

They pulled into a rest stop and parked in the remotest slot. He put a Yes tape in the 8-track, they dropped acid, and she stripped out of her clothes in record time.

Back on the highway a half hour later, as they were starting to get off on the acid, he said, "I wasn't going to call you. I don't know if I can go through this again."

"It will be different this time," she said.

"I want to believe that," he said. "And I am crazy about you; I feel it all coming back." He was driving eastbound on I-40, the big trucks leaving traces as they passed, the headlights from the oncoming traffic a symphony of light.

"I knew you would," she said, leaning toward him and taking his arm.

He found the gesture almost overwhelming, wanted to melt into it, fought to keep his eyes on the road, drive the car. His stomach felt knotty and tight, his whole body was tingling, and he shivered, though he wasn't cold. "It scares me, though," he said. "I mean, we love each other right now, don't we. And making love like that was . . . like nothing else I've ever known, amazing, beautiful. But we've been here before. Sometimes I think maybe we should just put an end to it all on a high note. Like right now swerve the car into one of those trucks and . . . done."

Jeanette pulled away from him and sat up straight in her seat. "Pull over and let me drive, Jack," she said.

"I'm not going to crash the car. I was just saying."

"I'm serious," she said. "You're scaring me. Let me drive."

"Don't worry. Here's our exit coming up. I'm getting off the highway. I'd never have the guts to do something like that, anyway."

A month later she was gone again. This time she'd completely left town. He felt like an idiot. And he had a major composition project due. *The Enchanted Pond* practically wrote itself.

AUGUST

*I*n the shade of a green and white striped tent on a low hillock stood the mourners: Avery with her husband, Dr. Sheridan, on her right and C.C. on her left, the priest at the head of the casket, Voss on the other side, alone, and at the foot the remainder of the small crowd.

Voss hadn't seen Avery since their meeting at the diner, and though she looked haggard, she stood erect, still with the perfect posture that had characterized her as long as he could remember, proud, strong, resilient, elegant as a single standing column in a Greek ruin. Beside her was the man Chance had learned to call Dad. Voss knew who he was, and they knew one another's voices over the phone, though they'd never actually been introduced. "The good doctor" Chance had called him when Voss was around. C.C. was made up heavily and a little sloppily. Voss looked at her differently after what Artie had told him the other night. That seemed long ago now.

His old bandmates, Kenny Claybourne and George Sinclair, in dark suits with sharply creased trousers, looked more like businessmen than rock musicians; their wives, in black, seemed strangely glamorous, as if they were dressed for a formal evening out. Bert, Voss's agent, stood with her feet apart, mannish in her black pantsuit. He didn't recognize any of the eight or ten others. All of them, he thought, including Kenny, George, and Bert, were there for Avery. Artie alone was there for him, and he had stepped away to speak with the paparazzi clustered on a small bridge a short distance from the gravesite. Voss watched the exchange from where he stood and was thankful for his friend's ability to manage such things. Still, he dreaded that gauntlet. In the August heat, he shivered.

He found it difficult to think of Chance inside that box. The painted face he'd seen at the viewing, with its cruelly sewn-shut lips, didn't look like anyone he knew. The hair was wrong, the blouse unlike anything he'd ever seen Chance wear. His mind kept jumping from image to image: her amazing birth in a German hospital; the toddler in the Berlin apartment; the time she explained to him that kids didn't speak English—only grown-ups did, except for her . . . kids spoke German. What was she, four? five? Then the long gap. Years of nothing until her reappearance in his life as a teenager, a beautiful young woman who reminded him of Avery when she was that age. But he couldn't connect any of those images with the mysterious entity being lowered into the ground.

At the funeral home, an hour before, the priest had droned on about a breach in the natural order of things when parents have to bury their children. He'd stayed away from the subject of suicide, and a stranger in the church might have thought Chance had died in an automobile accident or from a fast-acting fatal disease. People had been invited to share their memories of Chance Calentine Voss. Avery stepped up to the podium, but she couldn't speak, and after an agonizing minute of her standing there weeping, the good doctor led her gently back to her seat. Voss then stepped up. "I was just getting to know her," he said. "We had lost one another for a long time, which was my fault, and only found each other again a few years ago. We should have had more time." He'd composed the words carefully in advance, trying to be honest but not hurtful. He didn't want to say anything to hurt or blame Avery for the years she'd kept him away from Chance. He could have fought it, but hadn't, accepting the estrangement, he admitted now, with something like relief. There was no one to blame but himself. He stepped down, dry-eyed and quietly angry.

Others took their turns sharing tender moments and funny anecdotes. Not a single story was familiar to him.

Artie slid up beside him, nodded assurance that he'd held off the cameras for now. Voss turned to look at the cluster of photographers still waiting at the footbridge. His eyes scanned the tear-stained faces of the people gathered at the foot of the casket; most of them had known Chance better than he had. He looked away across the green lawns of the cemetery to the Hudson River gleaming in the sun like polished slate, on the other side, the New York City skyline. When the canvas straps unrolled to lower the casket into the ground, he couldn't recall anything anybody had said, only a collage of broken voices. Except for Artie and C.C., Voss had talked to no one about this. There had been no announcement in the papers, so the funeral was more or less by invitation. Bert, George, and Kenny must have called Avery. Nobody had called him—but then, how could they? Only Artie had his new number. As for Chance's friends, he'd only ever met Neil and Fade. Fade was being lowered into the ground in some other cemetery, and Neil was presumably in police custody somewhere.

As the crowd broke up, Artie put his arm around Voss's shoulders. "Listen, man, Avery thinks it would be better if you didn't come to the reception."

Voss stiffened. "Avery, or *Herr Doktor*?"

"That's not how it is, Jack," Artie said. "It's not you. It's those assholes who will follow you." He gestured toward the paparazzi now shooting the departing mourners as they crossed the bridge to get to their cars.

"Okay," Voss said. "So where do you want to go? I guess we could go to my place in the city."

"I can't," Artie said, his voice tensing up. "I gotta stay with C.C. I'm sorry, man. But . . . well, you know, I mean . . . you saw the other night. I can't leave her alone."

"Yeah, I know," Voss said.

As he crossed the bridge, a little guy jumped out at him with a pocket camera in his hand. "So, Voss," he nearly shouted, clearly wanting everyone to hear what he had to say, "you gonna write another suicide opera now?"

"What? Fuck you!" Voss said, stunned by the question. And then—the cameras clicking and buzzing, somebody pulling the little guy back, and Artie's strong arms guiding Voss to his car, opening the door for him, closing it after him. . . .

"These guys are probably going to follow you," Artie said. "Let them. Just go slow, don't let them rattle you. Once they see you're heading for the tunnel, they'll probably break off. I'm sorry I can't go with you. I'll call you later. I love you, man." Artie smacked the fender twice as if he were part of the ground crew launching a plane on a hopeless mission. Voss pictured a brief-ing scene from an old movie: "... some of you won't be coming back."

Voss headed out of the cemetery, trying to remember the route. If the paparazzi really did follow him, he wasn't aware of it. Within minutes he was passing into the long enclosure of the Holland Tunnel, the grimy, tiled passageway—so dark by day and so bright by night—that led under the river into the city. He remembered how, as a boy, he would watch for the blue line that marked the border between New Jersey and New York. He felt in the pit of his stomach that he was now crossing from one state into another, but what states they were he could not say.

As he emerged from the tunnel into the swirl of traffic around the Port Authority, Voss's cell phone rang. He picked up, fumbled to answer it, and the voice on the other end started right in: "So how's it feel? Now that the chickens have finally come home to roost?"

"What?"

The caller hung up. It had been a man's voice. An old voice, Voss thought. He steered for the car rental agency. He would dump the car, call Susan to get him a plane ticket, and get back across the country. He wanted badly to get fucked up, and if he stayed in New York he'd find a way, so it was time to get out of old Gomorrah on the Hudson, and head across the plains to his retreat above the western sea.

The cell rang again while he was waiting for his travel agent to call him back.

"I've waited thirty years to see you go through what I went through," the voice said.

"Who is this? Why are you calling me?" Voss said.

The line went dead.

Later, as he was leaving the car rental agency one of the clerks called his name: "Mr. Voss? You left this in the trunk."

It was the Strand bag with the private edition of Housman's poems he'd planned to give to Chance over dinner. He left it in his apartment where he'd found it the week before.

Artie called him as he was on his way to his gate at LaGuardia.

"You okay, bro?"

"I'll make it," Voss said. "I'm heading back to the fortress of solitude."

"I understand. I'm sorry about this morning. I wanted to go with you, but . . . I couldn't."

"I know. Where is she now? Is she okay?"

"Yeah. She's with Marilyn. They'll get trashed, but Marilyn will make sure she gets home safe."

"What about you, Artie? You all right?"

"Like Popeye, bro. I yam what I yam."

"Yeah," Voss said. He had never heard the Popeye line sound sadder. "So I got a plane to catch, man. Take care of yourself."

"You too."

On the plane Voss had a double scotch before the twilight takeoff, and slept most of the trip home, dreaming of highway ramps, and tiled tunnels that kept leading him to abrupt and unexpected obstacles, stopped trucks and striped barriers. He'd hit the brakes in a panic and wake up with a start, look out the window for a moment at the lights of strange cities below, then nod off again.

(♯)

At about ten in the morning, the doorbell woke Voss up. He pulled on a pair of jeans and found a uniformed officer waiting on his steps.

"Mr. Voss?" the young man said. "I'm here to take a look at your phone machine." He wore a crew cut, sharp-creased blues, a silver badge with too many points. "They told you to expect me, right?"

"I'm sorry," Voss said. "You got some ID? The uniform's nice, but I'm going to need to see something with your picture on it."

"No problem, sir," the young man said, producing a leather holder with his Sheriff's Department ID on one side and another seven-pointed metal star on the other. "You can't be too careful."

"C'mon in," Voss said. "Machine's over there."

The officer took a quick glance at it, made a note in his notebook, and said, "I'm going to have to take the whole thing. It's got a chip instead of a tape, so I can't pop it out. You got another phone?"

"Cell," Voss said.

"Okay. We'll pack this up and send it to . . ." he looked at his notebook again ". . . Hoboken. Let me make you out a receipt."

Voss's cell rang in the other room. "Just a sec," he said, and went to get it.

"Mr. Voss?"

"Yeah."

"Lieutenant O'Beirne. The local guy come by yet for your answering machine tape?"

"He's here now."

"Good. Any problems? Any more strange calls?"

"Guy called me twice yesterday. Said I was getting what was coming to me. Something like that."

"Anything like that ever happen before?"

"Not exactly," Voss said.

"I got a package in the mail. Clippings about back in '75, stuff like that. Mailed from Chicago. No return address. Any ideas about that?"

"Hold on."

Voss went back out to the living room. "You got everything you need?" he asked the officer.

"Yes, sir. Would you sign this copy of the receipt for me?"

Voss signed the copy, took the original, and walked the officer out.

"Lieutentant? You still there?" he said, walking into the kitchen.

"Yeah, go ahead."

"A package like that came to the monastery where I stayed about ten years ago. I never figured out where it came from."

"Okay. Let me know if you get any strange calls."

"Right."

"And by the way . . ."

"Yeah?"

"Somebody cleaned out your daughter's apartment. You know anything about that?"

(♯)

Gray light with the sea in it shone through the glass doors to Voss's deck, giving a nautical cast to the packing crate in the middle of the living room. The kind of heavy wooden box that would require a pry-bar to open, it had arrived two days after he had returned from the East Coast, and he'd let it sit there for a day more, dread trumping curiosity. Now he headed down to his basement where a toolbox had been left by the previous owner. He found a claw hammer and a large screwdriver, and after a few minutes of clumsy hammering and prying, he got the lid off the box. A cream colored envelope with his name on it sat on top of the Styrofoam peanuts which had already begun spilling out, some of them clinging to the lid as he lifted it. Inside the envelope he found a small pack of photographs and a note on fine paper:

$ *From the desk of Avery Calentine Sheridan* $

Dear Jack,

I've packed a few things from Chance's apartment. I got in there as soon as I could, which was a good thing, as you will see. Most of this stuff was yours from long ago, and I thought you might like to have it back. I think all of the records came from our old collection. Chance and her friends were real fans of retro music. I put the turntable in, too, in case you wanted to play them (nobody has turntables now), and, well, like I said, you'll see.

I'm sorry it didn't go better the last times we saw each other, but it was really an impossible time for both of us.

I don't know what else to say. I hope you are well.

Love,
A.

"Love." He hadn't expected that, and it caught him off guard. Then he read the postscript:

P.S. The pictures are from Chance's camera. The detective gave them to me and I made copies.

The photo on top was of Voss, Avery, and Fade sitting on the piano bench in The Cove, Chance between the two men, the center of focus in every way. He remembered the moment. They'd just finished dinner and he'd been about to start his first set when Chance said, "Wait, let me get a picture before we forget." She was trying to set up the camera for a timer shot when one of the waiters offered to take it for her. It was the night before they left. The other photos had been taken on the trip. There were two of Fade driving the van, one a classic road shot of the boy with the sea in the background, the other almost a silhouette, his face dark against an over-bright background of snowy peaks and sky. Voss flipped through the rest looking for more images of his daughter, but it was her camera, she had probably taken most of the pictures, and there was only one other with her in it. Almost certainly a timer shot, again Chance between two men, this time Fade on her right and Neil on her left. They were posed against the van on the side of the road. Behind them, flat ground for many miles—high desert—and in the distance, jagged mountains. Voss thought they looked happy. The rest of the pictures were mostly of scenery; about half of them appeared to have been taken through the windows of the van.

Voss set the photos on the coffee table before he could think about them too much. He returned to the crate, swept aside the top layer of clingy, white peanuts, and started digging. First, what looked like a picture in a frame, wrapped in the gray sheets of *The Wall Street Journal*. He tore the paper off and found a photograph of himself. He was leaning back and smiling, laughter in his eyes, a champagne glass in his hand. In the foreground, the bright sun overexposed the white tablecloth of a café table. An ice bucket with a half bottle of Moët glimmered on the left, and his leather jacket hung from the back of an empty bentwood chair to the right. Chance had taken the photo shortly after she'd moved into the Hoboken apartment, the first time Voss had visited. He pictured her with the camera in front of her face. It was only a couple of years ago. Well, maybe more—four? five? What had made him lean back and laugh like that? Something Chance had said? Something he himself had said? He thought of the old days when he and Hal and Avery were young. There had been a lot of laughter then. And clearly he'd had a moment like that with his daughter, yet he hadn't remembered it until seeing this photo. To be honest, he still didn't remember it. It was as if the photo was intent upon telling him what he had missed by not knowing her better. Or Avery was intent on telling him. He pictured her in Chance's little apartment. Giving orders to a crew of movers and cleaners. No, that wasn't fair. This tore her up, too. Now he saw her in his mind walking through the rooms weeping. She morphed from the angry, heavy Avery of those last days in Berlin when Hal died to that thin stiff figure he'd met at the diner on Route 46, the one he'd seen standing brittle at Chance's funeral, and who'd had Artie ask him not to come to the reception after. Of course she had to have help dealing with the apartment—her arms would snap if she tried to move a couch. So she'd gone around the rooms picking out things to keep for herself and things to send to him.

He reached deeper into the crate, his hand disappearing as if into a milky pool, loose bits of Styrofoam floating up and settling like mist. He felt a piece of rough cloth, an old tweed sportcoat. Avery had given it to him for his birthday during his last year at Forrester. Gray herringbone with leather patches on the elbows. He lifted it from the box and held it out at arm's length—what size was it: thirty-six? Thirty-seven? He remembered wearing it every day with jeans and Frye boots, a dress shirt unbuttoned to the middle of his chest. He wore a forty-two now, still lean for his age, but a far cry from those days. The sleeves were rolled up. Then he caught a whiff of his daughter's scent. He crumpled the jacket in his hands, brought it up to his face, and breathed deeply. She must have found it in one of Avery's closets and taken to wearing it. He'd never known. Something fell out the sleeve: a gray beret. This he could picture her in. He'd bought it for her in Monterey on her first visit to California. The year she'd turned eighteen. They'd gone to the aquarium and then to lunch on Fisherman's Wharf. A gray October day, drizzly, and bone-chillingly cold. He'd seen her shivering, and they stepped into a clothing store where he bought her a knobby sweater, heavy with lanolin, the wool so rough you'd expect to find twigs in it. And the beret. He'd quoted Neruda to her:

> *I remember you as you were last Autumn,*
> *you were the gray beret and the calm heart . . .*

"Do you quote that to your girlfriends?" she'd asked.

"Only after it's over," he had said, laughing, and he'd thought then—as he thought now—that he had no real idea of how to forge a relationship with this girl, who he could barely connect with the five-year-old watching German television. He couldn't remember where or what they had eaten, only that later, at the club that night, he'd played "Autumn Leaves" for her. That had come from the Neruda poem, too:

Dry leaves of Autumn whirled in your soul.

A sea breeze blew hard against the glass doors, bouncing them in their tracks and slipping through the crack between door and sill, blowing bits of Styrofoam around. The smell of the sea brought him back to the present, and he began digging deeper into the crate. He found the stack of records and the turntable. He flipped through the albums—a lot of old favorites: that first James Taylor, most of The Beatles, King Crimson, and Rick Wakeman. By now he'd stopped trying to keep the white peanuts in the crate, and they were spilling out into the room. Anita would be vacuuming them up for weeks. Down in the bottom of the box was a battered, hard-shell guitar case. He looked involuntarily at his left hand, the two stiff fingers a permanent reminder of that awful night in Berlin, and the reason he had to give up the guitar. Everything came together in this box, goddamn it. The case held the D-28 Hal had given him, the guitar he had dragged around Europe composing the songs that ended up on his first solo record. You could read his whole history in this crate, he thought, everything he'd ever done wrapped up in this package of stuff from his dead daughter's apartment, packed by his ex-wife. He lifted the case from the box, feeling its weight, not needing, or able, to open it just then, hearing the *plong* of the strings as he set it down by the door to his studio. Then he lifted the turntable out onto the floor. There was a record still on the platter with a disturbingly familiar silver and blue label. Voss felt something move inside him as he understood the full import of what Avery was sending him. What some part of him had known all along. Was this the music they'd played as Chance and Fade died? Had Lt. O'Beirne seen it? Had he ignored it? How had Avery managed to get it out of the apartment before somebody got hold of it? He lifted the smoky, clear plastic cover from the turntable to read the label: *The Enchanted Pond*. His head swam with vertigo and he felt as if someone had punched him in the solar plexus.

The Enchanted Pond

I was the one who could go either way. And I know there are people out there who say you choose, but you don't choose. Maybe I should have chosen. But I could go either way, and I went both.

THE ENCHANTED POND

Fantasy for Flute, Piano, and Voice

by

Jack Voss

Saturday, 20 October 1973, 8:00 p.m.

Lockwood Hall, Forrester College

Piano—Jack Voss

Flute—Valerie Flynn

Vocalists:

Soprano—Julie McIntyre

Tenor—James Vulpin

Baritone—Charles Boromir

Dancers:

Helena—Alice Changar

Prince Sigismund—Joseph DeLange

Boy—William Townsend

Fauns—Bobby Christian, Edward Szeleva

Choreography: Alice Changar
Set Design: Gianni Muscatello
Scene 1: A forest in Arcadia
Scene 2: An abandoned temple

The Story: A young Prince and his lover come upon a pond in the woods. "They say it is enchanted," the young prince, Sigismund, says. "Its waters have the power to make lovers love one another forever."

The young woman, Helena, kneels and runs her fingers through the water. "It is warm," she says.

The young prince removes his clothes. "We love each other perfectly," he says, "but we both have seen how after a time, many lovers' eyes begin to wander. If we bathe together in this pond we will ever after only have eyes for each other."

The young woman does not answer, but loosens her clothing and lets it fall around her ankles. She wades out into the pond; when she is waist deep, the prince dives in and rises, dripping beside her.

"Now we are joined together forever," she says, smiling.

"Not yet," he says. "According to the legend, we must share our love with the waters."

"And how do we do that?" the young woman asks.

The prince places his hands around her waist and draws her to him.

"Ah," she says, smiling.

As they lounge in the shallows after their lovemaking, the woman turns suddenly. "What is that rustling I hear?" she asks.

The sharp-eyed prince catches sight of a boy's head among the reeds and orders him to come forward. Embarrassed, but obedient to the commanding voice of the prince, the boy swims from the reeds, only his head showing above the water. "I'm sorry," he says, "I was following a frog and then I wanted a swim. I didn't see you until I was already in the water."

"Very well, young fellow," the prince says, "but do not hide yourself like this. Come here to the shallows and show yourself before us."

When the prince and his lover see the child before them, they smile gently at the state he is in. "The boy is as moved by your beauty as I am," the Prince says, smiling. Then he turns to the boy. "Don't be ashamed," he says. "When you are older you will share what you are feeling there with a woman and you will experience one of life's great delights."

"Such a pretty boy," the young woman says. "Someday you will find a pretty girl, and maybe you will bring her here."

"Now be on your way, young fellow," the Prince says, and laughing, he pulls the woman back into the water with him.

Years later, the boy, now grown, appears in the court of the prince and, now, princess. "I met you long ago," he says, "although you may not remember. I am alone in the world and I wish to serve you in any way you see fit."

The prince and princess look at him in puzzlement. The princess recognizes him first, and she feels her heart lift as she does. She turns to the prince and says, "Don't you recognize him? It is the boy who saw us in the water." She smiles shyly and looks down at the floor.

The prince looks the boy up and down and then studies his face. He smiles. "You've grown into a fine young man," he says. "If you are alone in the world, you need go no further. We will find a place for you."

Later, when the prince and princess are alone, she asks him, "Did you feel anything strange when you looked at our young friend this afternoon?"

"I did," the prince says. And then, since he and the princess tell each other everything, he goes on, "I felt a trembling in my heart not unlike the feeling I have when I look upon you, a thing I have never felt for anyone but you since we bathed together in that pond."

And the princess, with a look of genuine fear on her face, says, "I felt the same."

(♯)

Avery and Hal drove out to St. Louis the day before the performance. She was working for her father's firm now. They stayed with Voss at the big house on Lafayette. He met them at the door with a fresh ounce of Ozark pot held out before him, presented them to Artie and Darien Pynnoch, whom he introduced as The Statesman, and they fell back into the easy comfort of the months before he had gone into the Air Force. Hal had brought a bottle of tequila and half a dozen lemons; they sat around the kitchen table under the hole in the ceiling where the tub had leaked and the plaster had fallen, drinking shots with lemon and salt. Hank Bowman joined them when he came in, and later Duncan McGough and his girlfriend, Val. Voss and Avery switched to drinking beer after the first round, but Hal had shots with each successive round of people who came through the kitchen, and eventually passed out, his head on the table. They helped him to the couch, and then Avery simply followed Voss upstairs, undressed, and slipped into bed with him. "I've started to sag," she said to him as he buried his face in her soft breasts. They made love quietly, and afterwards he rolled over and slept the best sleep he'd had in weeks.

The production was a little awkward, unsure of itself, from the dancing fauns at the beginning, who established the back story of the pond with magic powers, to the lovers in chitons sinking behind fake reeds. Musically, it was cobbled together from bits of Stravinsky and Wagner, and it probably tried too hard to be classical. There were some nervous giggles at points Voss hadn't meant to be funny. But at the climax—as the three voices sang in soaring harmony while the dancers pantomimed the young man running a sword through the prince and princess and then stabbing himself with a dagger, all three then melting arm in arm into the pond—the audience seemed to be moved.

"I can't believe you wrote this," Avery said.

"I can," Hal said. "This is why the band never played your stuff."

"Thanks a lot, pal," Voss said.

"You know it's true. I never lied to you before, and I'm not going to start now. So you'll believe me when I tell you that this could be great if you rewrote it modern, electric."

"You're kidding," Voss said.

"No. There's some good songs in there. But the flute and the ballet dancing . . . they got to go, man."

"You know," Avery said, "he might be right."

"I don't know," Voss said.

"I'll help you," Hal said. "The Featherweights are dead. And the music store can live without me. I've got nothing to go back to. You know a guitarist and a good drummer?"

"You really think this can work as rock?" Voss said. "It's a fantasy. People want rock to be from real life. It has to have verisimilitude."

"What the fuck is vossimilitude?" Hal said.

"Verisimilitude," Voss said. "It means, like, you buy it as real life. Like, Tommy plays pinball, not polo."

"No," Avery said. "Vossimilitude. It's the name of your new band. And there's enough real life here for all of us."

Voss was about to ask her what she meant by that when he caught sight of Dr. Madison. She nodded slightly and smiled, then turned to leave on the arm of a distinguished looking man Voss took to be her husband.

Hal moved into the Lafayette house, and he and Voss went over the music for the rest of the fall semester. Over Christmas, they put a band together and started rehearsing. Voss played keyboards, of course, and Hal bass. The drummer was a guy Voss had met in Music Theory, George Sinclair; the guitarist, Kenny Claybourne, was the one he'd played with on that first jam session he'd joined at Forrester.

The second premiere was right after spring break. Gone were the fauns and the fake reeds, replaced by stacks of Marshalls, the music department's Hammond B-3 with Leslies on both ends of the stage, a massive drum kit, including two bass drums and a spectacular array of cymbals. The lovers were no longer on stage, but flickered behind the band in a film they'd shot in Forest Park just a week before with some acting students Artie knew; the boy was played by a girl in a tunic, like Peter Pan. Hal stood stage left, in skintight black jeans studded with stars, block-heeled boots, and a flower-print shirt that hugged his sleek torso, his beat-up Jazz bass hanging from a wide, black-leather strap, also studded with stars. Stage right, Voss looked out over the B-3, natty in a silk top hat, velvet jacket, and ruffled white shirt, working the pedals in powder blue suede shoes. Kenny was subdued in jeans, cowboy boots, and a faded flannel shirt, his white Stratocaster the only bit of flash. George wore a fringed leather vest that showed off his muscles, and he occasionally twirled his drumsticks like batons. They were a rock band, stepping into roles ready and waiting for them. Tight and confident after three months of practice, they set out to put on a show. From the first, quiet, flute-like notes of the organ to the crashing cymbals and reverberating power chords of the climax, and on to the dark resolution, they rode the groove like a locomotive rides the railroad tracks.

Thursday night's performance was sparsely attended. But a notice appeared in the morning paper on Friday, calling it a "rock version of the sex fantasy that scandalized some audience members last fall." That night, there were almost no empty seats, and the third and final night, Vossimilitude played to an overflow crowd. They had the audience standing on "Touch Her and You're Dead," one of two songs where Hal shared the writing credit with Voss, and after the last notes of the *Liebestod*—a slow, moody piece with swirling organ riffs and a haunting bass solo, the lovers committing suicide together and melting into the pond on the screen behind the band—the crowd sat in silence for a moment before erupting into a standing ovation.

The band members gestured to Voss to come out from behind the organ. He walked to the foot of the stage, in his shirtsleeves now, doffed his top hat with an extravagant sweep, and bowed deeply to swelling applause. Then the band bowed together.

After the applause died down, a man in a business suit called up to Voss from the floor in front of the stage.

"Mr. Voss," he said. "I knew you'd prove out."

Voss looked down and recognized the college recruiter Mr. Farraday had introduced him to two years before.

"I've got someone I'd like you to meet," the man said.

"I think you've got a record here," a man with a ponytail shouted up at Voss. "We need to talk." He handed Voss a business card. "Come to my office on Monday at around lunchtime."

"I'm in class until twelve-thirty," Voss said.

"Can you get downtown by one or one-thirty?"

Voss nodded and put the card in his pocket. He turned to Hal. "We fucking rocked, man," he said.

"Fucking A," Hal said.

"I just met a guy who wants to record us," Voss said.

Hal gestured with his head. Avery had come up beside Voss. She'd flown in a few days before.

"Record?" she said.

"Record," Voss said.

"When?" she said.

He showed her the card. "I'm supposed to have lunch with him on Monday."

She kissed him on the mouth, then held him at arm's length. "Don't you sign anything without letting me look at it. I'm an accountant, remember?"

"Don't worry, babe. You're the manager." It was the first time anyone had said it aloud, but it felt right.

Voss looked back at Hal. They were still standing on the stage. People were filing out of the room. He felt as if he had grown a foot taller and was glowing. Hal gestured again with his head and raised his eyebrows a fraction of an inch. Voss turned to look behind him.

"Keyboard man," a familiar voice said in his ear.

(♯)

The producer's office was in an old building in downtown St. Louis, about a fifteen minute drive from the house on Lafayette Street.

"Have you been up?" Avery asked Voss, pointing to the stainless steel arch as it came into view.

"Not yet," he said. "We should go sometime." It was one o'clock. He had cut his morning classes.

"Whatever you want," she said.

He looked at her and then back at the road. Was she deliberately echoing her remark of the other night, when Jeanette appeared after the show? "You're a rock star now, Jack," Jeanette had said. "Can I be your first groupie?"

"And so it begins," Hal had said, executing a deep, knightly bow to Voss, "Maestro." Then he pivoted neatly on his heel and strode across the stage.

Voss looked from Jeanette to Avery and back, out of his depth, still overwhelmed by the applause and the producer's invitation, and now. . . . He wondered what exactly he was supposed to do.

"Unless your girlfriend won't let you," Jeanette said.

"Jack does what he wants," Avery said.

"Maybe he wants both of us," Jeanette said.

"Tonight's his night," Avery said, slipping in closer to Voss, pressing her hip into his right side, and then turning so that her left breast rubbed across his upper arm. He could feel her nipple though her shirt. "You haven't introduced us, Jack," she said.

Voss's heart was pounding and he felt his face flush. "This is Jeanette," he said. "Jeanette, this is Avery."

"Jeanette," Avery said. "Jack's told me all about you."

"Oh, I'm sure he hasn't told you *all* about me," Jeanette said.

Voss found a parking space on Olive Street. In the elevator, he put his arm around Avery's waist, but she didn't move any closer to him.

"Do we need to talk about Saturday night?" he said.

"Not now," she said. "We need to be focused for this meeting. Remember, we don't sign anything today. Any papers he gives us we take home and go over with a fine tooth comb. I know some people we can call if we have questions. This could be the most important deal of your life. Let's not screw it up."

The office itself was like a private eye's office in an old black and white movie, with "Aron Productions" painted in black and gold letters on the glass pane in the outer door, a secretary in a skirt and hose, and a photograph of the building on the waiting room wall. In the photo, the tower silhouetted against a dramatic sky, it looked like the Empire State Building in miniature. The secretary announced them awkwardly through an intercom, as if she were an actress in a play: "Mr. Norman, Mr. Voss is here."

"Thank you, Sheila. I'll be right there," came a voice from the staticky speaker on the gray metal desk.

He emerged from the inner office, younger than Voss remembered from the other night. His tie was loosened and his sleeves rolled up, his shoulder-length mane of dirty-blond hair flowing loose. "It's Jack, right?" he said, extending his hand. "Bobby. And this is?"

"Avery Calentine," Voss said as Bobby shut the door behind him. "Our manager."

"Great," Bobby said. "Excellent. So many young bands have no management. It's good that you have someone to take care of that end of things."

Voss had the feeling that they were being bullshitted, that Bobby was putting on an elaborate show for their benefit.

Bobby turned to his secretary. "We'll be gone for a while, Sheila. If I'm not back by four, just take off, and I'll see you tomorrow." He turned back to Voss and Avery. "Ever been to Stan Musial's? Best lunch in town. You ready to go?"

Voss looked at Avery.

"It's on me," Bobby said. "I know you're poor college students. But I don't think you're going to be for long. Come on, where you parked? You got enough in the meter?"

"Who's Aron?" Avery asked as they headed out the door.

"It's my initials," Bobby said. "R. N. Robert Norman. But it's also Elvis Presley's middle name."

They put more money in the meter and then went to a nearby garage to get Bobby's car, a big white Buick convertible. Bobby must have seen them looking at one another again as he opened the door.

"Both of you take the back seat," he said. "I'll play chauffeur. It's not far. Just far enough to take care of this." He flipped open the ashtray and flourished a joint between his fingers, pushing the lighter in, starting the car as they waited for it to pop back out.

At the restaurant, Bobby was welcomed like a regular, a big-spending regular.

"You guys want a drink? Or . . . I say we get a bottle of champagne. Life is short and then you die."

A bottle of Piper arrived, Bobby ordered shrimp appetizers, and they all ordered steaks. Then Bobby held up his champagne shell for a toast: "You guys kicked ass the other night."

They clinked glasses and drank.

Then Bobby went on: "I mean, you were tight, professional, with some catchy songs. What was that one, 'I'll Kill You if You Touch Her?'"

"'Touch Her and You're Dead,'" Voss said.

"Right, 'Touch Her and You're Dead.' That's a keeper."

"Thanks," Voss said.

"And that bass player—awesome. He's got the looks and the chops. What's his name?"

"Hal Proczevski."

"Hal Proteus," Avery jumped in.

Voss looked at her.

"Proteus," she said again. "Don't worry, we talked about it. It's from Greek mythology."

"I know where it's from," Voss said.

"Wherever it's from, it's great," Bobby said.

After they'd eaten their shrimp, Bobby leaned forward with his elbows on the table. "Okay, so who the fuck am I, right? I'm not going to lie to you. I'm new at this. The old man's in real estate, big stuff, and I could just work for him—and I do, sometimes. I turned a couple of big properties over, and naturally he's telling me I should put the money into other properties, but I want to do something else. So I've got this warehouse on the south side, and it's being fitted with soundproofing and heavy duty electrical service even as we speak. We're building a booth. I found a studio in Detroit that's upgrading, and I'm buying their old set up. Mikes, mixing board, 8-track deck, the works—okay, so it's not the latest, but it's not junk, it was the latest two, three years ago, and it's still pretty fucking good equipment—The Beatles recorded *Sergeant Pepper* on a 4-track. And I've been talking to a guy I went to college with who's at Columbia Records now. He can't guarantee anything, but I get a demo to him and he'll listen. And I know him. We spent half our college careers getting stoned and listening to *Ummagumma* and King Crimson. He's gonna love your stuff."

(♯)

Vossimilitude was the first group to use the studio, the original four, plus Rick Darnell, a rhythm guitarist Bobby knew and pressed on them. Avery was never not there. She moved in with Voss in the Lafayette house, leaving behind her job in New Jersey. She kept track of the expenses, the charts, ordered food in, and smoothed out tensions between the boys.

"I want to record the whole thing first," Bobby said, "just like you played it at the show, but then we're going to have to cut it down to about forty-eight minutes, max."

"What?" Voss said. "They're not just songs—it's a rock opera, like *Tommy*. There's a story. We've got enough for a double album."

"Nobody starts out with a double album," Bobby said.

Voss looked at Avery for support.

"Let's take it one step at a time. First the demo, just like the show. We'll talk later about what comes next."

"Smart girl," Bobby said.

They worked mostly at night and on weekends. The first demo was ready in two weeks, and Bobby sent it to his friend at Columbia. By the time word came back, Voss and George, the only ones who were still in school, were in the middle of finals.

"It's a go," Bobby said over the phone. "When can you start on the real thing?"

"Double?" Voss asked.

"No, man. I'm sorry. Like I told you, nobody gets a double their first time out. But what they're offering is huge."

"What do you mean, huge?"

"Let me talk to Avery about that," Bobby said. "Is she there?"

"Yeah, just a sec."

"Wait. One more thing before you get her. He had two suggestions. I think you're gonna like the first one, and you're gonna have to trust me on the second, but he's right."

"Yeah?" Voss said, with a sinking feeling in his gut.

"Girl singers. A chorus. Just for a couple of songs. And I've got a line on three black chicks, sisters, who are kick-ass."

"Okay. And the second suggestion?"

"No German titles. That last song, Leeber . . . something?"

"*Liebestod*," Voss said. "Lovedeath."

"Whatever. Gotta be in English."

VOSSIMILITUDE
THE ENCHANTED POND: A ROCK OPERA

Jack Voss: Keyboards and Vocals
Kenny Claybourne: Guitars
Rick Darnell: Guitars and Vocals
Hal Proteus: Bass and Vocals
George Sinclair: Percussion
Ruby, Della, and Elizabeth Priestly: Vocals

Side A

Overture: There's Love Enough for All of Us (if we can live together) *(J. Voss)*	3:15
The Enchanted Pond *(J. Voss)*	4:12
I Was Just a Boy *(J. Voss)*	2:32
Stranger in the Castle *(J. Voss)*	3:45
The Beauty that I Saw *(J. Voss)*	:52
Who Was That? (I Saw That Look) *(J. Voss)*	1:17
He Cannot Look at Me (but she can) *(J. Voss)*	3:02
Touch Her and You're Dead *(J. Voss, H. Proteus)*	3:49

Side B

Why Can't We Try Another Way? *(J. Voss)*	2:57
Just Us Three (don't leave) *(J. Voss)*	3:19
We Never Knew *(J. Voss)*	:46
A Dark Place *(J. Voss)*	3:04
There's Love Enough for All of Us (but we can't live together) *(J. Voss)*	2:51
This World's Not Ready *(J. Voss)*	1:40
Send Us On, Then Follow (it's up to you) *(J. Voss)*	2:23
Our Crystal Pool (is now a pool of blood) *(J. Voss, H. Proteus)*	3:16
This World's Not Ready (reprise) *(J. Voss)*	3:57

SEPTEMBER

*R*obert Mitchum had just met Jane Greer in Acapulco when Voss heard the knock on the back door followed by the key turning in the lock. He jumped up, turned off the television, and ducked into his bedroom.

Anita had been cleaning for him for years, and by now she thought of him what she thought of him, but he still didn't like to be caught watching television in his underwear at ten in the morning. He slipped into a pair of shorts and a t-shirt, and carried his socks, running shoes, and a hooded sweatshirt into the kitchen where she was already cleaning up around the sink, the smell of cleanser sharp in the air.

"Morning, Anita. I'm off for a run."

"*Bueno, señor Voss,*" she said. "*Pero hace mucho frío.* Is very cold."

"That's all right," he said as he shrugged into the sweatshirt. "I'll warm up once I get going."

He sat on the back steps and laced his Nikes. Anita was right about the cold; probably in the high forties, but the bone-chilling damp of the Pacific sea breeze sucked the warmth right out of you. He jogged slowly down the hill toward the beach, taking it easy until he reached the hard sand at the edge of the water, his legs freezing. Then he picked up the pace, asking himself why he hadn't worn his running pants, and just what the hell he was doing anyway. He didn't like to be in the house when Anita was there. Not that she did anything to make him feel as if he was in her way—she was gracious and unobtrusive. But something about having her there—cleaning, laundering, tending the plants—made him feel awkward about his own way of passing the day. Unless he was actually practicing—and sometimes he did withdraw to the studio, a room Anita had been instructed to stay out of, and practice until she was gone—unless he was practicing, he felt embarrassed that he sat around listening to music, or reading, or watching old movies while she did something universally recognized as work. He knew it came from the old feeling that what he did was not really work, that it was more a form of play he was lucky enough to get paid to do. On the other hand, if agony and frustration were characteristics of work, surely composition was the hardest work he'd ever done, especially of late when it came with such difficulty, if at all.

On the beach the wind, cold off the sea, bit into his face and legs. It wasn't even October yet, but it felt like November. Sanderlings ran back and forth in front of him, like windup toys at the moving edge of the water. A couple of gulls were yelling at each other as they took turns tearing at some trash on the ground and gliding in place above it, hanging on the wind like kites on strings. Off to his right he caught sight of three pelicans flying in perfect formation, just clearing the tops of the waves. A handful of surfers in wetsuits bobbed on the swells, waiting. There were no other people.

Voss thought again about composing new songs, about not composing new songs. The music stand on his piano was covered with sketches of tunes, but he hadn't been able to come up with a new lyric in years. And since Chance's death it was even worse. Silly phrases he remembered her saying as a child would come to him, and then conversations they'd had during the few visits she'd made to the West Coast, the few he'd made to Hoboken. But he was determined not to use her death to create some sappy tribute. What about a genuine tribute then? Had he even known her well enough to list her virtues? Who was she really? How could she have ended that way? And that was the question all his musings took him to. An endless loop, like an acid trip going bad with hours still to go.

He told himself to forget about it, to lose himself in his running. His breath had settled down, he worked his shoulders to loosen them up, and then he began to stretch out his stride, slowing and lengthening at the same time—slowing down to speed up, he called it. He felt his body slip into the rhythm of an easy lope. But the voice in his head kept saying, *oh HOW could SHE have ENDed like THAT?* to the beat of his footfalls on the hard sand, *oh HOW could SHE have ENDed like THAT . . . ?* He tried to shake the voice, to go somewhere else in his mind, find another script for the rhythm of his long stride. In dreams he would run like this sometimes, and if everything was going right, he would keep extending the distance between foot strikes until he was virtually floating, then he would pitch his body forward like a diver and actually fly. He forced himself to change the voice in his head, to chant as he breathed, *in DREAMS someTIMES i RUN and FLY, in DREAMS someTIMES i RUN and FLY.* He loved those dreams—skimming along close to the ground, then arching his back to clear an obstacle and soaring up into the clouds—and if something woke him from one, he would do everything he could to re-enter it, but it almost never worked. Once the dream was broken, there was no return.

When he got back to the house, out of breath—he always sprinted the last bit up the road to his door— his upper body soaked with sweat, his legs red and wind-chapped, he headed right for the shower. As much as he felt awkward around her, Anita in fact knew his routines and would wait to clean the bathroom until after he had showered. When he emerged from the bedroom, in Italian loafers, jeans, and a soft, white dress shirt, she was working on the plants. Before he'd found Anita, Voss didn't have a single plant in his house. But not long after she'd started working for him, she offered all on her own to take care of the built-in flower boxes on the deck, copper-lined bins of dry dirt that occasionally sprouted a ragged weed or two. Under Anita's care, the boxes gradually developed into luxuriant gardens overlooking the ocean. Voss didn't know where any of the plants came from originally, and knew the names of only the dieffenbachia and the ficus, which he had learned back when he was living with Avery. Of the others— on which he often received compliments—he could only say, *that's Anita's department. She does a great job, doesn't she?*

"I'm going to work in the studio for a while," he said to her.

"Would you like me to make you some lunch?" she asked.

"No, thanks, I'm not really hungry," he said, though he was.

In the studio, he went through his warm-up routine, flexing and stretching his back, shoulders, arms, and finally his hands, a set of exercises that had evolved in the more than twenty years since his hand had been broken, but that still hurt every time he did them, the pain sharp and specific, and taking him back to those predawn hours in Berlin. It was funny, he thought, what you remembered and what you didn't. Some things you'd rather forget were permanently etched on the mind. Other things you'd like to remember, simply went cloudy, slipped away. He'd always had a head for songs and lyrics, could even remember the songs of the birds that sang from the trees around his place—could recognize the hermit thrush in an instant—he knew the cormorants, gulls, and terns that flew by, and the afternoon osprey, yet he could not seem to learn the name of a single new flowering plant. Their names would not stick. And sometimes, when he most wanted to remember Chance, he could not picture her face.

He sat down at the Fazioli and played a series of scales, still warming up, deliberately holding back from playing real music. Practice was practice, not play—he'd learned that from Dr. Madison. He focused on the right hand, then the left, injured, hand. Then on both together, not thinking ahead to what he would play but trying to be fully in the exercise. This was his meditation, his Zazen. There was little the monastery could offer that he could not find here in the careful repetition of these finger exercises. He straightened his back, lowered his shoulders, felt the rise and fall of the scales in his body, in his gut. He felt it in other places, too; it mingled with the rhythm of his breathing, and thoughts and memories rose and fell with his breath, with the scales, with the feeling in his gut, all one—images came to him, slipped away, came again, slipped away again, sometimes never to return, but replaced by other images that would have their own arcs of celebration and sorrow, of elation and grief. He was playing arpeggios now, up and down the keys, falling in and out of love, childhood love with Avery, sex and their easy closeness, happy and unhappy with Jeanette, unhappy and happy without her, sampling myriad guilty pleasures with Hal, the return of Avery, a river that seemed to flow through his years, watching Hal push that last time, seeing his little girl for the first time, losing her, having her come back into his life as a young woman, losing her again, this time for good. . . .

Anita was gone when he came out of the studio. He grabbed a Stella Artois from the fridge and made a sandwich. The practice had gone well, and he felt virtuous for having worked at it as long as he had, over two hours. But he had written nothing. He thought back to the days when songs would just come to him—a phrase on a menu, a scene glimpsed from the window of a train, a sense memory conjured up by a passing aroma . . . and he'd have a lyric. With it would come an obvious melody, suggested by the accents and vowel tones of the words themselves. A chord-progression to support the melodic line, and he had a song. Sometimes that would work unaltered; more often he would have to tease out a counter-melody as well, using tricks he had learned in Dr. Madison's composition class back at Forrester. Then, during the days of Vossimilitude, he'd play it for Hal, sometimes over the phone, and if Hal liked it, he would laugh, even if it was the saddest, bitterest song Voss had written to date. Hal's laughter meant, "Yes, you got it, my friend. The world is fucked up in just that way." And then Hal would come up with a bass line that would set off Voss's work, like Berry Gordy's bass line to "Whipping Post" set off Greg Allman's simple and overblown lyrics, gave them the solidity they needed. Four staves—enough for a jazz trio or a full orchestra.

Out of the Past was running again on AMC, but it was beyond the Acapulco sequence, which had just begun when he turned it off earlier—the love story, before the girl reveals herself to be a killer and more trouble than she's worth. Now it was in the dark, confusing, San Francisco sequence. Robert Mitchum was telling the cabdriver that he was pretty sure he was being set up. "Don't sound like you," the cabdriver says. "I don't know," Mitchum says, "all I can see is the frame. I'm going in there now and look at the picture."

Voss turned it back off and went out onto the porch. The sun was bright, but the wind still had knives in it. The day before had been balmy, in the sixties, and he'd sat on the porch reading. Now he picked up the book from the table where it lay face down open to the page where he'd stopped and brought it into the living room. It was a new book, a blistering attack on religious faith that yesterday had made him want to talk with Artie. But today he couldn't get into it. He finished his beer. He wanted a real drink. He wanted to get high. But he didn't have any pot, and he made it a rule not to drink hard liquor before evening. He hadn't bought drugs in twenty years, though sometimes someone would give him a little something to take home, a joint, a couple of mushrooms. And he had a medicine cabinet full of prescription painkillers, but he had to be careful. Once you were on the recovery train, you were expected to behave according to all the current addiction lore: no one believed in moderation for anyone who had ever had trouble with drink or drugs. You had to quit all together. It didn't matter that people had straightened themselves out without twelve step programs, that drunks had managed to cut down without going on the wagon for life, that heroin addicts had knocked off the heroin but still used other drugs from time to time without falling back into the pits of hell. But if your name was known, you were in all-or-nothing territory. Voss couldn't buy that. First of all, the public apologies made him sick. It was insincere, legalistic crap. He'd made one public apology in his life—and he'd made it again and again—but it was not for his own behavior. It was something else entirely and happened well before his first time in rehab, the time of his great fall. By then he was barely in the public eye. If his name hadn't been linked to Hal's, who was the real rock star, his own fall might have passed entirely without notice. He was a working musician, famous for a moment, never a superstar, never really hooked to a publicity machine, never blessed or cursed with a gigantic fan base that followed his every move. But he had written *The Enchanted Pond*, and that would haunt him forever.

He looked up a number in his address book, picked up the phone, and dialed it.

"I'm playing tonight at The Cove. You want to come down? I'll buy you dinner and . . ."

"And breakfast?" she asked.

He smiled into the phone. "Yeah, and breakfast. If you promise not to take advantage of me."

"No promises," she said. "Hasn't that always been our deal?"

"I guess it has at that," Voss said. "I'm going down to set up at about six-thirty. If you get there at seven-thirty, we can eat and talk. I'm on at nine."

(♯)

It was the first time he'd played The Cove since the suicides, but nobody at the club made any mention of Chance, though he could tell by the way they all spoke to him that they knew.

"You're here early," the bartender said. "Can I fix you something before you get started?"

"No, thanks," Voss said. "I feel like playing the organ tonight. Figured I'd better see that it's set up."

"Cool," the bartender said, "I haven't heard you play anything but piano for a while."

"Yeah," Voss said, feeling that he should say more but not finding any words.

When Bridget came in, he found that he still didn't have much to say.

"You took an awful chance waiting until Friday afternoon to call me for a date," she said.

"I know," he said. "I'm glad you could make it." Even he could hear the sadness in his own voice, although he hadn't meant to put it there.

She reached across the table and put her hand over his. "There's no place I'd rather be," she said. And then, her eyebrows knitting slightly in concern, "Are you all right, Jack? I heard about what happened, and I can't think of anything to say that doesn't sound stupid. I'm sorry. I really am."

"I know, Bridge," Voss said. "I don't want to talk about it right now. Maybe later, if you really want to stay. I may not be great company."

Bridget smiled. "You promised me breakfast, and I'm not leaving until I get it. I'll stay as long as you like—or as short. My weekend is wide open."

"Thanks," Voss said, and he poured more wine into each of their glasses.

Sometimes Voss wondered if the boys really liked it when he sat in. They played without him more often than with him, and they had their own routine. Yet they turned themselves over to him whenever he showed up, pretty much left the set list up to him. Tonight was a real departure. He let them choose the first two songs, stuff they didn't need him for, so he could hang back, take his time getting the feel of the big Hammond, adjusting the stops, working the pedals, exercising the old Leslie speaker that gave the B-3 its trademark warbling sound. Newer keyboards used electronics to get the same effect, but the Leslie did it mechanically, with a horn spinning on an armature for the midrange and the highs, a rotating baffle for the lows—state of the art in about 1965—and Voss was convinced he could tell the difference, far preferring the old technology.

The third number was Voss's call, and he surprised the boys by asking if they knew the changes to B.B. King's "Sweet Little Angel."

During the break, the guitarist stopped by Voss and Bridget's table. "Jack's trying to turn us into a blues band tonight," he said.

"I noticed," Bridget said. "But it sounds good. I liked your solo on 'Stormy Monday.'"

"Thanks, darlin'," he said to Bridget. Then he turned to Voss: "She's a keeper. Don't let her go."

Voss didn't say anything.

Later, at the house, Bridget caught sight of the arrangement of cut flowers on the dining room table. "Did you get those just for me?"

"Anita cut them this afternoon," Voss said. He looked at her looking back at him. "A smarter guy would have just said yes, wouldn't he?"

"Probably," she said. "But one of the things I like about you is your utter failure to be smooth." She unbuttoned her blouse, unzipped her skirt, letting them both fall to the floor in one motion, and stood before him in her underwear.

Voss thought for a second of Jane Greer, the light behind her as she walked into that Acapulco bar for the first time.

"I'm not smooth either," Bridget said. "Let's go to bed; I'm really *not* tired. "

Voss smiled. "I may disappoint you. I *am* pretty exhausted, and I'm in kind of a weird place, right now."

"I know," she said, casually unhooking her bra and stepping out of her panties. "You have disappointed me once or twice, but never in bed. If you just want to sleep, that's fine." She struck a pose, at once girlish and knowing.

"I didn't say that exactly."

(♯)

On Sunday afternoon, Voss was taking a bottle of champagne out of the fridge. Bridget stopped him.

"Before you open that," she said, "we have to talk."

Voss felt his heart sink, his stomach knot up. "Okay," he said. "What's up?"

"This may be our last time together," she said. "I can't keep waiting for you to call."

"I thought you said you didn't wait for me to call."

"Can we not joke about it, Jack? This isn't easy for me."

"I'm sorry. We always keep it light, don't we? It's what we do."

"Yes, it is. But I need more than that. It's not that I regret any of it. And if I thought there was a real chance, I'd keep waiting for you. . . . Jack, how long have you been back in town?"

"A few weeks, I guess. Been laying low."

"And you've had a terrible loss, I know."

"Yeah."

"And you never called me to talk about it, still haven't talked about it all this weekend. Jack, I can see it in your face, I can feel it in your body. You're suffering, but you won't let me in. I'm not part of your life, I'm an escape from your life. That's all I'm ever going to be."

"Bridge. . . ." He couldn't think of anything to say.

"There's more. I'm going to be honest with you, even though I don't have to be, even though you haven't been honest with me."

"I've never lied to you," Voss said.

"You never tell me anything," she said. "How could you lie? Anyway," she turned away from him, "I've met someone."

Voss suddenly felt a familiar sense of vertigo, the floor opening up between them, a vast, un-crossable abyss, the dizzying feeling of a relationship coming to an abrupt end.

"He's not perfect. But he loves me, and he really wants me to be a part of his life, and you don't, Jack."

"Do you love him?"

She turned to face him again. He saw that she was crying, though he hadn't heard it in her voice.

"You have no right to ask me that."

"I know. You're right. I'm sorry."

"So here's what I want to do," she said, an anguished smile under the tears. "I want to say goodbye tonight. I want to drink that champagne. I want to go to Salieri's for lambchops and grilled asparagus. Then I want to come back here and listen to you play the piano for me, and eat the raspberries and whipped cream we bought yesterday. I want us to make love and fall asleep in each other's arms. And if you wake up when I slip out of bed in the middle of the night to go home, I want you to pretend to be asleep. Can you do all that, Jack?"

"I'm going to miss you," Voss said.

"Do not say that," she said. "Please, nothing like that. Just romance me, Jack, one last time, take me out to a wonderful meal, play your music just for me, make love to me, hold me with your entire body. . . ."

"And say goodbye," he said.

"All of it will be goodbye."

Vossimilitude on Tour

You want to know who did what to whom and how and when? You want to hear that kind of stuff about us? Maybe you want soft light, and gauze filters, and white curtains swaying in the breeze, silhouettes of the lovers to the sound of a cello? Or do you want something more obsessed and desperate? Smoldering looks and then the wild leap on each other, the lighting more noir, the music churning and urgent? Or how about the porno version of the same thing, harsh light, body parts in tight focus, shitty jazz music and sucking sounds. Because that's where it gets to if you keep going. People fucking. It can turn sordid pretty fast when you talk about it. And I'm not going to give you that.

"Okay, cards on the table. Let's see who wins this competition," Hal Proteus said. "But I'm telling you, I've had a hell of a weekend, and I don't see how either of you are gonna beat it."

He, Voss, and Avery were passing a joint around in Hank Bowman's living room. The Lafayette house had broken up after the spring term had ended. Vossimilitude had played bars and clubs for most of the summer and fall; then the record popped. A major tour. Opening for The Moody Blues. And passing through St. Louis as local heroes. When Hank Bowman had heard they were coming, he'd insisted that they stay with him and Cynthia at their apartment rather than in some anonymous hotel. Avery, Hal, and Voss all had rooms booked at the local Holiday Inn with the rest of the band and the crew, but they had spent almost as much time here. *Tales from Topographic Oceans* was playing on the stereo.

Avery, sitting cross-legged on the floor, took a hit and passed the joint to Voss. "It's how many partners, right?" she said. "Not how many times."

"Yes, it's partners. You could just hole up with one guy and go for times— if the guy could keep up with you," Hal said, winking at Avery. "Partners is what counts." Proteus was stretched out on the sofa, his fingers intertwined behind his neck, his legs crossed.

"Just numbers or do we have to give names?" Voss asked, passing the joint to Hal.

"Well, I'm not sure I could give names, but you have to identify who it was. . . ." Hal took a long hit. "Like the burger girl at the snackbar, what's it called, the Bear's Lair? I don't remember her name, but I know who she is."

"The Bear's Den," Voss said. "She went with you? I thought she had higher standards."

"They all go with me sooner or later, Jack," Hal said. "Might as well get used to it." Again he gave Avery a look that made Voss feel a bit queasy.

"Who goes first?" Avery said, all business.

"Let's make it alphabetical," Hal said. "Avery, you first."

"Okay. Seven. Do I have to say who they were now, or after we see who won?"

"Now," Voss said. "Otherwise it's anticlimactic."

"All right. There was Darien. Duncan. Louis, acting teacher. The little guy with all the drugs, Swifty? Oh, shit. Who am I forgetting? Friday, Saturday after the show, oh yeah, Charlie the sound man. Jack, of course. And Hal. Seven."

"You slept with Hal?" Voss said. "Shit."

"You were the one who said I should get in on the game."

"Yeah, but . . ."

"No ties, you said. Gotta be free. Separate hotel rooms. No boyfriend girlfriend, just on the road together, come together when we come together, wasn't that how it went? What are you going to tell me, strangers are okay, but friends aren't?"

"No. Fuck. Forget it."

"Now, don't get sore, Jack," Hal said. "Let's get on with it. I'm next, and I'm afraid I've got Avery beat with nine. There's Avery. . . ." He grinned. "The burger girl, ooh, I think I'm in love with her. . . ."

"You don't even know her name," Voss said.

"Yeah, well . . . okay, then there's . . . where's Hank?"

"What?" Voss said.

"Hank, he's not here somewhere, is he?"

"No, he and Cynthia went out to get groceries for dinner, why?"

"Okay. Cynthia."

"What?" Voss and Avery said at the same time.

"Cynthia," Hal said. "That's three. The tall, skinny groupie at the show on Friday; I thought she'd be more into it, but it went pretty quick. I think she's in some kind of contest of her own."

"Four," Avery said.

"I can't believe you slept with Hank's girlfriend, fuck, fiancée," Voss said. "Just get on with it."

"Okay. The girls from the party the first night we were here, the one with the bottle of Southern Comfort who thought she was Janis Joplin—Sally . . ."

"Sassy?" Voss said.

"Right, Sassy. And her friend C.C. Tag team."

"Aw shit, Hal," Voss said.

Hal turned to Avery: "Jack's got a bit of a thing for Sassy, I think."

"No," Voss said. "But C.C., she and Artie are real close. I mean, I don't think they've ever made it together, but . . ."

Avery looked from Hal to Voss and back again.

"What's that, six?" Hal said. "So then there was another groupie on Saturday night—actually, I think she thought I was one of The Moody Blues. And there was another girl in the dorms, and your old pal Jeanette. Whoo. Nine."

Voss and Avery both looked at Hal.

Hal turned to Voss, who seemed to have crumpled. "You're up, man."

"Fuck," Voss said, "you win, okay? Why don't we just leave it at that?"

"Oh, no," Hal said, "it's not poker. You can't just fold. You got to show your hand."

Avery stood up and then sat down on the floor again.

Voss leaned forward over the coffee table, crumbled a couple of buds and began to roll another joint. "Avery and Jeanette," he said.

"Two, hah!" Hal said. "And both ex-girlfriends. That's just sad, man."

"Jeanette, huh?" Avery said. "Poor Jack." She shook her head.

Voss ignored her, licked the cigarette paper, twirled the ends of the joint, and lit it. "Flip the record, would you," he said to Avery.

As she lowered the needle on the other side of the record, they heard the door downstairs open, followed by the sound of Fritz, Cynthia's German shepherd, bounding up the stairs. The dog made the rounds in the living room, nuzzling first Avery, then Hal, and finally Voss, demanding affection from each of them, but quickly moving on to the next person in line.

"I saw Artie," Hank said as he cleared the half wall along the stairwell, "and Duncan, and Darien Pynnoch. They're all going to be here in about an hour. It'll be like a family reunion."

"Yeah, it sure will," Voss said, glaring at Avery.

"And we've got some serious food. Tournedos. I've got the makings of a béarnaise sauce. Asparagus. New potatoes. I hope you guys are hungry."

"And thirsty," Cynthia added, as she climbed the last steps behind Hank. "Beefeater's, Schweppes, fresh limes."

Avery rose from the floor. "Anything I can do to help?" she said.

"Something already smells good," Hank said as he set the bags of groceries down on the counter kitchen counter.

"Bogart it a while, bro," Voss said, handing Hank the joint. "We're way ahead of you."

"Thanks, man," Hank said. "Cynth, you want some of this?"

"No, thanks, sweetie," Cynthia called from the kitchen.

Voss wasn't sure, but he thought he could hear in that "sweetie" something that reflected whatever it was that made it possible for her to have sex with Hal while she was engaged to his friend. He realized that he had felt sorry for himself after his poor showing in the ridiculous contest, hurt that Hal had . . . with both Avery and Jeanette, but he now found himself feeling sorry for Hank, and even for Artie. He looked over at Hal, still stretched out on the couch as if he were the lord of the manor. In the kitchen he could see Avery and Cynthia mixing drinks. He understood nothing.

(♯)

On the way to Kansas City, Voss curled up in the back of the tour bus and slept. He didn't talk at meals, and when they got there, he ordered room service and didn't come out of his hotel room except for the show. Even on stage he seemed to hang back, so that it wasn't entirely clear who was fronting the band, him or Hal. He cut his solo short on "A Dark Place," and he hardly played at all on "Touch Her and You're Dead."

Back in the hotel at two a.m., he heard a knock at his door.

He opened it to see Hal with three women in tight shorts and high boots. Groupies or hookers, it was hard to tell.

"Something to cheer you up, dude," Hal said. "Ladies, let me introduce you to Jack Voss. Jack. . . . Okay, what're your names again?"

The girls introduced themselves.

"First one naked gets the first line," Hal said, "and if you don't hurry, it's going to be me."

He stripped off his shirt, unbuckled his belt, slid it out of his pants, and started twirling it around his head like a stripper twirling a boa.

"Hal," Voss said. "I don't know if I'm up for this."

"Not to worry," Hal said, misunderstanding perfectly. "Old doc Proteus has just what you need."

He sat down on the couch, pulled a glass topped end-table around in front of him, took a folded paper packet and a safety razor blade out of his pocket, and began to chop and measure out five lines of white powder. The girls were taking off their clothes, piling them neatly in the corner. Voss could see the marks left on their skin by the elastic of their underwear. The blonde was not, evidently, a natural blonde; her dark pubes had been shaved into a tiny heart. The redhead, however, appeared to be authentic, including the freckles across her small, pink breasts.

"How old are you girls," Voss asked.

"How old do you want us to be?" the brunette asked. She had large, dark nipples, wide hips, and a broad thatch of hair between her legs.

"Blondie," Hal said. "Show Jack your trick." He had rolled up a dollar bill into a tube and leaned down for the first line.

The blonde girl sat on the floor, drew her knees up, threaded her arms through them, and then stretched her legs behind her shoulders and rolled back. She looked like a yogi or an acrobat, except that, naked as she was, and hairless except for the little heart, Voss couldn't help but look at her open labia. Below them her anus seemed to wink at him like a pale asterisk opening into a black-eyed Susan and then closing into an asterisk again.

"The girl with the pneumatic asshole," Hal said. "And she'll take you any way you want, Jack."

"Or all ways," the girl said as she unfolded herself and knelt at the coffee table to snort her line, "just so the ass is last."

"Whoa," Hal said. "That could be a song, eh bro? The ass is last. . . ."

(♯)

After the show in Denver, Voss and Hal ended up in Hal's hotel room with a girl in cowboy boots and a denim skirt. In the limo she had flipped the skirt up to show them that she wasn't wearing anything under it.

"You take everything off but those boots, baby," Hal told her as he was opening a bottle of champagne.

"I'd better go," Voss said. "Third wheel."

"Fuck no," Hal said. "We can share. She's the girl of the golden west, aren't you, sweetheart? You don't want Jack to go, do you?"

"I've never been with two guys at once," she said. Then she took off her shirt. "But there's a first time for everything."

When Voss got back to his own room hours later, barefoot, his shirt obviously just thrown on, and carrying his boots, Avery was waiting by the door.

"What's up?" he asked. "Everything okay with the guys, the crew?"

"Yeah. It's not about that. Can I come in?"

"Sure," he said without enthusiasm, opening up to let them both in.

"It's about the contest in St. Louis," she said, ignoring what he'd obviously just come from. "I thought you wanted me to play. I thought it was your idea that I join in. It certainly wasn't mine."

"But I never said that."

"You never say anything! If you want me to know what you want, you have to tell me. I'm sorry you were hurt. What can I do to fix it?"

He was deeply confused. He had felt injured, and had folded protectively into himself, unable to ask for anything. Then Hal had drawn him into new levels of debauchery which Avery must have known about. "I'm okay," he lied, flopping into an armchair.

"Okay?" she said, shaking her head. "I don't think so, Jack. C'mon, I've known you almost as long as you've known yourself, and I sometimes think I know you better."

"That's probably not saying much," Voss said. "Because if I knew myself at all, I'd probably have a better idea of how to live my life."

Avery reached toward him, touched the side of his head, but he shrank away. "Don't patronize me," he said.

"That's the last thing I want to do, Jack," Avery said. "You think I don't know where you are or what you're feeling, and I'll admit that I didn't, until St. Louis. And that's partly because I didn't know what I felt." She knelt down in front of him, took his foot in her hand. It was a gesture of classical obeisance so striking, that even in Voss's bewildered state, he was moved by it. "Just let me say my piece," she said. "Okay?"

"Yeah, sure. Go ahead."

She tilted her head to the side, resting her ear against his ankle. "Jack, baby, I've loved you since we were kids. I would do anything for you. And some day, you're going to realize that you love me that way, too. But I'm realizing now that I don't have to wait. I thought that if you went away from me—like you did when you went in the Air Force, and like you did when you fell in love with Jeanette, like you're doing now with Hal and these groupies—that I had to go away from you, too. But the love doesn't stop. If I'd known how the contest would make you feel, I wouldn't have played it. I honestly thought you wanted me to be a part of it, somehow, like the night with you and me and Jeanette, in a way. But I should have known it wouldn't work. Jack, baby, Hal suckered us both. And I should have seen it. It was almost like he wanted to dirty me up, and I thought you would get some kind of kick out of it, like he did. I was wrong. But you know what? It's okay. Because I now know something I didn't know before. I know that I can fuck other guys if I want, but I feel less than when your hand brushes up against mine when we're walking side-by-side."

"Avery . . ." Voss said.

"No," she said, putting her finger gently on his lips. "Not yet. I haven't finished. I'm giving myself to you, Jack. If you and Hal want to have your contests, you have them. If you want other girls, you have them. Be a rock star. Fuck the groupies. Really, go for it. Or if you want Jeanette when she's around. . . ."

Her eyes were wet and she wiped them with the back of her hand.

"But I'll be here," she went on. "I'll be yours. Nobody else for me. I'm sorry that it hurt you that I played that game, but that's the last time I'll hurt you that way. Now, I want you to let me touch you, let me make love to you, let me give myself to you to seal this pledge, this promise. Okay?"

Voss leaned forward and placed his hand on the side of her face. She pressed her face against his hand and shivered.

"What are you asking me, exactly?" he said. "I can't make the same promise. I don't know . . . I don't think I know how to love like that. . . ."

"I'm not asking you for a promise back, I'm just asking you to accept my promise, asking you to let me love you."

"I. . . ."

"Stop," she said.

She was crying now, and Voss felt tears coming into his own eyes.

"Just lean back. Just don't push me away. Don't even move."

He took her head in his hands and lifted gently, but she pulled his hands away. "You just lie back. Let me do everything. Then, from now on I'll do anything you ask. The things you wanted me to do that I wouldn't do, I'll do them if you want. But now, just lie back. Don't lift a finger. Let me give you this, and then I want you to go to sleep. I don't want anything back. I just want to do this for you."

Voss leaned back, and Avery kissed the top of his foot. She picked up his other foot, stroked it, kissed it. He wasn't sure he'd be able to become aroused again, after what had just happened in Hal's room, but something opened inside him. It was sexual, but it wasn't only sexual. He felt her tears falling onto his feet. He closed his eyes and thought he heard the sound of a cello.

♯

Voss and Avery were inseparable for the rest of the tour. The boys played to the crowd, but Voss played for her, and after each show they went back to the hotel and an intimacy that made even exhausted sleep erotic; as long as some part of her body was touching some part of his—a leg thrown over a leg, her hand resting on the small of his back—with any connection, a soft, electric tickle kept them in deep communion and nearly constant arousal. Everyone they knew was happy for them, making comments like "It's about time they figured out that they loved each other," to which another might reply, "You mean it's about time he figured out he loved her—he was the only one blind enough not to see that she loved him all along." The other guys in the band would rib Voss gently for the way he shrugged off the groupies—he was now attracting more groupies than ever—but Avery laughed it off wonderfully: "With the pheromones you're throwing off, how could they not be drawn to you," she'd say, and sometimes when they were rolling around in bed she would ask him to describe them to her. "Tell me what you would have done with her if we weren't together," she'd say.

"C'mon, Avery, you know I want to be right where I am, here with you," he said to her the first time she proposed this.

"I know, but it will be fun. I want you to. It's just a fantasy, but I can make it real for you."

And he would close his eyes and draw a picture in words of the big girl who had flashed him from the front row, or the lanky beauty who latched on to him at the stage door . . . and Avery would become her.

"And what's your fantasy?" he asked her afterward.

"I'm living my fantasy," she said. "This is it."

Even when the boys would halfheartedly urge Voss to join them in a night of debauchery, they seemed actually envious of him when he went off with Avery. Only Hal would make negative comments, muttering backstage one night in Albuquerque: "It won't last; you'll see. They'll get tired of each other. Someone will stray. Nobody loves like that and doesn't get shit on eventually."

He said it loud enough that he clearly intended Voss and Avery to hear him, and Voss rose to the bait: "Like you would know anything about love, Hal?"

"I know you, and I know Avery," Hal said. "That's all I need to know."

To hear Hal say "I know Avery" sent a shiver of jealousy up Voss's spine, but he shook it off. "You don't know her like I do," he said, "no matter what you think."

"That's for goddamn sure," Avery added, as they climbed into the limo that would take them back to their hotel.

A sliver of moon was rising over the mountain to the east, and the white car had a light coating of red dust from the high plains.

"You coming, Hal?" Kenny called.

"I'll get a ride with the crew," Hal said. "I wouldn't want you to lower your standards."

As the car pulled away from the curb, Voss looked back to see the receding figure of Hal take a long pull from a bottle of vodka and give them the finger.

In Phoenix, Hal ended up in jail. As the manager of the band, Avery was the one who had to go down and post bail. Voss went with her, of course, and they got the story from the desk sergeant. Not only had Hal managed to find a brothel generally known only to the locals, but he managed to get into a brawl with a cowboy over the only girl in the place he wanted. She was at the station, too, and something struck Voss about her. She was pretty, Hispanic, but could have passed for Anglo. Slim and shapely, with long dark hair and low slung breasts, she stood about 5'6" in bright red cowboy boots. Voss found himself assessing her as he had begun to do with the groupies he would describe to Avery, but not until Avery herself pointed it out did it sink in that she was Avery's Mexican double.

"Jesus," he said.

Avery stood up on tiptoe and kissed Voss on the forehead. "Poor Jack," she said. "So smart, so talented, yet so dumb."

When they brought Hal out into the waiting room, he looked like another person. Maybe they hadn't really looked at him in a while. He seemed to have gained ten or fifteen pounds since the tour started. His gut was spilling over his belt, and his shirt, speckled with vomit, was stretched tight over it. He looked bloated and sick, obvious after-effects of a night of serious drinking, and he had a welt on his cheek that would probably blossom into a black eye in another few hours. He reeked, and his right hand was wrapped in a piece of cloth—a red table napkin, as it turned out.

"What the fuck, man," Voss said, screwing up his face. "I thought you never got sick?"

"Guy sucker punched me in the gut," Hal said. "Got spewed for his trouble."

"What happened to your hand?" Avery asked.

"He had a hard head," Hal said.

"Holy shit," Voss said. "You didn't break it, did you?"

"Might've," Hal said with a shrug.

Avery shook her head. "Will you be able to play tomorrow?" she said. "Or today, I should say. Our next gig is only about fifteen hours away."

"Ever the sentimentalist," Hal said. "Worried about your career, boss-lady?"

"That's all of our careers," Voss said. "What the hell were you thinking?"

"Look, loverboy, just put me in a cab and go home with the boss, okay? And thanks for your concern about whether I'm really okay. I'll play the fucking gig—don't dare break a contract with the dragonlady here."

A look passed between Avery and Voss.

"You don't need to talk about her that way, dude," Voss said.

"Forget it, Jack," Avery said.

"Yeah, forget it, Jack," Hal said. "You don't want me to break my other hand on your head, do you?"

Voss turned to the desk sergeant. "Can you call us a cab?" he asked. "We need to get to the Holiday Inn."

"I'll have a patrol car take you," the sergeant said. "Just don't kill each other on the way."

They managed to keep the tension from showing on stage, although Voss and Avery noticed Hal was high more and more of the time. Not that it seemed to affect his playing. The stage was a kind of magic zone for all of them—once the first notes went out into the auditorium and the lights came up on the band, it was just the music and the crowd. Voss felt he had become more of a conduit than a performer—the songs had their own momentum; they carried the boys through. When Voss wanted to add a new song to the program, they stepped up and learned it in an afternoon—it was mostly just an electric piano number for Voss, anyway. "Avery's Song," he called it. Perhaps the most surprising thing about it was the bass line that Hal came up with on the second run-through—sad, sustained, bent notes that held a heartfelt conversation with the bright chords on the Fender Rhodes and the tender lyric. But off stage, Hal and Voss hardly spoke.

OCTOBER

"Oh, man," Voss said into the phone, "I don't know. I'm the wrong guy for this, Artie. My own relationship with all that recovery business isn't good. You know I've never practiced what they preach. I still drink. I still smoke. I mean, I like to think I'm a man of moderation, but you want to get her in a program, those program people don't like me. They don't believe in me."

"That's exactly why I need you there. Otherwise I would never ask. You've got credibility with her. She'll listen to you."

The silence on the line between them throbbed. Artie was waiting for an answer. Voss stared out the window. It was the rarest of Pacific coast mornings: a low fogbank lay on the sea. If you were standing on the beach you would be in the middle of it, but Voss's house was high enough on the hillside to look out over it, like the view out of an airplane window when it climbed through the weather and came out on top, above the clouds. And Voss could hear the breakers hidden beneath the cloud sea that stretched out to the horizon.

"All right, man," Artie's voice came thinly out of the phone. "Forget it. I'll let you know how it goes."

"No," Voss said. "I'll come. I don't know how much help I'll be, but I'll come. Let me write down the time and place." As he turned to go back inside he caught sight of a white Styrofoam peanut clinging to the bottom of the drape.

(♯)

"I'm heading to New York next week, Bert. Have you got anything for me?"

"Jack Voss? Well, I'll be dipped in shit." She was using the speakerphone on her desk; Voss could hear the metallic echo. "I've been trying to reach you for weeks. Your phones are disconnected. Your cell appears to be dead. What's with that?"

"Aw, jeez," Voss said. "I'm sorry. Let me give you my new numbers. Somebody put my old numbers up on the internet, and I had to have them all changed." As he said it, he figured she'd connect it to Chance's death, and he let her. He could almost feel the change in her manner before she spoke again.

"I wanted to tell you how sorry I was about Chance, Jack. But I never got to talk to you at the funeral, and then you didn't come to the reception."

"I was asked not to," Jack said.

"Oh, shit. I'm sorry. I can't imagine. How are you holding up?"

"I'll survive," Voss said. "But that's not why I called you. . . ."

"And you kept working. You finished the record. Javi told me you nailed it."

"I missed a couple of days, but the . . . work was the best thing," Voss said. "What else was I going to do?"

"Right. So what can I do for you?"

He gave her the dates he'd be in New York, pacing around his living room as they talked. He could picture her flipping through her rolodex. Then he suddenly wondered if the picture was all wrong. He hadn't been to her office in years. All her contacts were probably on the computer now. Even his image of her—the brusque, New York woman in running shoes and a track suit—might be hopelessly out of date.

"It's pretty short notice, Jack," she said.

"Yeah, I know. Something came up, and I have to go for that, and I figured you'd want to know. I mean, you'd want a heads up, just in case there was anything."

"No, definitely. I'll make some calls. It'll be clubs. There's a new place out in Jersey. Would you go as far as Philly? How about Boston?"

"Sure," Voss said. "Why not?"

"And then you're coming back? You're in New York for New Year's like always, right?"

"Wouldn't miss it," Voss said, a little wearily.

"Okay. I'll get back to you by tomorrow afternoon. Now give me those new numbers."

He gave them to her.

"And don't be such a stranger," she said. "In times of trouble is when you call old friends, no?"

"Yeah," Voss said. "I'll talk to you tomorrow."

He hung up the phone and stepped out onto the balcony. The sun appeared and disappeared between ragged clouds, casting shadows on a restless sea. He studied the business card in his hand:

HOBOKEN P.D.

PATRICK O'BEIRNE, LT.
Investigations

(♯)

A hired car took him to SFO where he caught the morning flight to LaGuardia. He had to take off his boots, empty his pockets, spread out the contents of his briefcase. The usual, since 9/11. At least he didn't have to screw around with luggage. He dressed for the weather at his destination—today, that meant a winter raincoat and an umbrella—and brought whatever he was reading, any music he was working on, and that was it. When he arrived—the water taxi to midtown, and a taxi to the apartment on Park where he had all his New York clothes, a bathroom stocked with toiletries, everything he needed.

The water taxi he'd taken the first time on Artie's recommendation years ago. "You see a side of the city you don't see any other way," he'd said. And Voss had liked it so much, he'd made it part of his routine. The boat ride through Hell's Gate and into the East River connected his two homes, reminding him that New York was just as much a city on the water as San Francisco, and linking his New York apartment with its view of the bay to the south, to his Carmel house with its deck looking out over the ocean. He told everybody about it, but nobody had appreciated it like Chance. As he stepped aboard the boat from the pier at the old seaplane terminal, he remembered suggesting it to her the first time she'd come out to visit him on the West Coast. She had called him back as soon as she got home to tell him about how much she loved the experience. She had taken the small boat all the way down to the Battery, and then taken the ferry from there to Hoboken: "It was like going back in time," she'd told him. Going back in time, he thought. If only we could.

The wind had salt and fuel oil in it, and the boat rose and fell with the swells in Bowery Bay. Voss sat out in the weather and watched the crew help people onboard, calling out to them to time their steps with the last moment of the boat's rise. One guy waited too long, and almost fell, stepping off the pier just as the boat was lowering away from him. The crew caught him by the arms, and he laughed, a little drunk, Voss thought, in the early dusk of a November afternoon. They cast off and headed out past Rikers Island and under the TriBorough Bridge, the chop increasing as they cleared Astoria and the wind blew straight up the channel.

When he opened the door to his apartment the first thing he saw was the nine foot Steinway, which he had picked from the selection room in Queens years ago. Finished just for him, and tuned and regulated just for him, it was the best Steinway he'd ever played. He realized he hadn't touched it once during his last visit.

The second thing that caught his eye was the little silver model plane on the dining room table. On a chair next to it, the Strand bag with Housman's poems in it.

(♯)

"Arthur has talked to me about all of you," the facilitator said. He was a relaxed looking man in his thirties, corduroy trousers, a blue chambray shirt, a sweater vest. As if he were afraid he wouldn't be recognized as the professional in the group without his official counseling uniform. "You're all friends of Cecelia's. . . ."

Fuck, Voss thought. Arthur and Cecelia. Nobody called them that. It was Artie and C.C., for God's sake. Hank Bowman, sitting across the room, sighed heavily. Duncan McGough, sitting next to Bowman, listened earnestly. They had all been roommates in the house on Lafayette, the year of the first version of *The Enchanted Pond*, with the flute and the dancers. The only one missing was Darien "The Statesman" Pynnoch. And the women. Artie had kept Voss informed over the years. Duncan and Val had broken up while Vossimilitude was on its first tour. He was an architect now, still in St. Louis, but he and Artie had stayed close. Bowman had flown in from St. Louis, too. After his marriage with Cynthia had fallen apart, he'd joined the navy. Been all over the world. And ended up back in St. Louis, painting and teaching art at Laclede University. Voss had one of his paintings in the New York apartment, a seascape nearly six feet across, bold and abstract, Turneresque. Voss remembered when they had all sat around the living room of the house they shared, dreaming of having their own town. Well, that hadn't materialized, and they'd all had their moments of near ruin, but they'd survived, hadn't they? They'd come through.

There were other guys in the room, some of them actors, some people from the non-profit theater group where C.C. worked. And there were a few women, only two of whom Voss recognized—C.C.'s old friend Sassy, and Marilyn, their host. Age had not been kind to Sassy. Gray of hair and face, she looked ill. For an instant, Voss thought he could see her skull shining out through her skin, and he thought immediately: cancer. He tried to remember if Artie or C.C. had said anything about her in recent years, but nothing came. Marilyn, C.C.'s long time best friend, Voss had met several times before. A small, intense woman with a razor sharp sense of humor. Voss liked her.

The facilitator was droning on: ". . . there will be times when the tension in the room will make you want to laugh, it's a natural response, like the hilarity that sometimes overcomes people at funerals, but please try to resist it. This is more serious than a funeral, because we have the chance to save a life. And if we don't succeed, the next place you all see one another will be a funeral. . . ."

Artie was supposed to bring her in in ten minutes. Everyone would wait in the back bedroom of the apartment. Marilyn would meet them at the door and seat them at the big dining room table. Frank, the facilitator, would come in and introduce himself, say his piece, and then come and get the rest of the group.

"Won't she feel like we're ganging up on her?" Sassy asked.

"We are ganging up on her," Voss said before he checked himself.

Everyone turned and looked at him.

"Mr. Voss is right," Frank said. "We are ganging up on her. Because we've tried everything else. Once all of you come in and sit down, I'll call on you according to this list. Just tell her that you love her, and you miss her, and you want her to get help so that she can come back to being the person you remember. Use your own words, we don't want it to sound like you're reading from a script. You'll know what to do."

They all filed back into the bedroom. Bowman and McGough came over to Voss.

"It's good to see you, man," Bowman said.

"Yeah," McGough said. "It's been a long time. Wish it were under better circumstances."

They both spoke in that low voice people use when they meet at funerals and wakes.

"So how are you?" Bowman asked, "I heard you got in the hall of fame."

"No," Voss said shaking his head. "Just to induct Hal."

"Oh, sorry. And I heard something else about you. . . ." And then Hank and Duncan both seemed to remember about Chance.

"Oh, man," Duncan said, "I was so sorry when I heard about. . . ."

"I don't want to talk about it right now, okay?" Voss said before he could go on. "But I'm all right."

"Shhh," somebody said, and they stood there crowded together in the bedroom, no one speaking.

Soon they heard the doorbell. The door opened and closed, there was a murmur of voices. Voss thought he could pick out C.C.'s shocked response followed by the awful pleading voice of Artie that he had first heard that summer. Frank opened the door, and everyone filed into the dining room to see C.C. at the head of the table, her eyes flashing with fury, her lips clamped tight.

"Arthur," Frank said.

"C.C., honey," Artie began, "I know you're going to hate this, but I don't know what else to do. I've called all your friends here to help me convince you that you need help. Your drinking is out of control. You're hurting yourself and you're hurting me. You could have died last month. . . ."

"I had a seizure," C.C. said. "You trying to blame me for having a fucking seizure?"

Frank's practiced soft voice interrupted: "Cecelia," he said. "Please let Arthur finish. This isn't easy for him."

C.C. glared at him.

Artie went on: "I've booked you a place upstate where they can help you. I want you to go."

"Marilyn?" Frank said.

"Honey," Marilyn said. "I know you and you're in trouble. You know I love you dearly. It's time to let somebody help you, sweetie. . . ."

Voss saw something new form in C.C.'s eyes, and he began to feel afraid for everyone in the room, himself included.

Sassy was next. "C.C.," she said. "You know I'm not one to preach or tell anyone how to live their life. And I've probably matched you drink for drink since we were eighteen years old. But we both know you're in trouble. . . ."

"That's it," C.C. said and stood up so suddenly she knocked the chair down. Somebody reached to pick it up.

"Leave it," she said. "I've listened to all of this shit I'm going to. You fucking hypocrites. Every last one of you drinks. Is there someone here I haven't seen crawling on the floor, or sleeping next to the toilet. Him . . ." she pointed with her chin at Artie ". . . I've cleaned up his puke, I've wiped his ass. Okay, so now he doesn't drink much, but ask him when was the last time he wasn't stoned. Ask him if he got stoned before we came here. Marilyn? You think it's not drinking when you swallow your Listerine ten times a day at work? You think you do this to me they aren't going to do it to you next? Oh, and look who all Artie's found to come here and do his dirty work. All his old friends. HIS friends. Where were you when I was in the hospital last year having my ovaries sliced out? But you came to his show in that dump in Alphabet City. . . ."

Frank suddenly roused out of his shocked stupor, as if he'd never seen anything like this happen at an intervention. "Cecelia," he said, "these people are here now because they care about you."

"Shut up, you little wimp," she said. "You think a couple of psych courses taught you how to fix me? Go back to Connecticut or Long Island or whatever little waspy place where you grew up. Where I come from we don't need shrinks, just hard work and scratching a living out of the dirt. And out of that I got myself here, to New York and a career. You think you can tell me something about life I don't know?

"And the rest of you. Henry fucking Bowman. Did you bring some paintings to sell so you wouldn't waste the trip? And Iris? Are you here on your own or do you represent the office? Are you on the clock?"

She went around the table. Frank tried to stop her again, but she was unstoppable. Voss found himself hoping she would skip him somehow, that her fondness for him over the years would outweigh her fury and spare him the kind of surgical attack she was delivering to each of the people in the room. In fact she was saving him for last.

"And Jack," she said. "Jack Voss. The Keyboard Man. Rock star. Famous. Famous for what? For destroying how many lives with his little suicide record? Do you even know? They stopped reporting them because of the copycat thing. And now his own daughter commits suicide. You think that's a coincidence? Oh yeah, and how many times *you* been to rehab, Jack? Of course you wouldn't go to a place like the one where they want to send me. You get to work out a deal, huh, Mr. Prisoner of the Zendo. Then you make a joke about it. Are you clean and sober? Last time you sat in my living room drinking a glass of wine and smoking a joint you weren't."

She reached behind her, picked up the chair and sat down. "Fuck all of you."

Frank clearly didn't know what to do. He'd presumably had an image in his mind of how things would go—some tension, of course, some discomfort; tears and recriminations, then a contrite acceptance, a walk down to the waiting car surrounded by supportive friends. . . .

"Let's start again," he said. "It's natural for you to be angry at first, but you must see that everyone here came because they care about you."

"Oh, shut up. You're like a broken record," C.C. said. "Just get out of here, all of you, and leave me alone. I know how to take care of myself. I've been doing it all my life, with no help from you before now."

"We're not leaving until you hear us out," Frank said.

"Okay," she said, standing again, this time slowly and deliberately. "Fine. Marilyn, where's my coat?"

"I'm not getting your coat, C.C." Marilyn said.

"Then I'm leaving without it," C.C. said.

"Honey," Artie said. "Don't go. Please, baby. . . ."

It was that voice again. The voice Voss had heard back in August when they were watching the Convention. It cut right through him to hear Artie sound like that.

Then she was out the door. Artie grabbed her coat and his own from the front closet and charged out the door after her.

"C.C.? Wait, honey," he pleaded. "I've got your coat."

Everyone in the room looked at Frank as the sound of Artie's heavy footsteps on the stairs receded.

"It doesn't always work the first time," Frank said.

"Especially when you have no fucking plan," Voss said. "How long you been doing this? A week?"

A thin icy rain had fallen in the early morning hours, turning the road slick and the world inhospitable. WBGO out of Newark was playing "So What" from *Kind of Blue*. Bill Evans holding it down, the tether that kept Miles from floating away like a balloon. One of Voss's favorite recordings. But he couldn't listen to it now. He turned the radio off, checked the directions on the seat next to him and watched carefully for signs and landmarks. He would be there in about fifteen minutes. He didn't even know if Neil would see him.

Neil and Chance had been close friends since grade school, and he was the first of her friends Voss had met, when after six years of complete estrangement he was permitted to see his daughter. Avery had been a shadowy face in the window at that first meeting, establishing what would be their routine for these visits until Chance had her own place and it was no longer necessary for Voss to call for her at Avery's house. But Neil he had met on his second or third visit, when he came with Chance down Avery's front walk to Voss's waiting car.

"He's been dying to meet you," Chance had said.

Later, over burgers and fries in a little diner in Summit, Neil told Voss what a big fan he was. "When I first heard some of your songs," Neil said, "I was sure that whoever wrote them was gay, like me."

"I've been told that before," Voss said, smiling. "The first time by David Bowie."

"No way," Chance and Neil said, nearly in unison.

Voss had liked Neil, and as the gray stone prison came into view, he couldn't imagine the boy in there. Not effeminate exactly, Neil had been openly gay since he was in grade school, and Voss feared for him in this famously rough facility. Voss's knowledge of prison life came from movies, television, and crude jokes, all of which painted it as a harsh world in which homosexual rape of the small and the weak by the large and the brutal was the norm. The Neil Voss knew would be a helpless victim in such a world, as, Voss suspected, would he himself.

It was clear from the looks they gave him, that the guards didn't see many Ferraris pull into the visitor's parking lot. If the men who checked his ID and patted him down recognized him, they gave no sign, and as he heard the movie-familiar sound of heavy iron gates clanking shut behind him, he felt a sinking in the pit of his stomach.

He had been expecting to talk with Neil on a phone while sitting on the other side of a heavy pane of bulletproof glass, but he was directed to a large, high-ceilinged room with cafeteria style tables and chairs. Inmates were meeting with their families; children were running around, babies were crying, and on a catwalk around the upper story, guards with rifles watched the crowd closely.

Neil was ushered in by two hulking men in black and gray uniforms. His hair was greasy and unkempt, and his prison overalls were too big.

"I can't believe you came," he said to Voss. "You're the only one."

"What? Your family? Friends?"

"Chance and Fade were my only friends," Neil said. "And my family . . . they've been looking for an excuse to disown me for years. They'll never come here."

"What happened?" Voss said. "I mean, I don't know if I'm supposed to ask that. I guess I should ask you first if you're all right, or if you need anything."

"Do I look all right?"

Voss looked at the boy. He looked around at the other inmates, many of whom were clearly doing a lot of lifting. "You look small to be in here," Voss said.

"Fucking A," Neil said. "You don't know the half of it. But . . . I'll tell you what I need: I need a lawyer."

"You don't have a lawyer?"

"Court appointed. Not exactly the best law school, and not exactly the top of his class."

"That's a lot to ask, you know. If what the papers say is true. . . ." Voss looked down at the floor, dull, worn, green tile.

"Do you want to know?"

"What?"

"Do you want to know what happened? What we planned, and why and how it turned out?"

"Yes. I want to know."

"You're not going to like it."

"How could I like it? My daughter is dead. You're sitting here alive. What the fuck?"

Normally, Voss would try to get to a new venue at least an hour before he was scheduled to go on, but he'd left the prison with a lot on his mind. The weather had cleared and he had plenty of time to get to the gig, so he just set out driving, the way he and Hal and Avery would when they were kids. Even now you could find rural two-lanes out in the country where there was more open space than most people believed, their picture of New Jersey confined to that stretch of I-95 that went past the refineries of Linden and the sprawling runways of Newark Airport. Forty minutes west of that, you were halfway to Pennsylvania, in terrain that could pass for the horse country of Virginia or the rolling hills and alfalfa fields of southern Ohio.

The Ferrari hummed as he drove out 78, but really showed its mettle on the tight bends of the narrow roads that wound in and out of the Watchung mountains. Back in the sixties, the radio would have been tuned to WNEW FM, the station where Voss first heard Janis Joplin, James Taylor, Cat Stevens. But WNEW was no longer the station it had been then, and Voss rarely listened to contemporary music anyway. The station he'd been listening to earlier was now playing old Wes Montgomery, early stuff with Melvin Rhyne on the organ. Voss focused on the road, cornering carefully, pushing it into the turns, feeling the tires bite, shifting aggressively, but with care. He never drifted out of his lane, kept to within ten miles an hour over the speed limit. Occasionally a car would come up on his tail on a long straightaway. He'd watch the speedometer. Ease right to let them pass if the road continued straight, or if it came into a set of curves, he'd keep the needle right where it was and watch them fall back as he took the turns faster than they dared. It was a way of not thinking about what Neil had told him, which was exactly why he was doing it, but it was also a way of not paying attention to just where he was going and how long it would take him to get to Morristown for the gig Bert had found him. Then he heard his own name on the radio. The announcer was going down a list of jazz shows in the area, saying a few words about each one: ". . . and here's something you might want to check out: Voss, the one time leader of the famous '70s rock band Vossimilitude, will be playing the piano at Al Dente in Morristown. Voss is a player who has reinvented himself many times, and when he and a keyboard are in the same room, you want to be there. Fifty dollars at the door, reservations recommended for the dining room."

He pulled up in front of the restaurant with twenty minutes to spare, handing the Ferrari's keys to a very impressed looking boy in a black valet jacket.

"Voss himself," the owner greeted him, "I recognized you getting out of your car. Nice ride. I'll have the boys bring it back around and park it right in front. Makes us both look good."

"It's just a rental," Voss said. "And you must be . . ." he glanced at the sheet Bert had faxed him with the name of the place and the directions.

"Al," the man said, holding out his hand.

"Al Dente? You're kidding." The hand in his was soft and limp. Voss tried to release it without showing his distaste.

"Al Salamanca," the restaurateur said, a bit petulantly. "You want anything to eat before you go on?"

"Something light. You got a garden salad, maybe? A sprinkle of olive oil and a couple of lemons."

"Drink?"

"Just water," Voss said, looking around the place. Long bar, tiny tables crowded with tall chairs. Lots of dark wood. A back room with a full-size billiard table. White table cloths in the dining room, white cloth napkins folded into triangles on china plates. A waiter in black jeans and a starched white shirt was going from table to table lighting candles, and the little rubbery flames glinted in the polished wineglasses. The piano stood on a small riser against the wall between the dining room and the bar, a tall black Kawai studio.

"It's brand new," the owner said. "Three months. I don't let anybody touch it but the musicians."

Voss sat on the bench and raised the cover. The keys were filthy.

"Looks like the last piano player was eating a peanut butter sandwich while he was playing," Voss said. "You got some alcohol or a bottle of Windex?"

The owner seemed stunned, possibly insulted. Again. He called to the waiter. "Jimmy, can you help Mr. Voss out here? And I'll get him a salad."

Jimmy brought Voss a spray bottle of generic window cleanser and a couple of the cloth napkins. "He won't let any of us touch it," he said.

"Too bad," Voss said. "Pianos need to be played."

And tuned, he thought to himself a little while later, when he heard the first G chord resound flatly in the quickly filling rooms. But the action was quite fine. Light and uniform. Stable but not at all stiff. And consistently flat up and down the keyboard, so that at least it was in tune with itself.

He began with "Lolita," still in his mind from Wes Montgomery's version he'd heard during the afternoon. Rhyne's organ work didn't translate directly to the piano, especially this one, but Voss noodled around with his left hand trying vaguely to recreate the feeling of the old record. His right was picking out the melody, which Wes's guitar had presented so sparely. Only a couple of the diners seemed to notice when he brought the song to a close. Their sparse applause inspired a few others to clap, including a couple of people on the bar side. Voss didn't turn around, but he was sure fewer than half the people in the place were even listening. That was fine. He tried to think back to some of the other tunes he'd heard that day. "Body and Soul." He'd recorded that on his album of standards years ago. He knew it well, and as he played it, his mind drifted back to the talk with Neil that he'd spent the rest of the day deliberately not thinking about. No, he wasn't going to deal with that yet. Not now. He thought about the disastrous intervention yesterday, but that took him to C.C.'s vicious denunciation of him, which took him ultimately to the same place, Chance's death and the part he himself may have played in it. He stuck to old jazz tunes, mostly from the standards album, embroidering them, drifting away for long meditative breaks and then slipping back into the familiar melodic lines. A microphone on a boom hung above the piano's music stand, but he didn't sing at all during the first set.

When he took his break there was no place to sit at the bar, and the alcove by the front door was packed. Evidently the people who had eaten their dinner during the first set weren't about to give up their tables—not surprising considering the cover and the fact that the bar area was full—but the restaurant had taken reservations for a second seating. That left a small crowd of irate people clustered around the Maitre d's stand. Voss slipped into the kitchen and looked for a back way out to get some air.

He could feel the difference in the room when he began his second set. The tension fed into his own mood, and he began with "The Way You Look Tonight," slow and precise, the mournfulness and nostalgia built into the song magnified by the slightly flat piano.

"How about something a little more cheerful, man? You're bringing us all down," someone yelled from the dining room as the applause was ending.

Voss reached up and pulled the microphone toward him. "I guess that turned a bit gloomy," he said. "How about this?" He jumped into bouncy rhythm and began to sing "Straighten Up and Fly Right," doing his best fifties beatnik shtick:

Straighten up and fly right,
Straighten up and fly right,
Straighten up and fly right,
Cool down, papa, don't you blow your top.

He turned around to look at the place where the voice had come from and saw a large man in a white shirt with the collar loosened and the sleeves rolled up glaring at him. Some of the members of the audience were laughing at Voss's delivery of the song, and he realized in an instant that the big man had taken it as an insinuation that he was drunk and ready to go off. The song earned more applause than anything thus far, and Voss said, "The man asked for something lighter, folks. How was that?"

He turned on the bench to look out at the crowd. A few people murmured their assent. The large man, whose face was now red, then yelled out, "Got anything less than a hundred years old?"

Voss turned back to the microphone and said, "You know, I don't think this guy likes me." Then he perversely slid into Mose Allison's "Your Mind Is On Vacation," knowing he was escalating the situation:

You sittin here yakkin right in my face
Comin on exactly like you own the place
You know if silence was golden, you couldn't raise a dime
Because your mind is on vacation and your mouth is workin overtime.

The crowd loved it, but the man in the white shirt was fuming. Voss turned to see the other man at the table put his hand on the big man's shoulder. The women were sitting back in their chairs, as if they didn't want to be associated with him at all. It was clearly time to back off, to let it go. Instead Voss turned to face the piano and played an E7, then an E9, as low as he could play them. On the flat piano the low chords sounded like empty dumpsters being dropped by a garbage truck. With his right hand he played seconds up high, so that it seemed as if a little kid was just banging on the piano.

"Holy crap," the big man said. "We paid money for this?"

It was just what Voss had been waiting for. He worked the E chords up to the center of the keyboard, then played a B, followed by an A. His right hand twiddled a bit up high, and then came down to meet the left, delicately vamping on the chords, and he began to sing "Nowhere Man."

He felt the man coming for him, and he saw the bartender come right across the top of the bar. Al was moving in from the Maitre d's podium. Voss kept singing, confident that they would intercept the man before he reached the piano. He turned just in time to see the bartender and the owner put themselves in the angry man's path.

As he was being ushered out the door the big man shouted, "I guess I'll have to miss the suicide songs, asshole. Too fucking bad."

The applause when Voss finished the song was half-hearted. He tried to make a joke of it: "Sorry, folks. Show's over. Well, not this show." But the sour feel of what he had done had infected the place. He went into his own arrangement of "Lush Life," but he'd lost his audience, and people were leaving. By the time he'd finished the set, only one or two tables in the restaurant were occupied, and the bartender was rushing back and forth to the register to cash people out.

Voss played the late set to a mostly new crowd, but he felt like shit throughout.

When Al handed him his check, he said, "I should tear this up. You cost me money tonight. I hope you enjoy your ride home."

Voss went out into the empty street to see the Ferrari with all the side windows busted out. The leather seats were covered with glittering chips of glass and the windshield was spiderwebbed with cracks. A baseball bat, he figured, studying the placement of the two impact points and considering whether he'd be able to see well enough to drive it back to the city. Or could it have been the heavy end of a pool cue?

"You okay, dude?" Voss said into his cell. He was standing at the window of his apartment in the city, but he still hadn't had a new phone hooked up to the landline. "What happened after?"

"She packed a suitcase and split," Artie said.

"Couldn't you stop her? Why didn't you just take her someplace. Put her in lockdown?"

"I could never do that, Jack."

"What? You're twice as big as she is. I've seen what you can do."

"You know me better than that, Jack. She was pushed around enough as a kid. I never touched her without an invitation. Never muscled her. I couldn't do that."

Voss looked out at the cityscape stretching south, then white sun on gray water. A handful of container ships in the bay, a couple of sailboats, reefed down and heeled over, ferries churning between the Battery and the Statue of Liberty and Ellis Island.

"So where do you think she went?"

"I have no idea. I swear I have no idea. I've called everybody and she's not anywhere."

"Would she go back to . . . where's she from, Kansas?"

"Oklahoma. I doubt it. She doesn't talk to them."

"I'm catching a train to Boston later. You want to come over? Hang for a couple of hours? Talk?"

"I gotta be here in case she calls, or if she comes back."

"She's been gone two nights? Fuck, man. Where could she be? Work? Someone from there you don't know?"

"I doubt it. I know everyone she works with. They'd tell me if they knew."

"What's your best guess?"

"A bar. What I worry about is where she's sleeping. For all I know it's on a fucking grate somewhere."

"Did you call the police?"

"They're no fucking help. 'Did you have an argument?' they asked me. They're not going to look for her."

Neither spoke for a while. Then Artie broke the silence. "So how *you* holding up?"

"Okay, I guess. I almost got in a fight last night. Would have been my fault all the way. Provoked a guy. Got my car smashed up."

"You had an accident?"

"No, somebody broke my windows. I asked for it. I was looking for trouble."

"Why?"

"I talked to the kid yesterday and he gave me the runaround."

"What kid? What are you talking about?"

"Chance's friend. The kid that lived."

"Where'd you talk to him?"

"In jail."

"Shit, man. What did he say?"

"Everything and nothing. He'd tell me one thing and then change the story. I don't know if he's trying to be cagey or if he's just lost. Yesterday, though, I was pretty pissed."

"What could he have said that would piss you off more than you already were?"

"Same thing C.C. said at the intervention. *The Enchanted Pond*. I mean, he said a lot of things, but the thing that kept coming through was that I played a part in it. I wrote it and it came to pass. . . . Once again." Voss sighed heavily. "Plus there's a guy who called me a couple of times right after it happened and said it was, what the fuck, *the chickens come home to roost.* Like Malcolm X said about JFK."

"What are you going to do?"

"I don't know. Just try to get through it. Live with it. Right now I'm mostly trying to keep busy."

"Yeah," Artie said. "I know what you mean."

Soundtrack for Suicide

It was the record. The rock opera. The Enchanted Pond. We were living it without meaning to. Stuck. I was willing to leave, but she always said no. He couldn't stand it. He wanted to leave, but he couldn't handle being without her. Oh, God. It started out like the most romantic thing in the world. Magic. Breaking all the rules, crossing all the boundaries. But it couldn't last. And none of us could stand the way it was going to end. And the opera gave us the idea. Let's just end it together. Of course we weren't the first ones to get that out of it, were we?

The Vossimilitude tour bus was heading north out of L.A. on a Sunday afternoon when the news broke about the first suicides. The driver had been listening to the radio up front. He piped it into the back. Three kids in Iowa. A little town out on the prairie, where, in the girl's farmhouse bedroom, with Vossimilitude playing on the stereo, she and two boys, all in high school, had soaked their wrists in ice water and slit them with razors while their parents were at church services.

It had happened almost a week before, but the local police had not made the connection with the record. A reporter from Boise put it together. Now, as the band listened in the bus, he was being interviewed. "The record is what they call a rock opera, like The Who's *Tommy*," he was saying. "It tells the story of a desperate love triangle that ends in a triple suicide. Evidently the children got the idea from this record." All the color bled out of Voss's face.

"I can't believe they actually listened to the words," Hal said.

"It's not funny, Hal," Voss said.

Avery put her hand on Voss's hand and said, "It's not your fault."

He pulled his hand back and curled into himself, sitting in silence for the rest of the trip to San Francisco, where he didn't come out of his hotel room. Room service delivered food and liquor, and Avery went out for the papers. She slept next to Voss, but he didn't touch her.

At first the story wasn't as big as the Manson murders back in '69, but it got at least as much publicity as the deaths at Altamont. By Tuesday, the album cover was in all the papers, with its Maxfield Parrish style image of Sigismund and Helena standing at the edge of the pond, Helena with her hand at her collar, about to let her sheer chiton fall, and the boy peering from the reeds. The photo of the band posed with their instruments in the dark studio was almost as widely reproduced. On Wednesday, a second trio of young people attempted suicide in the suburbs of L.A., but the girl crawled to the phone, dialed the operator, and asked for an ambulance. *The Enchanted Pond* was on the record player, and the charred remnants of their tickets to the concert the previous Friday night were found in an incense burner on the floor. On Thursday, two boys shot each other in Topeka, leaving a note quoting the album's closing song:

> *This world's not ready*
> *Our love's not welcome here*
> *So let's go to the next world*
> *Where we won't live in fear.*

Bobby Norman kept in constant touch with Avery. "The record is flying off the shelves, but they want to pull it," he said to her on Friday. "We need to cut another one like yesterday."

Voss had picked up the phone in the living room. "Hi, Bobby," he said. "And how are you? How do you feel about making a record that people are killing themselves because of. How do you feel about being famous now for causing kids to commit suicide. Oh, right. That's not you, that's me. Fuck. Talk to Avery."

"I'm still here," Avery said from the extension in the bedroom.

Voss hung up and poured himself a drink. It was three o'clock Friday afternoon and they still hadn't heard whether the night's show was going to be cancelled, go on as scheduled, or, what looked more and more likely, go on with a replacement opening act. The Moody Blues had been publicly supportive, but Voss felt sure they were behind the idea to find another band to open for them.

There was a knock at the door. Voss answered it, and Hal walked in, striding right past Voss to the television, which he snapped on.

"Check it out, dude. We're more famous than ever."

Voss's picture was on the screen for a moment, then the band.

"Don't tell me there's been another one," Voss said.

Then they cut back to the announcer: "To repeat, city officials say that tonight's concert by the controversial rock band Vossimilitude will go on under extra security."

"This is a fucking nightmare. I never thought anybody would try to do what I wrote."

"I know, man," Hal said. "It's not your fault. But you gotta do something or we're toast. Get out there and tell them you're sorry. I know it's bullshit."

"I *am* sorry. That's not bullshit."

"Okay," Hal said. "Look, I'm just trying to help. We need to do something to make it look like we're not the devil here."

"We're *not* the devil. Fuck, Hal."

Avery came in from the bedroom. "Hal," she said. "I'm surprised to see you here."

"Not now, Avery," Hal said. "We gotta do something. And we gotta do it tonight. The other guys are talking about quitting the band."

"What?" Voss said. "What the fuck can we do?"

"We need to get everyone in here and talk about this," Avery said. "We'll come up with something."

The extra security measures delayed the show a good thirty minutes, as the crowd had to file through a gauntlet of police, and tickets were checked at the door and in the house. Finally, the lights went down. A single spot came up, a ray from the heavens lighting Voss, wearing jeans and a black shirt, standing alone at a microphone in front of the stage.

"I'm Voss," he said. "And I want to say a few words before we start. I wrote a story a year or so ago." He unfolded a piece of paper and referred to it from time to time as he spoke. "Actually, it was more of a fable. It was about how hard love can be when it doesn't look like mom and dad and the kids, when it takes another shape. In my story the lovers end up killing themselves. I wanted to show just how hard it can be. But I never wanted anybody to take that for a solution to their difficulty, their pain, their fear. There's been enough death. The world has enough ways to kill us, we don't need to add any. I'm sorry some people took my story the wrong way. I'm speaking now not just to those of you here in the audience, but to everyone who listens to Vossimilitude, to *The Enchanted Pond*: no more suicides, please. That's not the answer.

"Now, you didn't come out tonight to hear me talk, you came to hear music. That's what we do. And we're going to start tonight's show with a new song. We wrote it today, so bear with us."

The single spot followed him as he walked to the keyboards, his old Vox continental with the black naturals and the white sharps and flats, a moog, a Fender Rhodes, Mike Pinder's mellotron, and, for the first time on the tour, a grand piano. He spread some sheets of paper out on the piano's music stand and began to play. He started slow and soft, introducing the chord progression he and the boys had worked out just a few hours ago, the feel of the keys under his fingers reminding him of the old Steinway he played back at Forrester for Dr. Madison, but looser, the sound rich and clear. He sang the first lines of the new song:

> *The world it is hard on a love that don't fit,*
> *But love's what we're made for; don't give up on it . . .*

A deep bass note, bent and released, came in, sounding almost like a cello, and a second spot shone down on Hal Proteus. The crowd went nuts for a moment, then quieted again. Voss finished the verse, and Hal joined him on the chorus, their voices harmonizing the way they had since they first imitated The Beatles in Hal's basement ten years before:

Don't give up, old friend,
Don't give up.
Don't give up, new friend,
Don't give up.
We will find our own way,
We will live every day
We will find . . . our own way.

The other spots came up one by one as the other members of the band came in, George just playing the bass drum and the toms, no snare or cymbals yet, Rick playing the chords on his Rickenbacker electric 12-string, and Kenny playing slide on his white Strat. Voss sang the rest of the verses in a daze, as if he were carrying something very heavy. But at each chorus, he felt Hal's harmony lifting him up, so that by the end, when the other members of the band had quietly faded out and it was just Voss's soft piano chords, Hal's brilliantly tasteful bass line, and their voices in perfect harmony, Voss was in the music as he hadn't been in weeks. He hadn't forgotten about the suicides or the tension between him and Hal or the pressure from Bobby; those things were all still there, but they weren't inside him, they were outside, at some distance. Inside him were only the music and that thing that he and Hal could do together and it brought tears to his eyes. And it brought the audience to its feet.

The rest of the show went by like a luxury train, quiet on the rails, soft yellow light coming from the Pullman car windows, indigo sky sequined with stars. They had changed the set list, cutting out about half the songs from the B side of the album, and they finished with the beautiful "Avery's Song." If the crowd missed "Send Us On, Then Follow," or "Our Crystal Pool," they didn't show it.

During the intermission the Moodys congratulated them, and when they took the stage, Justin Hayward began the show by talking to the audience:

"Vossimilitude," he said. "Who says you have to come from England to be a great band? Eh?" The crowd applauded, a few whistled. "Those guys are artists, and it's been an honor to tour with them." Then the mellotron did its string-section thing, and they launched into "Forever Afternoon."

(♯)

By the time the tour reached Seattle there had been two more suicide attempts, both thwarted, one by a would-be participant who changed his mind, called the operator for help, and taped up the wrists of his fast-fading friends himself. In the other case, the last one that was publicly connected to the album, three high school students in Indiana had cut school in the afternoon, divided up a bottle of sleeping pills and washed them down with vodka. The girl's mother had come home early from work and found them unconscious on the living room floor. She called an ambulance, and both boys, who had eaten big lunches, were successfully revived after their stomachs were pumped. The girl, who weighed less than one hundred pounds and had taken the same dose as the boys on an empty stomach, was still in a coma.

Voss's remarks in San Francisco had been filmed. They were shown on national television and a transcription went out on the wire services, appearing in most major newspapers: "Rock Musician Pleads with Young Fans: Don't Kill Yourselves." Voss's picture made it onto the cover of *Time* with the caption, "When the Music is a Soundtrack for Suicide, Who Answers?" Inside was a surprisingly thoughtful article that began with an account of the suicides in eighteenth century Europe after the publication of Goethe's *The Sorrows of Young Werther*. Although there was a sidebar about a preacher in Georgia who was denouncing the band and calling for a public burning of their records, *a la* The Beatles in '66, the general tenor of the article was supportive of Voss and the band, saying that he had responded quickly and responsibly to the incidents and quoting the short speech that he was now making at each concert. The records hadn't been pulled from the shelves, but word from Bobby was they were going to let *The Enchanted Pond* go out of print.

"It's going to be a collector's item, man," he told Voss over the phone. "But we gotta get another album out. I've got a recording crew gonna meet you in Calgary. You've got two nights there, and we'll record both of them. We're not talking about a completely live album, but maybe we can get at least a couple of cuts. Then, after Chicago, back into the studio."

"How about a break? We've been on the road now for, what's it been? Feels like forever."

"It's been four months, Jack. I've got a house you can live in where you can walk to the studio. An old southside mansion. We're cleaning it up and putting in furniture now. You're gonna love it. Now let me talk to Avery, okay?"

(♯)

Although the suicides had briefly eclipsed the tensions that had been tearing at the band for the previous couple of months, by the time they moved into the house in south St. Louis, actually less than a mile from the house on Lafayette where Voss, Avery, and Hal had lived the year before with Voss's college friends, the cracks were starting to show again. The Calgary tapes had yielded a usable take of "Don't Give Up," though that song never sounded quite as good as it had that first night they'd played it in San Francisco. The live version of "Touch Her and You're Dead" was another keeper, and Bobby wanted to release it as a single as soon as they could come up with a B side. They decided on "Avery's Song," but although Hal had been playing beautifully on it throughout the tour, it took him a week to lay down the bass line. If it wasn't equipment problems, it was musical mistakes. On Friday afternoon, when he'd got through nearly the whole thing perfectly, dancing around the room as he played, he kicked over a bottle of beer, slipped in the spill, fell on the concrete floor and cracked the headstock of his bass.

Avery, who was in the booth, said something to Bobby, and then Bobby keyed the intercom.

"Go home and sleep it off, Hal," he said. "And how about coming in sober tomorrow?"

"What the fuck happened to 'Are you okay?'" Hal shouted back. "Fucking assholes. You get me another bass, and I'll lay this shit down right now."

Half an hour later, a borrowed Jazz bass in his hands, Hal hit every note. Perfect take. He waited in silence until the engineer nodded to Bobby, and Bobby's voice came from the booth. "Okay, Hal. That's a wrap."

"You're damn straight it's a wrap," Hal said, standing up from his stool. "And you ever tell me I'm too drunk to work again you can get a new bass player. And you'll find out pretty fucking quick that Vossimilitude ain't just Jack Voss and any old musicians. Now if you don't need me anymore today, I'll be back when I feel like coming back." He strode out the door and slammed it behind him. Avery and Bobby heard his new Harley roar away as they came out of the booth into the open area of the warehouse.

He came back on Monday with a handful of ragged edged pages torn from a spiral notebook. He hadn't been at the house, and Voss and Avery had wondered whether he'd split back to Jersey or someplace else.

"You guys want to make this record, these songs are going on it," he said.

Bobby and Avery were furious with him, but the fact was that they needed the material. Voss's songs weren't coming together. Weeks went by. He'd stop in the middle of a session to rewrite. Then he decided he needed a grand piano, and everything stopped until they could get one in and get it tuned. Winter had come, and they were running electric space heaters in the studio. Just a couple of days later the piano was out of tune again. Voss stood up quietly, abstractedly, and left the studio without saying anything.

It was Hal's moment to step in. He did, and except for an acoustic blues number from Kenny, the B side of the album became his. Voss came in and played what he was asked to. Mostly Fender Rhodes, reminiscent of Ray Manzarek's work on "Riders on the Storm," a sound that would later characterize Mutually Assured Destruction. He was getting high day and night, as they all were, but not even Avery was aware that in addition to the pot they all smoked in the house and the studio, Voss had bought a supply of acid and was more fucked up than anyone knew.

One January afternoon while they were recording an acoustic number by Kenny, Voss dropped a hit of blotter and drove to the Shaw Botanical Gardens, where he bought his ticket at four o'clock knowing that the place closed at five. Then, as the acid began to come on, he lost track of time. It had snowed in the morning, big sticky flakes that clung to the blades of grass and the smallest twigs. Voss thought of Housman's lines:

> *About the woodlands I will go*
> *To see the cherry hung with snow.*

The image brought to mind some Japanese woodcuts he had seen, and when he saw a sign for a Japanese garden, he knew that was where he had to go. As he walked the weaving path through the park, a light wind was blowing tufts of snow from the branches of the trees. As each tuft hit a lower branch it broke into a kind of snowy starburst, like fireworks. A pond came into view, the edges crusted with thin ice covered with snow, the open water black, the falling snow vanishing into it. Along the shoreline, against the white ground of the snow, intensified by the acid that was now coming on strong, the faint reds and yellows of the dry reeds glowed. The path took another turn, and the landscape that met his eyes was almost exactly like one of the woodcuts he remembered: an arched wooden bridge leading to a teahouse on a little island in still water. He came upon a small thatched shelter, out of the wind, and sat down and watched the snow blow into waves, clouds, not realizing that what he was watching was the development of a major winter storm. The wind whistled as it tugged at the roof of the shelter, and Voss thought of snowswept mountain passes and then a sacrificial altar made of ice where children, led there by the music and lyrics he had written, were cut to pieces and fed to white wolves. The wind was howling when he left the shelter, the snow horizontal, the cold biting. When he got back to the main entrance to the park, the tall, wrought iron front gates were locked, and he looked at his watch to see that it was already five-thirty. He watched himself not freak out, almost surprised at his own inner calm. He walked along under the high brick wall, out of the fierce wind, until he was opposite the parking lot where he'd left his car. With the help of a tree with low branches, his hands freezing in the snow, he climbed over the wall into the parking lot, immensely relieved to see that the parking lot gate was still open. Still peaking, he piloted his car out into the snowy evening, driving with exaggerated care to the West End, where he ducked into Gryffin's for a cheeseburger and an Irish coffee. He knew everyone in the place, and when he took out his notebook and started writing, they left him alone. The song came there and then, all in one sitting:

Locked in the Garden
Snow lies on the roses;
The leaves are shivering.
We are all locked in the garden,
And winter's blowing in. . . .

The album was finished a week later.

Vossimilitude II
Locked in the Garden

Jack Voss: Keyboards and Vocals
Hal Proteus: Bass and Vocals
Kenny Claybourne: Guitars
Rick Darnell: Guitars and Vocals
George Sinclair: Percussion

Side A

Locked in the Garden *(J. Voss)*	4:52
Avery's Song *(J. Voss)*	2:55
Famous by Mistake *(J. Voss)*	3:06
Stranger in the Castle *(J. Voss)*	3:45
Only When the Music Plays *(J. Voss)*	3:41
Don't Give Up (live) *(J. Voss, H. Proteus, K. Claybourne, R. Darnell, G. Sinclair)*	5:08

Side B

Black-Haired Beauty from Alburquerque *(H. Proteus)*	3:57
You Can Have Her, Friend *(H. Proteus)*	2:46
Kenny's Blues *(K. Claybourne)*	2:53
Nobody Tells the Bassman How to Play *(H. Proteus)*	3:01
Touch Her and You're Dead (live) *(J. Voss, H. Proteus)*	12:17

The 45 with the cut-down live version of "Touch Her and You're Dead" hit the radio stations a month after they had finished recording. To everyone's relief, the hunger for their music had not died down. It climbed up the charts like a vine, reaching the top in three weeks, and staying there for another two. Bobby and Avery worked out a deal to release another single before the album came out. "Locked in the Garden," haunting, Pink Floyd-like, caught a brief wave, and kept the buzz going for the album to come. The B-side, Hal's "Black-Haired Beauty from Albuquerque" started getting as much air play as the A-side, but there was no way to know which song was selling more records.

No one wanted to go back out on the road, but Avery and Bobby had them all under contract. It would be their final tour, New York to L.A., giant venues, huge crowds, and the fractious journey of a band that had in many ways already split up.

They sat in the green room of Madison Square Garden passing around a joint, talking frankly about what they would do next. Kenny was going to focus on the blues.

"There's some old guys who are still playing stuff like back in the thirties," he said. "After this tour is over, I'm going down south and record them. Put together a little crew, maybe two guys, an engineer and a driver, outfit a van, and cruise from town to town asking about old bluesmen."

"I'm going back to San Diego," George Sinclair, the drummer, said. "Something clicked for me there. It's like maybe I found the place where I belong, the place I could call home, cause I'm sure as shit not going back to south St. Louis."

"We're going to Europe," Voss said. No one had to ask him who was included in the "we" and who was not. "England, France, Italy. Visit Morrison's grave, maybe go to Hamburg and see the club where The Beatles got their start."

"How about you, Hal?" George asked.

"What?" Hal said, lighting up a joint he had just rolled.

"What're you going to do after the tour?"

Hal took a long pull on the joint. "You mean this tour's gonna end?" he croaked, holding in the smoke.

The door opened and Avery stuck her head in. "Five minutes," she said. Then she slipped the rest of the way into the room and shut the door behind her. "You know there's three cops like ten feet down the hall."

"What," Hal said, "you think New York's finest are going to arrest us five minutes before we're going out and entertain 20,000 citizens? Take it easy, babe. It's cool."

She shot a look at Voss. He just shook his head, mouthing silently, "Don't worry."

She looked at her watch. "Four minutes now," she said. "I'll be back to get you." She opened the door narrowly and slipped back out.

"You going to smoke that whole thing yourself, or are you going to pass it around," Kenny said.

"You pussies don't deserve it," Hal said. He took another hit, then passed the joint to Kenny.

When Avery came back in to announce that it was time, only a short roach was left. George offered it to her. She hesitated for a moment, then took it, saying, "Thanks. Now you guys get out there and rock." As they filed out, she sidled up to Voss and kissed him, deep and smoky. "Later, baby," she said.

Thanks to Avery and Bobby, Vossimilitude had one of the best contracts in the business, so that when the tour finally did end, with an unexpectedly spectacular show in L.A., after a series of lackluster performances across the west, they would be able to go their separate ways with enough money to do pretty much whatever they wanted for a few years at least. Bobby had come out to the coast for the last show. Aron Productions now had three other bands under contract, and the studio in St. Louis was getting a 16-track deck. He and Kenny had worked a deal creating an archival label for the blues musicians Kenny was heading off to search for. After that final show, they met in Bobby's hotel suite and celebrated. Rick was sitting on the floor in the corner listening to a demo of one of Bobby's new bands.

"They could use a good rhythm player, Rick. Let me know what you think," Bobby said.

Kenny was telling George again about the custom van he'd ordered and all the recording equipment that he was going to put into it.

Avery was on the couch watching Voss snort up a line of coke from the marble counter of the kitchenette across the room when Hal came in with a girl on each arm. She caught Voss's eye and together they assessed Hal's companions. One was short and shapely, with generous breasts and a round ass. She couldn't have been more than twenty, and was probably at the height of her beauty—her hourglass waist wouldn't last five more years, but right now she was a sweet morsel indeed. The other girl was at least six feet tall and skinny, with pointy nipples sticking out of her flat chest.

"Boys," Hal said. "Proteus is here with his nymphs, Short and Round, and Tall and Lean." He reached around the short girl and squeezed her right breast. She giggled. Then he pulled the skinny one's tank top aside and licked her nipple. She did a little shimmy and squeaked. A practiced gesture and its attendant sound effect.

"See what you're missing, boys," he said. "Jack."

Avery got up from the couch, walked over to Voss, took the straw and snorted up a line and then wrapped herself around him and kissed him deeply. She pointed at the short girl and whispered something in Voss's ear. Then she turned to Hal. "You're the one who's missing out," she said.

But Hal ignored her. "A little magic dust from the Andes? Make room for the shape-shifting sea god."

Voss walked Avery back to the couch and filled two champagne flutes from one of the magnums of Piper in the giant ice bucket.

Hal said something to his girls, and they headed out into the hall.

"Okay," he said. "You know I haven't mourned the death of this band and won't mourn it, though I know you will mourn the loss of me, so I've brought some things for you to remember me by."

The girls came back in dragging three shiny black guitar cases and one cylindrical case.

Hal picked up that one first. "George," he said, "from the dark continent, hand carved from monkeywood or some shit and topped with giraffe skin,

I don't know. They call it an African drum. You can smack the shit out of it and think of me."

"Whoa, man," George said, rising to his feet.

"Relax, dude," Hal said. "Stay where you are. Bring it over to him, slim."

The tall girl took the case from Hal and carried it over to George, who opened it to reveal a beautifully carved djembe.

Hal bestowed his gifts on the other members of the band, a sunburst Telecaster for Kenny—"just like Roy Buchanan's"—and an orange Gretsch Country Gentleman for Rick.

"Now, Jack," he said, taking the last case from the short girl, "I thought about getting you a piano, but since that would be hard to take to Europe with you, I decided against it. So . . . well I've seen you noodling around in the corner with Kenny's Guild, and I know it will probably take you about five minutes to master the guitar if you decide to, so . . . Here you go, man."

He handed the guitar case back to the girl who carried it over to the couch.

Voss opened it to find a Martin D-28.

"Songwriter special, bro," Hal said.

"I don't know what to say," Voss said.

"Forget it, man. And as for Avery and Bobby . . . I thought about getting you guys ledger books and matching red and black pens, but I figured you already had all you need. Now what I need is a drink, huh?"

He grabbed one of the magnums from the bucket, lifted it high, and drank right from the bottle.

"Now as I foresaw that you guys wouldn't be getting any gifts for me, I got my own as you can see." He gestured to the two girls standing next to the door. "And I'm going off to open my presents. *Adiós, compañeros.*"

He held his arms out to his sides, each girl hooked an arm in one of his, and the three of them slipped sideways out the door.

NOVEMBER

"Yeah?" The voice was a gruff challenge—*you'd better have a good reason for making me pick up this phone.*

"Artie, it's Jack."

"Jack," the voice softened. "How you doing, man? What's up?"

"So. Four more years, eh?" *The Chronicle* lay open on the kitchen table, headshots of a jubilant Bush and a weary defeated Kerry on the front page.

"Yeah. I couldn't watch it. I mean, I knew they'd find a way to keep him out, but I couldn't stand to see it. Fucking Ohio. People should go to jail for that; instead they'll end up the heads of federal agencies."

"Florida."

"Don't even mention that state to me. Brother Jeb."

"So, besides that, how are you? Any word?"

"She's in Oklahoma with one of her sisters. She got there last week. We talked on the phone a couple of times. She's still pissed, but . . . at least we're talking."

"And what about you? I mean, it must be a relief to know she's okay. I know it was tearing you up."

"Yeah, it's a relief somebody else is looking out for her. Although they're not exactly the best. . . . I don't know, man."

Voss heard Artie take a long drag on something and hold it in. It would be—Voss looked at his watch—eleven a.m. in New York.

"What else is going on? You working on anything?"

"I'm about halfway through a script on ancient naval warfare for The History Channel."

"That's right up your alley. Sounds like fun."

"It's not bad. It's the graphics that'll make or break it, and they're not budgeting near enough. But it pays the rent. How about you?"

"I don't know. Not much going on. I'm in kind of a dark place right now."

"Yeah. I understand."

"Hey, why don't you come out here when you finish your script? We can hang out. Wander up and down the coast a bit. Catch a couple movies. And there's lots of good food. Do you good to get out of that apartment."

"That sounds really good. I've got a couple weeks work left, but I'll call you when it's done."

"All right, bro. I'll be here."

"Later, man."

Voss poured himself another cup of coffee and walked out onto the deck. The sun glinted off the distant waves, but the breakers below were still in shadow. He pictured Artie in that dark apartment in Queens smoking a joint by himself at eleven in the morning. He knew his friend would never come to see him.

EUROPE

Suddenly one of the big boys was in front of me, maybe a seventh or eighth grader. You want to jump rope with the girls? I like to watch them. You want to be a girl, don't you? And then he pushed me. Put his hands on my chest and pushed me. And I started to fall. But there was another guy behind me, who sort of caught me and pushed me back into the hands of the first guy. And they started shoving me back and forth between them and I couldn't get my balance and I was scared and humiliated and tears came into my eyes because I didn't know why they hated me and wanted to hurt me and the next thing there was a circle of people around me all laughing. And she burst through and tackled the guy who shoved me first. Leave him alone, you bully. And some teachers closed in and I ran and one of the teachers caught me and took me inside and got me a drink of water and gave me the old, children-can-be-cruel speech.

Voss and Avery left for Europe the next day.

They went to the Poets' Corner in Westminster Abbey, laid a bouquet on Jim Morrison's grave in Pere Lachaise, read the sad, unidiomatic accounts of Keats's last days on typed sheets under glass in the house next to the Spanish Steps in Rome where he died. It was the spring of 1976. They learned to travel light. Money was not a problem, and Avery was a whiz at making arrangements; she would ship their big trunk to a first-class hotel in the next major city on their itinerary, and they would carry only backpacks and the guitar. Voss could already strum a few chords to accompany himself on silly songs he'd cobble together from the mangled English of travel brochures and guidebooks. *The Bay of Napoli is know for its blue,* he'd sing in a mock Italian accent, *reflexing the jewel of Isla Capri.*

They headed for Greece as the summer was beginning, college students showing up everywhere with their huge backpacks and sleeping bags. The narrow little cabin on the ferry from Brindisi to Athens was the smallest room they'd slept in since their *pension* in Rome, with not even a chair, so they climbed into the bunk and gave themselves over to the gentle rocking of the boat, first in languid sex, and then in blissful sleep. "This must be what it feels like to be a baby in the womb of a walking woman," Voss said.

"That's good," Avery said. "You should write that down."

In an Athens bookshop he picked up the *Iliad* and the *Odyssey,* which he had only read selections from back at Forrester. "You know, I don't think this is a war poem at all," he said to Avery on the boat to Mitilini. "I think it's an antiwar poem. All the blood and gore, it doesn't glorify war, it shows the brutality."

The islands of the Aegean called to them in no particular order. Something in *The Blue Guide* would catch Voss's eye, and they'd take the next ferry to Ios, Naxos, Paros, Santorini. The summer came to an end and the few college students they now saw had deep tans and traveled with only light daypacks and rolled straw sleeping mats.

"We have to go to Crete," Voss said, "and see the palace of Minos." And when they got to Knossos and walked among the brightly painted columns, up and down the inclined planes, through the hundreds of doors that inspired the story of Daedalus's labyrinth, he said, "It's what we were trying to build when we were kids in the sandbox, all walls and ramps and tunnels."

"You should write that down," Avery said.

From Crete to Rhodes, from Rhodes to Chios, where they sat on circular benches in a tiny mountainside amphitheater carved out of the living rock, in the center a kind of chair, like the stump of a tree, also carved from the natural rock—"The Stone of Homer" according to the guidebook. The mountain rose straight up out of the sea, and as you sat there you could taste the salt in the air, smell the pine sap from the gnarled, wind-twisted trees, hear the roar of the surf below and the cries of the gulls above. "I don't know if Homer was really blind," Voss said, "and I don't know if he ever really sat on that stone, but what a perfect place for a blind storyteller. It's all here."

"It's your next record," Avery said.

Voss strummed an open chord on his guitar, held it up into the wind, no longer the warm breeze of summer, and shook it. "I might have enough," he said as the chord faded in deep vibrato.

"When we get to Istanbul, I'll make some calls," Avery said.

They sailed through the Dardanelles, awash in history, marking the place where Leander swam across to Hero, and where Byron swam across just to prove he could do it. They stopped at Cannakale, went down to Hisarlik and Schliemann's excavation of Troy. A bus took them to Istanbul, where they met up with the big luggage trunk for the first time in two months. In clean clothes, Voss went out to tour Hagia Sophia and the Blue Mosque, while Avery stayed in the room and made her calls. When he got back, she had one word for him: "Berlin."

"Great," he said. "A lot of the best Greek stuff is there, in the museums. The Schliemann stuff that's not in Athens."

"Not for the museums," she said.

"What?"

"I got us a recording studio."

They had a month before the studio would be available. It was time to put all the notes and scribbles together into not just songs, but a sequence of songs. Avery found them an apartment with a piano, and Voss threw himself into the work. The first song to come together was "The Blind Storyteller," with its images of the old man sitting on the chair of stone singing into existence the sea below the cliffs, the gulls hanging on the wind, the smell of the pines, and an armada of black ships heading for Troy to bring back goddess-like Helen. It would start with that open guitar chord on the wind, then the piano, low and discordant at first, the crashing of waves.

> *His eyes no longer see*, Voss sang,
> *but in the sound of his words*
> *the colors are sharp and the sun is bright*
> *over the wine-dark sea.*

It was a ballad, all the stanzas ending in that same phrase, *over the wine-dark sea.*

He went into the studio with eight songs, but he felt confident that once he started putting the sound together with the session guys, enough other songs would come to complete the album. Avery was there every day. "I know you don't want it to sound like Vossimilitude," she said, "and you're right. But it's got to remind them enough of that to remember it's you. Blind Faith didn't just take Clapton from Cream to Delaney and Bonnie, it took the listeners, too. This is a bridge album."

"But 'Avery's Song' was already the bridge," Voss said. "And anyway, I'm not trying to create a completely different sound—it's just coming out that way. These guys are great, but they're not the boys I've been playing with all these years."

"You mean they're not Hal, don't you?" she said.

"You know how we could sing harmony. You were there when we first found out we could do it. And then there's the bass. That bass is going to take Hal wherever he wants to go. But it's not just that. Now that he's not around, I see how much I relied on him to tell me when the arrangements were working and when they weren't, even on my own songs."

Two days later, a slight young man with blond hair was waiting in the studio when Voss and Avery arrived.

The man half-smiled at Avery and turned to Voss. "I'm told you might want a little help with the arrangements," he said in a crisp British accent.

Voss looked at Avery. "I don't think we have that kind of money," he said, "do we?" He turned to the man and held out his hand. "I'm Jack Voss."

"Pleasure," the man said with a smirk. "I'm David Bowie. And I think we can work something out."

"I told him you'd do some session work for him," Avery said. "Keyboards, maybe a background vocal here and there. He's producing everybody."

"Not everybody," Bowie said, "but I do lend a hand here and there."

"So how long have you been working on this?" Voss asked Avery.

"She called me yesterday," Bowie answered for her. "I listened to the tapes last night, and I have some ideas."

He had a light touch, really. Got rid of the wind at the beginning of "The Blind Storyteller," but kept the open chord vibrato and the discordant piano. He added some choral effects, and he eliminated the bass altogether, letting the strummed acoustic guitar fill in. A bit of violin here, and some saxophone there, and the sound came together. While checking levels one day, the guys wandered into a riff that turned into another song when Voss put words to it; "In the Divided City" closed off side one. And with some changes in instrumentation—instead of the piano, a Hammond B-3; replacing the sax, a crunching electric guitar, overdriven through a vintage tube amp into howling distortion and modulated feedback—the same tune became "On the Other Side of the Wall," bringing everything together and finishing side two. It wasn't a concept album exactly, but it had a theme: artists in exile. From the tribute to Homer and songs about Keats dying in Rome, and Byron swimming the Hellespont, to the playful restaurant song in mangled English, and the pre-techno groove about session musicians from all over who were making music in Berlin, it was a statement.

"Literate and cosmopolitan," Bowie said. "Hard to believe yer a Yank."

"I couldn't have done it if I'd stayed in the states," Voss said.

"Let's just hope it will sell in the states," Avery said. "We're living on borrowed money."

"I can get you work," Bowie said, "if you don't mind playing dives."

"But I don't have a band," Voss said.

"Piano, a little crooning, cabaret stuff," Bowie said. "It'll do you good. Work on that voice. You can do most of these songs solo, and you've got a repertoire from before. Anyway, nobody really listens in the places I'm talking about, but they'll pay to have your name on the schedule. Just so you don't mind being hit on by *les boys*; this is Berlin, after all."

"You mean play the gay clubs?" Voss said.

"Yeah."

"But I'm . . ."

"Don't say it, Jackie boy," Bowie said. "You're already a hero to *les boys*. *The Enchanted Pond* is on all their bedroom stereos. Don't tell me you didn't know that. I thought you were gay until I met you."

"It'll just be for a while," Avery said. "They won't hurt you."

(#)

The club scene started late in the evening and ended well into the morning; Voss's schedule shifted to graveyard. He would get home at six-thirty or seven a.m., have breakfast with Avery and then go to bed, if he wasn't too coked out to eat or sleep. The gigs were fine. He wasn't paid a lot, but the tip jar on his piano filled up with deutschmarks on all but the slowest of weeknights, and he did hone his ability to sell a song without a band behind him. His piano playing improved, too. He usually played his own stuff in the first set, when solid citizens and curious tourists still stopped in to have a drink and take a look around. The second set was mostly Tin Pan Alley numbers, jazz standards, Hoagy Carmichael and Cole Porter, the piano surrounded by nattily dressed men in their forties and fifties who would sing along. Then, well after midnight, he'd back up the star of Der Trans-garten, a drag queen called Moo Moo whose signature number was Peggy Lee's "Fever." There was always a drink on the piano, Scotch these days; there was always pot, usually coke, and sometimes other drugs.

Avery began to worry. Sitting at home, watching German TV, and wait-ing for royalty checks that never seemed to come, she lost her enthusiasm for a boyfriend who needed to be cared for all the time. The great rebuild of a year ago—the night in Denver when she prostrated herself before him—had proved to be less enduring than she'd hoped. Yes, they'd had a honeymoon of sorts, an erotic connection for an amazing few months after, and then the carefree trip across Europe, which made them feel like teen-agers again. And she loved the poet in him, the Voss who scribbled lyrics on napkins in cafes. But by the time they got to Berlin, she had already begun to resent the way he'd come to depend on her making all the arrangements. Sometimes when he wanted her, it felt like the unending demands of a needy child. At first she kept her promise to be available to him whenever he wished, but one night she just couldn't go through with it, and she compromised by encouraging him to pleasure himself while she lay next to him. Soon he stopped reaching for her. At first it was a relief; then she started to worry that he was running around with the *frauleins*, coming home already satis-fied. But though he may have done that once or twice, it certainly wasn't his routine. The reality was that he was getting so wasted in the course of the evening that by the time he closed the lid on the piano and headed home, sex was the last thing on his mind.

"What all are you taking?" she asked him one morning over a breakfast of coffee and cigarettes.

"Nothing heavy," he said. "Joints, a little coke."

"A lot of coke, no?"

"I guess that depends on who you compare me to," Voss said.

"I compare you to me," Avery said.

"Are you saying you don't get high anymore?" Voss said.

"Not like you lately. Look at you, you're skinny as a rail. Your legs are jumping, your fingers tapping a mile a minute. You're fried out. It's scaring me. Can you even play when you're like this?"

"I can play," Voss said. "Look, do we have to do this now? I'm exhausted. I'm going to bed."

"You think you're going to sleep like that?"

"I'll take a blue Valium and I'll be fine. And I'll lay off the coke tonight, okay? Just let me get some sleep. And tonight why don't you come with me?"

"And be the only real girl in the room?"

"There's girls at Der Transgarten."

"Fag hags," she said, wondering again if he was fucking one of them, "and dykes. Not my scene. I'm surprised how well you seem to fit in."

"Aw, come on," Voss said. "I'm just trying to earn a living here." He took the wad of folded deutschmarks from his pocket and tossed it on the table. "And I'm not doing bad. That's last night's tips. Now will you let me go to bed?"

(♯)

Back in the states, *The Blind Storyteller* was making its way slowly up the charts. *Rolling Stone* called it "A solo project that almost makes up for the loss of a great band," and *The Village Voice* put Voss's picture on the front page and said, "Voss takes us to places the contemporary music scene hasn't gone before." But it still wasn't getting the kind of airplay that would make it possible for Voss to quit gigging. Then two things happened.

The first thing happened three thousand miles away. Hal started touring with his new band, Mutually Assured Destruction, and they played a hard-driving version of "Touch Her and You're Dead" for their encore at almost every show. Vossimilitude's last single, released the previous year—with their own, live version of the song—slipped quietly back onto the charts, and gradually climbed up to number four. The money would be coming in as soon as the royalty system caught up with the sales.

The second thing happened on the Nurnberger Strasse as Voss was coming out of Der Transgarten at five-twenty a.m. on a Sunday morning. Whether the five American soldiers on liberty from Templehoff or Clayalee had planned all along to kick a little faggot ass, or whether they had just happened to pass by the club as Voss, the manager, and the manager's leather-clad boyfriend stepped out onto the otherwise deserted street, the G.I.s jumped them from out of nowhere.

"*Guten Morgen*, faggots," one of the Americans said, the German words twangy and slurred. "*Was machen sie hier?*"

The three men looked up. Voss picked them out as off duty soldiers from their short haircuts and American blue jeans. The club manager spoke to them in German, but they clearly didn't understand. And whatever he said, they didn't care.

"Do we look like Germans to you, gay boy?" one of them said.

"What do you want?" Voss asked. "We're not looking for any trouble."

"Well, holy *Sheise*," said the first G.I., "he speaks English just like an American faggot."

"I am an American," Voss said. "And I'm not a faggot."

"Yeah, right. And I'm *der* fucking *Führer*."

The five G.I.s had Voss and his two companions backed up against the wall. The leather-boy started yelling back at the Americans, but the club manager tried to quiet him down. Voss's German had come a long way in the past several months, but he couldn't follow this conversation. Suddenly leather-boy lunged at the lead G.I. The soldier moved with the cool efficiency of a trained fighter, stepping to the side, grabbing leather-boy's arm, twisting it as he pivoted, and then dropping to his knees, taking leather-boy down with a crack.

"Which of you is next?" the soldier said, smiling as he stood back up, his foot grinding into his moaning victim's apparently broken arm.

The manager was talking German again. He stepped forward to help his friend up off the ground, but one of the other soldiers grabbed him and another punched him in the stomach, doubling him over. Voss did not move.

"That leaves you, sweetie," the leader said. "What the fuck should we do with you?"

"I'm not what you think I am," Voss said. "Why don't you just go and let me call an ambulance for these guys. Go back to your base, or wherever you're staying. I'll just say it was some German guys."

"You telling me what to do, fairy boy? You're worse than these German pansies, because you're American. You make us look bad."

Voss was on the brink of trying to tell them he was just the piano player, but seeing the hatred in the eyes of this guy who was clearly a trained killer, it occurred to him that if he said anything about playing the piano they would break his fingers.

"Look at you," the talkative soldier said, "you don't even have any fight in you. At least this boy had the balls to do something. You stand there with your hands at your sides."

"I'm not your enemy, man. I was in the Air Force," Voss said.

"Oh fuck. Now that I believe. The Air Force is all fucking faggots." He lunged toward Voss, who had nowhere to go but to paste himself even more tightly to the wall and turn his head away, cringing from the expected blow.

"Boo!"

Voss sucked in his breath and tears came to his eyes.

"I wouldn't dirty my hands on you," the guy said. "You guys take him. Don't kill him, he's an Amehhricahhn. But give him something to remember."

Strong hands grabbed his arms, pulling him away from the wall, and then Voss found himself surrounded by the other four men, who began shoving him from one to the other. He fell into one of them and thought he was going down to the ground, but the G.I. caught him, punched him hard in the ribs, and shoved him toward the man opposite, who did the same. Then one stepped in and hit him in the chest and belly, one, two, three, as if he were working a heavy bag. Voss's legs wobbled and his knees began to buckle, but again one of them caught him. As he was being held, the others took turns working his midsection, short jabs mostly, and Voss's thinking went muddled and soft. Eventually they dropped him to the sidewalk and began kicking him. He felt someone step on his left hand; then, through the constant dull ache of this pummeling, he felt a sharper pain on the side of his head, saw a blinding flash, and blacked out completely. The next thing he remembered was the distinctive *whee-low-whee-low* sound of European sirens and the bright light inside the ambulance.

Injury and pain are, above all, exhausting. Voss drifted in and out of consciousness. When awareness came, it was awareness of being alone, lost, hurt, and abandoned. Where was Avery? It seemed like they had been quarreling lately. Had she left him? Was she gone? Someone was calling him a faggot. Clean-cut boys were beating him up. His companions were two gay guys. Where was Avery? What was he doing with this guy all in leather? Faggot, a voice was saying to him. A doctor shone a light into his eyes. Voices around him were speaking German. Hours slipped by. He was on an IV now, knew enough about drugs to recognize the feel of the Valium they gave him. Thank God, he thought, for Valium, for Demerol. He could breathe again. He could sleep.

He awoke in a sunlit room, his hand in a cast, his abdomen tightly taped, the IV still in his arm.

"*Herr* Voss?" a voice said, "*Oigen sie bien*?"

"*Ja*," he said, "Yes. I can hear you." He felt tears come into his eyes, deep panicky loneliness engulfed him. "Where is Avery?" he said.

Nobody answered, and the darkness pulled him down again.

The next time he came up, Avery was there.

"You didn't leave me," he said.

"Of course I didn't leave you," she said. "What made you think that?"

"I don't know," he said. "I was so afraid."

"I'm right here," she said.

"I love you," Voss said, his voice cracking.

"I love you, too," Avery said, wiping away tears. "Now rest, baby. You're a mess. Rest and heal."

"I'm sorry," Voss said.

"What for?" Avery said. "You got mugged. What do you have to be sorry for?"

"I'm sorry for not being a better . . . I was afraid you'd be gone. Don't leave me. Promise you won't leave me."

"Jack," she said, putting her hand on his cheek, "I'm not going anywhere."

It felt so good to hear her say that, like a comforting wave rolling over him, and he passed again into the sea-swell of unconsciousness.

Awake again, with Avery sitting in the chair next to the bed, Voss looked down at the cast on his hand.

"Will I be able to play the piano?" Voss asked half-smiling through the abject terror of the question.

"That was the first thing I asked," Avery said, "and they told me, as well as I could understand them, that you will. They broke two of your fingers, a couple bones in the back of your hand, but apparently, once you get the cast off, playing is like the best therapy. Is that what you were most afraid of?"

"I was most afraid of losing you."

Voss pulled himself up into a sitting position. "What day is it? How long have I been here?"

"It's Monday night. You've been here since Sunday morning. I didn't get here until last night. Nobody called me. I thought you'd . . . I thought you'd gone out somewhere after the gig. I was so mad," she said with tears in her eyes. "Then I got a call from David asking if you were all right. Somebody told him you'd been hurt and he called me to find out about it. That was the first I heard."

"Avery," Voss said.

"And then they didn't want to let me in. Only family, they said."

Her breath was coming in gasps. She was beginning to break, Voss thought. "Avery," he said again.

She looked up.

"I know how to make it so that never happens again."

"What?"

He'd rehearsed the words in his mind as he'd faded in and out of delusion and pain: "Marry me," he said. "Become Avery Voss."

Her mouth went crooked and her tears flowed freely. "I still don't want . . . any more calls like that," she said, trying to get control of her breath.

"I know," Voss said. "I'm done gigging in the clubs. We'll figure something out. Just say yes, okay?"

"Yes," she said.

THANKSGIVING

Voss woke up shortly after three in the afternoon. The sensations he felt were familiar, but he hadn't felt them in a long time. Mouth dry and fuzzy, head throbbing, body achy, especially around the kidneys. He was in his own bed, at least. Years ago, he'd awakened more than once feeling like this and not knowing where he was. So, at least he knew where he was. What he didn't know was how he got there.

The last thing he remembered clearly was heading out his door and walking down to The Horse's Mouth. After that, nothing. Before that . . . he had been drinking a bottle of beer and eating a sandwich over the kitchen sink. He'd unfolded the newspaper and suddenly realized it was Thanksgiving.

Thanksgiving, once his favorite holiday. When he and Avery were in Berlin they had often hosted a huge, expat Thanksgiving dinner, hosting the lost and lonely, piling the table with food. But since the split, he had become one of the lost and lonely himself, and no one was looking out for him, it seemed. Except when he was physically injured, Voss had always seemed so capable, so in charge of his own life, that nobody thought of him as needing to be looked after. Nobody but Avery. Quite the opposite, in fact. More than a few people, Hal especially, seemed to think it was their duty to lure him into, not away from, trouble. To coax him into losing his precious control. He could not remember anyone ever saying to him, "Whoa, Jack, are you sure you haven't had enough? Are you sure you aren't hitting the—fill in the appropriate vice: booze, pills, pot, acid, clubs—a little hard?" Except Avery. He unconsciously ran his thumb along his ring finger, checking for the wedding band he hadn't worn in over fifteen years. And then, in a wave of nausea and emotion, the years caught up with him, the disappointments, the losses, Hal dead, his marriage over, the death . . . oh God . . . the death of Chance.

He showered, shaved, drank several glasses of water, and set out for the bar he'd aimed for almost exactly twenty-four hours before. It was only a ten minute walk, and the weather was refreshingly cool, the sea breeze light, sky mercifully cloudy. The place was nearly empty.

"Afternoon, Jack, how you feeling, buddy?" the bartender greeted him as he crossed the rough wood floor freshly spread with sawdust.

"I've felt better, Lou," he said.

"A little hair of the dog? Jameson's, wasn't it?"

Voss put his hand to his head. "Is that what it was?"

Lou was reaching for the bottle.

"No, no, no," Voss said. "I just wanted to be sure I didn't do anything too stupid or embarrassing. And that I paid my tab." He slipped gingerly onto a barstool.

"Fear not, my friend," Lou said, placing a napkin on the bar in front of Voss. "You were great. The life of the party, yes, but no fights, no complaints about pawing the ladies."

"The life of the party?"

"You played the piano, sang until you couldn't remember the words, and then passed out quietly in the corner booth. Jerry took you home. No problem."

"Okay. Thanks. So I'm all paid up?"

"You were very generous."

"Good. Well, I think I'm gonna go home and go back to bed, then. Can you order me a burger . . . no, make it a turkey club . . . to go? And a seltzer while I wait."

"Sure you don't want something to take the edge off that head?"

"A Valium would be good, but I'll settle for a couple aspirin or ibuprofen."

"I'm not supposed to dispense pharmaceuticals, you know. But I think I can help you."

Chance

You look around one day and you say, how did I end up with these people? I must have been switched at birth or something. I mean, how are they together? And how could they have had me?

Avery never told Voss that she had been on the point of leaving, that only the sight of him in the hospital bed had rekindled her love enough to consider going on. What was the point of telling him how close he'd come to losing her? She loved him, and he needed her now more than ever. For a while, she had to cut up his food for him, one-handed as he was, and then there was the long road back to being able to play. After the cast came off, she stayed on him about stretching his hands and arms in the morning and the evening and before and after playing. His fingers were still stiff two months after the assault, and his hand ached all the time, but he was managing to play, albeit slowly, most of the songs in his repertoire. Changing the time signature on some of them was a revelation, and he worked up a deeply mournful version of Cole Porter's "The Way You Look Tonight." He played it for Bowie one evening, and Bowie loved it.

"You know we could do a record of standards," Bowie said. "If you don't mind not playing your own stuff."

"How about half and half?" Voss asked. "Old and new."

"Do you have any new stuff?"

He had one new song. It was about the beating, and coming back from it. Dark, brooding, dwelling on the black images that had come to him in his delirium, the pain barely relieved by the hands that appeared to lift him up at the end.

"Bit gloomy," Bowie said. "Do you have a title?"

"Not yet."

"I think it's beautiful," Avery said.

"What if you went the other way," Bowie said. "Even more raw. Angry."

"I can do that," Voss said.

It was the high point of his recovery. The low point came the next day, when, while working on the song again, he reached for the guitar and found that he couldn't play it. While the fingers of his left hand could stretch out for the piano keys, the two that had been broken couldn't curl up to press the guitar strings against the frets. His guitar playing days were over. Avery had gone out to run errands. He took two Valium and plopped down in front of the TV.

She came back with groceries and the mail. "You got a letter from Hal," she called out before she noticed that he was sprawled listlessly on the couch.

"Let's see," he said.

She handed him the envelope. It had been mailed from New York and inside was a card of the Statue of Liberty laden with shopping bags, waiting for the subway. Inside was a short note:

> *Jack, old man. Heard about your troubles. Getting beat up is one thing man, but getting married?*
>
> *Is your hand okay? I hope you broke it on somebody's face. M.A.D.'s doing good.*
> *Take care, dude.*
>
> *Love and kisses,*
> *Hal.*

"Have we got any pot?" Voss asked Avery.

(♯)

Bowie found him some session work, and he worked on *The Songbook*, which ended up being all standards and the one new song, "Busted Up at 5 a.m.," a spare ballad reminiscent of Sinatra's version of "One for My Baby (and One More for the Road)." To Avery, his days in the studio were just as bad, if not worse, than his nights in the club. If you could imagine a drug, someone could get it for you. She knew Jack was doing things he wasn't telling her. The painkillers she understood—nights after he played a lot, the pain in his hand would wake him up from a sound sleep and he'd get out of bed and pace the apartment. She'd get up to find him smoking a joint and staring out the window.

"I wasn't cut out for pain," he told her one night. "Some people can handle it, I know, but I don't think I'm one of them."

"It won't last forever," she said. "Your mobility is coming back, and you're playing better. The pain will go away too, eventually. Give me your hand." She poured some lotion in her own palm and warmed it.

"I don't know how they do it," he said, as she massaged his hand, her fingers gentle and strong. "People with chronic pain. I think it could drive you crazy."

"You're not shooting, are you, Jack?" she asked. "I know some of those guys are shooting up."

He looked at her. "I've never mainlined, and I'm not going to start now."

"What *are* you doing, Jack? I need you to be careful."

"Careful is my middle name," Voss said.

"Let's go back to Greece," she said. "You're almost finished with the new record, right? And I just got a check from Bobby. Let me book us a trip. I'll find us an island spa. We can get healthy again, fatten you up, I'll trim down. Clean ourselves out."

Voss looked at the joint in his right hand, his left hand in Avery's hands, and then into her eyes. "You know," he said, "that's a great idea."

(♯)

On the ferry back from their island spa to Athens, Avery was seasick for the first time in her life. Voss was tan and fit and reveling in the sea air. It did her good to see him like that, but she felt truly miserable. An hour after they were on shore she felt better, and they toured the Acropolis in the afternoon under a bright blue sky.

"I feel like I haven't seen colors this clearly since I don't know when," Voss said as they looked south over the descending hills toward the Piraeus. "It's like the clarity of acid, but I'm straight, and I feel wonderful."

She stood next to him and squeezed his good hand. No words were necessary.

The next morning, when the boy brought in their breakfast with the pot of coffee she was immediately sick at the smell, and she knew. Terrified of how Jack might react, she waited until they were back in Berlin to tell him.

"You think we can stay this healthy for a while?" she asked Voss.

"I'd like to," Voss said. "I really would. I haven't felt this good in a long time. I'm gonna try, baby, I'm gonna try."

"I'm gonna have to," Avery said.

"I hear you," Voss said. It was Sunday night, and he was tuning the radio.

"For the baby," she said.

"What? Are you sure?"

"Pretty sure," she said, her voice betraying no doubt about the baby but vast trepidation about his reaction.

He sat back in his chair. The radio was about half tuned to the Sunday night oldies show—Gene Krupa's drum solo on "Sing, Sing, Sing" buzzed through the speakers. Voss leaned forward and tuned it in properly. Then he stood up and took both of Avery's hands.

"Dance with me, little mama," he said.

(♯)

It wasn't easy to stay clean, but Voss did his best, eventually settling into a fine moderation. He stayed away from the hard drugs, smoked only occasionally, and never drank alone. Chance was born in Berlin in February of

1981, two months after John Lennon was shot; Voss held Avery's hand and, through the blood and the goo, his eyes took in the nightmarish sight that turned into something amazing.

Chance was a perfect baby, wide-eyed and smiley when she was awake, and a great sleeper.

Avery breast-fed her, and it changed the way Voss saw his wife. Their sex life had come alive again after he'd cleaned up. They'd romped and frolicked long into her pregnancy, she'd tended to him lustily right up to the night she went to the hospital, and now, with baby Chance in her crib in the corner of the bedroom, their sex morphed into something tender and sweet, quiet, loving. Sure, he thought sometimes of hungry Jeanette, and of the days when he and Hal had bounced and sported with nameless stoned girls willing to do anything, but then he thought of Avery, soft and round and devoted to his child, and he believed he had proved lucky in the end.

The Songbook did well, but though his hand seemed to be getting better all the time, and his playing was clearly improving, he still wasn't writing. So the next project would be another record of standards, but this time with a big band. Or at least the record would sound like the music of a big band. The reality was that the band did not exist. The musicians existed—Berlin was full of musicians, and it seemed at one point that all of them were working for Voss—but the album was built track by track by guys who never played together. Avery worked out the business end. Except for songwriting royalties going to the heirs of the composers, all dead, the album would be Voss's alone. The other players would either be paid union scale for session work, or they would cut deals for Voss's services on their own albums, uncredited, of course. It took forever, and required of Voss that he be not only pianist, but also arranger, conductor, producer, and recording engineer. And it required that he sit in on payback recording sessions several times a month.

Avery, meanwhile, couldn't just sit in the apartment and be a mom. "I've gone over our finances," she said to Voss one night over Chinese food. "We're doing all right. But the money's just sitting in the bank. It doesn't make sense."

"So what do you want to do?" Voss asked. "Buy some property? Do we have that kind of money?"

"Actually, we do," she said. "But that's not what I want to do yet. I want to start investing."

"Hear that, Chance?" Voss said. "Mommy wants to invest. Put our money in Wall Street. We'll be rich."

"Waw Shree?" Chance said from her highchair. Voss put a plate of *lo mein* in front of her.

"No, Jack," Avery said. "Or, not exactly. But I've got my eye on a couple of things. There's this company called Apple. I read about it in *Time*."

"You mean The Beatles' record company?"

"No. It's a computer company out of California. I think they're going to be big."

"Baby, you went to school for that. I didn't. If you gave me a million dollars I wouldn't know what to do with it besides buy another piano. Or a Porsche. Silk underwear. I don't know. The money is your department, always has been. You want my blessing, you got it. Just, if we get so rich I don't have to work anymore, don't forget to tell me."

"Like you'd ever stop working," Avery said, a subtle jab at Voss for starting to take on club gigs again.

December

The rain was lashing at the windows, the wind bouncing the glass doors in their tracks, howling and pausing to catch its breath, then howling again. Voss stood in his underwear in the living room, drinking coffee from a black mug. He loved big weather. "Blow, wind, and crack your cheeks," he said aloud. Then he thought of Cordelia, her body limp in the arms of her father, her long hair hanging down.

He showered and dressed, poured himself another cup of coffee, and headed for the studio. The old guitar case still sitting by the studio door caught his eye. He remembered the night Hal had given it to him, the unexpected generosity in a time of awkwardness and tension. The black Tolex had faded to gray with age and ground-in dust. The buckles were stiff but sound. As he lifted the lid, the smell was first the smell of all old things, mold dried to powder in a hot attic. But that passed in a moment. What followed was the tang of guitar polish and a whiff of pot. He'd expected to find the guitar cracked and dried, with rusty brittle strings, unplayable after twenty-five years of neglect. Instead, he found a vintage instrument, polished, with state-of-the-art rustproof strings, and a humidifier in the soundhole. He took out the humidifier and picked up the guitar, strummed it. Resonant even with the wind trying to drown it out. Those deep bass tones of the old Martin dreadnoughts. Almost in tune. Had Chance played it? She must have. She'd talked about writing songs when she was still in high school. He'd tried to be encouraging, but he'd never asked to hear one. He flexed his hands. He'd responded to her talk of writing songs as he'd responded to amateurs over the years, eager to change the subject, loath to be serenaded once again by their juvenile expressions of angst. When he worked the Rock and Roll Camp, he would have to steel himself to listen to the paying customers, struggle to find something positive to say. With his daughter, he'd listened politely to her talk and then changed the subject before there could be a question of her playing something for him. Shit. But she must have kept on. The strings couldn't be more than a few months old.

He turned the guitar over—the scratches from his belt buckle were still there. He set it gently on the floor and opened the inner compartment in the case. A capo, a couple of picks, folded sheets of paper. He unfolded them to find lyrics and chord changes downloaded from the internet: "Hotel California," "Crazy," and "Teach Your Children." There was also a page torn from a spiral notebook with the lyrics to "Avery's Song" written out in longhand, and a photocopy of a fakebook sheet for "Autumn Leaves," the music simplified, a single staff with the guitar chords written in above it. He felt his left hand move to shape the changes, and, of course, felt the two fingers that wouldn't curl. It made him think of an old photo of Django Reinhardt, whose left hand had been badly burned. Django had taught himself to play all over again with his maimed hand, and had transformed the world of guitar music. Voss had given up at the first difficulty. But the guitar was not Voss's instrument, after all. He hadn't given up on the piano. Learning to play again hadn't been easy. The injury had changed his style, forced him to slow down, made him much more conscious of that left hand, at least for a while, until his technique could become almost unconscious again.

He put the guitar back in its case, took the humidifier to the kitchen and added water, then closed the guitar case and put it in the studio, next to the other guitars he had on hand should anybody came over and want to play. The nine foot Fazioli sat there in the middle of the room, the lid down, the keyboard closed. A DW drum kit sparkled on its riser, a row of amplifiers stood against one padded wall, two electronic keyboards leaned on end against a pair of congas. Out in the living room, a Yamaha baby grand waited for him whenever he wanted to play it. The dinner party piano, he called it, though he hadn't had a dinner party in a long time. All the toys in the world. He thought of Chance on her first visit about five years ago. He'd shown her the studio and she'd picked up the sunburst Strat admiringly. It never occurred to him to invite her to plug it in and play. He stood in the doorway between the living room and the studio. The rain slapped at the windows.

Das Totenschiff

I know you aren't going to believe me when I say that it wasn't sex, it was love. Sex was part of that love, but that's not where it sprung from, not what was behind it. And that was the problem. In the end it doesn't matter who you have sex with, it matters who you love. And we loved each other. That's what couldn't go on.

"You never liked Hal, did you?" Voss asked.

"You know better than that," Avery said. "Harold Proczevski I liked fine. Hal Proteus I tried my best to like," Avery said, "but he wasn't the same guy. Or maybe he was and I just never knew it until we all went on tour. Our life is different now." She gestured with her eyes toward Chance, who was watching *Sesamstrasse. Vay. Welt. Unsere schöne Welt.*

"Oh, come on. That was a long time ago. I've let it go, can't you?"

"I've let go of plenty," she said.

"Jesus, Ave, he's the oldest friend I've got besides you. I mean . . . grade school, The Featherweights. Even Artie I only met in college."

"When Artie comes to Berlin, I'll make dinner myself. Hal Proteus is not welcome in my house."

"Shit. I can't just blow him off. He came to Berlin to see me."

"I don't want him in my house." Avery said. "I don't want him anywhere near Chance."

"Okay, if that's the way it's going to be." Voss dialed the phone. "I'll be there in half an hour, bro. Don't empty the mini-bar." He turned to Chance. "Daddy's going to be out late with an old friend," he said to her, with one eye on Avery, who stood thick and glowering in the middle of the room. "How about a good night kiss, sweetheart?"

Chance reached her hands out for a hug without taking her eyes off the TV.

(♯)

A slim girl in faded jeans and a bikini top let him in to Hal's suite, and he took in the champagne on ice and lines of white powder on an ornate mirror taken down from the wall and laid on top of the formica coffee table. Hal Proteus came in from the bedroom with another girl on his arm. She was naked except for a black M.A.D. ball cap, and she clearly knew how good she looked in just her skin. Proteus looked bloated and unhealthy, wearing tight black jeans and an unbuttoned Hawaiian shirt. The girls were no more than twenty-five, both with long hair, one a blonde, the other a brunette.

"Only the best for my old buddy," Hal said. "You still into sharing, or do we need to pick?"

"I'm married, Hal," Voss said.

"Yeah, to Avery. She shared you a time or two, as I recall. And herself, in the old days."

"Times have changed. We have a little girl. We don't play around like that anymore. We didn't play around like that then, after the first few times."

"God, Avery with a baby . . . I never saw that coming. How fat did she get?"

"She's not a baby, Hal. She's almost six," Voss said, bristling at the all too apt question about Avery.

"You're kidding. Fuck, does time fly. Some things don't change, though. I mean, what Avery don't know . . ."

"No, man. It's not going to be like that. I thought you wanted to hang, maybe have me show you some of the clubs, local talent."

"I'm already tuned into the local talent," Hal said, smirking. "Eh, *Lieb-chen*?" The girls both looked at him and smiled. "But the clubs are definitely in our future. After a little vitamin C, for health purposes." He sat down in front of the mirror on the table, snorted the longest of the four lines, and passed the cut straw to the naked girl.

She snorted a line, dividing it between her two nostrils, and passed the straw to the other girl, who snorted her line in turn.

"You're up, pal," Hal said. "It's top quality stuff, and I took a big chance bringing it here."

Voss touched his finger to his tongue, touched it to the coke, studied it a moment, then tasted.

"Bolivian flake," Hal said. "Mountain grown, as they say. Pure goodness."

Voss felt the numbness on the tip of his tongue, the flavor, a little of solvent, but nice. This is what I need, he thought. I'm too tired to get through a night with Hal without it. And I've been good, lately. So damn good. Fuck it. He picked up the straw and sucked half the line into his left nostril. *Fuck you, Avery.* The other half into the right. *Auf wiedersehen, Chance, just for a couple of hours.* The burn hit first in his sinuses. He hadn't felt this in a long time. Then the burn was gone, and the melted flakes were draining down the back of his throat, cool and numbing. He closed his eyes and took a couple of long breaths through his nose. When he opened his eyes again the girl was holding a glass of champagne out to him. He dipped his fingers in it, put them in his nose and snorted to clear his nostrils and get those last few flakes; then he took the glass and drank it down.

"That's the old Jack I know and love," Hal said. "Now sit down and get to know Inga, or whatever her name is, there. I've got some business to attend to." He turned and steered the naked girl back into the bedroom.

"Dagmar," the blonde said, smiling.

"What?" Voss said.

"I am Dagmar. Not Inga."

"Jack."

"Jack," she said. "I have seen you at *Das Totenschiff.*"

"Are you a student?" Voss asked.

She looked at him and smiled. They both knew what she was. "Mássage," she said. "I study mássage. You like I give you mássage. You look very tension."

"You really study?" Voss asked. His experience was that hookers always claimed to be skilled at massage but usually didn't know a muscle from a bone.

"Two years," she said. "Svedishe, Shiatsu, Rolfing."

Voss laughed. "No Rolfing," he said. "Soft, okay? Just the shoulders."

"Take out the shirt," she said. She stepped into the bathroom for a moment, came out with a couple of towels and a bottle of lotion. She stood behind his chair. Her hands were knowing. They went right to pain points he didn't know he had, but then backed off, asserting their skill, promising relief. "Try relax," she said. "I not hurt you."

He tried, but his head was beginning to buzz with the coke. He was in deep shit already. Avery clearly felt betrayed by his spending the evening with Hal; if she knew what he was doing now, she would be furious. But he had tried to get things to go in another direction, he told himself. Anything that happened would be her fault.

Dagmar had stopped rubbing his shoulders and was spreading the towels on the floor. "Lie down," she said. "You need more relax."

He lay down on his stomach, determined to let it only go that far. She straddled him and began pressing her thumbs and the heels of her hands into his lower back, slowly working her way up toward his shoulders. She really did know what she was doing, patiently kneading his muscles. Soon her thumbs were digging deep under his shoulder-blades, opening him up, softening him. If it weren't for the coke, he probably would have fallen asleep. As it was, he just drifted between the world of bodily pleasure, a mountain melting, and the restless world of resentment and frustration. He knew better than to think there was affection in this girl's touch, but he couldn't remember the last time Avery had touched him at all except by accident. Soon she would ask him to turn over. He would do as she asked.

(✿)

As they were being led to their leather-upholstered booth at Anastasia's, the other guests stared at them unabashedly. Dagmar had put a sheer flowered blouse over her bikini top, and the other girl, whose name was Violett, was now dressed in five inch heels, a leather micro-skirt, and a red satin bustier. Hal didn't make things any better by insisting that the waiter bring a bottle of vodka to the table.

"The barman will make any drinks you wish," the waiter said, his accent more British than German.

"What we wish is a bottle of Stoli in an ice bucket," Hal said. "And some martini glasses. Charge me whatever you want. And take this for yourself, in expectation of your fine service." He handed the waiter a crisp hundred dollar bill. "You don't mind American money, do you?"

"No problem, sir," the waiter said.

"I thought not," Hal said. He turned to the girls." We'll be right back. A little business to attend to."

In the men's room, Hal produced a silver-covered glass vial that must have contained at least two grams of coke. He filled the matching silver cokespoon twice for each of them.

Voss came back to the table alone. "He's waiting for you downstairs," he said to the girls. They understood and rose together. The waiter arrived with a bottle of Stolichnaya in an ice bucket, four chilled martini glasses, and a tray of olives, sliced lemons, and lemon peels. Voss ordered two dozen oysters and caviar for four.

An hour later, they were in a cab driving around the Tiergarten, Violett on her knees, and everybody waiting for Hal to be done. "Inga," Hal said. "Come here, sweetheart. You don't mind, do you, Jack?"

Voss watched with a curious sadness as Hal began to take Dagmar's clothes off. He was jealous, aroused, and a bit hurt at the same time. Finally, Dagmar's tongue in his mouth and breasts in his hands, and Violett's head in his lap, Hal bucked and grunted and then pushed both of them roughly away. They dropped the girls off in the wasteland of the Potsdam Platz, giving them a wad of dollars and deutschmarks and the remains of the bottle from Anastasia's. Now, Voss thought, they might at least get to talk a bit.

"Time for some music," Hal said.

Two techno bars and a gay cabaret later, they were in Das Totenschiff, and they still hadn't talked, really. Nick Cave recognized them as he was finishing up "Black Betty." After the applause, he called them up on stage.

"Ladies and gentlemen, *Dammen und Herren*, look who's here, tonight. Voss you all know, of course. But unless I'm more fucked up than I think, that's Hal Proteus with him. Mutually Assured Destruction, man. You guys want to play some? Mick, you don't mind, do you? We'll make Hal promise to be nice to your bass. Voss, I know you've played that piano before." And before Voss really knew what was going on, he and Hal were sitting in with The Bad Seeds. "Well, there's one we all know, for sure,"

Nick Cave said, "if these boys will oblige us." He leaned over and said something to Hal, who was checking out Mick Harvey's rig. Hal nodded, adjusted the volume knob and the gain on the amp and started pounding out the bass line of "Touch Her and You're Dead." The audience roared. Mick Harvey had strapped on a Telecaster, and let Hal's riff go around one more time before he came in with the driving lead which he probably had learned years ago when every kid with a guitar up in his bedroom taught himself the most famous of the Vossimilitude songs. Voss worked at the piano. There was no mike, but it didn't really matter. Although he had written the music, doctored Hal's lyrics to make them work, and the song was credited to both of them, it was really Hal's song now. Voss knew that Mutually Assured Destruction still used it for their encore. He cringed a little on Hal and Nick Cave's attempts to sing together on the chorus, glad, in a way, to be off to the side at the piano, turned away from the audience, and he was caught by surprise when Hal slid from the chorus into saying "and . . . Voss on the eighty-eights. . . ." Then he bent to his job: give them something to float on, twelve bars, twenty-four if the rest of the band didn't come in. He watched his hands appear to play of their own accord—he hadn't played this song in . . . he would have to think about that later. It was coming out different. He threw in a new chord change, found a nice counter-melody—if he'd been the musician he was now back in '75, he would have written this in. Then, not hanging it too far out, he brought it back to what the rest of them knew, nodded to Hal, who came in with the bass line, and they finished the song together, to serious applause.

"Okay, okay, folks," Nick Cave said. "*Noch ein mehr.*"

Voss and Hal stayed on stage for "I Shot the Sheriff," and then the band took a break. Voss went back to the table, waving thanks to the crowd. Hal disappeared for a while, no doubt for a discreet toot. When he returned, Voss looked at him and said, "Dude, I'm dead."

Hal handed him the silver-covered vial. "No problem, old pal. Hal's got everything covered. You take care of business, and then I want to see the famous Rasputin."

"I don't know, man. I'm already in so deep. . . ."

"We don't have to do anything. You could see in the cab that I'm used up in that department. But I want to see the place. It's famous, right? So be a good boy and take your vitamins, and we'll head out. Okay?"

By the time they got to Rasputin, Voss's brain was screaming, and his body felt like it was going in a dozen different directions at once. The spoons of coke he'd snorted in the men's at Das Totenschiff had put him over the edge. Now he struggled to keep calm, as if he could by sheer force of will keep his heart from exploding. Hal had ordered another bottle of Stoli as soon as they walked into the brothel. Here, the bar had no hesitation—what you asked for at Rasputin, you pretty much got. But the vodka didn't calm Voss down at all, and surrounded by beautiful women decked out for every sexual taste, Voss couldn't focus his mind outside of himself—he was obsessing on his heartbeat, the pulse in his temples. It was too fast. His whole torso shivered with that fingernails-on-a-blackboard crawl. He felt panic rising. "Hal," he said, unable to tell if he was shouting or just talking, "I'm fucked up, man. I'm in overdrive. I think I've had too much coke, and the vodka isn't doing anything for me."

These are the moments when heroin seems like a good idea. Like a valium to ease you down from an acid trip. Yeah, heroin would ease him down from all this cocaine. It might save him, because without something, he was surely not going to make it through the next couple of hours. And there it was, in Hal's shirt pocket, evidently, for he was patting it and saying, "I told you I've got everything covered. Got just what you need to let you down easy. One of the stage crew at that last place fixed me up."

That was one thing you could say for Berlin, Voss thought, as easy as it was to get Central and South American cocaine in L.A., it was easier still to get A number 1 Afghani heroin here in Berlin.

"You got a kit?" Hal asked.

"I know where we can get one."

"Now you're talking, my man," Hal said.

"Hansa Studios, *mein Herr*," Voss said to the cab driver.

"Yes, sir," the cabby said, in English.

The night watchman knew Voss by sight and let them in. Marillion's gear was set up in the big ballroom in Hansa 2. In the moonlight, Voss could imagine it as the S.S. Officer's Club it was reputed to have been back in the 'forties—the high ceilings, the ornate moldings. He found Stony's amp in the corner. Inside was a suede bag containing the session man's work stash, a lighter, spoon, a length of surgical tubing, and half a dozen of the disposable syringes you could buy at any pharmacy—ah, Berlin.

"We'll have to take turns with the tourniquet," Hal said as he shook the brownish powder into the spoon, set the old Zippo on a wooden chair and lit it.

"No, man, I'm not mainlining. A shot in the deltoid will do me."

"You don't know what you're missing."

"Got to draw the line somewhere," Voss said.

"That's you all over, dude. Always drawing lines. Me? No limits, is what I say."

Voss unbuttoned his shirt and pulled it down over his left arm. He brought his arm across his body, and slapped his deltoid a few times, making himself relax the muscle. That was the trick, to be relaxed.

"You still got that vodka?" he asked Hal.

"Always prepared," Hal said.

Voss splashed some vodka on his shoulder, Hal handed him a loaded syringe.

"It looks like a lot," Voss said. "I mean, if it's pure. . . ."

"Trust your uncle Hal, bro. I've done this once or twice before."

Voss brought the syringe close, careful to get a steady, straight hold. Press and keep from tensing. The needle broke the skin and he slid it in slowly and gently. Don't tense, he kept telling himself. He looked up at Hal, who had the tourniquet around his upper arm, the needle in a swollen vein, as skilled as any phlebotomist. They pushed together. Hal turned white almost immediately, began to shiver.

"Oh, shit," he said.

"What? What? Don't tell me it's bad?" Whatever happened to Hal would happen to Voss a little later, as the drug spread through his muscle tissue and was absorbed.

"Oh, fuck, Jack. I'm fucked up, here. It's . . . I . . . Oh, fuck." Hal's eyes rolled back. He didn't say anything else.

At the moment when Voss wanted most just to close his eyes and go off to dreamland, he had to force himself to get up and make his way downstairs. He could feel the drug starting to flow through him. His body was like a machine that he had to force to operate, his legs seeming to move in robotic increments, like the second hand of a clock. Time slowed down, and he wasn't sure he would ever get down the stairs to the watchman. . . .

He came to in a hospital bed, foggy, dying of thirst. Avery was there. Along with a giant doctor or male nurse, one of those six foot five blond specimens that always made him think of Third Reich eugenics. That thought took him to Nazis and an S.S. ballroom somewhere, and then, oh shit. . . .

"Jack," Avery said. "Are you awake?"

"Avery," he said. "Oh, God, Avery. I fucked up, baby. I'm so sorry."

"Yeah, I know," she said, gently.

"Is Hal? Did they? Is he okay?"

"Hal's dead, Jack."

"Oh, shit," Voss said, and started to cry. "I'm so sorry, oh God, I'm so sorry."

"I know, Jack. But I can't stay. I'm glad you made it." She was crying, too. He noticed that she was holding his hand, squeezing it.

"I'm glad you made it," she said again, her voice cracking. "But I have to go."

She bent down and kissed him softly on the forehead. He felt her tears fall on his face. She rose and walked to the door of the brightly lit hospital corridor. She turned in the doorway.

"I'm taking Chance with me," she said.

CHRISTMAS

"Yeah?"

"You know, Artie, I've got to say you have the most unfriendly telephone answering voice of anybody I know."

"Jack? Sorry, man."

"It's like, 'what now, fuckface?'"

"Years of practice, dude-san. So where are you calling from?"

"I'm here in the city," Voss said, looking out of the window to the south, downtown under a low blue-gray overcast, a light chop on the bay, like crushed velvet, but cold looking.

"How long you staying?"

"Just until tomorrow—then it's up to Black Dome for Rohatsu Sesshin, a little spiritual tune-up, and the drunks on the boat for New Year's. What about you? What's happening? I'm sorry I haven't called in a while."

"It's okay. We're just staying in."

"So she's back? When did that happen? God, I have no idea what's going on with you. How is she? How's it going?"

"Yeah, we've got some movies lined up. C.C.'s gonna make tofurkey."

"And you can't talk."

"Exactly," Artie said. "What are you up to?"

"I don't know. I'm just going to chill out here, I think. So . . . Merry Christmas, man."

"Merry Christmas, bro."

"Give C.C. a hug for me."

"Will do."

Voss looked around the apartment. The Steinway stood closed at the far end of the long living room. He couldn't remember the last time he'd played it, certainly not since Chance's death, and he couldn't bring himself to walk over and open it now. It wasn't the piano itself, it was something about being here in New York. Back in Carmel, he'd found refuge in practice. Here, he'd only played gigs. It was time to go to the monastery, but he wasn't due there until tomorrow. There were other places in the city he could go besides Artie's. There were still people he knew. But that would be a bad idea. A very bad idea.

He looked at the Bowman seascape on the wall opposite the window where he stood. Hank had put all his frustrations about the years he'd spent at sea into that painting. He'd joined the navy to flee the world, he once told Voss, and all that happened was that the world went on without him, leaving him further and further behind. There was fury in the brushwork, death in the waves, and no pity in the ragged sky.

On the table in the dining room the little silver-painted model of the P-38 Lightning still sat. Voss walked over to it and saw the Strand bag with Housman's poems in it on one chair, the hobby shop bag with the model supplies and the other model kit on another. In with the paints and glue he found his makeshift pipe from five months before. There was pot in the freezer next to the TV dinners. He took the pipe and the parts from the P-51 Mustang into the kitchen.

THE DARK CASTLE

You want somebody to blame. You want to blame me. Okay. Go ahead. Blame me. And in a way it was my fault. They never would have done it without me. There never would have been a THEM without me. She would have met someone eventually, a nice boy who made her feel comfortable. She would have turned into her mother, as girls do. He would have found a girl and raised a family. Normal. Normal. Normal. But I couldn't decide. I loved them both and I put them together. Even that wouldn't have been so bad. But then I insisted on being a part of it. Insisted that it wasn't just the two of them and me, it was the three of us. And this world, no matter how progressive you think it is, doesn't have room for threes.

Up in the Catskills an old hospital with crenellated towers broods over a black river and a gray forest. In the winter the sun sets over the mountain at about four in the afternoon, and doesn't rise again until after eight in the morning. It's a dark place to try and find the light, but it's cold, which, Voss said to himself, must mean he wasn't in hell.

"You almost died from an overdose of heroin, man," Kurt said, the skull shining through the tight skin on his face. "Dude you were with did die. How can you sit here and say you're not an addict." He leaned back in the school desk that was almost too small for him and gestured to the rest of the people in the circle. "He's in denial. What's the point."

"You're the one missing the point," Voss said. "One, the heroin was bad. Cut with I still don't know what. Two, it was an overdose, an accidental overdose. Good heroin and the right dosage and I'm not here, Hal's still alive. No problem."

"Denial, man. Classic," Kurt said. He folded his arms across his chest and leaned even further back.

"Okay, Kurt," the doc said. "I'll do the diagnosing."

"Well, this is bullshit. I gotta come here and listen to this guy say he doesn't have a problem?"

"If I came in here shot, would you say I had a lead problem? If somebody fucking poisoned me would you say I had a . . . whatthefuck? An arsenic problem? A cyanide problem?"

"Poison is exactly your problem. First smart thing I heard you say."

"Fuck you," Voss said. "You got me all figured out, huh? You think I'm just like you?"

"You're not like me, because I admit what I am. I'm a junkie. And like it or not, you are too."

The rest of the group were tired of it, he knew. He was tired of it himself. Who wouldn't be? Everybody's seen the movies, read the stories. Rehab is always the same. Everyone has their demons, and they bring them to the program, but everyone has different demons, and sometimes the demons they bring are different each time they come. But Voss hadn't come in with a monkey on his back. There had been no withdrawal. No shakes. No night-sweats. His hand was killing him, but that was nothing new.

When the session was over, he went to the nurse's station.

"I need some Advil," he said.

The nurse checked a clipboard in front of her. "You can have two more at four o'clock, Mr. Voss. It's only two-thirty."

"You're kidding me," Voss said. "I'm not asking for Demerol, Dilautid, Valium. How about aspirin? Can I have a couple of aspirin?"

"You can have two ibuprofen at four o'clock," the nurse said. "I don't make the rules, Mr. Voss."

"You don't make the rules? That's original," Voss said. "Did you think that one up yourself or do they have you practice it when they issue you the Mickey Mouse PJs?"

"Is there a problem here?" a burly aide said, squaring his shoulders as he stepped up next to Voss.

"Oh my God," Voss said. "I'm trapped in a fucking movie. Where's Nurse Ratched and The Chief?" He walked away shaking his head. "I'll see you at four o'clock."

Back in his room he lay on the bed and massaged his hand. Theoretically, he could leave this place anytime he wanted, but he'd been strongly advised against it. By a woman named Bert who had showed up in his hospital room about twenty-four hours after Avery had said goodbye. "I'm your new agent," she'd said, "and if you want to salvage your career you'll do exactly what I tell you, at least for the next couple of weeks."

Avery had sent her, of course, and the plan they'd cooked up between them was to get him into this hospital, with a public statement of remorse and at least a tacit admission that he needed help.

"Why not go someplace here," he asked. "Baden Baden or something?"

"Your Visa's been pulled. There are no charges, but you're *persona non grata* in Germany, Jack."

"Okay," he said. "I'll go where you want, but no public apology. Who I apologize to is my own business, and it's not the public. Not this time. . . ."

So here he was, sentenced to a month in this dark, mountain fortress by his wife and a woman he'd only just met. He felt sorry for himself. In spite of what these folks seemed to think, he believed what success he'd had was due to talent and hard work. Okay, there was some luck involved, but he'd put his time in. And the bad things that had happened to him? They started with Jeanette, he would say. She'd torn him up. And why? Because he'd let her. He'd been naïve and trusted her. Was that a character flaw? And then he'd written *The Enchanted Pond,* and . . . what happened after that wasn't his fault, but he'd apologized for it anyway and done what he could to set it right. The beating in Berlin, that was just plain bad luck; wrong place at the wrong time. The drifting away from Avery? Okay, so after the beating he'd overdone it with the pain-killers a bit, but that was because he'd actually been in pain. His hand hurt all the time. Shit, it hurt now. But he had to work, didn't he? That's what they invented painkillers *for*. And he'd cleaned up in Greece. Hadn't done hard drugs for five years, for Christ's sake. If he and Avery drifted apart again with the omnipresence of Chance, well, she drifted as far from him as he had from her. Becoming more and more

Chance's mom, less and less Voss's lover. He wasn't saying he was perfect, far from it, but . . . he was here because of one fucking night.

Had Hal had a problem? No doubt. What was it they said in here? No boundaries. Hal had had no boundaries and no respect for the boundaries of others. He'd said it himself that last night: "No limits." Voss understood limits and, despite what everybody in here said, he was alive *because* he understood about limits. They wanted him to admit that he was out of control, when it was precisely his own control that had saved his life. If he had mainlined like Hal, he'd be dead. But the point was, and this is what all the rehab bozos couldn't get through their single-minded, narrow little brains, Voss had drawn his own line and was alive because of it. Granted, it was a near thing, but that was because the dosage was wrong and the shit was cut with something vile and poisonous. So. Bad judgment? Maybe in trusting Hal to dose him. Which brought it back around to the same thing that had caused his problems with Jeanette—he trusted too easily. *Hi, my name is Jack, and I put my faith in the wrong people.* He wasn't a fucking junkie. And he had no intention of swearing off the stuff. What fucking stuff? He didn't use heroin. There was no need to swear off something he didn't use. The night with Hal had been maybe the third time he'd ever used a needle in his life. And he'd only snorted it a couple of times. As for the coke he and Hal had been doing all that night . . . yes, he'd overdone it. But, again, that was hardly a regular thing either. And he wasn't a drinker, really. Not like the guys he knew who were actually drinkers. Bottom line, he was in here because that's what you do when you are in a big public scuffle and drugs or alcohol are involved. It was a show, a sop to throw to the tabloids. Something to endure until he could get back to business. He would start to look at it that way. What they wanted was an act. *Hi, my name is Jack Voss, and I'm a drug addict.* Fuck. He couldn't say it.

"We have a guest today," the doc said. "He's a trained therapist and an ordained Zen monk. William 'Chikuzen' McCauley. He's going to be offering a new kind of training here."

A wiry man in his forties with a shaved head and flowing, gray and white robes stood up to speak. "Thank you. I'm Chikuzen, and I'm looking for volunteers for an experimental program."

A skeptical murmur arose from the people in the folding chairs.

"I'm convinced that a rigorous program of yoga-based physical exercise along with regular meditation and mindfulness training based on ancient Japanese Zen traditions can teach people how to gain control of their addictive behaviors," the man went on. "I am a trained yogi, a licensed therapist, and an ordained Zen monk, and I'm going to be coming here three times a week to conduct this program. It's strictly voluntary, but if you agree to begin it, you have to agree to continue for the entire remainder of your stay here."

He followed this with a description of the training and the theory behind it. Then he took questions.

Voss spoke up. "What if you're not an addict in the first place?" he asked. Several of the people around him groaned. "What can this program do for you?"

"Good question," the man said. "The yoga is an excellent workout. It will increase your flexibility and strength, and it will help purify your body. The meditation and mindfulness training will help you learn to focus and concentrate better, and if you have anger issues, this will help you to control your temper; if you are an artist or a craftsman of any kind, it will help you do better work."

"What the fuck?" Voss said. "I'm in."

He learned how to do the sun salutation, which was wonderful for his shoulders and his back. Some of the exercises took him back to his piano classes with Dr. Madison—who had taught him to stretch before playing and not to slump over the keys—and to the physical therapy after his hand was broken. The meditation training was even better. He settled right into it. After the third or fourth session, Chikuzen pulled him aside on the way out of the makeshift Zendo.

"I've been watching you," he said. "Your meditation is solid, steady, natural. This is what you've been waiting for all your life, isn't it?"

He struck Voss as cocky, but knowing.

"May be," Voss said carefully, enunciating each word separately. "But you know I'm not like the rest of the people in here."

"May be," Chikuzen said, echoing Voss perfectly. "Where you going when they cut you loose?"

He talked more like an ex-con than a monk, Voss thought. "I honestly don't know," he said. "Stay with friends in the city for a while, maybe. I was living in Germany, but I can't go back right now."

"There's a *sesshin* starting the day you get out. Seven days silent meditation. Come to the monastery. It's twenty miles from here. Be my guest. It'll be a good bridge between this place and the real world."

"Same deal as here? Yoga and Zen?"

"More Zen," Chikuzen said. "But an hour of yoga every day. And you'll get to meet the Roshi."

"I'll think about it," Voss said.

"Do that. What else you got to do?"

(♯)

For some people, seven days of silence in a building full of strangers would be torture, but Chikuzen had been right—for Voss it was like finding something he'd been seeking for years without knowing its name. Early on during the *sesshin*, the Roshi, Chikuzen's superior, gave a talk on the theme of the self as a pool. When the pool is disturbed, the surface choppy, its surface is all we see. The purpose of sitting meditation is to calm the pool. As the pool grows calmer, we begin to see, through the ripples, reflections of the world itself. When we set aside all the thoughts and feelings that disturb the surface of the pool, it becomes like a mirror, and we see the world reflected clearly.

Not that this was easy. Voss had already learned to sit straight and count his breath. Simple enough. The calm half hour in the rehab center was a quiet respite from all the talk. But in the monastery the sittings lasted forty-five minutes, and during *sesshin* there were five, six, and eventually eight sittings a day. Voss would settle himself onto the black cushion, square his shoulders and stretch his back. Try to get his posture correct before the third bell, which meant no moving until the end of that sitting. Then breathe into his belly, letting it relax, one . . . exhale slowly, two. . . .

By the time he got to three or four he would be off on an excursion into memory. At first it was a replay of his final minutes with Hal and that nightmare trip down the stairs. Then he would come back to where he was, set that memory aside, and begin again.

One . . . two. . . .

Three . . . four. . . .

He was kneeling at one of the pews in St. Mike's. Hal was next to him. Avery in a pew across the aisle with the girls. Then Avery was sitting between him and Hal, one hand on each of them. He felt himself becoming aroused and then a whiff of sandalwood brought him back to the Zendo, to the gleaming hardwood floor before him, the people in gray robes on either side of him. He breathed deeply, trying to banish the images.

One. . . .

Rohatsu Sesshin I

Waking came slowly in the monastery, with the soft tinkle of distant bells. The sound reminded Voss of the bells that were rung during Catholic mass. Someone carried them, three or four small bells attached to a handle, ringing them continuously, through the halls of the monastery, up the narrow stairs, in and out of dormitory rooms, their music ebbing and then swelling again, a meandering tintinnabulation growing gradually louder, until finally they were coming down the hall to the room Voss was staying in. The door opened, the light came on to the almost fierce ringing, and then the bells floated back down the hall, fading, down the stairs, growing still fainter, until they stopped all together. People were rising from their bunks in the cold room, slipping quietly into dark, loose clothing, padding down the hall in bare feet or socks to use the bathroom, brush teeth, not looking at one another, not speaking, then shuffling downstairs, through labyrinthine passageways and cold staircases, to the drafty Zendo, where a few flickering candles were reflected in the gleaming wood floor. Always, a figure or two would already be seated on the black cushions, erect and still, there and not there, all attention, but not to this world. Voss took in the smell of sandalwood incense, the darkness outside, the cold of the pre-dawn, the silence, the whole monastery in prayer, in meditation, unbroken by movement or sleep, continuous as the silence that had been maintained since late last night when the *sutra* of the day was chanted. Rising in the dark to begin the day before the sun came up always had something special about it, keeping quiet to let others sleep, respecting the silence, the otherness of the sleeping body, whether it was your best friend in the sleeping bag beside you when you were ten and sleeping over, or your lover or wife sharing the bed when you were twenty or twenty-five, or now, a stranger to whom you hadn't even spoken, though you had shared a room and eaten side by side for, what was it? four days now. . . . Voss placed his zori in one of the cubbies at the back of the big open room, reminding himself to mark their location, made his way in his socks to his pad and cushion, and bowed. He would sit cross-legged for the first meditation period, then see how his knees felt. Facing the wall, staring at a point on the floor near where the wide, yellow-pine planks met the plain molding at the base of the plaster wall, he began to count his breath as he had been taught seventeen years before, settling in, trying to think of nothing. He was aware of everything that happened around him, although he did not move even his eyes to look. He heard and felt the other retreat participants come into the room, bow, settle onto their cushions, chairs, or benches. From time to time someone coughed softly, and he could hear doors opening and closing as people who slept out in the cabins came into the main building, bringing, he imagined, the chill of the night with them.

The young man whose cushion was to his right had brought in a chair for this hour, and the woman to his left was just settling onto her small kneeling bench when the first bell rang. Voss drew in a deep breath and straightened his back.

One. . . .

New York City

You tell yourself that love and friendship are the same thing, or versions of the same thing, different only in degree maybe. But in some ways they don't really match. Friendship is much more forgiving than love, though love is supposed to be the greater emotion. We were fine when we were all friends. But love, that word...

"What are you doing?" Artie said. "You'll never get that back together."

Voss had cleared a space on Artie's dining room table and was taking the back off of a tiny electronic keyboard. "C'mon," he said. "I graduated electronics school top of my class—3380th Technical Training School, Keesler Air Force Base, October 1970. What do you think I did in Germany, man? I mean the first time, before Forrester."

"You never talked about that." Artie threw his black backpack onto a pile of newspapers in the corner and flopped down on the tattered couch.

"Yeah, well. When I got to Forrester, '72, nobody wanted to hear about being in the service. Even if it wasn't Vietnam, it was. Which was probably true, I guess. We used to listen to the Russians. I wasn't a listener—never went to language school—but I handled the gear. I know a transistor from a diode, and I can run a soldering gun. Only gun they ever taught me how to use."

He had the white plastic Casio in pieces, but it was still working. He played "Für Elise" with his left hand, tracing the wires with his right. The notes came out of the two inch speaker with all the resonance and musicality of a touchtone phone.

"Is there a Radio Shack anywhere around here?"

"Somewhere," Artie said. "86th, I think."

"It's got thirty-seven keys," Voss said, continuing to disassemble the keyboard, "which isn't bad, but only two note polyphony."

"So you can't really play chords."

"Right, but I can fix that."

"And it sounds like shit," Artie said.

"It does, doesn't it? But I can fix that, too."

"So you gonna ask me how it went?"

"Shit," Voss said, finally looking up from his work. "I'm sorry, man. How'd it go?"

"It's on. 'Alcibiades on Trial' by Arthur Stephanos. Auditions start next week. I gotta go back and meet with the director, write the notice for the trades. . . ."

"Whoa, man!" Voss stood up and wrapped his arms around his friend. "Congratulations. That's amazing. I mean . . . it's not amazing, because you're good. It's . . . it's about time. It's fucking great."

When Artie came back later, a smell of burn hung in the air. It was after two in the morning, and Voss was still at work on the keyboard, tiny electronic components spread out on the table in front of him, a big black mark on the table next to the soldering gun.

"I owe you a new table, man. I'm really sorry. But I'm good for it, I promise. Listen to this."

He slid the keys—no longer in the casing but now attached to the other components by a tangle of thin wires—to the edge of the table and rested his fingers lightly over them. And then he was playing a warbling Hammond B-3, triads and sevenths with his left hand, a dancing lead with his right. Artie looked for the source of the sound and saw two clusters of speakers, still tiny, two and three inch taped together with black electrical tape. Voss reached up and adjusted a dial Artie didn't remember being a part of the original instrument. Now he was playing an electric piano.

"This is the future, man," Voss said. "I don't know why I never thought of it before. I guess I'm not an inventor, just a modifier. If I outfitted a recording studio with a couple of these, I could record an album all by myself."

"What about guitars, drums?" Artie asked, rolling a joint.

"Remember the Mellotron? The Moody Blues used it a lot. It was a fucking monster, weighed a ton, I remember when we toured with them. It was basically sixty-one tape players, each with a couple of different tapes. You hit a key and it played a tape, maybe of a whole violin section playing that note, maybe a flute. But now we've got a memory chip. It's a whole new world. . . ."

Artie shook a joint from his cigarette pack, lit it, took a deep hit, and held it out to Voss.

Voss waved it away. "No, thanks," he said.

Artie withdrew it quickly. "Oh, shit. Sorry, man. I keep forgetting."

(♯)

Artie and Voss sat on a bench in Carl Schurz Park, watching the joggers go up and down the walkway along the East River.

"You think she'll show?" Voss asked.

"She'll show or she won't," Artie said. "That's the most I can tell you."

"Pretty philosophical today, eh?"

They were waiting for the woman they called "Pink Shoes," a young mother they'd seen on and off over the past few weeks, pushing a baby in a stroller. The first time Voss had seen her she was wearing cork-heeled shoes of pink leather with pink ribbons that crisscrossed her legs up to the calf.

"There she is," Artie said. "She's in blue, today."

"You remember when Avery looked like that?" Voss said. "I think it's the posture, that long back, head held high, the breasts where they really go, not all straps and stays or silicone."

"I remember," Artie said. "The first time I met her, when she came with Hal to the Lafayette House. You really hadn't told me about her, and I thought she was with Hal, but when I saw the way she looked at you . . . Man!"

"And that ass," Voss said as Pink Shoes passed them and pushed her stroller along the walkway.

"World class," Artie said.

"The scary part is, I think I like seeing her because the stroller makes me think of Chance when she was a baby, and her body makes me think of the best times with Avery. I don't know if I'm torturing myself by waiting for her, seeing her, or if I'm comforting myself somehow. I mean, they're better off without me, right? I proved that I shouldn't be around either of them. Fuck."

"Don't do this to yourself, bro. You're clean now, right? I haven't seen you take a drink or a smoke since you've been back. You put it behind you. You need to work on the music. Let the rest go. Maybe Avery will want to see you again at some point, but you're going to have to give it time."

"No. It's over. She's not coming back; she's not letting me come back. Her lawyer found me this morning. She's filing for divorce. And full custody of Chance. And I'm going to let her have it. No fight. That would only make it worse."

"You going to have to pay alimony? Child support?"

"Yeah, but it's not bad. One thing I'll say for Avery, she understands money. She made me rich, man. I mean, I did okay with the music, but a couple of years ago she started investing, very careful, very fucking smart. The money I made, she made more money with that. A lot more money. We're dividing the assets down the middle and I'm set for life."

"Wow. So what are you going to do?"

"Find a good banker, get an apartment and a piano, computers, electronics. Keep making music, but now I can really do whatever I want. If nobody buys it, it doesn't matter."

"You always did whatever you wanted, Jack."

"Not as much as you think. I made compromises. Every step of the way, I made compromises. You remember the first album—I had enough for a double, but Bobby wouldn't let me do it."

"Yeah, but . . . was it all as good as what ended up on the record?"

Voss looked at Artie. "No fucking way," he said, laughing. "That double album would have been bloated with self-important, masturbatory bullshit."

"So let's talk about the rest of your compromises, dude," Artie said.

Voss laughed again. "I let David Bowie produce my first solo album."

"And he really fucked it up, right?"

"No, he made it a better album than I ever could have. Showed me things about my own songs I didn't see."

"Okay," Artie said. "I see a pattern here. What about the personal side?"

"I gave up Jeanette even though she still wanted me—along with everyone else." Voss shook his head.

"That's a good one; I remember that. Actually I remember that a couple of times. And?"

"I never had as many girls as Hal, even though I probably could have."

"Because you went with the girl who loved you and took care of you and made you rich."

"Yeah," Voss said, now laughing so hard he had tears streaming down his face.

"And?"

"And I changed the title of my *Liebestod.* . . ."

"Which you stole from Wagner. . . ."

"Right," Voss said, smiling. But then his face changed and he took a deep breath. "But that didn't turn out so well," he said.

"You couldn't have known they would take it like that. Nobody could," Artie said. "That's your albatross, man. I know. But you rose above it. You dealt with it like a man and then you moved on. I was proud of you."

Voss wiped his eyes with the back of his hand and looked up. A fresh breeze was blowing up whitecaps on the East River and the smoke from the few remaining stacks in Brooklyn streamed north in ragged lines. Anvil-shaped clouds were massing to the south. Joggers going that way had their heads tucked and were pumping their arms into the wind.

"Where'd Pink Shoes go?" Voss asked Artie.

"She rode the wind back to her pastel world."

"And I missed it," Voss said. "So goes the death of love, *Der Liebestod.*"

"Flush the toilet," Artie said.

"What?"

"*Liebestod,*" Artie said. "Flush the toilet."

"Fucking A," Voss said. "*Liebestod*: flush the toilet. That's fucking perfect."

When they got back to Artie's place on East 90ᵗʰ Street, they chanted the phrase as they marched up the five flights to his apartment, a call and response cadence:

"*Liebestod,*" Voss said.

"Flush the toilet," Artie answered.

"*Liebestod.*"

"Flush the toilet."

"*Liebestod. . . .*"

Circuits took almost two years to make, most of that time spent alone in the apartment. Voss would work out the music on the piano, then program it into a computer, where he'd manipulate the sound, not creating synthetic versions of existing instruments, but creating sounds that had never been made before. At least, that's what he told himself when he was feeling good about the project. On bad days he thought his new sounds were like the mythical creatures created by the illustrators of old geographies, not really new things, but monstrosities made up of bits of things already existing, dogs with the heads of cats, birds with rhino armor, ugly and too heavy to fly. Still he plugged on, going out to walk around the city with a tape recorder when he ran out of ideas.

Nights he played at The Last Straw in Soho, usually alone, though sometimes guys would sit in: a bass player from the old days in Berlin, a young drummer who wanted to work on his jazz chops. One night he stepped over to the bar between sets to see Artie sitting there with a pretty blonde.

"Look who's come back to New York," Artie said.

"Well, I'll be damned," Voss said, looking at her more closely. "C.C. You're all grown up."

"Aren't we all," C.C. said.

"Where you been all these years," Voss asked. "I think Artie's missed you."

"I was here before while you were in Berlin," she said. "I was in L.A. for a while, doing some film. But I'm a theater person. So I'm back."

"What are you drinking? Let me think—wasn't it Southern Comfort in the old days?"

"Don't remind me," she said. "This is just a gin and tonic for a summer night."

"Artie?"

"Harp draft."

"Aren't we supposed to be buying drinks for the piano player," C.C. asked, "instead of the other way around?"

"The piano player doesn't drink anymore," Artie said.

"Sure he does," Voss said, signaling the bartender. "I mean, like the lady says, it's just a gin and tonic for a summer night."

"I thought you were off the stuff," Artie said.

"I was." He turned to C.C., "I was ahead of schedule. It's a matter of pacing. I got ahead of myself, had done all my '87 drinking back around '85 or '86, and was well into my '88 and '89 by the time '87 came along. But I quit for a while and now I'm back on track."

The bartender brought their drinks.

"You'll never guess who she saw out in L.A." Artie said.

"Jack Nicholson? Meryl Streep?"

"Jeanette Del Rio," C.C. said.

"Really? How's she doing? What's she doing? Is she married?"

"She's doing okay. She's writing for one the soaps. Divorced. Still beautiful."

"Still crazy?" Voss asked. "Or, let me guess, well-medicated."

"I wouldn't know about that," C.C. said, "but she seemed all right. We had lunch. She asked about you."

"Still banging away at the piano." Voss looked at his watch. "Can you guys hang around? I've got one more set. Maybe an hour."

Artie looked at C.C. "What do you think?"

"We can grab a bite after," Voss said.

"Sure," C.C. said.

(♯)

"Jeanette? Jeanette Del Rio?"

"Speaking."

"It's Jack . . . Jack Voss."

"Wow, Jack. . . . How are you? Where are you calling from?"

Voss pushed the phone closer to his left ear and put his finger in his right. He couldn't tell from her voice if she was glad or just surprised to hear from him.

"I'm right here. In L.A. Laid down some piano tracks for some guys I don't even want to tell you their names. So how are you? What are you doing these days?"

"I'm fine, I'm great," she said, and then paused as if waiting for him to say something.

He waited, too.

"Working," she said, finally. "Which, for a writer is good."

"Like for a musician . . . which you used to be. I can still remember the first time I heard you sing."

"That was a long time ago, Jack."

"So, listen," Voss said. "It would be great to see you, but I'm only here until tomorrow. I thought maybe we could have dinner or something."

"I don't know. I mean, I just ate."

"Well, maybe we could meet for a drink, you could meet me for a drink. . . ."

"Jack. . . ."

"I'm at the Polo Lounge, in the Beverly Hills Hotel. I'll get a bite, and then you can meet me at the bar. Say around nine? It'd be really great to see you."

"Okay. The Polo Lounge. Around nine."

She didn't sound very enthusiastic, but Voss felt confident that once she saw him the old fire would come back. He replayed memories of past reunions as he ate his dinner, and afterwards found a spot at the bar where he could watch the door. A young woman was playing cocktail jazz on a piano in the corner—she had the technique, but she couldn't quite make it swing. Voss sat there, nursing a bottle of champagne, and wondered how much Jeanette had changed. Was she still the lean, small-breasted wildcat he remembered? C.C. had said she was still beautiful, and Voss pictured the way her eyes would light up when something interested her.

But nine o'clock came and went. Then ten.

Voss called her number again from the lobby, but her machine picked up. He didn't leave a message. He thought of the risk he had taken calling her in the first place, the recklessness of such a move. She had always been trouble for him.

The champagne gone, he ordered a brandy and soda. At midnight he went up to bed, cursing her to himself. In the middle of the night, however, he awoke thirsty and restless, and he found himself wondering if she had made the right choice in standing him up. What had he wanted from her now? Her body. Her fire. Maybe he had become a danger to her. Maybe, after all these years, he was the one who was trouble.

(♯)

Artie and C.C. were married in the smoky backroom of Peter McManus's Pub on 7th Avenue. Swami, an old friend of Artie's who was going to chef school at the Culinary Institute, had a certificate declaring him a minister of some church or other and had been asked to perform the ceremony. Most of the old Lafayette House crew made it. Henry Bowman, on leave from the Navy, had caught a hop up from Florida, Duncan McGough had driven in from St. Louis with a pretty girlfriend in her early twenties, and Voss pulled up in front of the bar in a canary yellow Lamborghini Countach.

He had arrived without a moment to spare, which was doubtless a good thing, since his intention was to invite Artie to skip it. "I've got a full tank of gas, a lid in the glove box, a cooler of champagne in the boot, and a gram in my pocket," he'd planned to say. "Anywhere you want to go, I'll take you." But somewhere between his apartment on the Upper West Side and 18th Street he had been delayed. If his last-minute arrival offended anyone, they didn't say so at the time. Two magnums of Mumms stood like sentries on the scuffed wooden table, a third, half full, sat in a sweating ice bucket. Voss poured himself a generous glass just as the ceremony began. Artie and C.C. had taken their vows from *The Taming of the Shrew* and exchanged plastic rings. C.C.'s old running mate, Sassy, wept copiously. As soon as Artie and C.C. broke from their kiss, Voss ushered them into the men's room for some lines, which Artie declined. Back at the table, he proposed a toast, raised his glass, and addressed the group:

> *Friends and lovers, husbands and wives*
> *We never forget you for all of our lives*
> *We meet years later, in . . . something something dives*
> *And slice up the past with sharp little knives.*

He looked around at the crowd, murmuring its disappointment. "But not Artie and C.C.," he added brightly. "May they succeed where everyone else, especially me, has failed."

Over the next hour or so he took everyone but the navy lieutenant into the john, made a drunken pass at Sassy, who handled him with good grace, and called Avery on the phone four times. When the party moved outside to watch Artie and C.C. climb into a taxi and head off into married life, he raised his glass again:

Friends and lovers, husbands and wives . . .

The taxi pulled out into 7th Avenue and everyone clapped, ignoring him.

"I think that's my cue to go have a little talk with the lovely ex," Voss said. "Or as I like to call her, the bitch who took my kid."

He folded himself into the Lamborghini and burned rubber through the red light at 18th Street. He was under arrest before he got to the Holland Tunnel.

He called Bert. Bert called an attorney. It took five hours, but they got him out.

"I owe you guys big," he said. "God, I just want to go home, get a shower, and sleep for a week."

"No sleep for you, buddy," Bert said. "This doesn't go away. You're in rehab by sundown today, or you're in jail."

"But I don't have to be in court until what, next month?"

"Jack, this is Mike Barker. Explain it to him, Mike."

"Mr. Voss," the lawyer said, extending his hand. "I wish we were meeting under better circumstances. It's not good. Driving under the influence, possession of pot and cocaine? You wait until your court date, it only gets worse. We put you in rehab today and talk to the judge."

"Back to the dark castle? Aw, fuck."

"There's worse places, Jack," Bert said. "Lots worse."

"Shit. Can I get cleaned up?"

"We're going to your place now," Bert said. "You can get a shower and pack a bag."

"Okay," Voss said as they pulled up in front of his building. "Give me an hour."

"We're not leaving you alone," Bert said.

"What, you're gonna watch me take a shower? Afraid I'll slip out the back window?"

"You were out of control last night. I'm not sure what you'd do."

"Aw, come on. Where would I go?"

Bert rode the elevator with him, and Mike came up after he parked the car.

In the bathroom Voss took a joint and a Bic lighter out of a Sucrets tin in the medicine cabinet, popped the toilet paper off the holder, and slipped them into the cardboard tube. Then he swallowed a ten milligram Valium dry and brought the prescription bottle out to Bert and Mike. Forthright. "So, you gonna count these or what?" he said. Petulant. "You know what my head feels like right now?" Confiding.

"Let's turn the prescription stuff over to the docs at the clinic. Then they'll work out what you can have and what you can't have."

"Okay, but at least let me have one now." Whiny.

"Just one," Mike said, dispensing a blue pill from the plastic bottle and handing it to Voss. "I'll note the time and tell the doc."

"Very lawyerly of you, counselor," Voss said, keeping up the sham of irritability.

He let Bert and Mike clean out his medicine cabinet. "Now can I take my shower in private?" he said. As soon as they stepped out he locked the door, turned on the shower and the exhaust fan, recovered the joint he'd stashed and lit it. He caught his reflection in the mirror and saw an aging high school kid sneaking a smoke in the boys' room. He was acting with the shallow, selfish cleverness of a junkie. He put out the joint and tucked the remaining half back into its hiding place. Standing under the shower, he thought back to the night before. How badly had he fucked up? Had he behaved inappropriately? No doubt about that. Had he ruined the wedding? He didn't think so. There was something else on his mind, but he couldn't put his finger on it. Had he resisted arrest, fought with the police officers? No. He'd been docile, polite. That wasn't it. He scrubbed himself and rinsed, then scrubbed and rinsed again. By the time he stepped out of the shower he had a good buzz from the pot and he could feel the first Valium softening the throb in his head, the ever present ache in the bones of his hand.

Bert took one look at his eyes as he came out of the bathroom and said, "Goddamn it, Jack."

"What?" he said.

She just shook her head and sighed.

Like a goddamned wife, he thought.

Mike came in from the other room. "The police charges aren't the only problem," he said.

"What are you talking about?" Bert asked.

"I just got off the phone with my office. Avery's lawyer has been calling all morning. They're going to ask for a restraining order."

"Fuck," Voss said.

"What else did you do last night?" Bert asked.

"I called Avery a couple of times," Voss said, remembering. "I may have been a little . . . I don't know. I was pissed. She won't talk to me; she won't let me see Chance."

"You told her you'd kick her fat ass," Mike said. "You told her you were coming and you had a baseball bat. They're making that out a threat. Christ, it is a threat."

"You know I'd never really do anything like that. Don't you? Bert?"

"Did you have a baseball bat?" Bert asked.

"What?"

"Did you have a baseball bat?"

"In the car. Yeah. I guess I did. I keep it there. Just in case. I mean, you can't carry a knife or a gun."

"Shit," Mike said. "You'll be lucky if you ever see your daughter again."

Three hours later, Voss woke up in the back seat of Mike's Audi. They had pulled off the thruway and were stopped at a light. He looked out into the gray rainy day, pictured the dark castle under the looming mountain. He remembered his last stay there and the week at Black Dome Zenji that followed.

"You guys still work for me, right?" he said.

"We're doing this for you, Jack. And it goes beyond work," Bert said.

"And I appreciate it. But I can't take that fucking place again. Fucking group therapy. It's torture. I mean thumbscrews and the rack, like they tie you down and make you listen to the Bee Gees. You're not crazy when you go in, you're crazy when you get out."

"You think you'd like jail better? We can turn around and swing by Sing Sing if you want to take a look."

"I want you to call this guy Chikuzen at the Black Dome Zen Monastery. Maybe you can work out a deal. Offer them a big donation. Get me out of the dungeon and into the monastery."

"You're asking me to bribe a monk?" Mike said. "Now I know you have gone nuts."

"Are we not paying for rehab? Call it room and board . . . tuition."

ROHATSU SESSHIN II

This was not a place that rewarded initiative, original thinking. Yesterday during work practice Voss was reprimanded—or it felt like a reprimand anyway—for changing the bag in a vacuum cleaner without being told. The day before that, a cook had berated him for washing mushrooms with water—*did I tell you to use water?* he had asked, breaking the silence with recrimination and poisoning the next hour's meditation with constantly rising thoughts of what he might say to the cook if he ever got the chance. In the world outside no one would have dared to speak to Voss that way, but here no one knew who he was, or if they did, they wouldn't acknowledge it. They respected his privacy in a way that almost no one else did. Once he let go of the urge to put the insolent cook in his place, Voss settled back into the melancholy groove this sesshin had taken on for him. Images of Chance as a toddler floated up before him, bringing quiet tears, then came memories of Avery that always seemed to end in arguments. Sometimes scenes from his erotic life swam into his mind's eye, and as the scenes flowed from one to another, his emotions veered from aroused nostalgia to sweet affection to deep embarrassment and shame. Then he would hear the distant caw of a crow, or the chatter of chickadees right outside the windows, or just the sound of the wind, and he would regain his sense of this whole place being sacred, the walls themselves exuding the quiet cool breath of monks who had lived here before, dedicating their lives to prayer, and himself a part of that sacredness in spite of all his imperfections, his base desires, welcomed into the harmony of breathing with the world, a kind of vibration, a chord mystical, like Gregorian chant, or the weird Zen chants that would make up most of the morning service to come later, chants Voss found beautiful except for the very end, the last note, when, according to the custom here, everyone trailed down the scale and faded in volume, like a character in an old movie falling off a cliff—Voss cringed every time they did it, tried to do it along with them, in unison, but it offended his musical sensibility. In fact, it sounded awful. One more thing to let go of, he thought, to surrender his sense that he knew more about music than they did.

BLACK DOME ZENJI

Her I knew since we were small. Seven or eight. Midway through second grade. She showed up in our class after Christmas. And we all knew right away. I don't know how we knew, if somebody told us or what, but we all knew it was just her and her mother. That her father was gone. But she talked about him. He's famous, she said. Someday he's going to come and get me, she would say, and take me with him around the world. Where is he now, we asked. He's in rehab, she said. What's that, some of the kids asked, but I knew. And I knew he wasn't coming back. Don't ask me how I knew; I just knew. Something in the way she said it. It was a dream. A fantasy. Not a plan. Not something she heard from him. Or her mother. After a while, she stopped talking about it.

"You're my prisoner," Chikuzen said, smiling as he and Voss sat cross-legged facing one another in the gray interview room, a stick of sandalwood incense burning before a gold painted Buddha.

"Yeah," Voss said. "Imagine that."

The deal Chikuzen had struck with the state was that the monastery would provide substance abuse training of a more intense variety than he could provide by visiting the rehab facility three times a week. Most of that training consisted simply of the daily mindfulness practice that was the routine of the monks. In addition, he would meet individually with Voss twice a week between dinner and evening Zazen. In their first session he told Voss his own life story.

Chikuzen, a few years older than Voss, had been trained as a chemist at Berkeley, had been part of a research team at Bayer, and had left it to work with Stanley Owsley, making the acid that fueled the Summer of Love. He'd broken with Owsley, concluding that psilocybin was a better product than lysergic acid, and he was on his way to Mexico in his brand-new Microbus camper with a propane-fueled drying oven of his own design, when the lab in Orinda was raided and everyone carted off to jail. He lived in the desert like John the Baptist, he would sometimes say, but in fact he grilled steaks on his hibachi, ate mushrooms with his girlfriend, and collected wildflowers. His "Mexican wanderings" took him through every kind of country, from coastal beaches to spreading green farmland, across high sierras, through cloud forest and dense lowland jungle to barren desert. He stayed away from the cities, but perfected his Spanish in the towns and villages.

He reentered the states through El Paso almost a year later with two large boxes of dried and mounted wildflower specimens that ultimately found their way into the collection at the St. Louis Botanical Gardens. The curator said his mountings were works of art. He also had a spare tire full of dried mushrooms, *psilocybe zapotecorum*. He was headed north. In Taos, he dropped his girlfriend off at a Dairy Queen and drove up to the Zen Center where he stayed for six months. He had seen his fair share of what the outside world had to offer, he thought, the university and the corporate world, American cities and the Mexican countryside, much of it pulsing softly with the glow that came from carefully measured doses of hallucinogens. Now he wanted to explore something else.

He was given a gray robe, taught to sit and count his breath, told about *satori* and *kensho*. He tried it straight for a couple of days and grew bored. Then he tried it with the mushrooms. It was much more interesting. He had been transported in time and space to medieval Japan. Some days he half expected to see Samurai come marching up the hill as in a Kurosawa film. Some days he felt that he was himself a Samurai who had laid down his sword and retreated from the world. He had a breakthrough during his first *sesshin*, about seven weeks after he'd checked in. This he could not describe to Voss. With luck and practice Voss would experience it himself someday. At any rate it changed the way he saw the world. It was probably not right to call it *kensho*, since he was riding a wave of hallucinogenic alkaloids when it happened. But the amazing thing was that a week later he found he could get back there without the mushrooms. They had only been necessary to find the way, like tinted glasses that revealed secret signs on a map. Now that he knew the way, he didn't need the glasses or the map.

The girlfriend wasn't waiting at the Dairy Queen when he came back down from the mountain. He went back to California and studied yoga at Esalen. There he met Roshi, a former psychiatrist from Queens who had spent five years at a monastery in Japan, and had come to Esalen to participate in a weeklong seminar on meditation. The two of them talked into the night. A year later Chikuzen made his first visit to Black Dome to become Roshi's student. Roshi gave him the name Chikuzen—shallow Zen—to be a constant taunt that he wasn't working hard enough. Time passed. After Chikuzen was ordained, Roshi suggested he go back to school and study medicine. He studied psychology instead, and earned an MSW and a license to practice as a therapist in the State of New York. This was how he was allowed to run his experimental program at the clinic. Eventually, though, he would be the abbot of Black Dome Zenji. Roshi had already promised it to him. In the meantime, he would try to teach what he had learned. He was confident that he could show Voss and others like him a way to be wide-awake-in-the-world without drugs. If Voss was willing to do the work he would reach a point where he would not need drugs anymore.

"I already don't need drugs," Voss said. "I like drugs, but I don't need them. I spent a week in the dungeon waiting for you guys to get me out. It sucked, but I didn't go through withdrawal. No cravings. You've done more drugs than I ever have. I just fucked up and got caught."

"Jack, Jack," Chikuzen said. "I know that. If I thought you were a real addict, I never would have allowed you to come here. Nobody knows what to do with real addicts. Look at any program, twelve-step, psychotherapy, drug substitution—like methodone—psychotropic medication . . . it's all the same. About a 2 to 10 percent success rate if we're honest. We are at a loss, my friend."

"So what are we doing here?" Voss asked. "I mean, I'm not complaining. I'm out of that hellhole, everyone with that *I'm Joe Blow and I'm a drug addict* shit. *Oh lord I am not worthy, say but the word and my soul shall be healed.*"

"Ah. Catholic to boot," Chikuzen said. "You and I have a lot in common. But we have one difference. I am a master of situation and dosage; you just think you are."

"If I wasn't careful about dosage, I wouldn't be alive today," Voss said.

"Maybe, but let's look at what got you in here this time."

Voss told him the story, what he remembered of it.

"So, let's look at the two parameters. First, dosage. How much coke did you do that night?"

"I don't know. Too much."

"How did that happen? Why didn't you control your own dosage? Nobody forced you to do another line, or another spoonful, whatever. What happened there?"

"I don't know. I was getting everybody high, getting high with them."

"Okay. Let's put that on hold for a minute. What about the situation. How did you end up getting arrested?"

"Driving."

"Why in the world would you combine driving with all that coke and booze?"

"You get drunk," Voss said. "Your judgment goes."

"Exactly. So when was the time to make a decision about driving? When you left the house with a couple grams of coke in your pocket. You take a taxi, we're not here now."

"So you're telling me moderation, and don't drink and drive. This is what you're offering."

"Why do you resent the stuff they do in the clinic, Jack? Because you don't recognize yourself in the way they want to describe you. Because you feel they will only be happy if you spout a line about yourself that you don't believe to be true: *I'm Jack Voss and I can't control myself, so I give myself over to a higher power to control me, and then everything will be okay. I'm weak and helpless and can't do what other people do every day, control my impulses.* I'm giving you something you can believe about yourself: *I'm Jack Voss and I've managed to get myself into some pretty deep shit a few times. I can't afford to let it happen again. And I can take some steps to make sure it doesn't.* They want you to surrender, Jack. I'm asking you to take charge. Own your life, be present for it, take care of it."

"Okay," Voss said. "And *satori*? *kensho*?"

"That's the part about being present. Appreciating and paying attention to each step of the journey, not fixating on destinations, accomplishments. *Satori* is being in the zone. You ever feel like you're in the zone? Everything's clicking, you're fully there, engaged in what you're doing. Some people call it *flow*."

"Yeah. Sometimes when I'm running. When I'm playing well. In the music."

"You're in the music. That's nice. That's what I'm talking about. Does it happen when you're high?"

"Almost never."

"Does it make you want to get high?"

"Not while I'm in it. Sometimes when it's gone."

"That's what we're going to work on," Chikuzen said.

"You got a piano?" Voss said.

"No."

"Because I will go into withdrawal from music. What if somebody were to donate a piano. You got a place for it?"

"Yeah, I think so. Would *somebody* be able to make it quiet?"

Thus Black Dome Zenji came to have a piano in a soundproof practice room. Voss would be allowed access to it for two hours every afternoon when there wasn't a *sesshin* in progress, which was about one week in every month. Bert contacted Bobby Norman, who located a construction crew; bonuses were paid and work was completed quickly. The piano itself, a Yamaha Studio Grand, arrived and was tuned three weeks into Voss's stay, but Apple Blossom *sesshin* was starting the next day. He would have to wait seven more days before he could play.

The *sesshin* ended late on Saturday night. Voss slept hard, rose at first light, and meditated alone in the Zendo for an hour before the Sunday morning service, at the conclusion of which he went quietly back to his room for his shaving kit, took a shower, and dressed in loose black pants, black Chinese shoes, and a long-sleeved black t-shirt. He could hear the distant rumble of voices in the dining room as he walked with measured steps down the hall to the piano room, its heavy, black-painted door marked with the Japanese kanji *Shugyo*: Practice.

He opened the door, stepped into the room, and closed it behind him. Total silence. The converted bedroom was floored with wide planks of gleaming oak, the walls tastefully quilted in fabric the color of sand. An ink drawing of a round-bellied flute player hung on the wall opposite the door, and a small altar with a carved ebony Buddha had been built into the wall to his right, a single *zafu* and *zabuton* before it. In the center of the room the piano stood, pulsing, Voss felt, with energy. He first went to the altar, knelt down on the *zabuton*, settled onto the *zafu*, brought his hands up before his chest in *gassho*, and bowed before the statue of the Buddha. Then he straightened up, took a stick of incense from the small pile that had been provided, lit it with the black Bic lighter that had also been placed there, and set it into the waiting bowl of fine sand. He bowed three times in *gassho* and then stood up. He turned silently and walked around the piano, faced the front of it where the bench was tucked under, raised his hands in *gassho* again and bowed to the piano. Then he pulled out the bench, sat down, lifted the cover as quietly as he could, reached toward the keys, and then pulled his hands back and let them rest on his thighs. Never in his life had the first note he played mattered so much. With this first note he would break the silence of weeks. Except that it had not been silence. With this note he would be adding a new thing to the carefully orchestrated soundscape created by the routine of the monastery. For five weeks, the only sounds he'd heard had been the bells and gongs, clappers and drums that portioned out the day, the rhythmic thumping of bare feet on the wooden floor of the Zendo during the walking meditations that came several times a day between sittings, the crack of the *keotsaku* when one of the monks went around the Zendo briskly striking the backs of those who wished it with the wooden stick, the deep scholarly voice of Roshi, giving his dharma talks, spinning out some Zen parable and elucidating it, the soft encouraging voice of Chikuzen calling out yoga positions during the third hour of the morning, the nearly whispered instructions during work practice, the birdsong that came in through the open windows of the Zendo on warm afternoons, the breathing of the sleeping bodies around him in the bunkroom. The notes Voss played now would bring a new dimension to an aural routine that went back thousands of years, that had been shared by monks in Japan, China, India, back to the days of Shakyamuni Buddha and before.

He raised his hands again and before he reached the keys he found himself remembering his lessons with Dr. Madison. This was not a time for music exactly, it was, as the symbol on the door made clear, a time for practice, and that was what she had taught him, now that he looked back on it: how to practice. He began with the stretching routine she had given him, concentrating on each movement, focusing as he would in counting his breaths in the Zendo, on chopping onions when he was on kitchen duty, or on sweeping the floor when that was his task. This would lead him to his first note; he wouldn't have to choose it, for the stretching was followed by scales, beginning with the C scale, a routine as strict as any in the monastery. He placed his hands lightly on the keys and struck middle C with his right thumb. The sound was almost overwhelming; a surge of emotion flowed up through his body. He listened to the tone fade and then he struck D with his index finger. He felt himself breathe, felt the music of one note fill the room, exquisite, powerful. His eyes filled with tears. He worked his way up and down the keyboard with infinite patience, striking the keys with the same pressure, listening to each note, attending to the way it resonated, letting it fade. First with one hand, then with both. C, then G, then D. As he played the A minor scale, the tears streamed down his face. That pianos existed seemed a miracle, this one a gift. He played a chromatic scale all the way up and down the keyboard. Every note had its own character, its own beauty. He had no music with him, so again he went back in his mind to Dr. Madison and the things she taught him. She had wanted to challenge him and had assigned him a piece by Satie. It was spare, without ornamentation, deceptively simple. Beautiful when played well, an emotionless student exercise when played poorly. But spare and simple were exactly what he wanted right now. He closed his eyes and took himself back there, picturing the sheets of music, feeling the notes in his fingers. He went through the entire piece in his mind, and then he took a breath and began to play.

(❦)

"I want you to tell me about what happened in 1975," Chikuzen said.

Voss had been in the monastery for three and a half months, staying on after his "sentence" was up. While most of the students there met with the Roshi at every chance they got, Voss still met only with Chikuzen.

"What are you, a shrink now?" Voss said.

"If I'd known about it before, I would have asked you about it a long time ago." He held out a manila envelope full of what looked like photocopied newspaper clippings. "This came in the mail yesterday. No return address, but it was mailed from Chicago. Do you want to see what's in it?"

"I don't know, do I?"

"Whoever sent it wanted to make sure we knew who you were. Funny thing is, I never knew about the suicides in '75. I was dividing my time between the monastery and trips to Mexico collecting. I guess I just missed it."

"I guess so," Voss said. "Let's see what they sent."

"And you never mentioned it in all the hours we talked."

"No, I guess I didn't," Voss said. Most of the clippings had been copied from the *Chicago Tribune*. They covered the first suicides, the ones that followed, the public apology, the attempts that followed. A *Newsweek* article from 1977 on copycat crimes was included. A sidebar circled with yellow highlighter suggested that the media had a history of not reporting some crimes, especially copycat murders and suicides, in order to stem the tide of violence. "The Enchanted Pond Suicide Case" was mentioned as one in which reporting was suppressed at the request of some influential psychologists working with the FBI. Voss felt sick when he read the following sentence: "Although only five cases were reported in the national media, some experts believe that as many as eleven cases occurred in the twelve months following the release of *The Enchanted Pond* with a total death toll of twenty-three."

"You want to talk about this?"

"There's stuff here I never knew about," Voss said. He continued to page through the sheets. The *Time* article that had praised him for his action at the time was there, too. The word "BULLSHIT" was scrawled across it in fat red letters. At the bottom of the pile was a report from just two years before: "Woman Dies 14 Years After Suicide Attempt."

"So she finally died," Voss said. "I often wondered about her."

"Maybe you should take all this stuff back to your room and read it, and we'll talk about it next time we meet," Chikuzen said.

(♯)

"This is a lot to carry," Chikuzen said.

"I didn't know I was carrying all this," Voss said.

"But you knew you were carrying something."

"I guess. I never wanted to think about it."

"Let's think about it now," Chikuzen said. "What made you write a work that ends in a triple suicide?"

And Voss told him the story of how he wrote *The Enchanted Pond*. He'd come up with the idea in a surge of jealous hopelessness. The seed had come that night in the car with Jeanette, having just had great sex, peaking on acid, and knowing full well that the wild high they were on, love or the illusion of love included, was bound to end. "Why not end it on a high note," he'd said to her. And when she left him again, he'd turned that idea into his opera, a work that expressed all of his own confusion about how somebody could love more than one person and somebody else couldn't stand it. The threesome was the given. The introduction of the bisexual member of the threesome was a trick, really, something to make it exotic, disturbing, to make it seem even more impossible than it might otherwise seem. He'd heard of guys committing suicide because they were gay. It was 1973, and he was living in the time of the sexual revolution. AIDS hadn't appeared on the scene. It seemed like every guy he knew had slept with every girl he knew, and a couple of the guys had also slept with guys, and girls with girls. He himself had never been that daring, that brave. He remembered the time in Hal's basement when Avery had jerked them both off, and though it had felt good as it was happening, only moments had gone by before he'd begun to feel awkward, guilty, ashamed, both for himself and for Avery. That had doubtless been another ingredient. And he'd known no other way to end his opera than with death.

But that was the opera. In life he had never seriously considered suicide. He guessed he simply wasn't the suicidal type. It had flashed across his mind a couple of times, as in that moment with Jeanette, but he'd never taken it seriously enough to pursue it. So when the suicides began in 1975, he was truly shocked. He was also twenty-six years old. The kids who were killing themselves were in their late teens, at a critical juncture in their lives. And if *The Enchanted Pond* seemed to give them a romantic way out, it was almost by accident. By mistake. He still didn't understand how they could actually do it. Even if they did it with pills, to lie down and sleep forever, never to wake up to another day, another morning sky, another first kiss, another great riff, another high. Why close all the doors? In the end, he was baffled, stunned at how much he didn't understand, at how such an act could seem like the right idea.

"So you went on record asking them to stop, to choose life," Chikuzen said.

"Yeah, and then I tried to put it behind me. Like a bad dream."

"But it wasn't a dream."

"No."

"And it kept going on."

"So what if it did? I did what I could. I never meant that shit to happen. What am I supposed to do about it now?"

"I don't know, Jack. What could you do?"

"Fuck, I don't know. Here's an idea: we'll bring the record back out. How many years is it? Almost time for a twentieth anniversary edition. Little essays by snobby rock critics. *Where are they now?* stories. Get somebody to make a film. Interviews. Old concert footage. A fucking reunion tour. And if they start killing themselves again, let them. Less of the weak in the world, we're better off. Like people who kill themselves because love is hard are going to do anything worth a shit anyway. . . ."

"You don't mean that, Jack."

"The hell I don't."

"Where's the anger coming from?"

"Where do you think? I was standing on the brink. I was gonna be the next Jackson Browne, Vossimilitude could have given The Eagles a run for their money. It was 19 fucking 75, we were coming up like a Saturn rocket.

They dropped the record, man. Those kids wrecked my career before I even had a career."

"What does that make you want to do, Jack?"

"It makes me want to break something. It makes me want to get fucked up."

"I'll bet it does. What are you going to do instead?"

"Go pound the shit out of the piano."

"Exactly," Chikuzen said.

NEW YEAR'S EVE

Voss told himself he didn't like to take advantage of his status, such as it was, but that was perhaps not entirely true. He felt he shouldn't take advantage, but, in fact, he enjoyed having the opportunity to do so. And it was somewhat gratifying that even at the monastery, where his anonymity was almost complete, he was in fact being treated as quite special. To wit: he was allowed to leave before the *sesshin* was over, something that was forbidden to everyone else. You could start late, and people kept arriving in dribs and drabs as the week went on, but you couldn't leave early. But, whether purely by the argument that he had a standing obligation to play a New Year's Eve gig on a cruise around Manhattan, or by virtue of the fact that he had donated quite a lot of money to the monastery over the years, Voss was allowed to leave after breakfast on New Year's Eve. At the conclusion of the morning meditation, he ate his portion of oatmeal in silence, sitting cross-legged on his cushion like everyone else, washed his bowls and utensils with the hot water that was brought around, drank the water with the last food particles, dried his bowls and utensils and folded them into the damp cloth. Then, when others were racing to use the bathroom before the next sitting, he quietly climbed the stairs to the room he shared with seven other men, stripped his bed, packed his things in silence, and, without saying goodbye to anyone, opened the back door of the monastery and stepped out into a blinding white world.

As his eyes adjusted he saw that well over a foot of snow had fallen. The sun shone fiercely, and Voss squinted as he trudged to his car, which he found half-buried in a snowdrift. He managed to get the door opened, tossed his bag in and located his sunglasses. Then he walked through the snow to the tool shed, got a shovel and broom, dug the car out, swept it off, and started it up. He tried to do all of these things as a continuation of the mindfulness practice he and all the other *sesshin* participants had been working at since the day after Christmas. After scraping the windows and making sure he could get the vehicle out into the road, he carried the tools back to the shed and headed down to Roshi's residence to say goodbye. Roshi was not in fact participating in the *sesshin*. He would come in and lead some of the meditations, give dharma talks, and have private audiences with the participants at the assigned times, but outside of that, he allowed the senior monks to run the show, and he spent most of his time away from the retreatants, most of whom would probably have been shocked to know that he did not share in their silence. In his own quarters he cooked and ate, read the newspaper and watched television. Voss knocked at the door, and after a minute or two Roshi appeared wearing gray sweats and slippers.

"So, Jack, you are leaving us once again. Have you had a good week?"

"Yes. It's been good. It's still not the same without Chikuzen, but it's been good."

"I miss him, too," Roshi said. "But in the end . . . it was for the good of the monastery. But you have suffered your own loss this year. A very great loss."

"Yes. I don't think I have fully understood it yet."

"We are always here. A refuge, if you need it," Roshi said.

"I know," Voss said. "Thank you. So. I have to go play. Work." He smiled. It was the first real conversation he'd had in six days, and the words felt charged with meaning.

"Is it the boat again?"

"Yeah, a musical cruise around Manhattan, they call it."

"I hope they give you a good instrument," Roshi said.

"Thank you, Roshi," Voss said, feeling moved out of proportion to the sentiment. "I hope the New Year brings you only good things."

"It will bring what it brings," the Roshi said, "for both of us. Let's hope, rather, that we are equal to what is asked of us."

"Yes," Voss said. Neither said anything more. Nor did they shake hands. After a moment Voss began to feel awkward. He tilted his head forward in a slight bow, then turned and walked back to his car. He drove for fully an hour before turning on the radio. Pier 42 in New York City was still two hours away.

(♯)

He'd asked for a Yamaha, and they'd provided him with a Steinway, so he had to spend a little time figuring what kind of Steinway it was. He'd played worse. And it was in tune. But it definitely wasn't a selection room piano. The action was stiff and the breakaway sudden, and he knew that by the end of the night his left hand would be killing him, but, although it would certainly affect his sound, he was determined not to let it affect his mood, which after the days of seclusion and silence, was calm, settled. He felt that he was seeing things clearly. Not that he had the answers he wanted, or that he had dealt with his emotions, but simply that he felt calm and saw the world with a kind of sharpness that had been lacking of late. The P.A. system was decent, and once he had adjusted the microphones over the piano, he could hear himself and felt confident that he would be heard by everyone once the place filled up. Not that it mattered that much. New Year's Eve was in many ways the worst night of the year for a gig. The audience would be increasingly drunk as the night went on, less and less interested in the music the closer it got to midnight. But Voss had taken the job years ago for two reasons: it paid well, and it gave him something to do. Bad as it might be to spend New Year's Eve playing music for a drunk crowd that didn't give a shit about what you played, it would be worse to have to spend the evening alone, worse still to have to go to a depressing New Year's Eve party where everyone was getting sentimental and reflective about the year that was coming to an end. Far better to lose himself in the music than to get sucked into that whirlpool. Especially this year. After setting up, he cut through the bar to the kitchen to get something to eat.

"Get you anything, Mr. Voss?" the bartender said.

"Call me Jack," Voss said. "I can't afford to get smashed; keep me set up with club soda and lime. And let's see . . ." Voss looked at the array behind the bar. "A split of Moët at midnight."

"Gotcha covered, sir," the bartender said, slipping a split round of lime onto the rim of the glass containing Voss's drink. "I'll set one aside for you—we ran out at the party I worked last year. I think they did it on purpose. At eleven-thirty, when everyone wants a little champagne, all we had were magnums."

"That sounds about right," Voss said. "Thanks."

In the kitchen, he stopped to watch a sous chef making crepes—the man was working four small iron pans in rotation. He ladled batter into two of the black pans and placed them on the burners, then he flipped the crepes in the other two pans and set them back down to finish cooking: scrape, clank, scrape, clank. Moments later he picked them up again and flipped the crepes onto the stack, ladled batter into the hot pans, set them back on the stove and returned to the first two, which were now ready to be turned. A Zen master of crepe-making, Voss thought. Perfect focus, impeccable timing. And he had a rhythm going: the clatter of pan on stove, scrape of spatula, tap of ladle on the rim of the bowl of batter making percussive music, a groove. Voss felt an accompaniment forming in his fingers.

"Hey, I know you," a voice called from down the line.

Voss turned to look. "Swami. I thought you hated boats."

The chef smiled through his thick black beard. "Yeah, I hate boats, but I like to get paid. Just like you, right?"

"Yeah." Voss looked at Swami's face, older than the last time he'd seen him, a bit fuller, but no more careworn. "You look good, dude. The last time I saw you was when? When we recorded that Laughing Falcons album in Antigua. And then I heard you were cooking for the Dead. Is that right?"

"That was a big job, man," Swami said, his black eyes twinkling. "There are so many of them."

"So where you been?"

"After Jerry died, I toured with the Further Festival one time, but it wasn't the same, so I came back east. Had a little joint of my own for a while, but that wasn't really my scene, so I'm back to being a *ronin*. It's kind of cool, really. I travel a lot. Do private parties, high-level meetings, the occasional cruise—but no blue water. I have an agent, man. Like, who knew chefs had agents?"

"Well, I'd say it agrees with you."

"You don't look so bad yourself," Swami said. "So what's new in your life?"

Voss's face fell and he took a deep breath.

"Aw shit, Jack. I'm sorry, man. I forgot. I read about what happened. Shit, I know you don't want to talk about that." He came out from behind the line and put his hand on Voss's shoulder, awkward. The two men did not hug. "You must want something to eat before you have to get to work. I've got some beautiful tenderloins here. Let me fix you a . . . wait a minute . . . steak Diane, no, au poivre. I've got some wonderful green peppercorns, you still like that? Ten minutes. You want a salad?"

(♯)

Voss felt the boat rock gently as it moved away from the pier. He was in the middle of his opening set, mostly quiet, slow songs. Music as elegant as the gowns and dinner jackets worn by many of the patrons, and about as personal. But this wasn't a concert, he reminded himself. It wasn't a recital. He was just one of the help, like Swami and the sous chef with the black iron pans. His name might have been a draw, but the night and the city were the real show: fireworks reflected in black water, the glittering Manhattan skyline for background. The sound was loud enough for those who wanted to listen, quiet enough for the rest of them to talk without shouting. A few people had made an effort to sit close to him, and he made a point of playing to them, pitching his voice as he sang the restaurant song from that first solo album all those years ago, smiling at the chorus of mangled English transcriptions he and Avery had found on menus in Italy and Greece:

> I'll have the hole fish cake in salt,
> With frisky potatoes and aubergine
> Bring a bottle of frozen bieri
> And dark cherries in thrashed cream.

Later he would play "The Christmas Song" and eventually "Auld Lang Syne," but for now he was having fun, getting used to the truck-like Steinway, easing it into the turns at first, getting the feel of the pedals, adjusting the mirrors. It was going to be a long night. He was settling in for the ride.

CARMEL

It's like the drug culture. They made drugs illegal, so when you tried them, just smoked a joint, even, you crossed the line. Now you were an outlaw. There's other lines like that. You cross them they've got a name for you. Fuck one goat.

Voss stayed at Black Dome Zenji until the beginning of 1994, a little over a year. When he got back to Manhattan, The Last Straw had closed. He asked Bert if she could find him any session work, and she said she could get him all he wanted, but he'd have to go out to L.A. That was fine, but he wanted to see his daughter before he left. Negotiations took over a month, Mike Barker meeting several times with Avery's lawyer, Bert talking with Avery herself, who still would not speak with Voss. . . . Finally, with the help of a patient judge, they worked out a visitation plan.

Chance had just turned thirteen, and she was the image of Avery at that age. It was disconcerting, and Voss felt a sense of vertigo, falling through a swirl of years, when he first saw her step out of the front door of her mother's house in Montclair. For an instant he thought it *was* Avery and watched for his little girl to follow her out the door. But the door closed behind her. No one else came out.

"We've got two hours," Bert said. "I'll get in back."

And then he saw her green eyes, the eyes he saw in the mirror every morning. It was Chance coming slowly down the front walk. Voss was frozen. This was his daughter. The little girl who had sat on his lap banging the keys while he played the piano. He had imagined himself bending down to receive her into his arms, but she was nearly as tall as he was, and suddenly a hug seemed out of the question.

She stopped about two feet in front of him and reached out her hand. He took it with tears in his eyes, and they shook.

"I'm going to call you Jack," she said. "You look just like I remember you."

He fought back the tears. "And you look all grown up, Chance. It's good to see you."

She turned a little bit away from him. "Hi, Bert," she said.

"Hi, sweetheart," Bert said, from the backseat of the Mercedes convertible.

"So," Voss said. "You want to go for a ride?"

"Okay," she said.

Voss opened and closed the door for her, then got in and headed toward Verona. It had snowed lightly the night before, but a warm front had moved through, and the afternoon had warmed to an unseasonable seventy plus degrees. A May afternoon in the middle of February. Along the ridges of the Watchung Mountains the last bits of un-melted snow glistened in the bright sun, and the cloudless sky was the color of a faded pair of jeans. REM's "Night Swimming" gave way to Whitney Houston singing "I Will Always Love You," and Voss hit the seek button on the radio.

"Do you have any of your music?" Chance asked.

"I'm sorry," he said, as the radio cycled through the channels—classic rock, country, rap, talk. "I almost never listen to my own stuff." He caught the sound of an acoustic bass and hit the button again. A piano came in, warm but pained somehow.

"That's gotta be Bill Evans," he said. "How's that?"

Chance listened for a moment. "A little slow," she said, "but I guess it's okay." She hugged her arms around herself.

"I can put the top up, if you're cold," Voss said.

"No," Chance said. "I'm fine."

Voss didn't wait to hear if Bert was fine in the back. "Great," he said.

"How do you know the way around here?" Chance asked.

"I grew up around here," Voss said. "We used to drive up here all the time as soon as one of us had a car. Didn't your mother tell you?"

"She never talks about you."

"I guess I can understand that."

"She never says anything bad. Some of my friends' parents who are divorced are always saying stuff about each other."

"I guess that's hard on them," Voss said. "Your friends."

"It sucks," she said.

"Your mom's a good woman," Voss said. "And me, I've made some mistakes. But I'm trying to do better."

"So are you going to start coming around now?" Chance asked.

"I'll try. But I'm going to be leaving for California in a couple of days, so it might be a while."

"Another seven years?"

Voss felt his heart drop into his stomach. "No, kiddo," he said. "I'll do better than that."

"Don't call me kiddo," she said.

"Uh, guys," Bert said, "I'm freezing back here. Could you put up the top?"

(♯)

Voss didn't mind staying in hotels when he was working, but between jobs he hated it. He considered getting an apartment, but truth be told, he hated L.A. And he already had an apartment in New York. So one morning he rented a Jaguar and headed up the Pacific Coast Highway. When he got to Carmel, something spoke to him. After a short walk on the beach, he pulled up in front of a real estate agency in the center of town. "Hello," the woman behind the desk said with a knowing smile. "Do I call you Mr. Voss or just Voss like on the records."

"Call me Jack," he said.

"I'm Bridget. How can I help you?"

"I'm looking for a place. A house, I think. With a view of the ocean."

"What's your price range?" the woman asked.

"You know, I'll have to make a call and find out," he said. "I honestly have no idea."

"Help yourself," she said, pointing to the phone.

"It's New York."

"Don't worry about it," she said. "I think we can afford the call."

He talked to Mike Barker, who gave him a number. "Probably not a bad idea to put some of your money in real estate," he said.

"So," Bridget said when he told her what he could afford, "you want to buy or build?"

"Show me what's out there," Voss said.

"You're in a hurry, aren't you. Why don't you tell me what you need first. No point in wasting time on places that aren't going to work for you anyway. Do you entertain a lot? Do you need a music room? A recording studio?"

"A studio would be nice. Probably room for a couple of pianos—one for recording, one out in the living room. A room for my daughter when she gets old enough to come visit. Serious kitchen."

"I think we can find something," Bridget said.

It was the third place she showed him.

"Built in the sixties," Bridget said as they drove up the steep driveway to what looked like a set of interlocking boxes, redwood, glass, and gray stone. Except for the sharp lines and angles and the glass, it might have grown there. "Local architect, much loved, very modern, Japanese inspired, local materials, finest craftsmen. The former owners hated to leave, but they couldn't handle the stairs anymore. Almost had elevators installed, but it would have meant chopping up the lines and they couldn't bring themselves to do that."

They climbed the stone steps to the door of varnished redwood planks held in place with iron bolts. Bridget unlocked it and then stepped back. "Open it," she said.

He expected the door to be heavy, but it floated open at his first touch, silent, and closed and latched behind them more quietly and firmly than the door of the Jaguar outside.

"It has four bedrooms, all huge. One would probably make a perfect studio. There's also a library, living room and dining room, chef-designed kitchen. . . ."

"I want to see the view," Voss said.

"Of course," she said, opening the doors out onto the deck and letting in the sound of the sea on the rocks below.

"This is where I was meant to be," Voss said. "How soon can I move in?"

"Oh, I think your credit's good, Jack. You can move in today, if you like. Though I expect you'll want some furniture. A bed anyway."

Voss laughed. "A bed would be good."

January, February, March

Voss spent the first three months of the new year commuting regularly between Carmel and L.A. More session work than he'd had in a long time. Chance's death was last year's news now, but the appearance of Voss's name in the media during the previous fall had evidently reminded a few people that he was still around. Or so Voss imagined. A rap group that had been sampling some of his old organ riffs asked him to play on their new CD. A young singer-songwriter out of Nashville who was trying to cross over from country wanted Voss on piano. At many of the recording sessions he was the oldest musician in the room by ten or twenty years.

Then Kenny Claybourne invited him to do an all-blues record.

"I've got an old flatpicker from the Piedmont and a guy from Mississippi who plays slide," Kenny said. "I could get a honky-tonk piano player and it would work, but you could do the honky-tonk more like a quote, and the rest of it your usual tasteful stuff. I figure all acoustic on one side, with the piano, and electric, Chicago, you know, with a B-3 on the other. These guys have been playing their whole lives on junk, we put some vintage Martins and Gibsons in their hands, maybe an old National, they're gonna sound unbelievable."

The men were in their seventies, their hands gnarly, their voices raspy. They didn't do anything fast, but they knew their instruments and they knew the blues; they were always exactly where they needed to be. You could see and hear their respect for each other and the songs they were playing: no showboating, no competition. Voss felt humbled by them, privileged to be a part of the music they were making together.

APRIL

V oss had the radio tuned to a Sunday morning music show which played hour-long sets built around a theme, sometimes obvious, sometimes not. This hour, all the songs seemed to be about time, and the host—who had an extensive collection of twentieth century music sometimes going back to the '20s— had already played The Stones' "Time is on My Side," The Chambers Brothers' "Time," and The Byrds' version of "To Everything There is a Season." Now Sandy Denny's voice was making its way through the ether, she was back from the dead, as if she had known even in her earliest days what it was like to grow old. It wasn't really the words—Voss knew the lyrics of the song well—it was the music and her pure and stirring delivery. "Who knows where the time goes," she sang, and Voss thought it must be the saddest song ever written.

He had been back in Carmel for several weeks now, and had nothing scheduled for the next few months. He opened a bottle of Calistoga water and took another aspirin. He'd been drinking more than usual, there was no denying it, and he'd smoked more dope in the past three months than he had in the previous five or ten years. There had been coke around when he'd recorded with the rappers and the kid from Nashville, but he'd managed to resist it, and Kenny and his group were a pretty clean bunch. But no work to keep him occupied was bad; he knew that. Once already since being back in Carmel he'd been stopped cold by the sight of a girl in the supermarket who, as she reached up to get a roll of paper towels from a high shelf, was the image of Chance, and of Avery when she was young, the dark hair flowing down the long back, the beautiful shoulders and perfect posture.

He'd called Artie several times but had got no answer. Bert had nothing for him. He ran on the beach, watched old movies, played the Fazioli, and thought of Chance and asked himself why.

On Friday he put on his leather jacket and got into the Lancia and drove to The Cove. He hadn't played there since the night Bridge had met him, the beginning of their last weekend together. Yet he only thought of her for a moment while the boys were setting up. He thought instead of the time almost a year ago, when Chance and Fade had come to Carmel. They'd come to hear him play on their last night in town. Which, now that he thought of it, was the last time he'd seen his daughter alive. So many last things.

He began with "Autumn Leaves," which he had played for Chance that night, just as he had the first time she'd visited him out west, when he'd bought her the gray beret. As he played, he relived the memory, embroidered it, filled in the gaps with imagination. What had they said to each other while he was playing? Had they responded to the music? He found himself longing for a connection with Chance, but now it could only exist in memories that were as spare as his evolving piano arrangements. He remembered playing "Stardust" that night too, and Joe, the guitarist, had put a microphone in front of him to see if he might sing, which he almost never did at The Cove. That night he had . . . for her. It was all coming back.

Between sets he'd asked Chance if there was anything she really wanted to hear. There was. She'd recently found his records in the basement and suddenly remembered him playing one of the songs in Berlin when she was a little girl. "Avery's Song." He hadn't played it in twenty years. But again . . . for Chance. He was surprised at how good it sounded, making him feel better about his voice than he usually did, and he went from that into "My Funny Valentine" and "Just Friends."

What must Chance and Fade have thought of him that night? Singing these terribly sad songs in a breathy whisper, like Chet Baker in his last days, intimate and shattered, shy and desperate, broken, yet still alive, the voice a reflection of the face, ruined and yet painfully expressive.

He imagined Fade sitting there in shock.

"What happened to him?" Fade asks Chance.

"What do you mean? He got beat up in Berlin before I was born. They broke one of his hands."

"No, not that. Somebody broke more than his hand," Fade says. "That was the most broken-hearted singing I've heard in my life. He's like a ghost come back from the dead to tell you how he died, how much it hurt."

"It's not that bad," Chance says.

"I don't mean it's bad," Fade says. "It's good. It's amazing, really. But he breaks your heart. I mean, doesn't he do that to you?"

"I don't know," she says. "He's my dad. I don't hear him the way you do. And mostly I realize that he's not the same as he was when I was little. I just remember being a little kid and him playing the piano all the time. But he doesn't sound like that anymore. I don't know. I guess it would break my heart if I let it, but I can't. I can't let it. You know?"

Or maybe they didn't say anything like that, he thought. He began to play "Stardust." Joe pushed a microphone over towards him, but he shook his head and looked down at the keys.

The old Bang & Olufsen turntable was sitting on a side table when Voss got back to his house in Carmel, *The Enchanted Pond: a Rock Opera* still on the spindle. He took the record off the platter, flipped it over, and put it on the turntable that was hooked up to his system. The overture blared from the speakers, bombastic, Wagnerian. He sat down with the album cover in his hands. The cardboard showed through at the edges, and the bright picture on the front had faded, but the darker photo on the back was still clear: the boys in the studio with their equipment. He looked at the faces, Hal's with an arrogant smirk and a twinkle in his eye, stoned no doubt. Kenny the serious musician-scholar, his fingers spread across the fretboard of his white Strat. He was actually making a chord, Voss noted. George sat on his drum throne like a Renaissance courtier astride his mount, his long hair shining and his drumsticks crossed before him like a symbol of something. Rick sat off to the side with his Gibson on his knee; Bobby's man, Voss thought, he was never really one of the gang. Voss himself sat behind the B-3, his Vox to his left, and a Fender Rhodes behind him, so that his own instruments walled him off from the other guys. In the black and white photo, his hair looked like a helmet of polished ebony, his black beard the chinstrap. He was what, twenty-three? Twenty-four? The same age Chance had been when she'd died . . . with this music on the record player.

How did you reconcile something like that? Was it payback for the kids who had killed themselves years ago? Some karmic law making sure that he didn't get to be a happy, proud parent? The songs segued smoothly one into another, "The Enchanted Pond" light and airy, a fantasy of Arcadia, "I Was Just a Boy" almost tender. The side ended with "Touch Her and You're Dead," Hal's song even then, driving, hard, tough-talking but ultimately as sentimental as Hal had always been. Voss stood up to flip the record, steeling himself for what they'd jokingly called "The Suicide Suite" while they were recording it. But two or three bars into "Why Can't We Try Another Way" he lifted the tone arm and moved it aside. Maybe someday he'd be able to listen to this music again, but not tonight. He carried the record to his chair and picked up the jacket. But when he tried to slip it into the cover it would only go halfway. Something was blocking it. He set the record down and flexed the album cover open. Folded sheets of notepaper. He reached in and drew the pages out, set the album cover aside, and sat down to read the handwritten letter:

Dear Jack,

I remember when you didn't come home. Mom said you had to go away, that you were sick and had to go to the hospital and stay there for a long time. And then we moved back to New Jersey. I think she hoped I would forget you, but how could I forget my daddy, who used to play the piano and sing me songs when I was going to sleep? Remember when you got me a little keyboard, a plastic thing, and told me there was music inside it and it would come out if I pressed the keys just right? I could make notes come out of it, noise, sometimes a scale. But when you picked it up it was like magic: there really was music inside it, beautiful music. I wanted you to show me the button to push to make it sound like that, but you couldn't. You taught me to play Twinkle, Twinkle, Little Star, *and for years after you went away I would play it, alone in my room, when I was sure mom couldn't hear. It was like you were dead, but then I saw you on TV. I ran and got mom, and we sat and watched. You played the piano and sang a song and an interviewer asked you questions and I thought you were sad, even though you laughed a lot. I asked mom why you never came to see us, but she was already crying.*

For a long time after that I thought you were a bad person. Then mom met Dr. Sheridan and she was happier and after a while they got married and he became my dad and we were like a regular family.

Then you did come to see us. And you cried when you saw me, but mom wouldn't even come out to talk to you.

You acted shy and sad around me, but I wouldn't let myself get mad at you because I wanted you to love me again. I could see why you wouldn't want to get back together with mom. But I dreamed that you would ask me to come to live with you. You would take me places with you, and I would get to meet famous people. It's embarrassing now, but when I was twelve that's what I wanted. By the time I got to be sixteen, I realized that wasn't going to happen. You would always say you were going to call, but then months would go by, so I made myself stop wanting it. Fuck those famous people, anyway, I thought.

But then sometimes I would hear your music it made me want to see you all over again. I looked you up in the library and read all your interviews. The interviewers never asked you about your private life—maybe you didn't let them. Only once, when somebody was asking about The Enchanted Pond *you said something that seemed to explain why you never came to see me. You said it was like Romeo and Juliet. I still remember your exact words: "They have to die. Because in real life love doesn't last. So they die at the high point of their love, and it's beautiful. But if they lived what would there be? Romeo busting his hump in a produce stand on a dirty Verona street, Juliet at home with a couple of screaming brats." So that's why you left, I thought. I was the screaming brat. You'll never know how much that hurt. So why did I make a copy of the interview and keep it with me?*

And I read about how a bunch of kids killed themselves because of your record and I didn't understand that at all.

And then that summer you came and took me backstage at your concert in New York, I think that was the happiest night of my life. Or the happiest night of my life as a girl. And in a way that made it possible for me to become a woman.

I never had any boyfriends in school. Just Neil, and he was always gay. I mean, he thinks he's bi, but we tried to be lovers because we were both so lonely, and it never really worked. He was sweet, but he couldn't really stay interested. (I could never talk to mom about this, or the good Dr., but it seems like I should tell somebody and you're like the only one.) So Neil and I were just friends, kind of like outcasts. He was the only boy I trusted enough to love, and he was the only boy who couldn't love me back in the way I wanted. We used to joke that we just needed to find a guy we could both love, and we would sit in the bleachers and talk about boys who might be nice to sleep with. Other boys came around, but I didn't want anything to do with them. But after you were in my life again, I thought maybe I could trust someone again, and that was when Neil found Fade. He met him in his design class at Steven's and brought him around to meet me.

The writing stopped about halfway down the page. But there was another page behind it, the writing larger, not as neat, but in the same hand. It appeared to have been written in fits and starts, perhaps at different times:

Neil and Fade don't know I'm writing this. They want our deaths to be a mystery.

I can't talk about what we're going to do. I've been working on this letter to you for a long time. I wrote the first part in my head a long time before I put it down on paper. But now we've come to this place. And if we keep going it's going to be a lot worse than Romeo and the produce stand.

We're going to make sure nobody ends up like that girl in a coma. It's like we're on a train and nobody can stop it.

I love you, Daddy.

Chance

MAY

"You got the statements from Chance's Visa?" Voss asked Larry Finn, his accountant.

"Sure, I got everything, Jack. Unless you pay cash, I end up with a record of it. Tax purposes. Whatever."

"I want everything you got on her from, I don't know, from when she was here last. March, April '04."

"Yeah, no problem. But what for?"

"I don't know. I want to see where she went. What she did . . . What she paid for, anyway."

He pressed a button on his desk. "Jane, would you bring me the Voss file? Thanks."

This always irked Voss. He wasn't a walk-in for Christ's sake, he'd made an appointment. Why wouldn't his accountant have the file on his desk when Voss came in? Because he liked the theater of asking his assistant for it.

The door opened and Jane came in with an accordion folder that she must have had waiting. "Here's this year," she said. "You need to go back further?"

Larry looked at Voss. "Last March, did you say?"

"Yeah." Voss turned to Jane. "If you don't mind."

"Two minutes," Jane said.

After she had come back with the right file, Larry took out a summary sheet. "Here's the Hoboken apartment: rent, which included heat and water, electricity, phone; and here's the charge card. The rest she did herself or else her mother."

"So you've got the phone records?"

"Not local," Larry said. "But long distance. Here's a call to Carmel, that's your number, right?"

"Yeah," Voss said. "I'll want those. And show me the charge card thing."

Larry handed him a Visa statement from January of the year before.

"What are these different dates? How do you read these things?"

"Never took care of the finances, did you, Jack?"

"Not since I was in college," Voss said. "By the time I had a charge card Avery was taking care of all the money."

"Lucky for you. . . . So here's the date of the transaction, and here's the date that it hit the bank. You want to know where she was on a given day, you just look at the first one. The day it gets processed in the bank doesn't matter."

"And what's this?"

"Cash withdrawal. We had a limit on the card. Worked it out with Avery back at the beginning—she didn't want Chance just having all the money she wanted any time. The card was supposed to be for emergencies. Two hundred dollars a pop. Five hundred a month max."

"Even for the trip?"

"Yeah, but it only applied to cash, she could buy whatever she wanted—food, gas, hotel rooms, whatever. . . . The total limit in the card was, let me look . . . five thousand."

"She could have bought a car," Voss said.

"A used car, I guess. You can't buy a new car for five thousand anymore."

"Not even a Fiat? An old friend of mine used to have a Fiat; I think it cost three thousand."

"When's the last time you saw a Fiat in the States, Jack? You're living in the past, my friend."

When Voss left he had a manila envelope full of copies of Chance's Visa statements and her long-distance bills from the last six months of her life. He still wasn't sure what he wanted them for, but he had them.

JUNE

North of San Francisco Voss started to get used to the car, a Mercury Sable with automatic everything, not his style at all, but his mechanic had convinced him not to take the Lancia. "Get something that don't call attention to itself," he advised.

On the seat next to him was a road atlas and a map of the U.S. and Canada, with Chance's charges and ATM withdrawals marked in red. He didn't know just what he hoped to learn by following her financial tracks, but he didn't know what else to do. He thought of Robert Mitchum in *Out of the Past*. "I just followed that ninety pounds of excess baggage to Mexico City." Of course, Mitchum was looking for a living girl. Voss was tracing the movements of a dead girl, his own daughter.

They'd gassed up Fade's van in Carmel the morning after they'd come to hear him play at The Cove. He'd seen them off, advising them on their choices of speed or scenery. They were going for scenery as best he could recall, and followed the route he'd recommended at the time: the coastal road through Monterey and Santa Cruz, up past Half Moon Bay and into the city, Golden Gate Bridge to Sausalito, and on up Highway 1. He followed the same route, point for point along rolling, feminine hills, plump and covered with soft grass. At Rockport the road turned inland for a while, rising up into sharp pine forests, the bones of the landscape beginning to show, coming back out to the coast at Eureka. Then a loose string of little beach towns where everything was made of weathered gray boards. The coast grew more rugged as he passed into Oregon. Great rocks stood in the surf like broken planets fallen from the sky, the low ones refuges for sea lions, the high rookeries for murres and guillemots, gulls, and the occasional puffin. Voss scanned them through a heavy scope bolted to the wooden platform of a scenic lookout, identifying each by its likeness in the poster provided by the state wildlife commission. He had lunch at The Seaview Café where Chance had spent $17.42 almost exactly a year before. The girl who waited on him was probably about Chance's age and had only worked there for a few months. "Everybody's new," she said. "New owners redid the place over the winter. All they kept was the name."

It had been difficult to put the question, to make himself ask a total stranger about his own daughter and her friends. That the girl knew nothing was a relief in a way, turning the asking into a kind of rehearsal for the time when someone would actually have something to tell him. He didn't know what he would do then.

He had the yearbook shot and the pictures Avery had sent him, and at the Windy Point Motel he took out the one of Chance, Fade, and Neil leaning against the van and showed it around in the lobby and the restaurant, but nobody remembered them. The next day they'd evidently met Neil at the Portland airport. Chance picked up two hundred at an ATM there, and they ran up a bill of $32.91 at one of the airport snack bars. Voss ate lunch there too, and though he expected nothing—so many people pass through airports—he made himself show the pictures to the girl who waited on him and the woman at the register. The next charge was two days later, in Seattle. That probably meant they had camped in the van, and Voss had marked his map with possible state parks and camping areas where they might have stayed.

He spent the night in a hotel just outside of Mount St. Helens National Park, having taken a drive up to see the devastation left by the eruption several years back. When he picked up a brochure at the park entrance, he was shocked to see that it had been twenty-five years. He remembered seeing the images on German television, the whole top of the mountain disappearing, the great plume of smoke and ash. *Vulkan ausbricht im Nordwesten USA.* Chance hadn't even been born. The earth had recovered, and fields of wildflowers spread out before him where he'd expected to see a wasteland.

In retracing Chance, Fade, and Neil's steps, he was doing what he remembered friends doing in the '70s, making the fabled trip out west in a van, something he'd never done before, he thought. Then he thought of the first Vossimilitude tour, Avery and Hal and the boys in the bus, the truck full of gear. Asbury Park, Philadelphia, Pittsburgh, Columbus, Indianapolis, St. Louis, Kansas City, Denver, Albuquerque, Phoenix, San Diego, L.A., San Francisco, Seattle.... For the first time, he realized that the route marked on the map in his hotel room corresponded to his own travels thirty years before, at least part of it did. San Francisco, Seattle, Calgary, Winnipeg. From there it diverged again. The Vossimilitude tour had gone from Winnipeg to Chicago; Chance, Fade, and Neil had stayed in Canada, reentering the U.S. in Buffalo. That he knew from Lt. O'Beirne. But they hadn't spent any money in Buffalo, or in nearby Niagara Falls, which surprised Voss. Maybe they'd just been in a hurry to get home by then.

In Seattle, someone recognized them. Actually he recognized the van first. "Almost like from the '70s," he said, looking at the picture. He worked behind the counter at a Tire and Lube about a mile from the motel where they'd stayed. They'd apparently had a flat sometime after they left Portland. "We fixed the tire and changed it out with the spare," the man said. "The three of them sat right here watching the TV for an hour. Very quiet. Polite. I remember they asked me if they could have a cup of coffee, like they didn't know it was for the customers. Did something happen to them? Are they in some kind of trouble?"

Voss had no ready response. The effort required to make himself show the pictures and ask his question had been so great that he had never considered the questions he might be asked in return. "No," he lied. "It's ... it's a family matter. Thanks. Thanks a lot."

He went out to his car where he suddenly found himself weeping. How was he going to do this? What was he looking for? Would he know when he found it? And having found it, whatever it was, what was he going to do with it? He wasn't a detective. He had no one to report to. Was he just torturing himself? He thought of Chance, Fade, and Neil sitting in the waiting room watching the television on the wall. It had been tuned to some kind of daytime talk show while he was there. They were so young. So innocent. They didn't even know that the coffee urn in the waiting area was for them. Polite, the clerk had said about the way they asked if it was okay to have a cup. And they were getting something fixed that a lot of kids would have let go. Repairing the spare. Responsible. Cautious. Smarter than he would have been at that age, he thought. How could this have ended where it had?

They evidently headed right out of town, because the next charge, the same day, was for gas just outside of Spokane, three hundred fifty miles east. Voss stopped at a Borders, where he bought a stack of CDs, then he got on I-90 and climbed into the Cascades, the snowcap of Mount Rainier coming into and passing out of view through the first hour, then dropping behind his right shoulder as he descended into Yakima and the Columbia River basin. Between mountain ranges he set the cruise control and listened to Neil Young and Crazy Horse, Neil's famous guitar, Old Black, making its trademark "jet engine in a thunderstorm" sound. He wondered what music Chance, Fade, and Neil would have listened to. What they had thought of this beautiful green country? Crossing the river north of Hanford he considered the things he'd heard Chance say over the years about the destruction of the environment. He wondered if they'd talked about the notorious nuclear facility. *I don't know how your generation can believe in anything*, he'd said to Chance on that last phone call. *Maybe we don't*, she'd said.

At the filling station outside of Spokane the wind was whipping down from the north, feeling more like February or March than early June. Voss showed his photographs to the pump attendant, a lean man in thick Carhartt overalls stationed in a booth on the island. The man shook his head. The heavyset woman behind the counter in the attached convenience store didn't remember them either.

"One of them yours?" She was probably about Voss's age, somebody's mother, he thought.

"The girl," he said.

"She run off?"

"No. It's a long story."

"I'm sorry," the woman said. "I don't mean to pry."

"It's all right. Is there a campground around here, say within an hour or so?"

"Which way you going?"

"Oh, right. I'm heading east. Idaho, Montana."

She told him of two places, and he dutifully stopped at each one, talking to the managers and driving around the serpentine roadways through the campsites. The season hadn't really started yet, and most of the sites were empty or occupied by RVs buttoned up against the cold, generators grinding away. He passed a big man grilling steaks under a striped awning and a young couple struggling to put up their tent in the wind. It was getting easier to show the pictures and ask his questions. He had conquered some of the awkwardness he felt at going up to total strangers. But each time he received a negative response, the whole idea of it seemed more absurd, futile. Still, he made himself keep going.

He stopped that night at a Ramada Inn outside Coeur d'Alene, getting dinner from the McDonald's on the other side of the strip, and watching *Now, Voyager* on the old movie channel. He'd seen it before, but he stayed with it until the first time Paul Heinreid lights two cigarettes at once and hands one to Bette Davis.

The next day, Voss showed his pictures around in Missoula, first in a downtown bar and then in a Western-wear shop.

"I remember them," said the portly man in white Western shirt and string tie in the boot department. "She bought a pair of Tony Lamas. This one tried to talk her into the red ones, but in the end she bought the black." He had pointed to Neil.

"Remember anything else about them? How they were acting?"

"They were just real nice, you know? Like they were having a good old time the way young people sometimes do, laughing and smiling. Not a care in the world. That one . . ." he pointed again to Neil, ". . . tried on two or three leather jackets. A couple of hats. Kind of clowning around. Didn't buy any, though."

"How about this one?" Voss asked, pointing to Fade.

"He was the quiet one of the three. Smiled and laughed with the other two, but didn't say much. I remember thinking that he was just a friend and the other two were a couple, but when they went out it was him and her was arm in arm and the skinny one was number three. Why all the questions?"

Something about the man caught Voss off guard, and he surprised himself by answering. "The girl was my daughter. She died last summer."

"I'm sorry, sir," said the salesman. "Accident?"

It was as if he couldn't keep silent. "Suicide. The three of them. Or it was supposed to be all three. This one didn't go through with it."

"You want to sit down for a minute? I could get you a glass of water."

"That's all right. I'm sorry. I'm all right. It's just that . . . it's not that often I say it out loud, you know?"

"Here. Sit down a minute. Chair's empty. Let me get you a glass of water."

Voss sat down in the chair, the shoe salesman's stool with its rubbered footstand in front of him. He looked around at the boots, the hats on shelves across the store, a glass display case with belt buckles and spurs, folding knives and silver jewelry. Chance, Fade, and Neil had been in this store, goofing around and laughing. He pictured Chance, perhaps in this very chair, trying on cowboy boots. They'd been remembered as cheerful, happy. The salesman returned with a glass of water. Voss thanked him and drank it.

"They seemed like nice kids."

"They were," Voss said.

(#)

"Road's only open to the Lodge," the ranger said, as Voss paid the entrance fee to Glacier National Park.

"When's it open the rest of the way?"

"A week, ten days."

"They got rooms at the Lodge?"

"Should have."

It hadn't occurred to Voss that the road they took north would be closed in June, though he had rarely been out of sight of snowcapped mountains for the last three days, and he'd been climbing since he'd left Missoula. As he drove along the edge of Lake McDonald he could see white shelves of ice leading out to the deep blue of the open water. The wind whistled at his windows, and he had to pay close attention for slick patches in the road, especially on the down-slopes, where it would be difficult or impossible to stop if he lost traction.

"They're plowing," he was told by the guy who checked him into the Lodge. "It'll be open in a couple of days. You can be one of the first to go through."

"Guess so," Voss said.

There was an old Yamaha concert grand in the lobby next to the bar, and Voss felt drawn to it as soon as he saw it. He hadn't touched a piano in weeks, and after he'd checked in and eaten lunch, he asked the girl at the counter if anybody played it.

"Piano bar, six to twelve," she said, pointing to a black and white poster on an easel. "Young guy. He's really good."

It was a little after three. Voss went over, pulled out the bench, sat down, and opened the keyboard. His left hand formed an A minor 7 chord. The action was a bit clunky, but the tone was rich and full. He played more sevenths: D, G, C. Just getting the feel of the instrument. Once again he was thankful that his left hand still worked on the keyboard, though he could not roll his fingers into a fist. He began picking out the notes to "Autumn Leaves" with his right hand. Slow. Warming up. But already connecting with the piano, feeling through it, expressing his private pain in this most public yet anonymous of places, but softly. He felt no urge to show off, no need for keyboard pyrotechnics, just the quiet search for the bluest jazz he could build around the song he had played for Chance. The world contracted to just him and the piano, and when he brought the song to its end he looked around, almost surprised to find himself in this place with its views of tall pines and snow-capped mountains. The bartender, a lanky man with a weathered face and a gray handlebar moustache, gave him a nod and a smile.

"Can I get you anything?" he asked.

"Club soda and lime," Voss said, pushing the bench back to stand up.

"I'll bring it," the bartender said. "Perrier all right? It's on the house if you play another one like that."

"Thanks," Voss said, sitting back down. He played Cole Porter's "Love for Sale," again slowly, all pathos.

"I know who you are," the bartender said, setting the drink down on a side table within Voss's reach. "You're that guy from that band in the old days. Vortex or Vertical or what was it?"

"Vossimilitude," Voss said. "Probably not the most memorable name ever."

"You guys were good, though. Man, I remember, what was the one, 'Touch Her and You're Dead.'"

"That was us," Voss said. "The first time anyway. It's been covered a few times, too."

"Mutually Assured Destruction, right? Hal Proteus. I remember when he died. And there was the other guy with him, the guy who lived."

"That would be me," Voss said. "That would be me."

Voss watched the light change through the tall lobby windows. As he got more used to the action of the piano, he came to appreciate its sound more, too. By five, he had left the American songbook behind and was just riffing along, drifting around the minor keys, running through his inventory of chord work with his left hand, letting his right hand dance off on its own. He knew he was playing well; he had always known when he was playing well and when he was not, even when he was high. That was one of the gifts he had—to know, even when high. He had played with plenty of people over the years who didn't have that insight into their own playing, who would get smashed and think they sounded great. And they did, sometimes. Some of them even sounded better—you weren't supposed to admit that nowadays. Hal probably played better high. But most players didn't.

The regular piano player showed up at about a quarter to six—his tuxedo left no doubt what he was there for. He recognized Voss, and sat in a nearby chair where he could watch his hands. Voss moved into E flat major. He was suddenly thinking of Dave Brubeck and Paul Desmond, and he started introducing Harold Arlen's chords. It would be a long tease, just as their version was, hinting at the melody, but never playing it outright until the end. The bar had begun to fill up, the noise level was much higher, and people were gathered on sofas and chairs around the piano. What was it we wanted out there above the chimney tops? What did those bluebirds have access to that we didn't? The song was always sad—Judy Garland capturing that sadness even when she was a girl, and nearly dying of it later when she would sing it as a tortured, tragic wreck. Voss didn't presume to know the song's secrets; perhaps they were different for everyone, but it was about longing for someplace we couldn't go. And for Voss right now, that was the past, the time before he'd lost his daughter, the time when it might have still been possible to actually be a father to her, to love her properly. His right hand played the little bluebird bit from the bridge: if happy little bluebirds fly . . . why oh why. . . . And then he slipped into the verse for the first and only time, soaring, thinking more of Paul Desmond's sax than Brubeck's piano, and aching, doing his best to make the piano wail: *somewhere over the rainbow.* He was working hard, playing loud, and the crowd had grown quiet. The music echoed from the tall glass windows as he brought it home. And then, it was over. Voss leaned back, slid the bench out, and stood up. People began applauding. The regular pianist came up and shook Voss's hand. "That was awesome," he said. "I never heard anyone play it that way."

"Check out Dave Brubeck and Paul Desmond," Voss said. "I don't remember which album."

Back upstairs, he ordered room service and flipped on the old movie channel. He caught the middle part of *To Have and Have Not*, staying awake just long enough to hear Hoagy Carmichael sing "Hong Kong Blues."

♮

He waited for the road to be opened, going out during the days to look around the campgrounds that were accessible, showing the pictures to rangers he met on the road. No one recognized the van or Chance and the boys. In the late afternoon he would play the piano in the lobby, and at night he would watch movies. One night at about two a.m., after falling asleep during *Ball of Fire*, in which Gene Krupa plays a drum solo on a book of matches, he sat up, turned the light on, and began to write a lyric:

> It's a black & white world in old movies
> I'm an ex-cop turned private dick
> There's a bottle of rye in the desk drawer
> A hat on my head and a gun on my hip
>
> And Hoagy plays the piano
> Bird comes in on the sax
> Gene scuffs a beat on the drum kit
> And I'd like to have some more facts

The next morning the clerk told him the road would be opening at ten.

The fierce sun glared off the glaciers and snowcapped peaks as he climbed the Going-to-the-Sun Road to Logan Pass. He took his time, pulling over frequently to take in the views. He couldn't remember what route the Vossimilitude tour bus had taken all those years ago, but it couldn't have been this one. He would certainly have remembered. At Bird Woman Falls Overlook an elderly couple showed him three mountain goats through their binoculars, black horns and hooves sharply defined against shaggy white fur. At Big Bend the wind ripped through his clothes as he squinted out into impossible vistas, the blue world falling away from him in all directions. At Two Dog Flats he had to stop for crossing elk. And each thing he saw as if with two sets of eyes, his own, and the imagined eyes of his daughter a year before.

By late afternoon he had crossed over into Canada, and the sun passed behind the mountains to his left an hour before he reached Fort McCloud, where he stayed at a small motel outside of town.

He spread his map out on the table in his room, studying it along with the Visa statement. He would reach Calgary tomorrow. Something had happened there. Chance, Fade, and Neil stayed three nights in the same hotel, but they had checked out and back in each day, charging three separate rooms to the card. They had hit the ATM two days in a row, taking out all that was left of the month's five hundred dollar allotment. Had they intended to leave town each day and then changed their minds over lunch? He tried to put himself in their place. They had crossed the border. They had had pot with them in Carmel. Had they smoked up the last of it in Glacier so they wouldn't be holding when they went through customs? Were they trying to replace their stash? Was it something else? He read Chance's letter again. *We've come to this place*, she'd written. *And if we keep going it's going to be a lot worse than Romeo at the produce stand.*

(#)

The woman behind the counter recognized Voss even before he handed her his credit card.

"Voss?" she said.

He nodded and raised one eyebrow: his yeah-it's-me-for-better-or-worse face.

She checked him in, gave him his key, and showed him how to find his room. He almost turned and went directly there, but then he reached into his jacket pocket and took out the photos and Visa statements.

"Would you mind looking at a couple of pictures . . . Toni?" he asked, reading the nameplate pinned to her blouse. "These people, they stayed here last year, right about this time. . . ." He consulted the papers in his hand. "June twenty-fifth to twenty-seventh. You don't remember them, by any chance?"

She looked at the studio photo of the beautiful girl and then at the timer-shot of the same girl with two boys leaning against a van. "It's your daughter, isn't it?" she said.

"Yes, it is. Do you remember her?"

"Only from when I saw that picture in a magazine." She pointed to the yearbook shot. "I don't remember her or the others from here. I'm sorry. I might have been doing up rooms when they checked in and out."

"It's okay." He took the photos back and glanced down again at the credit card statement. It was worn now, frayed, folded and unfolded many times. "Can you tell me how to find The Red Rooster?"

"Get back on the highway and go east to the next exit. Then south for about a mile, and you'll see it on the left—there's a big signboard shaped like a rooster. You can't miss it."

"Good place?" he asked.

"Great place," she said. "Best place around for a hundred miles, if you ask me. Get the ribs and stick around for the music. They go there last year?"

"Looks like," he said. "When's the music start?"

(♯)

"Can I have that table over there in the corner?" Voss asked the young woman who met him as he entered the bar. The place was almost empty.

"How about that one?" she said, pointing to a table right in front of a set of risers and a drum kit.

"I'd rather be a little further away from the speakers," Voss said. "If it's all right."

She seated him at the table he had originally pointed out.

"My name's Amanda," she said. "Can I get you something to drink?"

He ordered a draft beer, and when it came he ordered a half-rack of ribs. As he ate, he watched the guys in the band set up their gear. It took him back to his early days with The Featherweights. Too young to know how to be

part of a business, too hooked on the music not to try. An older guy was setting up the sound system, the latest Bose gear, with a mixing board, mikes
for the drums, monitors and mikes for all the band members. Nobody was
helping him. Until Voss saw him setting up his bass, he thought he might be
their manager or a paid techie. The rest of the band was mostly hanging out
around the bar, talking and smoking cigarettes. They kept looking toward
Voss's table, but nobody came over, so it was obvious they knew who he was.

The woman from the motel came in at about ten o'clock. She had recognized him earlier even in his casual driving clothes, worn jeans, old golf
shirt, moccasins. Now, dressed in black jeans, soft leather boots, and a gray
silk shirt, he supposed he looked more like himself.

She came right to his table.

"I see you took my advice," she said. "I think you'll like these guys."

"I'm sorry," he said. "I remember you from the motel, but I'm not real
good with names."

"Toni," she said.

"You were right about the ribs." He could see that she was waiting for
him to invite her to join him, but he wasn't sure he wanted company. He
saw her shift her feet and take a breath, then before she excused herself he
decided what the hell. "Let me buy you a drink," he said. "And you can
fill me in on the band. I sense some tension." He reached across the table,
grabbed his leather jacket off the chair and hung it on his own.

"What I didn't tell you is it's my little brother's band? He got all the talent in the family. And the other guys are great, too." She laughed as she sat
down. "But you're right about the tension."

Voss signaled Amanda, and she came over to take the order.

"You know who this is, Amanda? The famous Voss. Vossimilitude," Toni
said.

"Bull told me," Amanda said. "I'm sorry. I don't really know your stuff."

"That's okay," Voss said. "Toni showed her age by recognizing me."

"That's not very nice," Toni said.

Voss grinned. "Okay, then you must be one of those people who like
retro, old vinyl, like that." She was dressed in faded denim, cowgirl hippie-
chick. "You probably listen to James Taylor and early Eagles."

"And what if I do?"

"All right," Voss said. "Sorry if I offended. And please, call me Jack." He turned to Amanda who was standing there with her drink tray. "You better get her a drink fast before I get myself in more trouble."

"What can I bring you?"

Toni ordered a margarita and Voss asked for another beer.

"So, what tipped you off that the band had issues?" Toni asked when the drinks arrived.

"I look up there and I see an older guy with about five thousand dollars worth of the latest sound equipment and a bunch of young guys with beat-up gear, I know somebody's not on the same page as the rest of the band."

"Brock runs the local music shop," Toni said. "He's done a lot for these guys. They probably do take him for granted a bit."

"Every band has a story," Voss said. "Tell me theirs."

The band was called NorthSouth, the name being about the only thing that didn't change every few months. Jesse, Toni's brother, wrote most of the songs and played rhythm on a beat-up Washburn guitar. He picked up his first drummer and lead guitar player at an open mike night. That configuration, augmented a couple weeks later by Brock on bass and a high school kid on an electric piano, developed a local following and cut a CD before dissolving in a flurry of cancelled practices, half-staffed gigs, and recriminations over who paid for the studio time, and who never ponied up. Jesse didn't let that kind of thing bother him. He would play with half the band, with one accompanist, or alone. It was all the same to him. He had enough material for any gig. Tonight was a sort of reunion of the original band, minus the lead guitar player, who didn't answer anybody's calls. Rumor had it he'd been busted and sold his guitars to cover legal expenses, but nobody seemed to have any firsthand information. Brock, who had fronted most of the money for the CD and later quit the band for a while, was back. Though honestly, Toni didn't know how long he'd last.

The band members had wandered casually over to the stage, actually just one layer of risers, and were picking up their instruments, tuning up guitars, checking sound levels. Jesse called them together in a circle, no doubt finalizing the set list.

They opened with a blues in E. Standard stuff, Voss thought, but he liked the lyric:

North of the plains, south of the ice,
But too far north for you
I brought you home and paid the price,
You missed the warm sun didn't you?

This was my fine and private place,
I brought you here to share it.
You had enough and went away,
And didn't even shut the door—

The wind blows cold across the plains
And blows in through the open door.
In winter snow in summer rain
It blows in through the open door.

"Your brother writes the songs?" Voss asked Toni.

"Yeah," she said.

"And the music?"

"That, too," she said.

"Would these guys have been playing here a year ago?"

Toni tilted her head. Voss couldn't tell if she hadn't heard him over the music or if she didn't know what to make of the question.

"This time last summer," he shouted. "Would your brother's band have been playing?"

"Maybe," she said. "I think so. They just finished their CD and were selling it around this time. That's when your daughter and her friends were here, right?"

"Yeah."

Toni waited for him to elaborate, but he just sat there. "I don't know what it is you are looking for here," she said, "but you're going to have to give me a little more to go on—you're playing like a detective or something. Like in an old movie. Investigating a murder."

The band had ended the song, and her last words seemed to echo in the sudden quiet.

He felt himself shrink, as if the air had gone out of him.

"I'm sorry," she said. "I shouldn't have said that. I read about your daughter."

Jesse leaned into the mike: "This one's called 'Cougar on the Prowl.' It's dedicated to . . . well, you know who you are." He counted off, and the bass player started pounding out a driving rhythm. He wasn't Hal Proteus, but he wasn't bad.

Voss leaned across the table to be heard. "Forget it," he said. "The truth is I don't know what I'm doing. My daughter and her two friends were here last summer. I have it on her credit card statement. I'm just trying to see . . . where they went, what they did. But I don't know how to ask the questions."

"You have the pictures with you that you showed me before?"

"Yeah."

"Let me see them."

He reached for his jacket, took an envelope out of the inside pocket, opened it. Toni looked at the photographs again. "She was beautiful, your daughter," she said. "The yearbook picture doesn't do her justice, but this one . . ." She held out the group photo—Chance's arms around the two young men, all three of them laughing ". . . She's got a glow."

Voss handed her another picture he hadn't shown her earlier, just Chance sitting at a table in an outdoor café, the background a cold drizzly sky, dark hair under a jaunty gray beret, bright eyes, gypsy scarves, and a serious look.

"Wow," Toni said. She gathered the photos in her hand. "Let me show these to Amanda and Bull. Bull is amazing at remembering people." She got up and walked to the bar.

Bull, the owner of The Red Rooster, remembered them, and he came over to Voss's table. "They were here a couple of nights in a row," he said. "Let me think."

"Whatever you can recall," Voss said, almost broken again.

"These two," Bull said. "The dark guy and the girl. They were all over each other. In love, in lust . . ."

Toni shot him a look.

"Not sloppy or crude or anything," Bull said. "Sweet, you know. They were happy."

"And the other guy?" Voss asked, not sure he wanted to know.

"He's not so clear. I remember thinking they were a strange trio. Gay guy, I'd say, though I've been known to be wrong about that. He wasn't a flamer, and he seemed tighter with the girl than the other guy."

"They'd been friends since they were kids," Voss said.

"That makes sense."

"Can you remember anything else?" Voss asked, unfolding the credit card statement. "They spent a lot of money on the Friday night, barely half as much on the Saturday."

"Drinks," Bull said. "That first night they came in, they were really knocking them back. Pitchers of margaritas. I think they bought a round for the band, too. The next night they were a little shaky, took it a lot easier. Except for this one." He pointed to Fade. "He started slow, but then he had a couple of shots of tequila. It didn't seem to faze him, though. But something was different. I don't know." He looked around the room, checking the door, the bar, the service window where Amanda was standing waiting for somebody's order. "Like I told you, the first night these two couldn't keep their hands off one another. The second night he was all closed up, arms folded across his chest, legs crossed in front of him, you know. You learn to read people in this business. This guy was happy one night, but he was not happy the next. This is the end of the set." He gestured toward the band. "I gotta get back behind the bar."

Voss felt himself drawn to and recoiling from the next step. Something had happened, maybe it was just the ordinary push and pull of a relationship; maybe it was the turning point, the moment when something found its way into the organism that would eventually destroy it. A bacterium, a virus, a poison. How much did he want to know? How much could he bear to know?

"Let's show the picture to the guys in the band," Toni said. "Maybe they remember something."

Voss doubted it. Unless something really went haywire in the audience, you didn't remember the folks out in front.

The boys were back in the alley next to the dumpster, passing a joint around. The rich scent of the marijuana competed with the sour vinegar smell of fermenting soft drinks and garbage.

Jesse handed the joint to Toni, who held it out to Voss. "Or don't you do that kind of stuff anymore?"

"No," he said. "I'll take a hit. Thanks."

"So?" Jesse said to Voss, "You scouting? Looking for talent?"

Toni answered for him. "He's not here about that. He's in a whole 'nother place."

"Sorry," Voss said.

"That's okay," Jesse said. "I figured. Brock'll be bummed."

Toni looked around. "Where is he?"

"At the bar."

"So what are you here for?" the piano player asked, passing the joint to Toni again.

"This," she said, handing him the photos. "It's his daughter that died in that suicide thing last year. She was here last summer."

"I know it's a long shot," Voss said. "But if you recognize them. . . ."

"They were here," the drummer said. "Buying drinks, looking to score."

"Score what?"

"Just about anything, I'd say. I think Smitty hooked them up with some coke."

"Smitty doesn't sell to strangers," Toni said. "He's scared to death of cops."

"You ever see twenty-year-old cops in a traveling three-way?"

"What?"

"Ask anybody," Billy said, passing the photo to the others in the circle. "I'm going back inside and get a drink."

The rest of the boys looked at the photos. "Oh, yeah," the piano player said. "I remember watching them dance. It was weird, man. The girl, it was like she was into both guys. The gay one. . . ."

"You don't know he was gay," Toni said.

"Gimme a break," the piano player said. "Everybody knew he was gay, and he was hot for the straight guy. Remember them out on the dance floor?"

Voss listened, detached, as if he was hearing a story that had nothing to do with him. When they got back to the table, Toni seemed embarrassed by the casual way the boys had talked about Chance. When the guys were ready to go back inside, she held on to the photos. "There's one more guy I want to talk to," she said, "but it's better if you don't come."

Back at his table he ordered another draft. The band was going over their list for the second set. Jesse was tuning his guitar and the bass player was fiddling with the mixing board.

Toni came back in through the front door and joined Voss again. "What did you know about her relationship with the guys?" she asked.

"They visited me in California before they headed north," Voss said. "Chance and Fade were in love. Neil wasn't with them, but I've known him for a long time. He was Chance's best friend. I guess he was as close to her as a gay guy can be to a girl. Closer than a straight guy can be, for all I know. I don't know what he thought of Fade. I expect he was protective of Chance; they'd known each other since grade school."

"People who saw them say they were closer than that," Toni said. "Is that something you want to know about?"

"I honestly don't know," Voss said. He looked at the pictures as Toni gave them back to him. His daughter. He had so few memories of her. The little girl in Berlin. The grown daughter in the last couple of years. All that missing time in between. And now, no more ever again. "Whatever you found out," he said. "Tell me."

"They bought some coke," Toni said, "from a local dealer."

"Is that all?" Voss said, almost relieved.

"The guys say they were a threesome. Dancing together. I don't know."

"And the second night," Voss said, almost to himself, "Fade was coming apart."

Toni looked at him. "You don't look so good," she said.

"Yeah," he said. "I've felt better. I think I'd better get going. If I stay here another ten minutes, I'll be here when the place closes down, and I don't need that kind of night."

"I understand," she said.

"Listen, you've been great. I wouldn't have been able to . . . You were a big help. I owe you. I don't know how . . ."

The band began to play a fast number, Jesse strumming like Pete Townsend.

"I'm going to get out of here," Voss shouted. He put a fifty down on the table. "That should cover everything. Get yourself another drink."

He picked up his leather jacket and left with it draped over his arm, hunched, unsteady, old.

♯

Toni was at the counter when he checked out in the morning.

"I was hoping you'd be here," he said.

"Well, here I am."

He handed her a page of the motel's notepaper. "This is the name of a producer in L.A. If your brother wants to give him a call, tell him I gave him his name. I'm pretty sure he won't take the whole band, so . . ." He shook his head. "It's a tough business."

JULY

Voss drove across Saskatchewan in the dark, as Chance, Fade, and Neil had done the previous year, as the Vossimilitude tour bus had done thirty years before. He couldn't remember just why they had been driving at night—the rush to get to Chicago, where they were to meet a recording crew? Whatever the reason, it had led to an experience he had never forgotten. The guys were dozing, and he and Avery were tracing their route on the map. They'd noticed how the lights of a city could be seen in the wispy clouds even when the city was a great distance away. Medicine Hat had been a glow on the horizon thirty miles before they got there. Regina had loomed for what seemed like hours before coming into actual view, and they swore they could see the light from Saskatoon, eighty miles north of their route. Now they were seeing a glow to the north again, but when they consulted the map they could find no city to correspond with it. The nearest thing in that direction was . . . nothing. Somewhere up there was Husdon Bay, and beyond that the North Pole, but nothing to account for the light in the sky. They asked the driver to stop for a minute. Out on the side of the road they stood looking north, and as their eyes grew more accustomed to the dark the light in the sky grew brighter. It moved, a hand with long wispy fingers, and they realized they were seeing the northern lights, Aurora Borealis. Colors appeared and disappeared, blue and pale green. The fingers turned to rivers in the sky, a hint of yellow, a deep violet.

"My God," Avery said. "It's beautiful."

"Should we wake up the guys?"

"In a minute," she said, putting her arm around his waist and moving closer. "Let's just have it be ours for a little while."

Voss put his arm around her shoulders. She kissed him on the neck. Did he turn to kiss her? He couldn't remember. Could he tear his eyes away from the sky long enough to find her lips? It didn't matter. They stood together on the rim of the world and the sky danced for them, trailing scarves of colored silk against the background of the whirling universe.

They didn't have to wake the others, they awoke on their own in the stopped bus. Before long the whole gang was standing on the side of the road, chattering, lighting cigarettes, cracking beers, passing a joint around. And then the lights were gone. The Milky Way, which had been there all along, came clearly into view, the familiar summer constellations, the scene Voss was seeing now as he stood on the side of the road thirty years later.

And somewhere along here, Chance, Fade, and Neil had stood, too. Chance had told him that in her last phone call. "We saw the northern lights," she'd said.

"I saw them once," Voss had told her. "With your mother."

What had Chance made of that? Was that another grain of sand on the scales of fate? Had she thought, *they had a moment like this, too . . . and look what happened to them*?

Lake Huron, gray and oceanic, fell behind him on the right, clouds massing over the water. Voss looked down at the road atlas open on the passenger seat. Niagara Falls pulled at him. He had never been there, and neither had Chance, as far as he knew. Approaching New York from Ontario as Chance, Fade, and Neil had, and out seeing the world as they had been, it only made sense to see the Falls. Yet all the evidence of their expenditures suggested they'd blasted through this region, and Lt. O'Beirne's report of their hassle with customs had them crossing into the country at Buffalo, not Niagara. Why had they passed it by?

As Voss came through Toronto, Lake Ontario hove into view on the left, another inland sea, big, windblown waves breaking on the waterfront. And then as he crossed the Peace Bridge into Buffalo, a glimpse of Lake Erie, its chop blown into white streaks. He arrived at customs in a summer thunderstorm. The young man who asked to see his papers couldn't have been more than twenty-five; the look on his face was as starched as his uniform. Voss handed him his California driver's license and his passport.

"Purpose of your trip to Canada, sir?"

"Research," Voss said. "Checking out the music scene."

"Sign anybody," the officer asked, his face opening up into a hip smile.

"Not this trip."

In a pull-off area to the right of the inspection lanes Voss could see a couple of young kids, their t-shirts soaked through, standing in the rain while men in gray plastic coats went through their vehicle, an old Volvo station wagon.

"Welcome home, sir," the young man said, handing Voss his license and passport. Another officer crossed in front of Voss's car, keeping a large German shepherd on a tight leash, and headed toward the beat up Volvo. Voss raised the window and pulled out into the rain, squinting to make out the signs for I-90. Billboards for Niagara Falls hotels vied for his attention, shabby appeals to honeymooners and lovers made shabbier by the pouring rain coming briefly into focus and then blurring to the jerky, irritating rhythm of the wiperblades. A semi blew by, throwing Voss into an impenetrable cloud of spray, visibility zero. Then he caught sight of the interstate sign, swerved abruptly, made the turnoff by inches.

A half hour out of Buffalo, the rain cleared up and Voss began to feel a reluctance to end his journey. Chance, Fade, and Neil had evidently driven straight through to Hoboken from here, but there was no reason he had to. At a filling station off the interstate, he consulted his road atlas for a scenic route, a red or blue line through rural New York State, maybe through Binghamton rather than Albany. At dusk he found himself in northern Appalachia, ramshackle houses right on the road, rusting farm equipment in weed-grown fields, an old school bus with smoke rising from a flue-pipe, squalid trailers, the burned shell of a double-wide. Then, as the light failed, he watched the squalor vanish. Old cars up on blocks became indistinguishable from bushes or hillocks; appliances on front porches melted into shadow, fireflies sparkled in dark green yards, and vignettes of rural American life appeared in the windows of lamp-lit rooms. He felt that he had slipped through a time warp. At one house a heavy man pushed himself back from the dinner table as a woman in an apron began to clear the dishes. At another, a blond boy with a crewcut stood in an open doorway surrounded by dogs. Other windows were lit with the flickering blue light of televisions, and in one carport a trouble light hanging from the ceiling illuminated a man bent under the hood of a pickup truck. Colors were fading to gray, yet the electric light was gold, and the images made Voss think of Vermeer and Rembrandt. Once again he was glimpsing the calm beauty of ordinary life.

He thought of Artie and C.C. Almost a year ago he had gone to their place in Queens for a taste of that calm beauty. But that evening hadn't turned out the way he'd expected it to, and its revelations had been swept away the next day in Hoboken. He was still in a daze when Artie had made his desperate attempt to get C.C. into rehab, which had backfired in the worst way. Who knew where she'd been and what had happened to her between that day and her appearance at her sister's house in Oklahoma? What was Artie going through now that she had returned to him? Voss couldn't imagine the agony of watching your spouse disintegrate into fractured alcoholic incoherence and unrecognizability. That was Artie's particular hell. The loss of Chance was his. Maybe everybody had their own.

He rounded a bend and saw a golden picture window with gauze curtains go dark as he approached; then another window in the same house lit up as he drove past. People were going to bed, turning out the lights as they left day rooms for night rooms. He was nearly alone on the road, his rental car ticking along dependably. He'd turned the radio off about half an hour before after searching in vain for something listenable, but only now did he notice the quiet of the evening. Up ahead, a thin, yellow sliver of moon climbed slowly through the tree limbs. The Earth was rolling along through space, and he was riding the roll, moving eastward on the eastward turning blue-green planet, tiny under the star-strewn heavens. As long as humans had stood up on their hind legs, they had gazed up at this same sky looking for answers. And only the delusional found them.

"Everything happens for a reason," Avery's priest had said at the funeral. That was the delusion of this age. Voss rejected it outright. Yes, you could find a causal chain to explain just about anything, but that wasn't the kind of reason they were talking about. What had he learned in philosophy class all those years ago at Forrester? Causality was one thing, teleology another. Identifying the presumed causes, as an accident investigator might report the causes of a plane crash, so that that particular sort of event might be prevented in the future . . . sure, you could do that. But finding an intention behind the event, its role in some great master plan—that, Voss could never believe in. C.C. hadn't become an alcoholic so that Artie could become a better person. Chance hadn't died so that Voss could discover something about himself, or so that some other destiny could work itself out. *Because of?* Yes, Voss could buy that. *So that?* No, sir.

He passed a green neon sign that said Log Cabin Restaurant & Motel, the word Vacancy flashing red below it. Slowly he eased the car to the shoulder of the road and turned around. The motel, too—a semicircle of individual log cabins—made him feel that he had wandered into another time. A larger log building housed the restaurant and office, a neon Budweiser sign lighting up one of the windows. Seven or eight people were in the dining room, and they all turned to look at him as he came through the door.

"Kitchen's about to close," the manager said, when Voss asked about a room. "If you're hungry you might want to get your order in first. Then we can get you registered."

"Thanks," Voss said, pausing to be directed to a table.

"Just sit anywheres," the man said. "I'll send Judy out."

For some reason, he cringed as he sat down, half expecting a girl of Chance's age to come through the kitchen door and ask him what he wanted, but Judy turned out to be a little round woman with red hair and a pink apron. Her voice was like the low notes of Ian Anderson's flute, more breath than music, and Voss had to lean closer to hear the daily special.

"You want the salad first or you want it all together," she asked.

"Just bring it as soon as it's up," Voss said. "I don't want to keep you here later than I have to."

"That's all right, hon," she said, smiling with her eyes as well as her mouth, "I don't have to be anyplace."

Later, as he stood under the stars at the door to his cabin, Voss felt once again that he had slipped into another era, a more comfortable and kindly era. The moon, now a silver sickle, had climbed well above the trees. To its left, Cassiopeia sprawled on a black velvet couch. As Voss scanned the sky for something else he might recognize, the bright neon sign went off, and the last people in the restaurant came out, got into an old station wagon, and drove away. The parking lot was dark now, his car the only car there, his cabin the only one occupied. As his eyes adjusted to the completer darkness, he could just make out the edges of the Milky Way. He'd come well over a thousand miles since staring up at the sky the other night, but the stars were right where he'd left them, dependable, indifferent.

The inside of the cabin was decorated with hunting and fishing prints, the twin beds covered with red plaid blankets. The walls and ceiling were knotty pine, darkened with age. Voss didn't know places like this still existed. For a moment, he wondered if he still existed or if he had been translated to another dimension. But he knew that was not the case. In the morning he would awaken to a gray gravel parking lot and see an overflowing dumpster alongside the restaurant wall. Chance would still be dead. He would still be alive. If he could trade his life for hers, he thought . . . if he could trade his life for hers . . . But it didn't work that way. There was no reason. No plan. No enlightenment. Just this life. This beautiful world. This private hell.

By midday Voss was in the Catskills, the highway climbing and descending, crossing green ridges and black rivers. The sky was pale blue, cloudless, hazy. He turned north.

At around two in the afternoon he knocked on the door of Roshi's residence.

"Jack," Roshi said. "No one told me you were coming."

"I was in the neighborhood. You got a minute?"

"For you? Sure. Come in."

Voss had never been inside Roshi's house before. It was actually older than the Temple, a Japanese style structure that had been built in the early '70s. The classic mountain bungalow, decorated in the mission style, dated from the '20s. Roshi, in faded jeans, house slippers, and a City College sweatshirt, led him to an armchair upholstered in green leather.

"I was never really your student," Voss said, as he sat down. "But I thought, maybe. . . ."

"Chikuzen was my student, and you were his. Now he's gone, that makes you mine. Besides, you've done a lot for us over the years. What can I do for you?"

"You know my daughter died last summer."

"Yes. I'm very sorry."

"It was strange. We weren't that close, really. She lived with her mother for a long time. I missed huge chunks of her childhood. And then, we were starting to get to know one another. And she killed herself. Or she had one of her friends kill her."

"That's very hard," Roshi said. "It leaves a lot of things unfinished."

"It's not all. Maybe you know this, maybe you don't. Years ago I wrote some music, an opera, a rock opera. It ended in a triple suicide. And back then some kids . . . they did it, what I wrote, played the record and killed each other. I don't know how many died. Could have been more than twenty. Rumor has it some of them were hushed up. Fear of copycats. And now my daughter and her friends . . . same thing. My record was on the turntable."

"That's a lot to carry," Roshi said.

"That's exactly what Chikuzen said. But that was before my daughter. . . ."

"What have you done? To try to come to grips with it?"

Voss told him about Chance's letter and his attempt to follow their footsteps and understand.

"What religious tradition were you raised in, Jack?"

"Catholic. But it was never . . . I was never. . . ."

"Those first things you hear are strong, though. They stay with you. Catholics believe in confession, right? You have to confess to be forgiven."

"Yeah. I always hated that."

"And then the priest gives you a penance to do. Say some prayers, something."

"Yeah."

"Have you confessed?"

"Who to? God? Some priest?"

"Who's been hurt by this?"

"Me. Avery. Fade's parents, I'm sure. Parents of the kids from back in '75. Neil."

"Neil?"

"Neil. The boy that didn't die. He's still in jail."

"The boy who might have killed your daughter?"

"Yeah."

"I can't get you out of this, Jack. I'd say sit with it, but I think you've been sitting with it for a while. And you've searched for answers. Maybe you haven't found any, but the search itself is good. Searching is a way of becoming whole again. But now you have to do something. I don't know what, but I think you do."

"I can't do some flamboyant thing that brings the spotlight back on me," Voss said. "I already thought about a Suicide Prevention benefit concert, but it's too complicated. It could just bring more attention to the old music and then maybe more suicides. I can't do that."

"Then do something quiet. Something only you know about. Or do several things. But make sure you keep at least one of them to yourself, that you make one private act of atonement and penance and never tell a soul."

"What?"

"Let that be the focus of your search, now. Search for what you can do."

CHANCE, FADE, AND NEIL

Voss remembered how Chance and Fade couldn't keep their hands off one another when they'd visited him in Carmel. "We're gonna take a little nap," Chance would say after lunch, and they'd go off laughing to the guest bedroom. He'd go into the studio to be sure he couldn't hear them.

But not long after leaving Voss's place they are sharing a room with Neil. Do they refrain from having sex at all? It seemed unlikely. Do they make love quietly in the dark on one bed while Neil, on the other, tries to pretend it isn't going on? Voss remembered doing that in his dorm room with Jeanette, Artie over in the other bed. And then one night, maybe outside of Calgary, after their first evening at The Red Rooster, the night they danced and bought rounds for the band, Chance—it would be Chance—says something. "Look at him, over there." She makes an exaggerated sad face. "It's not fair."

"He doesn't want to sleep with you," Fade says, laughing.

"But I'll bet he'd like to sleep with us," Chance says.

Fade says nothing. Chance stands up, naked, takes two steps to the other bed, and crosses an invisible line. She draws down the blanket that covers Neil, takes his hand, and leads him back across that line into the bed with her and Fade. And maybe all they do is sleep.

The next night they go back to The Red Rooster. Fade is moody and drinks heavily. Bull said he wasn't happy. But, according to the boys in the band, they score some coke. That helps Fade get over his inhibitions. The details don't matter. They are far from everyone they know, in another country. They become a threesome. They work it out, somehow. Who knows what exactly goes on, but Neil loves Chance and Fade both; Chance loves Neil and Fade both; Fade loves Chance like crazy. They drive across Alberta, Manitoba. One night, they stop the car to look northward at pulsing lights in the sky, shimmering green and blue, interlacing, holding hands.

Maybe it starts to turn sour in Buffalo, that dark and sooty city so much further from the East Coast than it sounds like it would be. Their car is carefully searched as they cross back into the U.S., and they are questioned at length, especially Fade, whose olive skin and Middle-Eastern name seem to count for more than the fact that he has a New Jersey driver's license. If it was going to be so hard to get back into the country, why didn't they warn him back at border between Montana and Alberta? He doesn't have a passport because he is an American citizen, born in Hackensack, for God's sake.

"But you haven't lived here all your life, have you?" one of the guards asks.

He is tempted to answer with the old New England joke—*not yet*. But he doesn't. "My parents are Persian," he says. "They came here when the Shah was deposed. I was born here and this is the first time I have left the country."

"Where did you get your accent?"

"What accent?" he asks. "My parents, maybe, I don't know. I spoke Persian with them at home."

"Is this your boyfriend?" the guard asks, pointing with his chin at Neil.

"No, he's not my boyfriend. I'm not gay. She's my girlfriend. Why are you asking me these questions?"

"Sit down over there," the guard says. "We have to check on some things."

The three of them sit on gray metal chairs and watch through the glass as a German shepherd is led around and through Fade's van. They hear the dog bark, and then watch one of the men pull the ashtray out of the dashboard. Fade looks at Chance. "There's nothing but cigarette butts in there, babe. Don't worry."

"We know you had drugs, that you were smoking in the car. But you don't have them now, so we're not going to hold you. You want to leave the country again, son," the guard says to Fade, "I advise you to get a passport."

"Welcome fucking home," Fade says, once they are finally on their way. "America the beautiful."

Neil reaches up from the back seat and puts his hand on Fade's shoulder. Fade shakes it off, swerving, and almost losing control of the vehicle. "Don't you fucking touch me, fag. . . ."

"Fade," Chance says.

"Don't talk to me. Nobody touch me, nobody fucking talk."

They drive straight across New York, seven hours. Nobody says anything; it is just understood that they won't be going to Niagara Falls as planned, won't be stopping at a motel, won't be sharing a bed. Fade pulls up in front of Neil's apartment; he doesn't even get out and help him with his gear. For his part, Neil collects his stuff in silence. "See you," he says, kissing Chance but turning to climb the stairs to his place without making eye contact with Fade.

The next day was the last time Chance and Voss spoke. She had called to tell him she was home safely and to thank him for the charge card. She hadn't indicated anything unusual except to mention that the guards at the border had given Fade a hard time, taking him for an Arab, no doubt. Voss commiserated with her and they spoke for a couple of minutes about the beauty of Canada. She told him about seeing the northern lights. And he told her about his upcoming trip to New York for a recording session. They agreed to get together when he was there.

"I love you, sweetheart," he'd said.

"I love you too, Jack," she'd replied. No *Daddy*, just Jack, in keeping with his role in her life, her mother's one-time husband, her biological father, but after the first six years, never again her daddy, except in the letter—the letter she might have already written when she called. Why did she revert to that childhood name for him when she was looking at the end? Because it was the act, finally, of a child, of children?

EARLY AUGUST

*A*rtie opened the door wearing a torn black t-shirt and a pair of jeans that hung loose from his hips. He and Voss hugged each other, but Artie's heart wasn't in it, Voss could tell.

"C'mon in, man," Artie said, stepping to the side of the narrow hallway." It's not pretty, but it's nothing you haven't seen before."

"So what happened," Voss said. "Like I said on the phone, I've been off the grid. Bowman finally got hold of me through Bert. She's in the hospital?"

The place was an epic mess, the clutter of the summer before still there beneath a year's worth of additional dust, magazines, and dirty clothes.

"Car wreck," Artie said. "She almost killed somebody in the other car, and she's in pretty bad shape."

"She was driving? Whose car?"

"It's a long story. I'm just glad she's finally in a hospital."

"She gonna be okay?"

"The broken bones will heal. The big question is still the booze. They had to do a chemical detox to operate on her—ruptured spleen. And she should be going straight to rehab once she's out of the hospital. But I don't know what's going to happen when she comes home. I want to be able to support her, but . . . I will support her. I'll never leave. But I feel like I'm just going through the motions, and I hate that."

"I don't know. I think going through the motions is better than not going through the motions. You can't promise to stay in love with someone forever—shit happens, feelings change. But you can promise to stay, not that I've ever done it. But you're doing it. That's my definition of loyalty."

"She's my wife. But I'm in a deep hole. Can't seem to get out of it."

"You're a good man, Artie. Most guys, they wouldn't still be here. What was she like before the accident? Binges, or all the time? I haven't seen her since that fucked up intervention. Shit, that's the last time I saw you. That guy did not know what he was doing."

"It got worse after she came back." Artie said, "She was pretty much keeping a blood level. Steady. But by the end of the night she'd get ugly. Then weepy. You saw it that night last summer."

Voss remembered. C.C.'s dream of a Kerry win, Artie's excited calls for "red meat," and then his sad pleading when C.C. headed out for her secret drinks. He remembered seeing the notice on the screen of the suicides in Hoboken. Someone had survived. He thought for a moment of Neil in his oversized prison clothes.

Artie sat down on the filthy sofa, opened an Altoid tin of pot, and started rolling a joint. The television was tuned to C-SPAN, and John Roberts was being questioned by the Senate Judiciary Committee. "Done deal," Artie said when he saw Voss watching for a moment. "Rubber stamp." Then he licked the rolling paper, twisted the ends, and lit it off.

"You've done everything you could," Voss said.

Artie handed him the joint and he took a hit.

"A lot of guys would have given up," Voss croaked, holding in the smoke.

"I could have done more. I should have."

"What else could you do? She's on her own path. You tried to get her to give it up. You tried to get her into a facility somewhere. Now she's in one, or she will be. What else could you have done?"

"I could have gone with her." He held up the joint. "Quit this. Go through a program together."

"That's hindsight," Voss said.

"She was a drunk the whole time I knew her, all the years we were together. Maybe it suited me."

"Don't do that to yourself, man. You're better than that. You can beat yourself up with that forever, but it doesn't do any good. Believe me, I know."

"I know you know. I'm sorry. But I'll admit, I don't know what it's going to be like when she comes back. I've run out of tears, man. I'm fucking worn out." He took another hit of the joint. "But it's good to see you, bro. How you doing?"

"I don't know. These people who talk about closure? There's no fucking closure."

"Now that I do believe," Artie said, handing the joint back to Voss.

Voss took another hit of the joint and then held it out in front of him. "So, if you don't mind my asking, how much of this *are* you doing?"

"Too much," Artie said.

"Yeah, that's what I thought."

"What are you doing, Jack? What are you doing to deal with it?"

"You really want to know?"

"If I didn't want to know, I wouldn't ask," Artie said.

"Well, one thing I'm doing is trying to understand. I just followed their route, that whole last trip they took. Went where they went. Asked about them."

"Like a detective? You?"

"Sort of. I showed people their picture. Some people remembered them."

"And what did you learn?"

"I don't know. But I keep thinking about Neil."

"Who?"

"Chance's friend. The kid that lived. I keep thinking about him and wondering if I can help him somehow."

"Are you crazy? He was part of something that got your daughter killed. He might have killed her himself. How would you help him?"

"I don't know yet, but there's gotta be something I can do. I worry about him sometimes."

"Jack, you are a profoundly strange man."

"Look, I don't know what exactly went on, but I'm pretty sure Chance was a willing participant in it. She loved those guys. They loved her. Whatever happened between them, it wasn't murder."

"Avery would shit if she heard you talking like this."

"I don't know. Maybe. But Avery's nothing if not rational."

"That's exactly the problem, bro. Avery's rational. This is not rational."

"I mean, she'll see that what they did was not something you . . . I don't know."

"No, see, you're being rational about something that's irrational. . . ."

It was the old Artie, Voss thought as he listened. The guy he went to for advice when they were in college. The guy he hadn't really seen in years.

"Those kids were in the irrational when they did what they did," Artie went on. "You're trying to be rational about it. And that's cool. Shit, I admire your ability to separate your feelings from your thoughts on this subject. But Avery, she's so deep into being rational that she simply isn't going to be able to see their irrationality the way you do."

"Slow down, okay?" Voss said. "You're losing me."

"It's like Nietzsche, man. You've got to allow a place for the irrational, for the Dionysian, in order to make sense of this. Avery, man, she's not going to go there."

"Well, I don't think the kid deserves to die. I don't want to see him sent to the chair, or the gas chamber, or hooked up to the IV of death. . . ."

"Jersey hasn't executed anybody in, like, forty years."

"Okay, then I don't want to see him spend the rest of his life in a cage. He's not a criminal. Even if they convinced him to help them in their suicide pact, he's never going to do that again. I talked to him—he's carrying enough guilt for ten men."

"And what about you, Jack? How much guilt are you carrying?"

"I've got my share. I wasn't much of a father."

"That's not what I'm talking about, and you know it."

"What?"

"*The Enchanted Pond*. It was their script, wasn't it?"

"Who told you that?"

"C'mon, man. I know you. I know that opera. I was there when you wrote it. And I remember what happened in '75. I read the papers. I'm amazed it hasn't made the front pages."

"It will. If there ends up being a trial. It's bound to come out. Fuck."

"It's not going to be easy, that's for sure."

"I never thought. When I wrote that. Goddamn, that fucking piece of music set my career in motion, and it's dogged me ever since. Berlin, when I got my hand broken, I never would have been playing that club if not for *The Enchanted Pond*. And now. . . ."

"It's not your fault, bro. You're right. You never thought. You couldn't have foreseen. No one could."

"Thanks, but when it hits the papers, I don't think it's going to play that way."

"No, probably not. But I'm here to tell you, bro, and I want it to be loud and clear: it's not your fault."

"Yeah," Voss said. "I know you're right. And you know what? C.C. isn't yours."

They sat there side by side on the stained and tattered couch in silence. Artie picked up the remote and started flipping through the channels. He stopped at an old Alan Ladd film with Veronica Lake.

"I remember when C.C. looked like that," Artie said.

"So do I," Voss said. "She was beautiful."

"Yes she was."

"Listen," Voss said. "Let's get out of here. It was shaping up to be a beautiful day when I was on my way here. Let's get out in it. I'll get a car. Drive over to Jersey."

"I don't know. I'm pretty wiped."

"I know. But when do we get to do shit like that? Come on. Grab a jacket and let's just go."

"Let me get a shower first," Artie said.

Two hours later they were tooling through the Holland Tunnel, westbound, in a red Mini-Cooper.

"I ever show you where I played my first gig?" Voss said.

They took the Pulaski Skyway over Kearny Marsh, crossing the Hackensack and Passaic Rivers, passed by Newark Airport, and headed out 78 toward Union. Voss hadn't been there in he wasn't sure how many years. He got off the highway at Burnet Avenue. Apartments and condominiums everywhere.

"This used to be all greenhouses," he said. "I walked by them on my way to school."

"It's the same where I grew up," Artie said. "Farms and empty lots now all broken out with yuppie colonies, like acne, or fucking herpes."

Voss turned up Laurel Avenue. "I dream about this landscape," he said. "There was a tunnel under the railroad tracks, and sometimes I dream I'm going through it." He pulled up in front of St. Michael's School. "I wasn't sure it would still be here," he said. "It was huge in my memory, but it's not that big."

"We were smaller then," Artie said.

"Yeah. I also remember it as dark, and it still looks as gloomy as ever."

"So where was the gig?"

"Right here. School assembly. I played my accordion. There was a nun who played the piano like a drum major in a marching band: One, two, three, four, boom, bam, blang, boom. I've heard player pianos with more rhythm, more emotion."

"What did you play?" Artie asked.

"Huh?"

"On the accordion. What song?"

"Shit, let me think. 'I'm an Old Cowhand.' I had a cowboy hat and toy pistols, too."

"Nice," Artie said. "Perfect."

They drove past the old candy shop where Voss, Hal, and Avery used to buy bubble gum and Smith Brothers Cough Drops before school, and Voss showed Artie the house he grew up in, also much smaller than he remembered it, the whole neighborhood shabby and neglected.

"I remember one time when I was a kid," Voss said, "I heard a weird bell out in the street. Not like the Good Humor truck or canned music of Mr. Softie, but almost like a ship's bell. And I came outside and there was this guy with a horse and cart and he was a knife sharpener. You brought out your knives and scissors and he would sharpen them for you. And the housewives on the street came out to him. I only saw him the one time."

"From another era."

"Yeah. I told that story once when The Statesman was around, and he told me I shouldn't tell it because people think we're old enough already."

"Right. Did your mom bring out her knives?"

"I don't remember."

"You know, I don't know anything about your folks," Artie said. "You never talked about them."

"They were old when they had me," Voss said. "More like grandparents. The old man died while I was in the service. My mother died while I was living in Germany with Avery. They never met Chance. I guess it's sad, but I kind of left them for good when I went in the Air Force. Except for when I was real young we never really understood each other at all. In a way, I think the '60s was too much for them. I look around now and I think I know how they felt. You're born into a world you think you understand. A world that makes sense to you. I mean, it's yours. But if you live long enough you find yourself in a world that is stranger and stranger. It seems like it should be the other way around, that the longer you live the better you understand the world. But I look at the world right now and I don't know. . . . Maybe it happens to everybody who gets to be forty or fifty."

They drove by Union High, went down 22 past Caruso's Music, and stopped at a drive-through for cheeseburgers, fries, and milkshakes.

"Where to next?" Artie asked.

"I want to go and visit the grave," Voss said. "Chance's grave. I haven't been there since the funeral. You mind?"

"No. It's okay."

"Here's another strange memory," Voss said as they drove down a Hoboken street of tall narrow houses with almost no front yards and steep concrete steps leading up to ornate doors. "When I was like eight or ten years old, somebody brought me to a place that looked like one of these, and we went into a downstairs apartment, with the entrance under the front steps, and the place was dark and the furniture all had lace doilies on the backs and the arms, and this old couple lived there. I have no memory of who they were. And the woman came in with a tray with little glasses of sherry, and she gave me one. It tasted like medicine to me, but okay, and I drank it and it was warm going down. Probably my first drink. I don't remember ever going back there or who they were or why we went. But I can still see the place, feel the gloom of it, and feel the warmth of the sherry."

"I went to places like that when I was a kid," Artie said. "People from the old country. Aunts and uncles. Some of them didn't speak English."

They were taking care of each other in the quiet way that men sometimes do. Driving around. Getting something to eat. Talking, but not about their feelings, just sharing memories, showing each other places and things. At

Chance's grave they stood side by side and passed the stub of a joint back and forth, looking across the Hudson at the city, the windows of the tall buildings reflecting yellow and gold as the sun went down behind them.

"Remember when we dreamed of having our own town?" Voss said.

"Yeah. With our own theater and recording studio and everything. Our own private world."

"What the fuck happened?"

"Life happened."

"Yeah," Voss said. "Life. You ever hear people say that if they had it to do over again they wouldn't change a thing?"

"Yeah."

"I fucking hate that. If I had it to do over again and I knew what I know now, I'd sure as shit do a couple of things differently. Not everything, but some things. That goddamn opera."

"But it doesn't work that way," Artie said. "Even if you got to do it over again, you wouldn't know what you know now. You never get to know how it's going to turn out. That's the way it works. You're always flying blind."

HOBOKEN

The Enchanted Pond is not the explanation. It was not the reason. It was a shape things took. A vessel we poured all the other things into. In The Enchanted Pond the lovers make a suicide pact because the world can't accept them, because there's no place for them. But the world never accepts you. Or if it accepts you in one way, it rejects you in another. At least that's my experience, and I believe it is pretty much universal. If that were enough to make people kill themselves the human race would have died out long ago. There was more. We couldn't accept the world. And we were too small, too weak, too tired to change it. We couldn't accept that we were getting old. That we were losing our fire. Turning ordinary. Talking about BMWs and iPods and catching ourselves laughing along with the laugh-track on TV sitcoms. The war made us sick, but we weren't doing anything about it. We were talking about careers. He was working on his portfolio. She was talking about asking her famous dad to introduce her to some people in the music business. I was going to be a teacher. But it all seemed so pointless. All a winding down. You want to tell yourself that fifty is the new thirty? That people are acting and living as if they were younger well into what used to be considered middle age, old age? To us, twenty was the new thirty. Our youth was coming to an end, and what came after had no appeal at all. Ordinary life in a sick self-deluded, so-called civilization. Like the country, we had reached our peak, and we didn't feel like watching the long decline. It's like when you're talking to your best friend about would they pull the plug on you if you were a vegetable. We said we would. We just moved the date up a little. But it was the same thing. You start laughing along with the sitcoms on TV and it's all over anyway.

(♯)

What happened in the short time between their return to Hoboken and that final day? Did Fade try to leave Chance and fail? What amplified the typical human failure at love to the point that death seemed the only way out? And who first suggested that they die together rather than live apart?

It would have been Neil who brought *The Enchanted Pond* into it. "Your father's opera is about us," he says to Chance. "Or it could be. Two guys and a girl. All in love. Enchanted. Doomed. Blessed. Cursed."

"I haven't listened to that in years," Chance says. "Or, I don't know, maybe I never listened to it. Mom never had his records in the house. And I only really heard what they played on the radio."

"You've got to listen to it. I'll go get it."

"Now?"

"Now."

The next day she plays it for Fade. "You've got to hear this," she says. "You're not going to believe it."

"What is it?"

"It's my father's rock opera from the '70s."

"What about it? What am I not going to believe?"

"Just listen."

And that is the seed. It grows quickly. A doomed fantasy. A fantasy of romantic doom. Fade tries to shrug it off, but Chance won't let it go. One night after making love, still coupled, she whispers in his ear.

"I want to ask you something."

"Now?" Fade says, arching his back to see her better.

"Don't move away," she says. "Stay right where you are. You're right where I want you."

"What do you want to ask?"

"What's something you've never done before with anyone that you'd like to try?"

"Huh? What are you asking me?"

"What would you like to try that you've never done?"

"Why?"

"I'll do it," she says.

"You don't even know what it is," Fade says.

"I know you," she says. "At least I think I do."

"And what do I have to do in return?"

"Let Neil back in," she says. "Just to be with us, to touch us. He loves us both. You don't have to do anything you don't want."

"I love you," Fade says. "I don't love Neil."

"You don't have to—no, don't pull back, please, baby, stay right where you are. You don't have to love him. Just let him love you. You liked it when we were in Canada."

"I'm not gay," Fade says.

"I know you're not, silly. You're macho enough for all three of us."

But he isn't. It eats at him. What does it mean? Who is he? What is he? Is he like Neil? No, he can't be like Neil. Is Neil his boyfriend, like the customs inspector said? Can people look at him and know he lets another man fondle him, suck him off while he fondles his girlfriend, that he has lain back and closed his eyes until he doesn't know who is doing what to him?

Maybe it didn't go that way at all. Only Fade and Chance could say, and they were both dead. But even if they had survived, would their accounts have matched up? At some point every experience is so subjective that even the person who experiences it can't account for it accurately. What color shirt was your attacker wearing, the policewoman asks, and the victim can't answer, or answers incorrectly. How many people were there? Or, the question we all get wrong, how long did it take? Does this mean our precious memories are a kind of theater in the mind? Movies we play inside our heads, rewinding them when we want to see a scene over, slowing them down to see something more clearly, hitting the subtitle button when we can't make out what someone has said? No. That DVD model suggests that the actual substrate of the memory is unchangeable, the lost dialogue recoverable, that the victim can just play the scene over again in her mind and remember that the shirt was blue plaid, the pattern on the pockets diagonal to that of the rest of the shirt, the collar frayed at the tips. But that doesn't work. The remembering mind is its own digital editing station, with its own capacity to alter the memories themselves. The shirt was, um, green—click: it's green. His hair was long and greasy—click: there it is, hanging down in brown strings. Finally, after too many of these edits, filling in details where there were none, inventing a specificity that wasn't there in the first recall, our memories become fabrications. We remember events from our college days and look around at the people who were there—George, Kenny, Artie and C.C., Avery, Hal. But wait, Hal was still back in New Jersey then, and Artie didn't get together with C.C. until later. We take out the photographs, but no one has written dates on the back, so we sit there, saying, "What year was that? Do you recognize that apartment? Who's that guy in the purple shirt, the girl with the big hoop earrings?"

Neil told Voss what he told him. It was, at best, Neil's honest recollection, his attempt to reconstruct events as accurately as he could. And even at that, who knows how true it was. At worst, Voss knew, it was a deliberate reconfiguring of events, colored and shaped to communicate a particular interpretation of what happened. Maybe he wanted to arrogate blame to himself that wasn't really his. Maybe he wanted to clear himself of blame. Was he driven by Guilt? Shame? Loyalty to Chance? To Fade? By fear of the consequences should he be found guilty of murder? He'd told every possible version at one time or another, to Voss or to Lieutenant O'Beirne. Chance killed herself and Fade killed himself and then Neil took the gun and couldn't do it. Chance killed Fade and then killed herself and Neil took the gun and couldn't do it. Chance killed Fade and Neil killed Chance but when it came his turn he couldn't do it. Or Fade killed Chance and then killed himself and Neil took the gun and he couldn't do it. Or Fade killed Chance and handed Neil the gun and Neil killed Fade and was supposed to kill himself but he couldn't do it. Or Neil killed Chance and Fade and then pointed the gun at his own head but he couldn't do it. The only part of the story that didn't change was that when it came Neil's time to kill himself, he couldn't do it.

The bottom line was that on the twenty-ninth of July in the year 2004 in a Hoboken apartment decorated with batik curtains and books, side B of *The Enchanted Pond* playing on the stereo, a .22 caliber bullet pierced the temple of Chance Calentine Voss, passed through the parietal lobe of her brain, ricocheted off the inside of her skull, tumbled through the delicate neural web of her mind, and came to rest two centimeters from her pituitary gland. Her body went limp, her breathing and her heartbeat ceased, the light went out of her eyes, and all thinking, remembering, hoping, and imagining ended, all suffering and all enjoying was over, all seeing, hearing, feeling, smelling, and tasting stopped together and forever. Shortly before or after that, the same gun fired the same caliber bullet into the skull of Fadil al Muti. Neil watched both of his friends pass out of this world, their eyes going blank, their lovely bodies becoming so much meat. It was his turn to do the same to himself, and he couldn't do it. He went to the phone and dialed 911. The woman who took the call had to ask him to turn the music down. It was roaring:

> *Our crystal pool, our magic pool*
> *Is now a pool of blood*
> *Our bodies melt into the pond*
> *Our souls rise out of the world.*

Voss and Hal's voices in eerie harmony, the organ wailing, the bass like horses' hooves pulling a caisson.

LATE AUGUST

"At least I paid the alimony and child support," Voss said. "I wasn't a deadbeat dad."

They were sitting at a corner booth in the Park West diner, coffee in thick cups on the table in front of them. Muzak in the background: a thin orchestral arrangement of "Bohemian Rhapsody."

"No," Avery said, "you weren't a deadbeat dad, you were an absentee father. And you know, people would tell me we were lucky, Chance and me, because so many guys just abscond, but you never made us want for money. But you know what? We didn't *feel* lucky. Or I didn't. So you paid what the court ordered. You paid more. You were generous. With your money. But with your time? Where were you?" She looked down at her hands, long fingers, the serious diamond from the doctor.

"You made it clear you didn't want me around," Voss said. "What was I supposed to do?" He opened his hands on either side of his coffee cup.

"I know. But you laid down so easy. It was like you were relieved to be rid of us. You didn't even put up a fight."

"I thought I was being a gentleman. What good would it have been to fight you? You didn't want me around Chance, and I couldn't blame you. I was no good. I was weak and would have been a terrible influence."

"Sure, but you didn't have to be that way. You could always be whatever you wanted to be. You're a goddamn rock star, Jack. You're in the freaking Hall of Fame. . . ."

"No, I'm not," Voss said, "Jesus."

She looked at him like she didn't understand. Then she just went on, "Anyway, you've written songs that will last forever. You mean to tell me you couldn't straighten up and be a father to Chance? All you had to do was make an effort—instead of making drunk threats."

Voss took in a deep breath and let it out. "I've never known how to fight, Ave. I never had to learn. I've been lucky and unlucky. I've worked at what I loved. . . ." Only after the words came out of his mouth did he realize what he had said, and before he could say anything else, Avery pounced:

"Exactly," she said. "You gave your all to what you loved: your music. Us, you didn't love. Maybe you thought you did, told yourself you did, but if you had you would have fought for us. And that you didn't do."

They sat in silence for a long moment. Then Avery spoke again: "I mostly let it go a long time ago. You were who you were. To see you when you were wrapped up in the music was beautiful. I loved you and you let me. I knew who you were. I guess I'd known since we were kids. But Chance deserved better."

"I was just getting to know her," he said.

"Whose fault was that?"

"Oh, for Christ's sake, Ave—give me a break."

"Why should I? It's not for me to do, Jack. Believe it or not, I understand that you need somebody to comfort you, to ease your pain. And I know you are in pain. It's not that I don't believe that. But I can't be the one to help you now. Go to one of your girlfriends. Talk to Artie. Go to a therapist. Go to your Zen master, or whatever he is. Believe me, I know what you're going through, but I can't give you what you want."

"And I can't give you . . ." Voss exhaled, his shoulders slumped, and then he straightened his back and sat back in his chair. "She was a beautiful, smart, charming girl, Avery. You did that. You did well."

"Yeah," she said bitterly, "I did well."

"They got the idea from *The Enchanted Pond*," Voss said. "They used it for their fucking soundtrack. You knew that."

"I knew," Avery said.

"It's like they thought I would get it. I would understand. Some kind of tragic gesture I would approve of. But that was just a story, you know that. I never approved of that. God, Avery, I went on the radio and television to tell people that suicide wasn't the answer. Okay, so later I fucked up and nearly died, but that was an accident. I would never kill myself on purpose, never wanted anyone to."

"I know," Avery said.

"I mean, you write a song where somebody jumps out a window doesn't mean you want people to jump out of windows, you think it's a good idea."

"I know," Avery said.

The waitress came and refilled their cups. Voss poured cream into his and stirred it.

"Jack," Avery said.

He looked up. "Yeah?"

"You didn't invent their unhappiness. You got it right is all."

"What?"

"You just got it right. Back then and now. People who are stuck in impossible situations feel like death is the only way out. People who ache like that want the aching to stop. And you told them it was romantic to do that."

"I was hardly the first to say that."

"Yeah, but you said it in their language."

"Then why don't I understand it?"

"Your life-force is strong, Jack. You're like the weed that comes up through the crack in the sidewalk. You dragged yourself down those stairs in Berlin. Why didn't you just lay back and die?"

"I wanted to just go to sleep that night. But you don't do that."

"*You* don't do that, Jack. Neil—may he burn in hell—I think he is like you. He led the charge and then stepped aside and let them go over the cliff."

"I never led the charge."

"Keep telling yourself that, Jack. Don't you get it? You were always the leader. Everyone looked up to you. Bent over backwards to impress you. Hal and I, we were trying to impress you ever since we were kids. But you just moved along on your own path, oblivious to us. You think Hal would have become a musician if you weren't already one?"

"C'mon, Avery. Hal was a wild man. I wasn't like that."

"No. You weren't. You were always in control. Which makes you all the more responsible. But you never took responsibility. And when things got too close to the edge, you saved yourself. Like Neil. The time came, he said no. Fade was weak, maybe already broken. And Chance, I just don't know. I think she did it for Fade. I think she made a mistake. . . ." Avery picked up a napkin to blot her eyes. "But Neil, he stuck around, going along with everything, until it was his life that was threatened. Only then did he finally say no. Too late for my little girl."

Voss reached out his right hand to place it over her left, which lay flat on the table. She drew it back.

"No, Jack. It's too late for that, too. I have another life. I'm Mrs. Sheridan now. There's nothing left to tie me to you."

Voss looked at her. "I guess I should go," he said.

"Yes."

As Voss settled with the cashier, he could see Avery's head silhouetted against the window. She did not look toward him. He signed the receipt, put his wallet in his pocket, turned toward the door, and made his way out to his car without looking back.

(♯)

Voss hadn't been in Chicago since the concerts in '75 and '76, and he hadn't seen much of it then. Now he was picking his way around Evanston in a rented Cavalier. The name and address Lt. O'Beirne had given him were written on a MapQuest sheet Susan had faxed to him. The house was of blond brick, the numbers in blue tile set into the front steps. He rang the bell and waited. He rang again.

From within a voice called, "Hold your horses."

The door opened. "Yeah?"

Voss had expected a man in his eighties, and that's what he saw—short and stocky, white hair in a crewcut, maybe a Marine forty or fifty years ago.

"Mr. Kestner?" Voss asked. "Do you know who I am?"

The old man looked him up and down. He studied Voss's face. "Never in a million years did I expect you to show your face here," he said. "You got some nerve."

"I wanted to tell you I was sorry. I am sorry."

"You know she died? After fourteen years, she died. And that's been fifteen or sixteen years ago now."

"I know. I got your message."

The two men stood at the doorway, one outside looking in, one inside looking out.

"You want to come in?" the old man finally said. "I can walk pretty good, but I can't stand in one place too long anymore."

Voss hesitated, looked up and down the block.

"I'm not gonna hurt you, son," Kestner said with the calm authority of a man who could if he wanted to, even at eighty.

Voss followed him into the house, past a staircase, through a living room that looked like it hadn't been used in years, to the kitchen in the back. Fat orange and green tomatoes lined the windowsills, and Voss could see through the screen door into the backyard: tall, staked tomato plants, a stand of corn behind them, neat rows of what might be peppers.

"You want a cup of coffee? It's decaf—that's all I'm supposed to have now—but I make it pretty strong."

"Thanks," Voss said.

Kestner poured coffee from an ancient electric percolator into two Chicago Cubs mugs.

"Cream?"

"Sure, thanks."

The old man got a can of Pet Milk from the refrigerator. It had two little holes punched in the top. He poured some into his coffee and then handed the can to Voss. When Voss had finished with it, his host put it back in the refrigerator and sat down. Voss was staring at the coffee cup.

"I guess I got a thing for lost causes," Kestner said.

"What?"

"The Cubs."

"Oh."

"You a religious man, Mr. Voss?"

"Call me Jack," Voss said automatically. "What? No. I'd have to say no. I went to Catholic school, but . . . it didn't take."

"My wife was Catholic. They believe that suicide is a mortal sin, that if you commit suicide you will never get into heaven. You will burn in hell forever. All she ever wanted was for our little girl to wake up long enough to make her confession. She prayed over that girl for fourteen years."

"I'm sorry."

"I wasn't raised with much in the way of religion. Went to church for weddings and funerals. I thought religion was supposed to be a comfort to people in times of trouble. Never knew it could be a torment."

"Is she still alive, your wife?"

"So you don't know everything?"

"No, sir. I just know what I read in the stuff you sent. That was you, wasn't it? And the calls?"

"Yeah, that was me."

"How'd you get the numbers?"

"A guy who used to work for me. Knows all about computers. Says he can find anything."

"I guess they can nowadays," Voss said.

"I just wanted to let you know there were still people out there. . . ." He breathed deep and let it out again. "And now your little girl is dead, too."

"Yes. Like yours."

"You still got a wife, son?"

"Divorced," Voss said.

"Oh."

"And your wife, sir?"

"Lizzie. She died."

"I'm sorry. When?"

"Fifteen, sixteen years ago."

Voss waited. He took a sip of his coffee, which had grown cold.

"She wore herself out trying to get that girl to wake up. I knew she wasn't ever going to come back. But my Lizzie went through hell. I don't know if I believe in heaven, but hell I believe in. And Lizzie believed in it. But I think if my little girl had died first she would have killed herself just to be with her. Hell or no hell."

"But your wife died first?"

"She just gave out. And after a while I had them turn off the machines. Lucky nobody got in a hubbub about it, like this woman in Florida last spring."

The two men sat at the table, sipping their coffee, Voss, pushing sixty, feeling like a boy in the company of this man a generation his senior. Outside in the garden chickadees and titmice chased each other around a feeder on a post.

"I never knew what to do," Voss said. "I never thought anybody would actually go and do what I wrote. When it happened I didn't even think of the parents. I tried to do what I could to stop it."

"Whatever you did back then wouldn't have been enough for me," the old man said. "All I had to keep me going was my anger. I wouldn't have let it go. And I still got plenty of it, but now I sit here with you and I see that you're not the one I can be angry with anymore. You got what I wished for you, and may God strike me dead, I'd take back that wish now if I could."

(♯)

"You can go ahead in, Mr. Voss," the receptionist said.

"Thanks, Jane," Voss said, rising from his chair in the waiting room. "And why don't you just give me the file, so Larry doesn't have to call you again on the intercom."

The young woman smiled, reached under her desk, and handed Voss the accordion folder. "You've got him figured out," she said.

"Larry," Voss said, closing the door behind him. "I've got a tricky job for you."

"Okay. But sit down first." He watched Voss put the file folder on the glass-topped desk. "You want a cup of coffee or something? I can have Jane get you something."

"No. I'm good."

"Okay then," Larry said, leaning back in his chair. "Tell me about this tricky job. Let's see what we can do."

"I want to get a good lawyer for Neil Webster, and I don't want anybody to know I'm paying for it."

"Neil Webster?"

"He's still awaiting trial in New Jersey. I don't have to tell you who he is, do I?"

"No. I know who he is, but Jack, Jack, Jack. This isn't a tricky job; it's an impossible job. Guys like you don't do things like this without anybody finding out."

"And what exactly are guys like me?"

"Guys who are in the spotlight, under the microscope, you know, in the public eye."

"One, you are exaggerating my fame by about a power of ten. And two, how many cases can you think of in which people make donations without saying anything about it and suddenly are in the papers?"

"Yeah, yeah, yeah," Larry said. "That's true. Most of the famous donations are made with a press release in advance. Who gives a bunch of money and doesn't want anybody to know about it? Except maybe you give it to Al-Qaeda or something. So maybe we can find a way to do this."

"But we can't be too casual about it," Voss said. "Your first instinct was right. He shows up in court with a high-priced lawyer, people are going to want to know who's paying the tab. Here's my idea: you find somebody to set up a defense fund, ask for donations. But keep me out of it. Nobody's going to think I'd do this, so they shouldn't come looking, but it's got to be quiet. I don't want to be on TV explaining why I'm footing the bill for a lawyer to defend the guy who might have shot my daughter."

"So why *are* you doing this, Jack?"

The window behind Larry looked out on the picturesque little village of Carmel. Tanned men and women in boat shoes and pastel golf shirts walked from shop to shop. It would be hard to get further away from a triple suicide in a seventy-five year old Hoboken apartment building.

"I think whatever the kid was doing," Voss said, "he was doing what Chance wanted him to. He's not the type to come up with this. Or he's the type to talk about it, but not to follow through. And I don't think he wanted to do it, but the other two convinced him, and when they weren't around to keep convincing him, he realized he didn't want to die. But they were already dead. There was nothing for him to do. So he called the police on himself. He's not a killer, Larry. He doesn't deserve to spend the rest of his life in some hellhole getting used and abused by guys he can't possibly fight. I know the kid. The least little delinquent is tougher than he is."

"You could be talking about a lot of money, Jack."

"Well, you know how much I've got. Can I afford it or not?"

"Yeah, you can afford it. But it won't be painless."

"That's okay. But like I said, we don't want more media attention than necessary, so I think we need to find somebody local. We can't go bringing in somebody from the West Coast or anything like that. Somebody with a low profile who knows his way around New Jersey. No showboating. Quiet professionalism. You think you can find somebody?"

"Yeah. I don't know anybody offhand, but I know people who will know. I'll ask Mike Barker, if you haven't already talked to him. . . ."

"No. Mike and Bert are too close to Avery, and I don't want her to know."

"Yeah, I can understand that. But sooner or later, Jack. . . ."

"I know. You're probably right. But later is better. I can't talk to her about it. I don't think she wants blood, but she'd like to blame somebody. I think she'd like to blame me and Neil both. Neil is a little easier. But she's known him since he was a kid, and somewhere inside she knows he just got caught up in something bigger than him. Like I said, I don't think he ever wanted it to go that far."

"Who's he got now? Public defender?"

"I don't know, but that's what I'm guessing."

"And when's the trial?"

"Again. I don't know, but it ought to be coming around, don't you think? It's been a year."

"Okay, Jack. I'll make some calls, get the ball rolling."

"Don't break any laws. But please do everything you can to keep my name out of it."

"Got you."

"Thanks."

"And Jack?"

"Yeah?"

"You've still got some surprises in you, I'll give you that. Most guys lost a daughter wouldn't be doing this."

"Yeah. Well, life is more complicated than most guys think."

(♯)

Voss didn't know if this would work. And he wouldn't be able to watch it closely, would have to stay well clear of the proceedings. The best thing would be if he were on tour, but Bert was not optimistic about that.

"It's not you, Jack, it's the market," Bert said when he called her. "They want new people to do new stuff, and old-timers to do their old-time stuff. I can get you a nostalgia gig in a small house any time you want it. Refurbished theaters from the '20s—fifteen hundred to twenty-five hundred seats. There's one in every decent-sized city. Piano bars, jazz clubs now and again. You want to put together one of those all-star bands, I can get you one hundred gigs a year, easy. But a full blown tour with new stuff, you're not that kind of draw."

"Is that it? I go out and play old stuff for tired crowds of people my own age who are trying to relive their youth—or nothing? C'mon, Bert, there's got to be something better than that." He was standing out on his deck, the sun a flat, white disk in blue-gray haze, sea and sky merging, no horizon. Below, the slow churning of the waves against the rocks.

"Not in this country."

"Then where?"

"How far are you willing to go? I can get you something in Japan. Maybe back in Germany."

"I can't go back there," Voss said, pure reflex.

"It's changed a lot. You wouldn't recognize it."

"Still. I don't know."

"What's the issue date on the new album?"

"September something."

"I can get you on the morning shows, they'll let you play a song or two, but you know they're going to want to ask you about Chance."

"I'm not going to talk about that."

"I know you're not. I've known you long enough to know that. But what's really at issue here, Jack? Do you need the money?"

"No, I'm okay money-wise. I need something to do, Bert. I need to work. I've spent enough time alone in my house, my car. And I'm starting to write some songs again, not just instrumentals. So I need to play for people. I'm going crazy here. I'm not talking about arenas. Even arts centers, clubs would be great."

"The kind of clubs you're talking about are dying out, Jack. Blues clubs, jazz clubs, there's now as many in the whole country as there used to be in Chicago alone. I can get you gigs, but I can't build you a tour."

"So what do I do? I'm not going to Japan, Germany. . . . Shit."

"Look, I know what you're saying. And I know you're probably beginning to feel like I'm not working hard enough for you. So let's say this: you think about what you might be able to put together. Give me a description. A set list. A roster of musicians. And I'll think about how and where we might get you an audience. I'll tell you right now, you're going to have to do some old stuff."

"Yeah, yeah. Okay. There's some old songs I still believe in. But nothing from *The Enchanted Pond*."

"I'll leave that up to you, but you know that's what they're going to want. 'Touch Her and You're Dead.'"

"Definitely not that one."

"Okay, I'm sorry. But you know what I mean. Something—the old songs, the old sound—just to get them ready for the new, so they remember who you were, who you are."

"Yeah, who I was."

"Shit, Jack. Sorry again. You know me. I'm blunt. You do what I ask, get me a set list, some names. I'll bend over backwards to find you a gig. You know I will."

"Okay, Bert. Give me a couple of days. Let me think about it, make some calls."

"I know you still got it, Jack. We've just got to figure out a way to let the audiences know that, get some buzz going. I'll be waiting for your call."

"Who I was," Voss said aloud to the evening. "I'm sick of who I was. I'm not who I was. But who the fuck am I then?" He went inside and opened the door to the studio. The big Fazioli beckoned, but he needed the open doors, the air, and the dying light. He turned to the Yamaha in the living room, sat down, played the ugliest chord he could think of. Then he hit a couple of random keys at the top end, hard, letting them ring out, hang in the air with the low rumble of the breakers outside. Discord. Clashing notes. And then he set out to resolve them, not in a hurry, but slowly, patiently, never quite easing the tension, playing on the edge of harshness, barely music, but laying down hints of where it could go if he let it; the sharp cacophony of an angry Ornett Coleman. His left hand ached. He was playing loud and fast, all over the keyboard, making mistakes, hitting notes even more wrong than the ones he meant to hit. It sounded like a thunderstorm, like a house falling down, like an avalanche, like a subway train screeching around a sharp curve, like a fifty car pile-up in the fog, and then the wind blew in, the long low howl of a blizzard that wasn't going to let up for hours, for days, but its roar was steady, it was breathing; a living, breathing, angry beast at the door, and, as anger will, and fear—for it came to him that no small part of his emotion was fear—it slowly wore down to weariness. He slowed the tempo. Simplified the chords, paring the sevenths and ninths down to the familiar triads, majors and minors. He played that original chord again, softly, teasing out the pieces and settling each of them down to rest. His breathing had quieted. The storm had passed, and he played just a little of the green world shaking off the rain. Then he stopped. It had grown dark. He stood up, walked out onto the deck, and looked out at the ocean under the first stars. Listened to the sea surge against the rocks. A car careened down the twisty road behind his house, tires squealing and a girl's voice whooping with excitement. He sighed, sat down on one of the recliners, and watched more stars appear one by one. So much squandered beauty, he thought.

He thought again of the road. Europe. Asia. That's what Bert had said. What about South America? He'd never done that before, but people were doing it now. Start in Rio. Work on his jazz chops. Put together an international combo. Top people who nobody in the states knew about. One of those Cuban guitarists. A Latin drummer. Some horns. No frills. He could open with "The History of the Organ." Now you could do it on a single, well-programmed keyboard instead of the two tons of equipment it used to take. Move on through some familiar pieces, rearranged for the new band. Stuff Chance would have liked. Work up some new pieces to feature the talent—world music stuff. That was the direction things were going. It would be work, exhausting, demanding, but that was exactly what he needed—work. And maybe, with any luck, every once in a while the music would take him to that place where everything seemed to make sense, where loss turned into the blues, confusion into jazz, ambition into melody, and you could ride out anything, feeling that you were in touch with the inner workings of the universe. Maybe you didn't understand them. Maybe you didn't like them. But you were in touch with them, you flowed with them, and you could feel, at least for a time, that you were where you were supposed to be, doing what you were supposed to do. No, it wouldn't make up for the failures, it wouldn't fix things with Avery, wouldn't bring back Chance, but it would give Voss a sense of purpose, it might bring some good moments into the lives of the people who came to listen, it might help the careers of the players. But, no, that was all a way of trying to make it seem unselfish, and it wasn't unselfish. Voss was a selfish man, and there was no point in deluding himself with the idea that he was doing this for anyone but himself. It would be an escape and a refuge, and that was what he needed now. And when it came to an end . . . when it came to an end, the next thing would present itself and he would deal with it then. He had a plan. That was enough for today. In a few minutes he would go inside and pour himself a drink. He'd find an old black and white movie on the television and fall asleep in his chair. He would like to cry, but it wouldn't happen. Tomorrow he would call Javi and Charlie B. in New York. Maybe call Kenny in L.A. Then he'd call Bert again and start to set things up. He was doing what he knew how to do. He would keep doing it until he couldn't do it anymore.

Discography

Vossimilitude	
The Enchanted Pond	1974
Locked in the Garden	1975
Voss	
The Blind Storyteller	1977
The Songbook	1978
Ride the Music	1983
Circuits	1990
Prisoner of the Zendo	1995
Ordinary Life	1997
Practice	1998
Tearing the Cover Off	2005
Last Song for Chance	2007

Bonus Tracks

Cleveland: The Rock and Roll Hall of Fame
Hal Proteus, Performer
Inducted 2004 by Voss
Transcript of Induction Speech:

Ask somebody three separate times what was the first piece of music that really moved them and you will likely get three different answers. But ask a musician what was the first riff or lick they learned, and they will remember. I'm a keyboard man, and for me it was the organ part on "Whiter Shade of Pale." For guitarists of my generation, it was Keith's riff on "Satisfaction," or Eric's on "Sunshine of Your Love." And there was a moment in time when every kid with a guitar was holed up in his room trying to learn "Stairway to Heaven" note for note. And the bass players? They were learning Hal Proteus's riff on "Touch Her and You're Dead." That riff alone would have been enough to make Hal famous. But, as you all know, he followed it up with brilliant playing on every song he ever recorded, from his great backing on songs like "Locked in the Garden" and "Avery's Song," to the innovative bass leads he played on "Black Haired Beauty" and all three of Mutually Assured Destruction's albums. His influence is still felt. In fact, hip-hop musicians sample his bass riffs more than any others. I think he'd like that.

Hal and I were best friends since kindergarten. We watched The Beatles on Ed Sullivan in his living room, and we formed our first band when we were still in grade school. Hal was so small when he got his first bass, that he could barely reach first position, so he learned to play high on the neck from the start. The seeds of the Vossimilitude sound, those high bends on the bass, were sown in Hal's basement when we were still kids. We played together for family members sitting politely on their couches and for thousands of screaming fans in packed arenas.

Hal Proteus drank deep from the cup of life. Then he poured another cup. And when that was empty he ordered another bottle.

Mostly he got away with it. He was larger than life, a man of huge appetites, incredible energy. I know because he carried me. I was barely life-size. If you were wondering what the platform boots and top hat were about back in the Vossimilitude days, that was me trying to be as big as Hal.

I still miss him. I miss the way he could find a bass line that complemented my melody on the keyboard. I miss the way it felt to sing harmony with him—I've never found a better singing partner—and I miss the way he would look at me after I said something like this and say, "Enough of all the hearts and flowers shit, Jack—let's make some noise!"

Interview with Terry Gross—May 1995

A figure on the American pop music scene for over twenty years now, my guest today is known as a musician's musician. Voss burst onto the scene with his 1974 rock opera *The Enchanted Pond*. Since then he has put out six more albums of his own music and has played keyboards on innumerable records from David Bowie to The Defibrillators.

Terry Gross: Voss, it's really a pleasure to have you here.

Voss: Thanks, Terry. It's a pleasure to be here. Please call me Jack.

T.G: Okay. Jack. You have had an extraordinary career in pop music, from your debut Vossimilitude album in 1974, *The Enchanted Pond*, one of the most controversial albums of all time and still one of my favorites, to your new release, just out last month, *Prisoner of the Zendo*. I'd like to begin by asking you what's your favorite of your own records?

Voss: That's a tougher question than it seems. As a working artist, I almost make it a point of professionalism for my favorite to be the one I'm working on at the moment, but that's dodging the question. And there's always been a lot of pressure to repudiate *The Enchanted Pond* because of the suicides. But the truth is that there's a special place in my heart for that album. It's not just that it was first, but it was a kind of gift—a complex and difficult gift, but a gift just the same. I think artists—maybe scientists, too—are sometimes able— it's tempting to say *allowed*, but then who allows it, God?—they're sometimes able to produce a piece of work that is actually beyond their capabilities at the time. And then they don't really know how they did it. *The Enchanted Pond* was like that. I wrote those songs— some of them I had help from Hal—I wrote them in a daze. I had been out of the Air Force a little over a year and was going to college on the G.I. Bill. It was the early '70s—that magical time between the sexual revolution and AIDS. . . . And I was reading these poets in class—a lot of them I couldn't stand at the time, like Dryden, Swinburne, but some I went crazy over: Yeats, Housman, Keats. "La Belle Dame Sans Merci" was a perfect lyric, I thought. And then, in another class, I was reading Ovid. And, like everyone sooner or later, I had a disastrous love-affair. All of those things combined to give me the idea for the story of *The Enchanted Pond*. I wrote that stuff before I really understood what it was about. It took me a long time to be able to write like that again. In a way, I never did.

T.G.: A lot of people said—and still say—you were ahead of your time with the gender-bending stuff. But you're saying you were ahead of yourself?

Voss: I was never ahead of my time; I was a product of it. And I was really pretty shy when it came to the gender-bending. Look at David Bowie, or Elton John . . . or, well, he may be a bad example, but. . . .

T.G.: Lou Reed.

Voss: Yeah, look at someone like Lou Reed. He was hanging it out there. I was just telling stories about characters I made up. And their attempt to live out a threesome doesn't exactly come out very well in the end. You hear David Crosby's song "Triad" and you think, hmm, maybe it could work. You don't get that in *The Enchanted Pond*. It's more like those stories where you get a wish and it turns into a curse. Two people who have eyes only for each other is fine. Three is a problem, right? So the enchantment turns into misery, damnation. . . . Which, I guess, is what led to the tragedies.

T.G.: The suicides of kids imitating the final scene in the opera.

Voss: Right.

T.G.: Well, why did you end with everybody dying?

Voss: How else does a doomed love story end? Even Romeo and Juliet—they have to die. Because in real life, love doesn't last. So they die at the high point of their love, and it's beautiful. But if they lived what would there be? Romeo busting his hump in a produce stand on a dirty Verona street, Juliet at home with a couple of screaming brats. And I imagined it could only be worse for my lovers, so I killed them off. I never imagined that anyone would . . . I mean, it never occurred to me. I've been atoning for it ever since.

T.G.: That was your first album. But Vossimilitude wasn't your first band. You had a band with Hal Proteus before.

Voss: That's right. Johnny and The Featherweights. I was sixteen. We wore pegged pants, featherweight shoes—you remember those?—pastel on pastel shirts with high-roll collars, and bell-sleeve sweaters. Pompadours. Sort of a hood version of Jay and the Americans.

T.G.: I can picture it. What kind of songs did you play?

Voss: Covers, of course. "96 Tears" was our signature tune. Beatles covers: "Ticket to Ride" and "We Can Work It Out." Hal and I loved the harmony on that one. And always some slow songs, or you didn't get the school dance jobs. "Massachusetts." "Spooky." "She's Not There." And later, "Crystal Ship."

T.G.: I think I went to those dances. But you weren't playing the piano then, were you?

Voss: I had one of those Vox Continental organs, black naturals and white sharps and flats, it had these spindly legs that you screwed in, and I played it standing up.

T.G.: You and Hal Proteus went way back, right? When did you meet?

Voss: Hal and I met in third grade. Harold Proczevski. We were thrown together in a way. Neither of us had any brothers or sisters. We built model airplanes together. Then, after seeing The Beatles on The Ed Sullivan Show, we decided to form a band. He started out on the bass because of Paul McCartney, and I was already playing accordion. I saw Paul Revere and the Raiders on TV, and had to get one of those organs. . . . And it turned out that we could sing harmony. But after he died, and I almost died, I spent a lot of time reevaluating my life, including my friendship with him. He was a tremendous talent on the electric bass, in his hands it was a lead instrument, and he was a wild man. An American Keith Moon, they used to say. I never knew Keith Moon, but I'd say Hal Proteus was not a happy man, that he was self-destructive in the extreme, and that I was drawn to him like to a whirlpool. I almost drowned. If I had been a better friend to him, I might have stepped up and said something, but he made self-destruction seem like a lot of fun. The night he died, I just went along with everything he did, and it almost cost me my life.

T.G.: Are you saying you weren't a wild man yourself?

Voss: I was never the wildest man, put it that way. To people who haven't lived the fast life of a touring rock musician, I'm sure I seem like I've had a pretty wild life. But if you ask the guys I've toured with, they'll tell you, I'm really not that wild—even then I wasn't that wild.

T.G.: You went into seclusion after Hal Proteus died. What were you doing?

Voss: I wouldn't say I went into seclusion; I was already more of a studio musician and session man than a performer. I went into rehab. And through that I started to explore Zen. I moved to New York, and fortunately, I had enough money that I didn't need to work. But I still went out. I played in a little club a couple nights a week. I made *Circuits* during that time. And I spent time with friends, walked to the grocery store. . . . Then I slipped up again and ended up back in rehab, and then in the monastery where I basically changed my life. I started to develop the habit of practicing. I used to practice in the Berlin years, but only as a means to an end, now I practice as an end in itself. It's my meditation.

T.G.: Like Zen?

Voss: Yes, it's very much a Zen thing. I go back to the monastery every now and then for a kind of spiritual tune-up, but the piano works better for me than silent meditation. "Piano is my practice" would be a Zen way of saying it.

T.G.: The new album's dedication says, "To Chikuzen, who taught me to choose life." Chikuzen is actually William McCauley, who was recently dismissed from the Black Dome Zen Monastery for distributing controlled substances and for sexual violations. Was he another Hal Proteus?

Voss: No, I wouldn't say that. There is a Zen saying: when the student is ready, the teacher will appear. I think it goes the other way, too. When the student appears, the teacher can emerge. Chikuzen was the teacher I needed at the time. The human flaws that caused him to lose his position at the monastery are what made it possible for me to listen to him. They gave him a kind of credibility. I knew of his history with hallucinogens. It was one of the ways we connected. The things I learned from him maybe I could have learned from somebody else, but I doubt it. I would never have listened. I feel badly for him right now. I owe him a lot.

T.G.: Did he give you hallucinogens during your studies with him?

Voss: No. I'd already been there. And I don't want to get too deep into this, but if he was giving people mushrooms, it wasn't just to get a buzz on. I know he's not perfect, but who is? You ought to get him on here sometime. I think you'd be surprised.

T.G.: Okay. Let me go back to something you said before. You said you practice as an end in itself. What does that mean exactly. How are you coming along? How do you rate your own skills?

Voss: High second-rate, but that's not the point. I mean, when it all shakes out, I have to acknowledge that I'm second-rate. A second-rate songwriter, a second-rate singer, a second-rate piano player. Worse, it's only because of lucky timing that I am even that. In the days of the great composers, I would not have had a career at all as a writer of music—I can barely read Beethoven's scores, can't imagine writing one. In the days of Caruso, I would not have made it even as a lounge singer—I don't know how to project, my voice doesn't have the clarity of the old crooners in the early days of records. In the world of classical pianists, I could not earn a living. Jazz is my great love, but I can't do what Oscar Peterson does, or what Keith Jarrett does, or, you know whose playing I really admire? Bruce Hornsby. But fortunately for me, I have an audience left over from my rock years, and their standards aren't that high. No, that sounds like I'm putting them down. Let me put it this way, my fans have been very indulgent of my failings.

T.G.: You're pretty hard on yourself, Jack. Have you always been that self-critical?

Voss: Probably, yeah. Or for a long time, anyway. I've seen a lot of great musicians come and go. The way I see it is we're now in the late days of rock. The standards of musicianship are not that high, and where so many of the luminaries haven't lived very long, I have survived to be a kind of elder-statesman in a field dedicated to youth. I have learned to make the most of what voice I have, and after forty years I have learned to coax out of myself a kind of piano playing that is more emotive than technical and supports my singing nicely. I still take voice lessons, and I'm still learning. The most important thing, though, is that when I'm playing, everything else goes away. That's why I say it's my practice. When I'm playing, especially when I'm playing alone, just me and the piano, I hook into something bigger than me.

Prisoner of the Zendo

"So you're here as part of your sentence?"

"Strange judge."

"Wise judge."

"Call me The Prisoner of the Zendo, like the old movie."

"Sounds like a murder mystery."

"Everybody but one gets up after Zazen. Who did it? Who saw it?"

"Blood on the Zendo floor."

"Someone is murdered in a room full of people and nobody sees it happen."

"A detective comes here, questions all of us."

"*Were you there? Yes. Did you see anything? No . . . maybe the killer's feet? The killer's feet? Well, somebody walked around the Zendo with the kyotsuke, I thought it was Chikuzen, but he says he wasn't there. I saw his feet when he walked by. You couldn't see his face? I was looking at the floor. . . .*"

"And then he's going to want to know what a kyotsuke is. *It's a stick to whack you on the back to wake you up and release the tension in your muscles. You mean somebody walks around and hits you with sticks?* The detective would think we were all nuts."

Rich Man's Speed

"Think of it as rich man's speed," Hal said as he used a double-edged razor to chop lines of white powder on a pocket mirror. "You've taken speed, haven't you?"

"Sure," Voss said.

"Same thing, basically, but a lot more fun all around. Why do you think people are willing to pay so much for it?"

"Touch Her and You're Dead"
by J. Voss and H. Proteus

That's my baby sitting pretty over there
I know she's lookin' fine, so go ahead and stare
But if you get to thinkin' you might take her to your bed
Look into my eyes, friend: touch her and you're dead.

    [Chorus] Touch her and I'll cut across your throat with my knife
    Touch her if you're tired of this ol' earthly life
    Touch her and I'll shoot you down with my gun
    You even think of touchin' her, my friend, you better run. . . .

She does things for me that I can't do without
She does things you can only dream about
But if you think she'll do those things for you instead
Look into my eyes, friend: touch her and you're dead.

[Chorus]

When you've got a girl this hot you got to be on guard
For other guys who sneak around and play in your back yard
But if I come home late at night and hear a stealthy tread
Look into my eyes, friend: touch her and you're dead.

[Chorus]

Our Own Town

"We need to get our own town," Duncan said.

"Huh?"

"Yeah. Like down in the Ozarks or something. We buy a hunk of property, make our own town, invite artists and writers and musicians to live there. Build a theater. . . ."

"But each of us needs to have his own house," Bowman said.

"Oh, yeah, sure," Duncan said. "Big houses. Yours has a studio, Jack's has a conservatory, Artie's a library. Lots of room to have friends over."

"And it's our town," The Statesman said, "So we write our own laws, have our own police department."

"Why do we even need a police department?" Voss asked.

"We don't want people coming in and rob us," The Statesman said.

"Let's see how long we can go without the authoritarian apparatus of the fascist state," Artie said.

"How would we survive in this town of ours?" Voss asked.

"We follow our callings. Make art. Artie writes and puts on plays. Bowman paints. Voss makes music."

"We could grow our own food," Val said.

"And pot," Duncan said.

"Which would be a reason not to have police," Artie said.

"Or to have our own. I nominate Artie for Police Chief."

"Seconded."

"All in favor. . . ."

The ayes rang out almost in unison.

"Ayes all around. Artie, do you have any words of wisdom for us?"

"It's a new day. If I may quote the great sage, John Lennon: 'Smoke pot, smoke pot, everybody smoke pot.'"

"Amen," Bowman said.

"What about an anthem? For our town," Duncan said. "Jack could rewrite the words to the 'Star Spangled Banner.'"

"It's just a town, not a country," Artie said.

"*Oh, say can you see, in the Ozarks at night . . .*" Voss sang.

"You gonna do the whole thing, Jack?" The Statesman said, "There's like, what? Twenty verses?"

"Four, but nobody sings any but the first."

"They took the tune from an old Brit drinking song," Artie said.

"It's awful hard to sing for a drinking song," Val said.

"But when you're drunk, you don't care," Artie said. "Anyway it was to spit in the eye of the British."

"So, I know there are a lot of drinking songs, I mean, maybe the first song was a drinking song. But are there any smoking songs?" Voss asked.

"One Toke Over the Line," Duncan said.

"Don't Bogart Me," Artie said. "From *Easy Rider*."

"So when are we likely to see some pot anyway?" Duncan asked.

"I don't know," Artie said. "Maybe next week. The whole town's dry. Even the seeds and stems are gone."

"*. . . what a fine little town . . . we have hid up in these hills. . . .*"

"Keep going, Jack," Duncan said.

"Yeah, no. The more I think about it, the more I think Hendrix did it better without words when he played it at Woodstock."

"No, man, that was great. But your words are, too. People need words. They don't get things unless you explain it to them. They're stupid," The Statesman said.

"Except for us, right?" Duncan said.

"Well, I don't know about you," Voss said, "but I've had my moments."

"Jeanette," everybody said in unison.

"Yeah. So I'm going to have to count myself in with the stupid people."

"Me, too," Artie said.

"Aye."

"Aye."

"Aye."

"Aye."

Biographical Note

Born and raised in New Jersey, John Van Kirk attended Webster University and Washington University in St. Louis, served as a navy helicopter pilot, and received his MFA from the University of Maryland. He teaches writing and literature at Marshall University in Huntington, West Virginia. His short stories have earned him the O. Henry Award and *The Iowa Review* Fiction Prize and have been published in numerous magazines, journals, and anthologies. This is his first novel.